PRA

MW01193918

"An attorney investigates the death of her mentor, leading her into the darkness of his past in Schaffer's mystery novel. Schaffer creates a vivid world with realistic and understandable characters, especially Noli, who is the heart of this large cast. A satisfying, fast-paced whodunit with two strong female leads."

—*Kirkus Reviews*

★ ★ ★

"In the tradition of Robicheaux and Clete and Spenser and Hawk—but female—two unstoppable women—a hard-edged PI and a high-powered attorney—partner up to find out who killed the beloved Fitz. Through twists and turns, beaches, vineyards and coastal redwoods, historical layers and modern changes, Santa Cruz, the story's setting, is described in such engaging detail that, for this alone, *Mortal Zin* stands as a notable debut by Diane Schaffer."

—ROBIN SOMERS, AUTHOR OF *Eleven Stolen Horses* AND *Beet Fields*

★ ★ ★

"On her first day home for a visit, Noli Cooper learns her friend and childhood mentor has been found dead on a nearby beach. Suicide? Or murder? Solving this mystery is only the tip of the iceberg in this captivating story, which weaves wine history and war history as danger increases for Noli and the people she loves. In the same way Louise Penny's mysteries leave readers craving a fresh croissant or a cup of hot chocolate, *Mortal Zin* will make you want to settle in for an uninterrupted read with a glass of zinfandel and your own private charcuterie."

—KATE WOODWORTH, AUTHOR OF *Little Great Island*

Mortal Zin

A MORTAL ZIN MYSTERY

DIANE SCHAFFER

Sibylline Press

AN IMPRINT OF ALL THINGS BOOK

Mortal Zin

A MORTAL ZIN MYSTERY

DIANE SCHAFFER

Sibylline Press

Copyright @ 2025 by Diane Schaffer
All Rights Reserved.

Published in the United States by Sibylline Press,
an imprint of All Things Book LLC, California.

Sibylline Press is dedicated to publishing the brilliant work of
women authors ages 50 and older.
www.sibyllinepress.com

Distributed to the trade by Publishers Group West.

Sibylline Press
Paperback ISBN: 9781960573933
eBook ISBN: 9781960573162
Library of Congress Control Number: 2024941256

Book and Cover Design: Alicia Feltman

**Sibylline
Press**

This book is dedicated to
Michael and Lynne Muccigrosso

Thanks for sharing your vineyard in the sky

CHAPTER ONE

Thursday, September 24, 2009
Santa Cruz County, California

Her dog was restless. As dawn seeped through the fog, the girl unzipped a few inches of her sleeping bag, extended an arm, and caressed his fur. Damp. A faint odor of peroxide rose from his undercoat.

"Hey, Joey. It's okay."

Ears cocked, nostrils twitching, the dog pointed his muzzle toward the south end of the cove, but the mist blocked the girl's view.

Yesterday evening, as the fog rolled in, the sun-worshippers had brushed sand from their towels and fled. The girl had settled beneath a stone ledge, a hidey-hole both dry and invisible. No bums. No drunks.

Seaward, the waves *shooshed* over boulders far out in the cove. Low tide—very low.

Good.

She crawled into the open. A fish-garbage stench hung heavy in the damp air. Shivering, she peeled away her jeans. The abalone poacher had vowed to provide a wetsuit so she could harvest without freezing.

Another broken promise.

From her pack, she withdrew a sheathed knife and clipped it to the neck of her T-shirt, stowing scissors and a garbage bag in her back pocket. The dog whined, still focused on the south end. Like as not, he'd scented a dead animal, and he wanted at it. He'd rolled in a seal carcass last month, and it had taken weeks for the stink to fade.

"Heel!"

Reluctantly, the dog obeyed.

She loped toward the surf line. Beyond was the naked seabed, an alien planet where she was the lone explorer. Tide pools gleamed metallic. Boulders loomed, black and spiky with mussels. The sand was cold and hard.

Joey lagged behind, whining and pissed.

Rounding a whale-sized rock, she knelt beside her meal ticket: a tiny forest of sea palms, *Postelsia palmaeformis*. She'd been a whiz at biology. Mr. Billings had wanted her to enroll in college.

All seaweed is algae, that's what Mr. Billings had said. But you could see why these were called "palms." Each specimen gripped the seafloor stones with a holdfast resembling a mass of tiny roots. Each tubular trunk was about a foot tall. Leaflike blades radiated from the top of each trunk.

Bracing one knee in the sand, she commenced the harvest, clipping one palm stem at a time. She imagined Mr. Billings' classroom. Last month, when school resumed, had her absence worried him?

She yanked her attention back to the slippery work. *Snip, snip, snip.* The sack filled. Slinging it over her shoulder, she called for Joey.

Gone.

Inserting thumb and forefinger between her lips, she whistled. Whistled again.

Waiting for him, she ran her tongue over sea palm residue on her lips.

Fish-flavored celery. Gotta wonder how Chef Antoine turns 'em into a gourmet dish.

A minute passed. Too long. If Joey was into something rotten, she'd never get to town. No one picked up a hitchhiker with a stinking dog.

Back at the ledge, she stowed the harvest. With a scrap of towel, she cleaned her feet, then donned her jeans and hoodie.

She whistled again.

A yellow ghost dog emerged from the fog, sending a chill down her back. Then she laughed, remembering she'd bleached Joey's fur.

"What is it, boy?"

He swerved and yipped, backing away, begging her to follow.

Drawing her knife, she followed him past boulders, driftwood, and rotting kelp. She squinted through wisps of fog, where light and shadow splintered and mixed. Nothing. Then, at the far end of the beach, something.

Joey raced ahead and attacked a pale mass.

Sea gulls screeched as they dove for his muzzle. He yipped in pain, backed away, and shook them off. Again, he charged. Snarling and biting.

As the gulls swirled, she caught a glimpse of blue.

Grasping a branch of driftwood, she joined the combat, her stomach clenching with every sickening *thud*. Wounded birds wobbled away. Others spread their wings and lifted off, hovering greedily, just beyond Joey's bite.

She could see it now, a man's body. Blue windbreaker, jeans, and gray tennis shoes. A bit of gray hair. A thick, reddish-gray beard. Bloody holes where his eyes had been. Bile rose. She knelt and retched the meager contents of her stomach. The dog leaned his warm body into hers, licking her ears, her cheek. She wrapped her arms around him, burying her face in his fur.

The gulls reclaimed their prize.

She struggled to her feet and scanned the cove. In a shallow tide pool, a wine-colored dinghy swayed from side to side. On its bow, *Mortal Zin*.

She recognized the dinghy. She'd watched it enter the cove yesterday, guided by the man now lying dead.

Where was the boy who'd come with him?

CHAPTER TWO

Later That Morning

As Nollaig Cooper drove her rental car away from the airport, the high-rises of San Jose, California—the capital of Silicon Valley—faded from her rearview mirror. The steering wheel was firmly clasped in her left hand, a large takeaway coffee in her right.

Yesterday—or was it the day before?—she'd boarded a plane in Milan. Should have been a direct flight to New York, but mechanical problems had forced a landing at Heathrow. Then came a storm delay, transfer to a new flight, lost luggage, and a missed connection to San Jose. Through all the delays and the time in the air, she'd worked, winding up the last details on her cases for a Dublin law firm. When she touched down in California, she wanted to be free.

And she was. She was thirty-four, and she was planning a new chapter in her life.

The weather was unseasonably hot for September, the air brown with smog. Traffic moved briskly along a highway that would be bumper to bumper at rush hour. Heading south on Highway 17 toward the Santa Cruz Mountains, she passed mile after mile of urban sprawl. She recalled her father's stories of the thousands of acres of apricot, plum, and apple trees that had blossomed here, even as late as the 1950s.

It had been called The Valley of the Heart's Delight.

Her return to California had begun with a call from her godfather, Peter Hanak, nearly three months before. He reached her at Heathrow, where she was waiting to board a flight for Rome. A man of few words, he opened with, "I'm planning a surprise party for Tina's sixtieth. Any chance you can come?"

"Umm, September … let's see … Nope, I'm booked with—" She laughed. "Of course I'll be there."

"Excellent! Can't wait to see you."

"How's the '08 vintage?"

"Trouble. Tell you all about it when you get here."

"What's wrong?"

"You know the wine business. Good years, bad years."

And the three months passed. Sure, she called the Hanaks several times. But Peter ducked all questions about the 2008 vintage. He'd never acted like that before, and she was worried he might have lost the entire year's work. It would be a relief to be there in person, find out what was going on. Help, if she could.

And there was another reason she was visiting. Fitz, her childhood mentor, a crusading lawyer with his own legal practice, had offered her a job. She'd be meeting with him for dinner that night.

She reached Los Gatos, gateway to the Santa Cruz Mountains. Highway 17, which continued over the summit to Santa Cruz and Monterey Bay, began its twisting ascent over forested foothills. Four lanes wide, split by a concrete divider installed to reduce head-on collisions, the road was affectionately called Blood Alley by the locals. But its curves were so embedded in her memory, she wound into the tight turns with ease.

As the road climbed, the air cooled. She could smell the Pacific Ocean, out of sight beyond the summit. Her father had always opened the car windows at exactly this point in the drive. He'd say, "Just imagine, the trail we're following is ten thousand years old!" He'd wax poetic about Ohlone traders hiking the trail from Monterey Bay to San Francisco Bay, packing obsidian, cinnabar, dentalium shells, feather capes, and seal skins. This route had connected forty small tribes of a culture that flourished for thousands of years in a land of unsurpassed abundance.

Of the Franciscan fathers and Spanish soldiers, riding the same path on horseback between the missions at Santa Cruz and Santa Clara, he spoke darkly. "The few Ohlone who didn't die from European diseases, they enslaved."

At other times, his focus would jump to 1848, "when America bought the land we now call 'the Southwest' from Mexico. Loggers and miners from Scotland and Wales drove wagons and ox carts along this same trail, branching out into the mountains, staking claims. Other settlers came, too: the French, the Italians, the East Coast migrants. Farms, orchards, and vineyards took root on the scarred land. It became the new state of California."

Dad's ability to bring history alive for his students had made him the most beloved teacher at Santa Cruz High School. Twenty years had passed since he died, but she could still hear his voice.

At Bear Creek Road, she exited, feeling the highway tension drain away. She was nearly home. She drove west through a second—or maybe third?—growth forest of madrone, laurel, and oak. Here and there, massive stumps remained, testimony to the ancient redwoods cut down to build San Francisco. With bravado, loggers had sawed through the magnificent trees' fifteen-foot-diameter trunks, not knowing those trees had begun reaching for the sky when Christ was born.

Then again, maybe it wouldn't have mattered to them.

Soon Noli spotted her turn, marked with a new sign, almost a billboard. She braked and signaled left. Waiting for a gap in the oncoming traffic, she studied the sign:

Andolini Vineyards
And Winery
Founded 1855
Tasting Room open daily 11-7

Approximately five feet tall and three feet wide, it displayed an Italian family crest in four quadrants: a castle on a hill, a knight in armor, a falcon, and a cluster of dark purple grapes. The crest was pure fiction, designed and installed by the new owners. Previously, the only marker for Andolini Road had been an arrow on a mailbox. Peter had liked it that way.

Gunning the engine, she shot a gap between two BMWs, surprised to find Andolini Road had been paved. To her left, the original Victorian mansion gleamed with fresh beige paint, its gingerbread highlighted in green, gold, and mauve. Six years ago, it had been derelict. Adjoining the mansion, a newly built carriage house was signed Tasting Room. The parking lot sported a churning cement truck and a portable construction shed.

The new owners at Andolini had deep pockets.

Beyond the buildings, row upon row of trellised zinfandel vines marched across the flank of Loma Buena Mountain. Ruby and gold leaves glistened in the morning damp. The vines were splendid, heavy with purple clusters awaiting harvest. Would the Hanaks' vines look as good?

The pavement ended. She proceeded at a crawl over the rocky limestone road, crossing the unfenced boundary where Andolini vineyards gave way to Hanak property: a forest of second-growth redwoods so tall, the morning sun was reduced to twilight. She lowered the window, inhaling the spicy, loamy scent of her childhood.

These few acres of redwoods belonged to the Hanaks, but originally, like all the Hanaks's land, they had been part of the Andolini Estate. In 1873, after modest success in the gold fields, a Sicilian named Marco Andolini had purchased several hundred acres of logged-over hills from a lumber company. Legend had it that Marco's oxen died from overwork before he'd cleared the final stumps. Since he'd already staked out his prospective vineyard, he'd called out to the eager sprouts that circled each stump and invited them to touch the sky. Someday, he vowed, this reborn forest would yield lumber for the homes of future Andolinis.

A man of vision, old Marco. But time had proven the founding of a dynasty required more than dreams and a willing arm.

Clenching her jaw, determined to make it on the first try, Noli turned onto a steep, uphill track—euphemistically termed "the driveway"—and gunned the engine. Her rental sedan attacked the slope, slid backwards, found traction, and burst forward onto a level graveled clearing.

Before her stood two geodesic domes, both made of redwood, one aged to silver-gray, the other a fresh reddish-brown. A broad deck wrapped its arms around the two structures, uniting the new and the old. Redwoods with trunks as stout as cathedral columns surrounded the domes, as though protecting them from harm.

This was the home of Peter and Tina Hanak. Her safe place. The place where, as a traumatized and badly burned fourteen-year-old, Noli had been given a new life.

She killed the engine, slid from the car, and stretched her travel-weary limbs. Her heart ached as she assessed the new dome, which had been built since her last visit. A wheelchair ramp sloped toward the parking lot, a reminder that multiple sclerosis had deadened Tina's legs.

The adrenaline that had fueled her drive from the airport was fading. Craving a few hours' rest, she pulled her carry-on, briefcase, and jacket from the back seat and climbed the plank steps to the older dome. For the first time in her life, it struck her how small a structure it was. Yet, here she had lived with Peter and Tina from age fourteen until leaving for college. It couldn't have been easy for the Hanaks, surrendering their privacy, bringing a teenager into what was essentially a one-room living space. But she'd never felt anything but love: the longed-for child they'd never had.

Reaching for the latch, she found a note wedged between door and frame. She pulled it free. The door was locked. Unusual, but the Hanaks had left yesterday, and they hadn't known her exact arrival time. The note was addressed *Noli*. Opening it, she recognized the sloping penmanship.

Noli, call me. It's about your father. Top priority. Fitz

Her father had died twenty years ago. What could be so urgent? Couldn't it wait until dinner? She pulled her cell from her briefcase and selected Fitz's number.

No service.

Of course. There was never cell service at the domes. She knew that.

She circled past the domes and climbed a well-worn footpath. In minutes, she'd left the redwoods behind and crossed a stretch of chaparral with an array of four solar panels. Beyond these rose a south-facing ridge, where, in all its autumn glory, stood her godparents' prize zinfandel vineyard: two hundred vines, more than a century old. They called it Old Marco's Hill.

From a distance, the thick and twisted trunks resembled dwarf olive trees. But they were indeed grape vines, their branches woven in circles to form a goblet-like rim. Shoots cascaded from these rims, carrying reddish-gold leaves and dark purple grape clusters. Nets draped from overhead scaffolding protected the fruit from marauding birds and raccoons.

One stout vine, in the center of the first row, could claim to be the leader. Peter had christened it "Bacchus." Smiling at the memory, she rolled her sleeve up to her elbow, ducked beneath the net, and plunged her arm into Bacchus's cascading leaves. Where two branches formed a deep V, her index finger registered a cold, metallic edge.

She remembered the day when she'd followed Peter to the old vineyard. Showing her how he wedged a house key in Bacchus's forking trunk, he'd said, "You'll always have a home with us, Noli."

Now, she plucked a single grape from the nearest cluster and popped it into her mouth. Juice flowed across her tongue, dancing with the distinctive flavors of the Hanaks' terroir. Then she registered the heavy tang of tannin, too heavy, the constant challenge when Peter blended his vintages. And then she sensed the fullness of sugar. These grapes were nearly ready. For this, she was grateful. It had been too many years since she'd made it home during harvest.

Feeling the sun warm on her shoulders, she traversed the western edge of the vineyard to a redwood bench which offered a view over the Hanaks' land. With equal measures of excitement and apprehension, she surveyed her godparents' miniature kingdom. The vines seemed magnificently healthy. Of course, early stages of disease could be difficult to spot, and she was no expert. Peter had said, "There are good years and bad years ..." Had he lost the entire 2008 vintage? That would be a difficult blow to absorb. Pride never permitted Peter to admit to their financial struggles, but Noli knew that Tina's MS treatments were daunting. They'd had to delay building the modern winery they desperately needed. And of course, there was the cost of the new, accessible dome. Just how close to the edge were they?

Her stomach, always unreliable, started to churn. Breathing deeply, she lifted her eyes to the horizon, across the Andolini Valley, across the receding ridges beyond, focusing on a narrow strip of blue wedged between Earth and sky. The Pacific Ocean. It was only eleven miles distant, but, as the locals joked, "You can't get there from here." No single road traversed the Santa Cruz Mountains, whose topography resembled a rumpled quilt.

Her love for this beautiful land ran deep, but its apparent tranquility would never fool her. At wild intervals, invisible faults in the ground sheared and reassembled, tossed by colliding tectonic plates in the Earth's crust. The San Andreas Fault followed the crest of the mountains, spawning lesser faults both east and west. Twenty years ago, one such fault, the Loma Prieta, had erupted and changed her life forever.

With a creeping foreboding, she remembered Fitz's note. She tested her cell phone and found it had service at this exposed altitude. She dialed his number. After ten rings, she left a voicemail. "Hi, Fitz! Got your note. Call me on the old dome's landline or wait till we meet tonight. Can't wait to see you!"

Ready to catch a few hours' sleep in her old bed, she began the downhill hike to the domes. Her cell pinged. But instead of an answer from Fitz, it was a text from Fitz's best friend, Munch Gutterson.

Can you come to the store right away? It's important.

She wanted to tell him she was severely jet-lagged and would look forward to seeing him later, but it was so unlike Munch to make this kind of request that she hesitated. Maybe Fitz was at the store? Wanting her to join them?

She texted: *Is Fitz there?*

Just come.

Munch was unable to speak, but he could hear. She could call him, politely beg off. Instead, not quite knowing why, she texted: *On my way.*

As she made her way down the mountain, she thought for the millionth time how fortunate she was. When the worst had happened, her father's Band of Brothers had closed ranks around her, much like the redwoods guarding the domes. After fighting in Vietnam, they'd all returned to Santa Cruz County to pursue their dreams. For Munch, success was owning a surf shop and living as Santa Cruz's top surfer dude. Peter's dream was this award-winning vineyard and winery. Fitz had earned a law degree and, for three decades, had fought for the underdog.

And her father? He'd founded a commune where vets and their families could live in nature and heal.

When she reached the domes, she took a shortcut by boosting herself onto the deck at the back of the new dome. As she straightened, she noticed white discoloration on a few of the boards, a striking contrast to their natural redwood hue. Puzzled, she looked closer. The white appeared to be paint that had been mostly scrubbed away. Backing up to take in all the white boards at once, she could see two words had been graffitied there:

Die Traitor

She stared at the threatening whisps of white. Someone had chosen the spot carefully, placing the words where the Hanaks' living room window looked out on the deck. Anger surged through her, and she imagined finding the creep who'd done it and making him replace the damaged deck planks—after he'd offered an apology to Peter.

But why had he done it?

CHAPTER THREE

At the Santa Cruz Yacht Harbor, parking was unusually easy. Lousy weather for sailing, surfing, or even sitting on the beach. For a moment, Noli rested her head against the steering wheel, allowing waves of exhaustion to drain away. When she opened the car door, a damp wind chilled her instantly. Less than a mile out over Monterey Bay, a wall of fog was advancing landward. Waves slammed the jetty at the harbor mouth.

She donned her suit jacket, grateful for the added warmth, and headed for Munch's store. A gray-shingled building, perpendicular to the jetty and backed against the beach, offered four storefronts; she chose the one where an orange neon sign flashed, Way Open.

Inside, a buff twenty-something man was arranging a display of skimboards. On his green T-shirt, turquoise letters proclaimed: Eat, Drink, Surf.

He gave her business suit a curious, top-to-toe assessment and said, "Need help?"

"I'm looking for Munch."

"In the back."

She threaded her way among new and used surfboards. Overhead, wetsuits hung like beheaded corpses. The air was pungent with neoprene, fiberglass, petrochemical waxes. At the stockroom, she swung the door open, calling, "Munch?"

On her left, shipping boxes were stacked to the ceiling. To her right, Munch sat at a small table; across from him, a man in the uniform of a Santa Cruz sheriff's deputy.

Munch rose and enveloped her in a welcoming hug, then held her at arm's length, pretending to look her over. A legendary surfing champion, he still dressed in flip-flop sandals and board-shorts. But his well-worn T-shirt couldn't hide the toll that time—and a love of beer—had taken on his stomach. His Dutch Boy face was deeply tanned and even more craggy than she remembered. His blond ponytail had turned silver. One thing had not changed: a thick, ropey scar ran the width of his neck, where a piece of Viet Cong shrapnel had removed his larynx.

His ocean-blue eyes, which she remembered as bright and twinkling, were red and swollen.

The uniformed man stood, saying, "Sheriff's Deputy Alonzo Villanueva. You must be Nollaig Cooper?"

"I am."

"I'd appreciate a few minutes of your time."

Munch nudged her toward a chair and sat beside her.

Resuming his seat, the deputy said, "Ms. Cooper, I have sad news. The body of John Fitzpatrick was found at Cruces Cove this morning. I understand he was important to you. I'm sorry for your loss."

She tried to ask, "How?" No words came. Bewildered, she frowned, thinking for a moment that this was a nightmare in which she was mute and immobile, at the mercy of those around her.

Munch squeezed her shoulder, then walked to a sink, filled a glass with water, and brought it to her.

She sipped. Cold water trickled down her throat.

At last the words came. "How did he die?"

"We aren't sure." The deputy leaned forward in his chair, his expression open and compassionate. He was young, trying to do his job. "Munch says you've been in touch with him?"

"By 'aren't sure,' do you mean he might not have died of natural causes?"

Ignoring her question, the deputy asked, "When did you last speak to him?"

She tried to remember. Her brain felt like mush. "It was about a month ago."

"Did Mr. Fitzpatrick mention anything that worried him? A problem at work? Or with a friend? A girlfriend?"

Uneasy now, she looked at Munch. Munch nodded, encouraging her to be open with the deputy. "On the contrary, he was happier than I've ever known him to be. He was planning to marry."

Villanueva said, "When Mr. Fitzpatrick told you about his fiancée, did he allude to any problems they might be having?"

"No, nothing like that," Noli said. Seconds passed before the implication of the deputy's questions hit her. "You think he killed himself?"

Villanueva sighed. "We have to look at that possibility, Ms. Cooper. I'm sorry. Just one last question. Can you suggest other friends of Mr. Fitzpatrick we should talk to?"

She wasn't going to mention the Hanaks, not until she'd had a chance to talk with them herself. "Deputy, I haven't lived here for more than a decade."

Deputy Villanueva stood, pulled a business card from his pocket. "Thank you, Ms. Cooper. Please accept my condolences. If you think of anything that might help our investigation, even a small detail, please call me."

Accepting his card, she asked, "Who's in charge of investigating Fitz's death?"

In a neutral tone, as though stating the weather forecast, Deputy Villanueva said, "Detective Rinzler."

"Detective *Aaron* Rinzler?"

Two beats of silence while Deputy Villanueva studied her face. "Do you know Detective Rinzler?"

She set her jaw. "Not personally. No."

Villanueva gave her a long, inscrutable look, then turned and left.

CHAPTER FOUR

Thursday, 1 p.m.

Reluctantly, Luz Alvarado handed an enlarged photograph of a blond eager-eyed girl to the gray-whiskered manager of rundown apartments on 32nd Avenue. The man leered at the photo of Crystal Langley as if undressing her with his eyes.

Luz wanted to kick him in the *cojones*. Instead, she said, "She's only fifteen. This is how she looked six months ago, but maybe she dyed her hair. Or cut it. She might have piercings or tattoos. Have you seen her?"

"No. This one I'd remember."

Luz retrieved the photo. He'd left dirt smudges around the edges. She handed him her business card. "Contact numbers are on the back. Call me if you see her." She caught the manager's bloodshot eyes one last time. "There's a reward."

He licked his lips.

As she walked away, she prayed to a god she didn't believe in: *Don't let him be the one who finds her.* She checked her watch. Time to change outfits and interview the surfers at Pleasure Point. A girl on the run could do worse than shack up with a beachboy.

She drove her beat-up Corolla along Portola Drive and parked behind a row of storefronts. No one around.

From her ever-ready disguise box, she chose a Forty-Niners cap, a denim jacket, ripped jeans, scuffed sunglasses, and a faded brown T-shirt. She wound her long hair into a bun, covered it with the cap, and checked her appearance in the rearview mirror. Thus far, she hadn't used the cap or glasses, and she'd only worn the jacket once, five days ago. With any luck, the locals wouldn't realize they'd seen her before.

Lacing up a pair of black high-tops she'd scored for $2.50 at Goodwill, she tried not to feel discouraged. Fitz had warned her to be patient.

"Kids hide better than adults—no job, no Social Security number, no car. If they use their phones, we track them down in a day. But Crystal left hers at home. Not a good sign." Fitz spread a frayed map of Santa Cruz on the worktable and circled cheap housing near the amusement park, the harbor, and Pleasure Point. "Crystal's best friend says she bragged about 'going to live on the beach.' She's pretty, and as far as we know, not strung out on drugs. These are the places she's most likely to find someone who'll take her in. The aunt claims she's smart, so you probably won't find her panhandling on Pacific Ave., but it's worth checking once in a while. Our ace in the hole is the German shepherd. She takes it everywhere."

Luz thanked the universe for giving her Fitz as an employer. He took the time to teach her what he knew, and he'd helped her qualify for a PI license far more rapidly than she'd ever dreamed. She was determined to make him proud of his investment in her.

Slinging her backpack over her shoulder, she locked the car. A blast of chilled ocean air swirled up the street, cutting through her denim jacket. Shivering, she checked the waves. Tall, but crumbling into a north wind. Bad conditions for surfers. Still, there were a couple of loners on the sand, staring out at the bay. She approached one, a sunburnt blond man wrapped in a beach towel. "Mind if I sit down?"

Shading his eyes, he smoothed the sand to his left. "Be my guest. Bring a board?"

She sat beside him and mimicked his stare, watching the white caps. "Nope. Just watching."

"Not much today. What's your name?"

"Kelly. Yours?"

"Bob. Haven't seen you around."

"I hitched from Fresno. Looking for my friend, Crystal." From her jeans pocket, she pulled out a small photo of Crystal and herself, photoshopped to look like they'd been together. "She has me worried. Maybe you've seen her? She has a German shepherd named Trace."

He sniffed. "I maybe saw a girl like this. Downtown. But her hair was short. Black."

"She could've changed it."

"Yeah. Well, her dog was white. Not a German shepherd."

"Where downtown?"

"Laurel Street, near Chez Antoine. Green eyes, just like these. I tried to chat her up, but she kept walking."

"When?"

"Last week. Tuesday, maybe Wednesday."

Luz's cell vibrated. "Excuse me." She stood and opened the cell. It was Mrs. Maldonado, Fitz's secretary. She walked to the road before answering.

"This is Luz."

Silence, then the sound of a woman weeping.

CHAPTER FIVE

M unch led Noli to the front of the store. His assistant was gone. He posted a Gone Surfin sign on the front door, grabbed a small, battered laptop, retrieved a large shopping bag from behind the counter, and locked the door. Nodding toward the Crow's Nest, the iconic restaurant at the harbor's entrance, he set off. She had to stretch her legs to keep up with him.

A foghorn called *oogah-oogah* in a deep voice, beckoning any boats still out on the bay to return to safe harbor. She followed Munch through the heavy redwood door of the restaurant. A zaftig waitress with spiky bleached hair, wearing an I'm-not-over-the-hill-yet outfit of hip-hugging jeans, halter top, and nose ring, gave Munch a hundred-watt smile. Her name tag read, Shananda.

Shananda's gaze lingered on Munch's red-rimmed eyes as she said, "Yo, Munch. Want a table by the glass? Not exactly a crowd today, as you can see."

"By the glass" meant a table overlooking the harbor's mouth. Prime real estate. But Munch nodded instead toward a sign that read, *Bar closed until 6 p.m.*

Shananda looked puzzled. "You want lunch?"

Munch nodded as he swept past the sign and mounted the staircase leading to the bar. Noli followed. The bar was empty. Expansive windows offered views across the beach to the ocean, but he circled to the right and selected a table secreted against the north wall. Here, the window offered a view across the parking lot and up the harbor.

Shananda approached, pad and paper in her hand. "Your usual, Munch?"

He reached for her pencil and pad, scribbled a note.

Shananda studied his face for a few seconds, walked to the bar, and returned with a bottle of Jameson in one hand and two glasses in the other. "Ice?"

Munch shook his head.

"Besides this, you want your usual?" she asked.

Munch nodded.

Shananda turned to Noli. "For you?"

Longing for warmth, Noli answered, "Coffee and a bowl of chowder—piping hot, please."

"You got it." Shananda gave Munch a worried look before walking away.

Munch poured double shots of whiskey into both glasses. He raised his glass, mouthing, "Fitz."

Noli tried to raise her glass to meet his, but her hand shook so badly, the whiskey spilled.

Munch waited.

Wrapping both hands around her glass, she succeeded in lifting it to tap his. "To Fitz."

Munch knocked his back in one gulp.

Hoping the smooth Irish alcohol would help steady her nerves, Noli took a sip. The warmth that spread from her tongue to her toes felt welcome. But nausea quickly followed. She squeezed her eyes and concentrated on breathing until the queasiness passed.

When she opened her eyes, Munch was keyboarding in a two-finger frenzy. He'd used a laptop for years, but never learned to type.

Wrapping her arms around herself, trying to grasp that Fitz was gone from her world, she mindlessly scanned the shops wedged into the marina parking lot. Bait and tackle, boat rental, coffee kiosk, deli. When she was a kid, the buildings had been shabby and weathered. Now they boasted new paint and crisp awnings. In the harbor, a lot of expensive yachts. No surprise. Silicon Valley was just an hour's drive away.

In the 1960s and '70s, many Vietnam vets—including Fitz and Munch—had chosen to live on sailboats in the relative privacy of a funky harbor, forming a tight community. They knew their neighbors understood when flashbacks tore their heads apart. Had they been pushed out? She wanted to ask Munch, but he was still keyboarding. Finally, he turned the laptop around.

Coast Guard brought *Mortal Zin* to their dock 2 hrs ago.

Jack Breezy—guy who lives on Fitz's dock—got guard to talk. Suicide note found on boat.

Fitz died by suicide? She closed her eyes, remembering her last conversation with him:

"*How's business, Fitz?*"

"*Excellent. I'm representing a new union, one for vineyard workers. Best of all, I've got a new PI, a dynamite young Latina.*"

He'd paused, and she'd heard him inhaling deeply, pulling air through a cigarette. "*Wish me luck, Scout. I'm going to ask Pilar to marry me. It's time to retire. We want to enjoy whatever time we have left. I need a successor. Someone like you.*"

When she was growing up, Fitz had called her Scout in honor of the brave little girl in *To Kill a Mockingbird*. She'd never called him Atticus, after Scout's father, a lawyer who'd stood up to a racist lynch mob, but that was how she thought of him. In any case, Fitz hadn't called her Scout in years—for a corporate lawyer, the name wasn't a good fit.

"I'm honored, Fitz. But I really don't know what's next for me."
"Just think about it, okay?"

To her surprise, she had thought about it. She'd been going through a dark time and was ready for a change. She'd expected they'd talk about it when they had dinner that night.

She realized Munch was watching her, waiting for a response. "When I talked with Fitz, he was truly happy." She expected immediate agreement from Munch, but instead, his eyes slid away to look out the window. Her stomach went squishy. "Do you believe Fitz would kill himself?"

Munch tapped the computer keys. The gash across his throat throbbed bright red.

Sure, if he was sick. Cancer or something

"He wouldn't tell you first? I don't believe it."

Munch spread his hands on the table, his fingers moving up and down as though playing a slow tune on a piano. A tear escaped his brimming eyes and slowly traversed the network of broken veins on his nose. She waited, knowing how hard this was for him. He and Fitz had grown up like brothers in a rigid foster home. Both of them orphans, they'd been each other's confidant and protector.

His fingers crept back to the computer and typed,

You're right

She took his hand. "You know it's not your fault, right? No one could protect Fitz from all the people who wanted him dead."

Munch nodded without much conviction and released her hand.

"Did Jack know what the suicide note said?"

Munch shook his head and started typing.

Something else. Jack heard Pilar yelling at Fitz late Monday night. Sounded furious. So cops say Fitz

depressed cause their fight

"Where were they—Fitz and Pilar?"

Fitz's boat. Jack is berthed on same dock.

"He couldn't make out her words?"
Munch shook his head.
"Did Fitz think he'd lost her?"

Maybe. Also afraid not make good husband. Scared Pilar
be disappointed.

Fitz scared? That was a notion so strange, it was like being handed a new piece to a jigsaw puzzle she'd already assembled. What else hadn't she known about Fitz?

The waitress brought their orders. Munch pushed his computer aside and dug into his burger and fries. Noli dipped a spoon into her chowder. The first taste seemed comforting, but when it hit her stomach, the queasy feeling returned.

She pulled Fitz's note from her pocket and passed it to Munch. "Fitz left that for me at the Hanaks'. Do you know what he meant?"

Munch shook his head.

"Maybe some news about the war?" Her father, a Quaker, had served as a medic in the Vietnam War. "I hear there's been a new release of documents."

Munch turned his hands up in a "beats me" gesture.

Struggling to keep her emotions under control, she pushed thoughts of her father aside and returned her attention to Fitz's death and the suicide note.

"Did Jack Breezy learn how Fitz's body was found?"

Munch typed, Anonymous call this morning

Cruces Cove, where Fitz's body had been found, was several miles up the coast from Santa Cruz. "Was the *Mortal Zin* anchored outside the cove?"

Munch nodded.

"But his body was on the sand?"

Munch shrugged. He didn't know.

"Aaron Rinzler, the guy in charge of the investigation, he's the guy Fitz tried to get fired, right?"

Munch nodded. His jaw muscles twitched. He poured another shot, downed it, chased it with coffee, and returned to keyboarding. Thinking he was laying out the background on Rinzler for her, she said, "I remember the story, Munch."

Munch nodded but kept typing.

Fitz's beef with Rinzler had begun when Fitz was fresh out of law school. Rinzler had come into the Santa Cruz County Sheriff's Department as a rookie. He'd immediately begun intimidating Latino kids in Watsonville, a town in south county with a large population of Mexican American families. When the parents of two boys he'd beat up complained, Rinzler hid behind his badge, claiming the kids were lying gangbangers. Back then, there were no cell phones with video capability, so the kids had no proof. Fitz charged Rinzler with police brutality and tracked down a handful of adult witnesses. Fitz won, but Rinzler wasn't fired, merely sent to sensitivity training. Still, the blot on Rinzler's record was enough to impede his advancement, and he'd used every means at his disposal to make Fitz's life difficult. Over the years, the hostility was re-stoked every time Fitz defended a client Rinzler had arrested.

Munch turned his laptop toward Noli:

We might have an ally in Alonzo Villanueva. The deputy you just met. He's a local kid. Few years ago Fitz helped his older brother, Angel, get out of the Norteños gang. But Alonzo's only been a deputy for a couple years. He won't have any pull.

Noli nodded. "All the same, he might share information with us. Rinzler isn't going to investigate unless the killer walks into his office and confesses."

Munch nodded, poured himself another shot, and resumed typing.

Her thoughts turned to the evidence they would lose if Rinzler shut down the investigation. No fingerprints from the *Mortal Zin*. No search for witnesses at Cruces Cove, nor at the harbor when Fitz boarded his boat and sailed away.

Munch swung the laptop toward her.

Jack is walking harbor. Looking for anybody who saw *Mortal Zin* leave yesterday

"Good." Thinking Munch might have known what Fitz had planned for the day, she asked, "Did you see Fitz yesterday morning?"

Said he was taking day off to work on old apple barn at Tina and Peter's. Wants to make it into house for Pilar. They wanted to surprise you. Fitz buying old orchard from Tina and Peter. Retire there. Plant grapes.

That would be—*would have been*—perfect. The Hanaks would have capital to build a new winery. Fitz and his bride would begin the new adventure together. But now...

Fighting tears, she said, "Instead, he sailed to Cruces Cove. Why?"

Munch shook his head.

"When I worked for him, Fitz used the Cove for picnics. He often sailed the staff of Legal Services up to Cruces for an afternoon off. He'd anchor the *Mortal Zin* outside the cove and row us to the beach in the dinghy. He was the only person I knew who could navigate that cove—it's full of submerged rocks."

How did sailing to Cruces Cove fit with Fitz's stated intention of going to work on his mountain property? Had he just changed his mind, decided it was a beautiful day for sailing? Or had he decided to end his life in a place he loved?

"The most important thing right now is to stop Rinzler from shutting down the investigation. We haven't got much to go on, but we can scare him into believing it *could be* murder, and that we're watching his every move to see that he does his job. I'll confront him in the morning. In the meanwhile, let's find out everything we can. I need to meet with Fitz's new investigator. You know her?"

A smile broke through Munch's grief. He typed:

Luz Alvarado. Newly licensed PI, works for Fitz 3 days a week. He says she's great! She still works a second job, late shift at the Pelican Bar, on weekends.

Noli remembered the Pelican Bar. Run-down and welcoming, just a block from the harbor. It was home away from home for the men and women who lived on, or regularly sailed in, their boats. "I'll call her. Can you hang out there tonight, ask around? If we can find witnesses who saw Fitz, we might have stronger position with Rinzler."

Munch gave a thumbs-up, then, pointing to the men's room, he walked away.

Noli peered through the window, surveying a deserted harbor. Daylight had turned an eerie gray. She closed her eyes and reviewed her conversation with Munch, hoping her jet-lagged brain had absorbed everything he'd said.

Munch reappeared just as his assistant came bounding up the stairs and announced, "We've got a busload of surfers from Fresno."

Munch answered with a nod. His assistant turned on his heel and departed.

Munch slid onto his seat and typed,

How long can you stay?

"As long as it takes."

Munch placed the shopping bag he'd carried from the store on the table.

Old bottle Andolini zinfandel for Peter n Tina. Take it for me?

"Wow. Where'd you get it?"

Networking.

"Hell of a network, Munch."

He smiled, looking just for a moment like the forever-teen-ager she remembered. Then her brain registered *old* and *zinfandel*. Munch, a beer enthusiast, knew nothing about wine.

"How old is *old*?"

1982

She bit her tongue. Having grown up in the Hanaks' vine-yard, she knew zinfandel didn't age well. A cabernet, if crafted for aging and stored properly, might be hitting its prime. But zinfandel? No way. Munch had bought a bottle of vinegar.

He was studying her face, sensing her hesitation. Lowering his eyes, he typed:

What's wrong?

"I, uh, was just thinking how difficult it is to age zinfandel."

Dont worry. Fitz drank 2nd bottle. Wine fantastic.

Unlike Munch, Fitz knew wine. There must be a misunder-standing, but this wasn't the time to sort it out. "Wonderful! Sure you don't want to wait, bring it yourself?"

Sooner, better. Tell Peter I might have more bottles by tomorrow. Fitz said he's very discouraged.

Discouraged? Who wouldn't be? If he'd lost an entire vintage and was the target of graffitied death threats? She considered asking Munch about the threatening graffiti, then decided to wait. Stay focused on challenging Rinzler, for now.

CHAPTER SIX

Thursday, 3:30 p.m.

As Noli stepped out of the Crow's Nest, fingers of mist wove through the parking lot, chilling the air. She jogged to the rental car and laid Munch's wine carefully on its side on the back seat. From the rectangular bulge in the sack, she guessed the bottle was encased in a block of Styrofoam, a professional barrier against damage during transportation.

She pulled out her cell and called Fitz's office.

"Legal Services, Inez Maldonado speaking," said a teary voice. "How may I help you?"

"My name is Nollaig Cooper. I'm calling Luz Alvarado on a matter of great urgency."

"Ms. Alvarado is out. May I take a message?"

"Ms. Maldonado, you don't know me, but I worked for Fitz—John Fitzpatrick—many years ago. You're crying, so I'm guessing the sheriff's deputies have already notified you of his death. Am I right?"

"Y-y-yes."

"That's why I need to talk to Luz as soon as possible. What's her cell number?"

"If you give me your number, I will take a message."

Noli complied and ended the call. She strode to the first dock, the one belonging to the Coast Guard. The *Mortal Zin* was chained there, tied with so much yellow tape it looked gift-wrapped. Its dinghy, also yellow-taped, bobbed on the water behind.

In front of the *Mortal Zin*, where the Coast Guard cutter should have been docked, there was empty water. Given the speed with which the fog had come, the Guard was likely answering a distress call. She needed to interview one of the guards, but they weren't likely to return any time soon.

She moved to the edge of the dock, as close to the *Zin* as possible. A beautiful mahogany and teak sloop, forty-two feet long, it was a rare beauty and the pride of the harbor. It had been Fitz's *home*. In the misty light, she imagined Fitz standing topside, reaching out a hand to steady her as she jumped aboard.

And it hit her afresh, the knowledge that he was dead. Stunned for a moment, she felt as though her heart had ripped, leaving a gaping hole that could never be repaired.

Fitz, I swear I will find your killer.

She took a deep breath, straightened her back, and paced the dock, examining as much of the *Zin's* deck as she could see. The light was poor, but there was no obvious sign of a struggle: nothing broken, no blood. But what of the cabins below?

No one was around to see if she ignored the yellow tape and boarded the *Zin*. So tempting. But there was a shiny padlock on the hatch, so even if she jumped the tape, she couldn't get below.

Disappointed, she remembered Munch saying Jack Breezy would be casing the harbor, hoping to find someone who'd seen Fitz sail out. Maybe he'd already succeeded?

She scanned the docks and quay for a man who might be Jack. No one in sight, but the harbor was a narrow thumb of water curving inland for a quarter mile. Jack might be at the far end.

The docks were named in alphabetical order, running up the west side and down the east. Entrance to each was protected by a tall fence and a locked steel-mesh door. L Dock, the next after the Coast Guard's, was deserted, as were the next two.

Moving deeper inland, she came to O Dock. Twelve slips on each side. She thought she spotted movement behind the curtain of a Catalina 32 named *Mi Sueño*. She tried the dock's mesh door. Often it was left unlatched by boat owners expecting guests, but no luck today.

"Hello, *Mi Sueño*!" she shouted. "Can I talk with you?"

No answer.

"Hello, O Dock! Anyone home?"

She waited. No response. Every vessel was battened down. The adjacent docks were similarly deserted.

If she couldn't interview the owners in person, maybe she could reach them by phone. The harbormaster, who handled the renting of slips as well as the policing of the harbor, must have a directory, and his office was only a few yards away.

She strode to a gray, two-story clapboard building attached to a four-story observation tower. When she was halfway up the stairs, her cell rang. Hoping Luz Alvarado was returning her call, she whipped the phone from her pocket, but the screen displayed the number of a colleague in Dublin.

She silenced the phone and opened the door.

A slender young man seated behind a low counter said, "Can I help you?"

"My name is Nollaig Cooper. I'm an attorney." She pulled out a business card. With any luck, the man wouldn't look too closely at the address. "I'm looking into the death of John Fitzpatrick, who lived on the *Mortal Zin*. Did you know him?"

"Fitz? Sure. Everyone knew him."

"Were you here yesterday?"

"Sorry. My day off."

"I need phone numbers for the owners on B, C, and D Docks."

His forehead wrinkled. "I'll have to ask the harbormaster." He walked down a short hallway, knocked on a door, and stepped through. In less than a minute he returned, followed by a stocky, middle-aged man who came directly to the counter and offered his hand. His complexion was both florid and tanned. "Chuck Krieger. Friend of Fitz for thirty years." His handlebar mustache danced as he spoke.

"Nollaig Cooper. Fitz was a family friend. In my younger days, I worked for him."

"Matt says you want a phone list?"

"Exactly. I'm looking for people who saw the *Mortal Zin* prepare to sail out yesterday."

"You don't buy the suicide verdict?" he asked.

"Do you?"

"Hell, no. Fitz's the last guy on earth who'd kill himself over some woman."

"What woman would that be?"

"His fiancée. Don't recall the name. But Jack Breezy heard 'em fighting a few days before Fitz died. Blabbed all about it to the sheriff's deputies." The harbormaster shook his head in disgust.

"Any other theories floating around?"

"Not that I've heard. But I haven't been over to the Pelican for two nights running."

"Did the sheriff ask you for a directory of boat owners?"

"No, he did not." He looked her in the eye and paused, as if to say, *I'm thinking what you're thinking.*

"I need to start calling right away."

"And I'd like to help. But owners' phone numbers aren't public information. I'd be booted out of here if even one of them found out how you got his number." He drummed the fingers of one hand on the counter while he stared out at the harbor. Then his face brightened. "Ever sail in the regattas?"

"Sure. I used to crew for Munch."

"Things haven't changed. Wednesday and Sunday, each boat races the others in its class. Don't know which ones went out yesterday, but odds are someone saw Fitz. So here's the deal: Weather prediction for Sunday looks promising. Lots of folks are likely to show up. If you're here around eleven, you'll catch them before they sail." He pulled a card from a plastic holder on the counter and wrote on it. "My home phone and cell. Anything I can do—that won't lose me my job—call me."

She thanked him politely, thinking Sunday was too long to wait. With any luck, Jack Breezy or Munch would find at least one witness by night's end.

As she walked out, she checked her watch. Four thirty. The legal offices would close soon, and Luz had not called. She dialed the number again.

"Legal Services, Inez Maldonado. How may I help you?" The receptionist's voice was still shaky.

"Ms. Maldonado, this is Nollaig Cooper again. I haven't heard from Ms. Alvarado. Is she in the office?"

"I'm sorry, Ms. Alvarado is not in. Perhaps you can reach her in the morning."

Hoping Luz would return her call before then, Noli set off across the public parking lot to the one reserved for boat owners. She located Fitz's perfectly restored Woody station wagon, which showed no sign of having been searched by the sheriff's deputies.

Again, memories rushed to her mind. Waxing the Woody's side panels with Fitz; riding along Highway 1 with Fitz, talking over a complicated case; Fitz picking her up at the airport in the old days, saying, "Good to have you home, Noli."

She squeezed her eyes shut, wiped away the tears, and banished the memories.

She tested the driver's door. Locked.

Fitz never forgot the details of a case, but he was forever losing his keys. So he'd devised a backup system: the keys to his life were magnetically clamped to the underside of his Woody. Several false keys were included to make things difficult for a thief.

She ran her finger along the rim of the left-front fender and found three magnetic boxes. By the time she'd combed all the fenders and both bumpers, she'd harvested a total of twelve, all of them crusted with dirt and oil. Her heart sank. None of the boxes had been opened recently. Either Fitz's memory had improved, or none of these keys would open his office door.

CHAPTER SEVEN

Thursday, 6 p.m.

Luz's tears had dried, replaced by a furious need to act. She planned to text Munch soon, but first she wanted to find a lead to Fitz's killer.

She stood in Fitz's office, surrounded by boxes, file drawers, and stacks of loose paper. She picked up the nearest document: *Clements v. Greenblatt, Inc.* Inside, page after page of legalese. It would take hours just to learn what was at stake, much less whether Greenblatt or Clements had motive to take out a contract on Fitz.

She bit her lip. *Think, Luz! Think!*

Where had Fitz gone yesterday? Booting up the computer, she opened the calendar for Wednesday, September 23. He'd written, *Day Off, work on property.*

Property? Must be the land where he and Pilar were building a house, somewhere in a vineyard. So how did he end up at the beach?

His email might shine a light on it.

He'd kept a little notebook filled with passwords. He'd told her, *If you ever need access to computer files, use it. Every password is written in reverse.*

She'd felt honored, being trusted in that way. Now she wondered, *Was he expecting trouble? Wouldn't he have warned her?*

She scanned his inbox. Today's emails were simple, most pertaining to a missing persons case he was handling by himself. Yesterday's mail was more of the same. From Tuesday, one message was marked *High Priority*. The sender was Raul Espinoza, a professional labor organizer for the new Union of Vineyard Workers. Fitz was to be Raul's counsel.

Raul's message read, *Please confirm you'll attend. Meeting with the Tri-County Vineyard Owners Association, 10 a.m. Oct 8. Soquel Inn.*

Before she could call Raul, her cell chimed. It was her brother, Eduardo, a Santa Cruz city cop, away on training in Sacramento. Had news of Fitz's death already reached him?

Lifting the phone to her ear, she said, "Yes?"

"Sit down, Luz." It was a command, yet Eduardo's *Big Brother* voice contained warmth as well as authority. "You're not going to like this."

"Just tell me."

"They're calling Fitz a suicide."

"What?"

"He left a suicide note on his boat."

"Bullshit."

"I'm sorry, Lucita. It's hard to accept."

"They're wrong."

In a kind tone, Eduardo said, "Lucita, I know a lawyer in Watsonville who could use your help right now. I'll call—"

She cut him off. "First, I find the man who killed Fitz."

"*¡Maldita sea!*" he swore softly. "I knew you'd—"

"Rinzler didn't even search Fitz's office, Eduardo. What does that tell you?"

"Lucita, you don't know—"

She cut the connection.

The sound of tires on the gravel parking lot brought her to the window. An unfamiliar sedan pulled in. Its headlights died, then the dome light came on. An auburn-haired woman was clearly visible in the driver's seat. No passengers.

From her second-story vantage point, Luz had a view of the woman's lap as she sorted through a pile of keys, selected several, then turned off the dome light and exited the car. Who was she?

The woman headed in the direction of the back door.

Luz switched off the desk lamp.

★ ★ ★

At the back door to Fitz's office building, Noli tried four keys with no success. But the next key slid into the keyhole and turned. Encouraged, she swung the door open and entered a hallway dimly lit by a blue safety light. She trailed her hand over the nearest wall, searching in vain for a light switch. She pulled her cell from her pocket and used it as flashlight.

There was a staircase to the left, leading to the second floor. Silently, she ascended. She pulled Fitz's keys from her pocket. At the first door on the right, Fitz's office, the second key she tried turned easily. With a sigh of relief, she pushed the door open and reached for the light switch.

A hand gripped her wrist and twisted her arm behind her as a blow to her knees sent her down.

Her head slammed the floor.

Pain rocketed from cheek to shoulder.

Her cell skittered across the floor, illuminating an empty office chair.

A knee pressed into her back, pinning her in place.

"Who the fuck are you?" It was a woman's voice. Low and threatening.

At first, she couldn't summon any words. Was this Fitz's killer? If so, what chance did she have? No one knew where she was. She managed to croak, "Nollaig Cooper."

"Where'd you get the keys?"

"Fitz hides them in his Woody."

A few moments of silence passed before the weight lifted from her back.

The overhead light came on.

Noli placed both hands on the floor and rose to her knees. The room spun, then settled. Her assailant sat at the desk—Fitz's desk—staring with penetrating brown eyes. The woman's face was finely sculpted: high cheekbones, full lips. Her skin was brown, her black hair wound in a tight bun. She wore black jeans and a baggy sweatshirt. She was young, maybe mid-twenties. Motionless, she radiated the confidence and tense energy of a cat watching its prey. Pointing at the open door, she growled, "Get out."

"Are you Luz Alvarado?" Noli asked.

"I said, get out."

"I'm here to help."

"With what?"

Noli rose to her feet, aware that she was swaying. Grasping the corner of the desk for support, she said, "The sheriff's calling Fitz a suicide. He's going to shut down the investigation."

"Says who?"

"Call Munch Gutterson. He'll tell you."

"*You* don't know Munch. He can't talk."

"Text him!"

Not taking her eyes off Noli, Luz pulled her cell from a back pocket, hesitated, then double-thumbed a message. Setting the cell on the desk, she crossed her arms and leaned back to wait.

Noli eased into a shabby chair, one of two facing Fitz's desk. Behind the desk and to one side, rainbow-colored ellipses danced across a computer monitor, as though to remind her of how much she needed Luz's cooperation. She took a deep breath, swallowed her rising anger, and made a show of surveying the office. It looked the same as his Legal Services office had twenty years before. Utilitarian, with an overlay of chaos. Dented, serviceable furniture. Stacks of paper on every horizontal surface.

A hardback book lay atop the desk, open and face down. She craned her head to read the book's spine: *The History and Mystery of Zinfandel* by Charles Sullivan. Aware that Luz was watching her, she extended her hand slowly and picked up the book. Inside the book's front cover was written, *Property of Peter Hanak*. Post-Its protruded from the book like a furry yellow fungus. She felt a stab of sadness, recalling what Munch had said: Fitz had looked forward to planting his own vineyard on the land he was buying from the Hanaks.

Luz's cell chimed. She read the text, presumably from Munch, then leaned back and surveyed Noli from head to foot. "That was a really stupid thing you did, coming here alone."

"Shit, Luz! I couldn't wait till you deigned to call me."

Luz shrugged.

Searching for a positive opening, Noli said, "Fitz told me how impressed he was with you. How long have you been a PI?"

Ignoring the question, Luz asked, "Why did you leave him?"

"Come on, Luz! Every minute that passes, the murderer is—"

"Tell me or go."

Noli held Luz's unwavering gaze, trying to comprehend what was wanted. Was it a question of loyalty? Trust?

"All right. Here's my story. I grew up on a commune in the mountains near here. Fitz was my father's close friend. They served in Vietnam together. Fitz was like an uncle to me, and he's the one who got me interested in the law. I started working for him when I was still in high school and continued right through law school.

"When I passed the bar, I realized I wanted to see the world. I was offered a position with an international firm based in Dublin." She paused, trying to read Luz's reaction. But Luz's expression was impassive. Deciding full disclosure was the only hope of winning Luz's trust, she continued. "And Luz, I needed the money. My stepmother was being treated in a private mental hospital. It cost far more than Fitz could pay me." She took a deep breath. "I want to emphasize Fitz encouraged me to go. He *insisted*. He knew I'd come home when I was ready."

Luz's expression was skeptical. "It's been more than a decade, right? Are you telling me you don't like your work?"

"In the beginning, I loved it. The travel, the challenge. But lately?" She searched for the right words. "I do mergers and acquisitions. Multidimensional puzzles. I'm good at it. If I do my job well, I help corporations become more efficient. But lately, too often, that's meant workers lose their jobs while stockholders get richer."

Luz's rigid posture softened just a bit. "So you're done with it?"

Noli spoke softly. "Didn't Fitz tell you? He asked me to come back. He wanted me to take over so he could retire."

Surprise flashed across Luz's face before she could retrieve a look of indifference.

Noli said, "I've told you the truth. You need to know he trusted me."

Luz looked away, considering. Finally, she asked, "Do you have any idea who killed him?"

Noli answered, "No. I was hoping you might have some leads."

"Not yet." Luz swiveled to the computer and began keyboarding. The screen opened to a calendar.

Feeling a surge of hope, Noli said, "Fitz backed up his calendar on his computer? And you have access?"

"Yes."

"He had a lot of confidence in you."

"Maybe he knew he would die soon."

It was nearly midnight when Noli pushed her chair away from a file-laden table in Fitz's office. She glanced at Luz, who sat at Fitz's desk, scrolling through old emails. For hours, they'd been working under an unspoken agreement: it was Noli's job to search for leads in the legal files and Luz would search the email.

Noli said, "I'm going to make a fresh pot of coffee, Luz."

"Like I said, I don't drink coffee."

"Tea?"

"No caffeine. Is that so hard to believe?"

"In my world, yes." Noli settled for the stale half-cup left in the coffee carafe. She stared at an open file, trying to focus her weary eyes on a case file from earlier in the year. A fifteen-year-old boy had run away from his home in Redding. Fitz had reunited boy and mother, obtained a restraining order on the abusive stepfather. Stepfather moved to Florida. Not a likely suspect.

As she edged around the desk to pull more cases from the file drawers, she watched Luz. Luz's face was fierce, as though she were locked in combat with a hostile computer. Her fingers were slender and tapered, the nails bitten to the quick.

Sensing Noli's gaze, Luz looked up. "Find anything?"

"Not yet," Noli said. "The open cases are either runaway kids or abusive husbands and stepfathers. I can imagine the abusers going after Fitz, maybe trying to punch him out. But so far, I've found no one who could've planned a fake suicide."

Luz's cell rang. After a rapid conversation in Spanish, she said to Noli, "You know about Fitz's fiancée, Pilar, right? That was her son. Pilar's gone to a retreat in Guadalajara. It'll be a week before we can talk to her."

Noli said, "So she's in seclusion, deciding whether to forgive Fitz, not knowing he's dead."

"Yeah."

"Luz, I've got to catch some sleep. I—" At the look of disdain on Luz's face, Noli felt a surge of anger. Taking a deep breath, she continued, "Look, I haven't slept in a couple of days. I'll be back here as early as possible in the morning. Can we talk then about how we're going to work together?"

Returning her eyes to the computer, her voice flat, Luz said, "Tomorrow."

Noli looked at the stack of case files yet to be examined. The lead to Fitz's killer could be there, on that table. But if she tried to keep going, it could slip right past her.

CHAPTER EIGHT

Friday, 5:30 a.m.

A blast of reggae music ripped Noli from black, dreamless sleep. The air was cold and damp. The bed, hard. The music, very near. Seconds passed before she remembered she was in a Santa Cruz motel.

On the wall above her head, the occupant of the room next door pounded in anger.

She yanked the clock radio's cord from the wall and shouted an apology. She'd forgotten the first rule of sleeping in a motel: Always check the alarm clock.

She cancelled the alarm she'd set for seven thirty on her cell and headed for the shower. Shampooing her hair beneath near-scalding water, she considered how to approach Detective Rinzler.

Rinzler was a bully. He understood power. And the only power she could wield was the threat that he was being watched, and that incorrect police procedure would be challenged. His career had already been damaged by bad publicity; she would make him believe it could happen again.

She opened her carry-on and removed a plastic zip bag containing a clean silk blouse and fresh underwear. She'd learned years ago to have backup clothing in case her luggage was lost. She touched-up her rumpled slacks with the motel's iron, pulled them on, then ventured to the bathroom mirror to assess the damage to her face.

It could be worse. A purple bruise had formed at the outer edge of her left cheekbone, extending toward her jaw. Much of it would be covered by her chin-length hair.

Could she and Luz work together? Last night, after the initial confrontation, Luz had been cold but polite. They'd shared their progress—or lack thereof.

Time would tell. Luz had promised to stake out Cruces Cove all morning; if they were lucky, she'd find someone who'd been there on Wednesday and had seen Fitz arrive.

Noli rubbed moisturizer on her cheeks and treated her red-rimmed eyes to two drops each of Refresh. As she blinked and peered into the mirror, she had the brief sensation of seeing her father there, a mirage that often came to her when she was exhausted. While it was true that she had her Irish mother's auburn hair and green eyes, her bones were modeled after her father: high forehead; straight brow; long, thin nose; sturdy chin. Only her full lips softened the severe countenance of his Quaker ancestors.

She headed out for some breakfast. Aromas of coffee and toast led her to the motel's overly sanitized breakfast room.

With a mug of pretend-gourmet coffee and some steaming instant oatmeal, she took a table where she could be alone. An earlier patron had left a copy of the *Santa Cruz Sentinel*. Inside, on page two, was the report of Fitz's death.

FORMER LEGAL SERVICES DIRECTOR DIES

An anonymous tip yesterday led sheriff's deputies to the body of a well-known attorney on the beach in Cruces Cove, eleven miles north of Santa Cruz on Highway 1.

According to an unofficial source, a suicide note has been found.

John Fitzpatrick, 66, a Santa Cruz native, served in Vietnam and subsequently attended Boalt Hall School of Law at UC Berkeley. He returned to Santa Cruz as an attorney for, and subsequently director of, Santa Cruz Legal Services (1977–1987). After leaving Legal Services to establish a private practice, Fitzpatrick continued working in the public eye, most notably as lead attorney in the class-action suit against Immigration and Naturalization Services (now USCIS) on behalf of Beach Flats residents.

Fitzpatrick was also a prominent leader of the local chapter of Veterans for Peace and a vocal advocate for veterans.

When contacted, Joe Cortines, current director of Legal Services, said, "It is impossible to overstate John Fitzpatrick's contribution to social and economic justice in this county. I am stunned and heartbroken at the news of his death."

Noli read the article a second time, pondering the contrast between the public figure it described and the low-profile caseload Fitz had carried recently. Maybe somewhere there was a notebook containing details of his political work?

Probably not. Fitz had been legendary for his ability to keep everything he needed to know in his memory.

She ripped the article from the paper and folded it for later. There was one big advantage to having Fitz's death publicized as a suicide. The killer would assume he was in the clear and might not bother to cover his tracks any further.

Shortly before nine o'clock, Noli parked in front of the Santa Cruz County Office Building. Five floors of concrete, solid enough to withstand an earthquake, the building was graced with just enough architectural detail to escape being labeled "grim."

Her cell buzzed as she crossed the parking lot. A text from Peter. *Couldn't reach you at the domes. We'll be home by eleven tonight.*

She answered, *See you soon.* She was worried about the impact of Fitz's death on Peter and Tina. Not only had they lost a dear friend, but there was the money Fitz was to have paid for their unused land.

Praying the Hanaks wouldn't learn of Fitz's death until she could talk to them, she refocused on the immediate challenge. In the lobby, a directory indicated the sheriff's offices occupied the third floor. Waiting for the elevator, she gulped a deep breath and pasted a grim smile of confidence on her face.

On the third floor, she exited the elevator into a small waiting area before a counter staffed by two women in uniform. She approached the counter, gave her name, and explained she had important evidence relevant to the death of John Fitzpatrick. She wished to speak to Detective Rinzler. No, she would not be willing to speak with one of his deputies.

Detective Rinzler, she was told, was not available.

She said she would wait until the detective could speak with her, seated herself, and read the day's news on her phone. When a half-hour had passed, she removed her laptop from her briefcase and subscribed online to the *Santa Cruz Sentinel*. She set up a search on "John Fitzpatrick" for the past three years and began reviewing the results in reverse chronological order. On March 20 of 2009, the anniversary of the Iraq invasion, he and Peter had hosted a program on local television called "Eyes at the Front." Their guests were soldiers who had returned from Iraq. Quotes from the soldiers made it abundantly clear that, although they'd volunteered for the Army to support their country after 9/11, none had returned believing the invasion of Iraq was justified.

In the days following the paper's coverage of the TV program, angry letters to the editor had excoriated Fitz and Peter—both of them decorated soldiers—for their lack of patriotism. And while it was true that letters in support of Fitz appeared as well, the conservative-leaning *Sentinel* had given triple space to the attacks. Fitz, Peter, and the Iraq vets were called "gutless whiners" and "enemies of freedom and Christianity." The op-ed editor had summed it up, "They were an embarrassment to the brave Armed Forces of the USA."

The graffiti on Peter's geodesic dome flashed into her mind. "Die Traitor."

Continuing her search, she found similar programs had been held in 2008, focusing upon Afghanistan, and two in 2007, one each for Iraq and Afghanistan.

"Ms. Cooper?"

A uniformed woman at the counter was calling her. She shut down her computer and came forward. She was escorted through a locked door and down a hallway to an open door with a plaque announcing *Detective Rinzler*. As she entered, he rose courteously to offer his hand. He was a man of medium height, his blond but graying hair cropped to near invisibility. "Ms. Cooper? Please take a seat."

Unlike many middle-aged cops, Rinzler had stayed in shape. His handshake was firm, his gray eyes intense. She warned herself not to underestimate him.

When she was seated, Rinzler displayed the type of false smile that any attorney deciphers as trouble. He said, "I understand that you have information regarding the death of John Fitzpatrick."

She opened her briefcase and removed a page of Fitz's handwriting, taken from an old case file. Placing it on Rinzler's desk, she said, "Thanks for seeing me. Here's a sample of Mr. Fitzpatrick's handwriting. I'd like to know how it compares with the suicide note you found."

Rinzler kept his eyes on her, ignoring the paper. "Ms. Cooper, this morning's newspaper may have given you the impression—"

Noli interrupted him. "Word travels fast in the harbor, Detective. The Coast Guard found a suicide note on the *Mortal Zin.*"

"I can't comment on—"

"My apologies. I'm not asking for comment. I'm telling you John Fitzpatrick didn't commit suicide. He didn't write a suicide note. I'm *asking* you to get a handwriting expert to study this writing sample and the supposed suicide note."

If Rinzler was rattled, he didn't show it. He leaned back in his chair, regarding her carefully. She expected him to ask her how she knew Fitz, but as it turned out, he'd done his homework. "Am I mistaken, or did Deputy Villanueva interview you yesterday?"

"He did."

"And you are an attorney?"

"I am."

"Then surely you understand I cannot discuss the progress of an ongoing investigation."

"I'm relieved to hear the investigation is *ongoing*, Detective. Might I ask when the inquest will be held?"

"Not until the toxicology reports have come in. Four to six weeks, I'd estimate."

Noli pulled a business card from her briefcase and placed it on his desk. "If I can be of further assistance in your investigation, please call. My cell number is written on the back of this card. I look forward to hearing that John's *murderer* has been apprehended."

When Rinzler did not reply, she stood and turned to leave. To her back, Rinzler said, "How long will you be staying in Santa Cruz, Ms. Cooper?"

She paused long enough to look over her shoulder. "As long as it takes, Detective Rinzler."

As she walked down the hall toward the exit, an office door opened, and Deputy Villanueva emerged. Spotting her, his eyes widened in surprise. He nodded and was about to pass by when she touched his arm. "Deputy Villanueva, I've just left a sample of John Fitzpatrick's handwriting with Detective Rinzler."

Villanueva watched her face, uncertain how he was supposed to respond. "Thank you. We appreciate—"

"John was left-handed, like you. I knew him well. His writing is quite distinctive."

A flicker of understanding lit Villanueva's eyes.

CHAPTER NINE

Friday, 2 p.m.

Noli climbed the stairs to Fitz's office, planning to continue reviewing case files. She hoped Luz was having luck at Cruces Cove, and that Luz would show up for their meeting. The office was locked, but there was a note taped to the door: *Noli—See Abbie Wheeldon. Office 6.*

Recalling that Wheeldon was Fitz's longtime friend and personal lawyer, Noli knocked at the door marked #6. A warm contralto voice called, "Come in."

"I'm Noli Cooper. You're expecting me?"

Abbie Wheeldon circled her desk to offer her hand.

Noli had forgotten how impressive Abbie was. If handed a shield, a spear, and long braids to replace her close-cropped hair, Abbie would be Brunhilde come to life. Close to six feet tall, she was Noli's height, but broad-shouldered and well-muscled, with bust and hips in proportion. Her amber eyes were riveting, though puffy and red-rimmed at the moment. According to Fitz, Abbie was a formidable opponent in the courtroom.

Abbie said, "We met when you were a teenager, right?"

"Sailing with Fitz," Noli said. "How did you know I was here?"

"I called Luz this morning, soon as I saw the paper." Abbie motioned Noli to sit, then slumped into her own chair behind the desk. "You've heard there's a suicide note?"

"Yes. Do you think he killed himself?"

"No fucking way."

"Did Fitz ever hint about threats on his life?"

"No," Abbie said, with a rueful smile. "Fitz was *macho*, in his own way. But Aaron Rinzler comes to mind. You know about him?"

"Yes."

"He's in a perfect position to cover up his own dirty work," Abbie said.

"Any recent fuel for Rinzler's grudge?"

"None that I'm aware of." Abbie sucked her lips. "Look, I'm not being objective. I despise Rinzler, but I don't think he's got the balls to murder Fitz. On the other hand, I can see him sharing a beer with himself as he labels Fitz's death a suicide and walks away."

"Munch and I came to the same conclusion," Noli said. "This morning I paid Rinzler a visit."

Wheeldon's eyebrows rose. "And?"

As Noli described her meeting with Rinzler and the chance encounter with Deputy Villanueva, Abbie smiled. "Well done. He's on notice now." Abbie rose from her chair and paced. "Fitz's been in private practice for what, eight years? Nine?"

"Something like that."

"You'll be reviewing his case files?"

"I began last night. So far, only deadbeat dads, runaway kids, a few abusive husbands and stepfathers. No likely suspects."

Abbie checked her watch. "I'll give you a hand this evening. Unfortunately, I leave for New York in the morning. My mother's having heart surgery." She circled back to her chair. "You worked with him, so it's not news to you that Fitz kept shitty paperwork. Especially on cases he was working *pro bono*. He called those 'helping a friend.'"

"And he relied on his amazing memory, which left the rest of us behind."

Abbie gave a rueful chuckle. "Yeah."

For a few beats they were silent, each lost in memories.

Noli wrenched herself back to the present and said, "This morning the *Sentinel* mentioned his public role as a spokesperson for Veterans for Peace. I dug through the angry letters and guest editorials from those days. Did you and he ever discuss the matter?"

"Never." Abbie scraped a hand through her hair in frustration, then pulled a file from her desk drawer. "I am the executor of Fitz's will." She opened the file and glanced at the first two pages. "Fitz set aside much of his estate in a trust—we can talk about that later." She withdrew a sealed white envelope from the file and handed it to Noli. "Fitz instructed me to give you this when he died."

Noli slid it into her pocket. "I'll read it later."

Abbie closed the file. "How much longer will you be in California?"

"Maybe forever."

"Good." Wheeldon leaned forward. "Look, Fitz refused to look out for himself. Don't make the same mistake. The killer will know soon—if he doesn't already—that you're looking for him—or her."

"Understood."

Exiting Abbie's office, Noli saw the door to Fitz's office stood ajar. Luz's voice and a deep male voice echoed down the hall. She knocked briefly before entering.

Luz's visitor was a heavyset Latino man, early thirties, black hair slicked from his forehead to the nape of his neck. His sculpted beard set off an aquiline nose. His jeans and shirt were crisply ironed. All in all, a handsome man who took care with his appearance. He rose from his chair and offered Noli his hand.

"Raul Espinoza, organizer for the Union of Vineyard Workers. Fitz was representing us."

"Noli Cooper. I used to work with Fitz."

In a flat voice, Luz announced, "Raul has something he'd like us to hear."

Noli took the chair beside Raul and pivoted to face him.

"The vineyard owners took out a contract on Fitz," Raul said. "I'm sure of it."

Noli blinked. It took a moment to switch gears from Abbie's measured discussion to Raul's impassioned indictment. She asked, "Who exactly are 'the vineyard owners?'"

"The Tri-County Vineyard Owners Association."

"Have they threatened you or Fitz?"

"I got a threatening phone call in the middle of the night Wednesday. Some guy whispered that I'd be sorry if I showed up for the bargaining session. The same person might have gone after Fitz."

"Did you notify the police?"

"Waste of time. But I saved the recording."

"You didn't recognize the voice?"

"No. Tomorrow night I'll be interviewing a grower who's sympathetic to the union. Maybe he heard someone threaten Fitz."

Luz snapped, "Why should he tell you anything?"

"I knew him in college," Raul said. "He's honest."

Luz shook her head. "Seriously? He was just a kid when you knew him."

Unfazed, Raul stood, saying, "Good to meet you, Noli. You'll be hearing from me about the growers."

The door closed behind him. Luz waved her hand as though waving away an unpleasant smell. "He is so—he thinks the Earth revolves around him."

Wondering why Luz was so dismissive of the organizer, Noli looked at her more closely. Luz's eyes were dull and sunken. "Did you get any sleep?"

"*No es importante.*"

"Luz, investigations take time. You've got to—"

Luz bristled, so Noli bit her tongue.

Luz stuffed her notebook, cell phone, and pen into her backpack and cinched the strap. "I was at Cruces Cove all morning," she said. "Didn't find anyone who was there Wednesday afternoon or evening. No luck for Thursday morning, either. I'll go back tomorrow at dawn." She stood and swung her backpack over her shoulder. As she headed out the door, she said, "My shift at the Pelican starts in twenty minutes."

So glad we could talk, thought Noli.

CHAPTER TEN

Peter Hanak guided his truck south on Highway 1, oblivious to the seacoast beauty streaming past. He stole a glance at his wife, asleep in the passenger seat. Ordinarily, Tina loved to watch the scenery as they drove between San Francisco and Santa Cruz: beautiful beaches, tan cliffs, showy surf, sometimes a breeching whale. But two days at the Multiple Sclerosis Clinic had worn her down. As always, the doctors had emphasized the need for rest. And, as always, she had claimed she was extremely careful to rest, sidestepping the issue of her full-time job.

Cushioned by a neck pillow, her face seemed relaxed. Sleep eased the pain lines. He would give anything—anything—to carry her pain for her, to see her walk again. But that would never happen. Still, if this year's harvest succeeded, maybe he could persuade her to retire.

For the hundredth time, he ran their finances through his mind. The result was inescapable. After losing the '07 and '08 vintages, Hanak Winery was on the ropes. Fitz's money would bail them out of debt, but this year's vintage was the last chance.

He stole another glance at Tina. It would break her heart if they had to sell. She had worked so hard to make their dream a reality.

He turned inland, winding east through the mountains, driving by instinct through Ben Lomond, his jaw so tight with worry that his teeth ached. As he came to Andolini Road, he lowered his window and shouted at the fake coat of arms, "Marco Andolini was a *peasant!*"

The sharp turn slammed Tina's head against the door. Half awake, she grunted.

Feeling like an idiot, he took her hand. "Sorry! Did I hurt you?"

She rubbed the side of her head. "I'll live. It's you I worry about. Raging at Daniel like that will give you a stroke."

He was being a jerk. Yes, he loathed Daniel Arnant. Loathed the glossy makeover Arnant had given the old Andolini Winery. But he knew Arnant wasn't the reason Hanak Winery was failing.

As they drove past the manicured Andolini estate, trucks and vans pulled out of its parking lot. Several vans bore the company sign, *Executive Cement and Tile.*

Tina said, "They're sure working late! I wonder when Daniel's new cave cellar will be finished. His harvest party's soon, isn't it?"

Peter didn't answer, wouldn't speculate on Arnant's "improvement" of the natural cave that had served the Andolini family well for three generations.

When they reached the domes, he lifted her wheelchair from the truck bed and positioned it by the passenger door. She leaned toward him, wrapping her arms around his neck while he lowered her into the chair. She was light in his arms, lighter than she ought to be.

Suddenly desperate at the thought of losing her, he said, "With Fitz's money we'll be out of debt. This year's grapes are the best ever. Let's tell the hospital you're retiring."

She held his face in both her hands and kissed his lips. "You keep forgetting. I like my job." With that, she pivoted her wheelchair and muscled it up the ramp to their new dome. He'd watched her go, her silver hair flowing behind.

She *used* to like her job—that much, he believed. She'd been a wonderful nurse. Who would know better than he? But after the last MS flare-up, the one that put her in a wheelchair, she'd left nursing to become an administrator. A number-cruncher. A form-filler-outer.

She hadn't spoken a single word of regret. But hell, "like" her job? *She* worked so *he* could pursue a dream. That was the simple truth.

Determined to be cheerful, he followed her, scanning the parking area for a rental car. Seeing none, he decided Noli had headed to the store for supplies. No doubt she'd be back soon. Nothing would be better for Tina than a reunion with her beloved goddaughter.

CHAPTER ELEVEN

C hecking the file drawer labeled *2007*, Noli said, "Only two more files."

Abbie gave her a thumbs-up.

Thus far, they'd identified four suspects. Two abusive fathers had sent written threats against Fitz's life, although there was nothing to suggest the threats were more than bluster. In addition, there was 1) an industrial spy he'd exposed, a man who'd sent three threatening emails; and 2) a con man he'd sent to prison in 2005, who'd been released last month for good behavior. The con man's ex-wife had sent Fitz an email before the man's release, asking to meet with Fitz to discuss protection. Luz had flagged the email before her shift at the Pelican.

Abbie said, "None of these losers are worth your time. Let me call a couple of PI's I work with. They can do the follow-up."

"How much do they—"

"Never mind. I'll foot the bill." Abbie stood and stretched. "I'll have time to brief them before my plane takes off. They'll be told to report to you."

Noli's cell rang. "I have to take this, Abbie. Might be a while." She backed into the hall and closed the door.

"Hello, Peter."

"We can't wait to see you, kiddo. Where are you?"

"In Fitz's office. Peter, I have some bad news."

"Why don't you come on up to the dome?" he said. "Tell Fitz he can't keep you." There was a forced cheerfulness in his voice. She remembered Munch saying Peter had been "down" lately, and her heart sank even lower at the prospect of telling him about Fitz.

"Fitz is dead. They found his body in Cruces Cove yesterday morning."

Silence on the line. She imagined Peter's face, the stunned disbelief, and wished she had waited to tell him in person.

"Dead? How?" he asked.

"We don't know yet. The Coast Guard found a suicide note on the *Zin*. Luz—Fitz's assistant—has sources who tell her it was alcohol and barbiturates."

"But that's..." Peter said nothing for several beats.

"Peter, has Fitz said anything to you about problems? Being depressed?"

"No! He was happy. Ready for a new adventure. He and Pilar were—" His voice broke.

She waited a few beats, then asked, "When did you last see him?"

"Wednesday morning. He stopped by on his way to inspect an old barn on the property he's buying from us. If its beams are still good, he might—he would have turned it into a cottage." Peter's voice broke again. "He texted me later that morning. It says, *Call me ASAP*. What if he needed help? If I'd just—"

"Peter, whatever happened to him, it happened in Cruces Cove. Nothing you could have done." She paused to let him think it through, hoping he would absolve himself, then continued. "There's more. The detective in charge is Aaron Rinzler."

"Rinzler? He'll fucking dance on Fitz's grave." A loud thump echoed over the phone, as though Peter'd slammed his fist into something. "Jesus. Can this get any worse?"

Tina's voice came on, sad but steady. "Noli, will you be coming home tonight?"

Home. A tiny, consoling warmth blossomed in Noli's chest. Making up her mind, she said, "I am. But don't wait up for me. See you in the morning."

When Noli stepped back into the office, Abbie said, "We've reviewed through 2007. Let's have a look at the rest of the file cabinets." She approached an unlabeled cabinet and opened the top drawer. "Pens and pencils. Wite-Out." Next drawer. "Yellow pads." Third drawer. "Reams of paper." Last drawer. "Candy and cigarettes." She chuckled sadly and shook her head in disbelief. "Fitz's office supplies are quite tidy."

The remaining two cabinets were labeled alphabetically. Noli checked the drawers marked *A-C* and *D-E*. "Old cases, 1997 to 2006. Any of these could involve a pissed-off psychopath he crossed years ago."

"Possibly," Abbie said. "But horror movies to the contrary, psychopaths rarely wait three years before they snap."

"Unless they've been in prison."

"Right. Might be worth checking that."

Noli's cell rang. *Unidentified Caller.* She considered letting it go to voicemail, but then realized it could be Luz calling from work.

"Hello?"

"Is this Nollaig Cooper?" A male voice, muffled.

"Yes." She put him on speaker and moved closer to Abbie.

"Detective Rinzler has terminated the investigation into the death of John Fitzpatrick."

"I'm not surprised," Noli said. "To whom am I speaking?"

"A friend. I've left you a package by the back door. Don't call the police."

The line went dead.

She looked at Abbie. "A trap?"

"Possibly." Abbie killed the overhead lights.

They moved to the window, each standing to one side, peering into the dark. "See anyone?" Abbie asked.

"No." The parking lot wasn't well lit, and the hedge behind it could have concealed a small army.

They waited.

Noli thought of Deputy Villanueva, how he'd looked at her in the hall outside Rinzler's office. She said, "I'm bringing it in."

"I'm coming with you," Abbie said.

Before descending the stairs, Abbie turned off the hall lights. By the soft blue of an emergency light, they made their way to the back door.

Abbie whispered, "Crouch low. I'll open the door enough for your arm."

Noli knelt.

"Grab it fast. Ready? One, two, three!" Abbie opened the door slightly, blocking further inward motion with her hip.

Blindly, Noli patted the ground outside until her fingers touched something smooth. Her heart threatened to pound its way out of her rib cage. Eventually her fingertips encountered a package—flat but thick. She pulled it inside.

Abbie slammed and locked the door. She clicked the overhead light switch.

Noli held a fat manila envelope, large enough to hold a legal file—or a bomb. It was heavily taped. No address, no writing of any kind.

"I don't like the look of it, all that tape," Abbie said.

"Then move away," Noli said. "Go up to your office and close the door."

"I'm not leaving you with—"

"Do it, Abbie. My cell phone is in Fitz's office. Take it with you for evidence."

Abbie hesitated. "All right. Give me a minute." She climbed the stairs.

Noli waited while Abbie's footsteps echoed from the second-floor hallway. A door closed.

Was there a right way to open a letter bomb? Yes, in an armored chamber complete with a robot.

Slowly, Noli stripped layer after layer of tape from the envelope's glued flap. Now came the move that would detonate a bomb: Open the flap.

She told herself she was being stupid. How likely was a letter bomb? Still, her hands were shaking. With thumb and index finger, she tore the corner of the flap. Waited.

Nothing.

Beads of sweat rolled down her cheeks.

She inhaled and ran her index finger under the flap.

The crackle of glue releasing.

She pulled the contents into the light. No gelignite, but a bomb of a different kind: a photograph of Fitz's body. He lay on a beach. Blue windbreaker, blue jeans, and gray tennis shoes. Bloody eye sockets. A thick, reddish-gray beard.

There, in her hands, was the reality of his death.

Shaking, she looked at the second page. A close-up of his head. Eyes gone, mouth hanging open, brown-stained smokers' teeth. Next, a photo of his torso. No rips or holes, no obvious blood.

"Noli!" Abbie shouted.

"I'm coming."

Abbie met her at the top of the stairs.

Noli waved the envelope at her. "You're not going to believe this." Racing to Fitz's office, she cleared the worktable with a sweep of her arm and spread the envelope's contents. Several shots focused on the area surrounding Fitz's body. The dry sand was churned up. Near him lay a blanket, its edges weighted with stones. She recognized the blanket's old-fashioned cactus-and-sombrero pattern; it was the picnic blanket Fitz kept on his sailboat. Atop the blanket, a fifth of Tres Hermanos Tequila lay on its side, uncapped. It looked empty, but she couldn't be certain. A bag of tortilla chips and two wrappers from Señor Tico's Burritos had blown flat against a small cooler.

Other photos covered the wider scene. A sailboat just like the *Mortal Zin* was anchored out beyond the mouth of a cove. Her sails were furled. Close to the beach, a wine-colored dinghy floated in a tide pool. A zoom shot revealed its name: *Mortal Zin*. Why was the dinghy in the water? Fitz would have pulled it well up the beach, above the expected high tide line. Had high tide come after he was unconscious?

"Do you recognize the location?" Abbie asked.

"Cruces Cove," Noli said.

Had Fitz been alone this time? The liter bottle of tequila suggested not. Perhaps there were footprints near the blanket? But there was no way to know how many people had tracked through the scene before someone reported his body. Which made her wonder what evidence had been carried away before the sheriff secured the scene.

Abbie pointed to a photo of several objects displayed on a white cloth. Wallet, credit cards, drivers' license, Medicare card, some paper money, a ring of keys, and a plastic vial. "Almost two hundred dollars in his wallet. This wasn't robbery gone wrong."

Noli pointed to the plastic vial. It had a screw-on cap of the childproof type, like a prescription pill container from a pharmacy, but was unlabeled. "Does that look empty to you?"

Abbie lifted the photo into the light and squinted. "Yeah. Even so, they can test the residue."

Noli stacked the photos they'd already examined and spread out the remainder. These had been taken at the northern end of the cove, the opposite end from Fitz's body.

A sturdy wooden staircase led down from the parking lot. Behind the base of the stairs, a deep rock shelf overhung dry sand, creating a sort of cave. Close-ups showed what might be footprints in the sand there, as well as a broad scrape that began under the ledge and extended into the open. The hiding place of Fitz's killer?

"Oh, no!" Abbie gulped and dropped into a chair. The photo on her lap showed a pale gray circle with a scalloped rim lying on a dark background. Within the circle, two rows of white letters said:

Dear Pilar

I'm sorry!

Noli stared at it, reaching for a memory of the scalloped circle. In seconds it came. "This is the mirror in the head—the bathroom—of the *Mortal Zin*. My guess, they took the mirror to a lab, and this photo was taken with indirect lighting. That's why the background's just uniform darkness."

The letters were as perfectly formed as an elementary teacher's writing lesson— nothing like Fitz's handwriting, which was nearly illegible and, like most left-handed writing, heavily sloped.

"No way that's his writing," Abbie said.

"A mirror is a vertical surface. Paper is generally horizontal," Noli countered. "That might account for the change."

"Not that much," Abbie challenged.

Noli raised her left hand and mimicked printing on a wall. It seemed there would still be a slant, but she couldn't be certain. "Okay, let's assume the killer wrote the note. There could be fingerprints in the head. If only Rinzler had looked!"

Abbie said, "There won't be prints if the killer knew what he was doing."

Together, they stared at the photo. Noli thought about the uneven texture of the white letters. They reminded her of spray-painted graffiti on a wall, but on a mirror, you couldn't spray paint—it would drip.

She closed her eyes and pictured walking into the head. On her right, the sink. Above it, the mirror. To her left, a tiny cabinet for soap, shampoo, and toilet paper. Soap!

"What if these words were written with a cake of soap? That would explain the letters being white and uneven."

Noli picked up a stapled set of papers they hadn't yet examined. "Here's the coroner's preliminary report. Time of death estimated between five and eight p.m., possibly unconscious for as long as two hours before death. No trauma. I guess that means no one shot, knifed, strangled, or beat him." She swallowed hard before continuing. "There's technical stuff, summarized as 'Consistent with alcohol and barbiturate intake.' Samples were sent to a lab." She tossed the report onto the table and reached for her coffee.

Abbie refilled her cup and sipped, making an obvious effort to calm herself.

"Maybe you were right," Noli said. "Rinzler could be behind this. He could have had one of his guys write the suicide message, then photograph it."

Abbie frowned. "That's gutsier than I'd give Rinzler credit for. Keep him on your suspect list if you want, but honestly, I'd be surprised."

Noli said, "I would have expected to see the contents of Fitz's phone."

"Another indicator of how quickly Rinzler pulled the plug?"

"Maybe. But the phone itself isn't in any of the photos."

"Then either they don't have the phone, or your mysterious helper decided not to share it with you."

Would Villanueva have reason to exclude the phone list? "Maybe he was afraid he'd be exposed if we followed Fitz's calls." Noli flipped through the report, scanning quickly. "A

911 call was received September 24 at nine fifteen, reporting the body of a man at Cruces Cove. Woman's voice, refused to identify herself. The location of the phone is a Safeway store, 211 Mission Street, Santa Cruz. Pay phone?"

"We'll soon know." Abbie reached for Fitz's office phone, dialed, listened, set the phone back in its cradle. "Recorded message for the store manager. They open at six."

CHAPTER TWELVE

Saturday, 1 a.m.

One hour to closing. Luz surveyed the tables in the Pelican Bar and Grill, remembering how she'd been planning to quit as soon as Fitz took her on full time. As things were now, she'd stay on a while. Truth was, on a good night she made more money here than she did as a PI.

Noli Cooper had sent a text saying she had good news. Luz knew she ought to return the call, but her heart remained in a black funk.

Munch had come in earlier than usual. He'd canvassed the room, showing each newly arrived customer a card on which he'd written three questions:

Were you at the harbor Wednesday, midday?

Know anyone who sailed in the Wednesday regatta?

Or anyone hanging around in the harbor Wednesday between noon and 5 p.m.?

He hadn't had any luck. Now he was sitting at a long table with seven other guys who'd known Fitz, drinking and sharing stories. When she delivered their drinks, she overheard two men say they'd been on the docks late that day, probably starting around three o'clock. They swore the slip reserved for the *Mortal Zin* had been vacant. Munch looked up to catch her eye; she nodded.

She seated a few late arrivals and took their drink orders. By the time she looked for Munch again, he was sitting with two short, sweatshirt-clad gringos who were killing their second pitcher of amber. The gringos were middle-aged, one dark-haired, the other bald but sporting a scraggly beard to his chest. She'd seen them at the Pelican before, but not often. She didn't know their names.

Long Beard signaled to her. Pointing to Munch, he said, "He needs a glass. Got any nachos left, *chiquita*?" His speech was slurred.

Luz pretended to smile past the word *chiquita,* asking, "For how many?"

"All of us."

When she returned, the men were deep in conversation. Just as she set the nachos plate in the center of the table, a stout, gray-haired man burst into the bar and hailed Munch. Sliding into the fourth chair, he was welcomed by the others. "Hey, Goose!" and "Long time no see."

He said, "Sorry I'm late." He handed Munch a shopping bag.

Munch wrote on his notepad and passed it to Goose.

"Sorry, Munch. The price is firm."

Long Beard grabbed Luz's arm. She pulled away. He winked, his eyes twitching at the corners. "Another pitcher and a glass, *senorita. Pronto.*"

As Luz turned away, she heard Goose say to the group, "Saw the write-up on Fitz this morning. What the fuck?" She wanted to hear their answers, but instead returned to the bar to fill their order. When she returned with a pitcher and a clean glass, Munch was holding a wine bottle up to the light, examining the label. On the pad, he wrote, *Same stuff?*

Goose replied, "A year older. Should be as good as the first two."

Luz was puzzled. She'd never known Munch to show any interest in wine. She pulled a towel from her apron and wiped a pair of empty tables, keeping the men in her field of vision. From his wallet, Munch counted a pile of bills, which he pushed across the table to Goose. Goose kissed the money, chugged his beer, and left.

Munch's companions called for their tab. Long Beard doled out cash, leaving her a fifty-cent tip on a hundred-and-eighty-dollar tab.

Munch remained at the table. Rather than interrupt his thoughts, she toweled the bar and filled the dishwasher. When she was ready to close, Munch came to the bar, set the bottle of wine down, pulled out his wallet, pushed a twenty-dollar bill across to her, and wrote:

For you. They're jerks.

"Thanks, Munch. The coffee's still good. Can I pour you a cup?"

He nodded.

While Munch drank his coffee, she counted her tips. When he'd finished, she asked, "Those guys friends of yours?"

Only Goose. Vet, used to live in harbor.

"He's a wine dealer?"

Munch smiled.

Goose inherited mansion with old wine cellar.

"You're drinking wine now?"

Nope. Gift for friend.

Munch stowed the tablet in his pocket and gestured at the door.

"Yeah, me too," Luz said.

Munch walked her to her car and shyly patted her shoulder.

She watched him shuffle toward the docks. An old man. If he survived the grief of losing Fitz, how much of him would be left?

CHAPTER THIRTEEN

Saturday, 5 a.m.

Noli lay on her teenage bed in the loft of the old dome, unable to sleep. In her mind, she reviewed the photographs from the sheriff's case file: Fitz's corpse, a cactus-print blanket, a tequila bottle, Señor Tico's burrito wrappers, an unlabeled plastic vial, a dinghy in the surf, the *Mortal Zin* anchored beyond the cove. The suicide note in its scalloped frame. Of all the details the photos offered, she could find only one solid lead: The murderer had known about Fitz's relationship with Pilar.

She considered waiting for dawn, but Peter and Tina probably hadn't slept either. It would be good to join them. Maybe Tina had already made coffee.

Wearily, she swung her legs into the morning chill and fumbled for the light switch. At the foot of the bed rested a battered cedar chest containing her Santa Cruz clothes. She selected a long-sleeved tee, soft enough to ride gently on her scarred back. Then heavy jeans, a padded wool shirt, and wool socks. The clothes should have been musty, even damp. Instead, they smelled of sunshine. *Thank you, Tina.*

Beneath the clothes were her old work boots. The leather was unexpectedly soft and pliable. *Peter oiled them.*

Descending from the loft via a metal spiral staircase, she viewed the circular main floor. Little furniture remained: an old sofa, a desk, and a wooden chair. One lamp. The kitchen area held a small refrigerator and a hot plate, sufficient for the hired help who sometimes slept there. Warmth still emanated from the wood stove where Peter had dampened last night's fire.

With one of several flashlights kept by the front door, she stepped onto the deck, hoping to see a light in the new dome, a sign that she could join Peter and Tina. But it was dark. Were they asleep, or perhaps lying awake in bed?

Not Peter. With the harvest fast approaching, he'd be working, and she had a good idea where to find him.

Shaking the kinks out of her arms and legs, she aimed the flashlight beam down a two-track leading to the storage barn. Striding through the damp night air, she made a plan. Although Fitz had died on the coast, he must have come up to his mountain property on Wednesday morning before the regatta, else he couldn't have left the note on the dome's door. Might the neighbors have seen him? Could they pin down the time he had left?

And more, she wanted to see the property Fitz had been so in love with.

Her thoughts turned to Abbie and Luz. Soon Abbie would be meeting with her two PI's, setting them on the trail of the four unpromising but need-to-be-checked potential suspects they'd gleaned from Fitz's case files. And by now Luz would have read the long and detailed text Noli had left her, describing the sheriff's case file and asking her to follow up first thing in the morning on the call from the Safeway manager's phone. It was a *request*.

Imagining the ensuing problems if she and Luz couldn't work together, Noli felt her stomach clench. She stopped, slowed her breathing, and tasted the resinous perfume of redwoods. She played the flashlight beam across their giant trunks, three and even four feet in diameter. A hundred feet overhead, stars glittered in a gap in the overstory.

She promised herself she'd do whatever it took to work out a partnership with Luz.

Moving on, her steps were silent, cushioned by a deep layer of redwood duff. Soon the storage barn came into view, a building so old that shafts of light escaped through its shrunken slats of siding. She remembered the first time her father brought her here. How old had she been? Five? Six? The memory played in her head like a movie—

Passing through the forest, she held tight to her father's hand, guided only by the flashlight. They came to an ancient wooden building, the kind a witch might live in.

He released her hand, stepped forward, gripped a handle, and pulled with all his strength until a door slid open. He stepped inside, leaving her alone in the dark.

She was scared, but she decided to be brave and count to ten.

When she reached six, a single bulb flickered to life inside. Her father beckoned to her. She entered, seeing at once that the light was too dim to reach the dark corners of the barn. Spiders lived in dark corners. She pressed closer to her father. He lifted a stack of dusty crates and carried them outside, where he handed her a hose. When he turned a spigot, water gushed from the nozzle. Together they began to wash the crates.

Peter, in pajamas and unlaced boots, clomped down the path, shouting, "For crissakes, Jonathan, it's the middle of the night!"

Laughing, her father had called out, "It's the Mad Hungarian, as I live and breathe!"

The memory brought a gentle warmth to her chest. She pulled the barn door aside and shouted, "It's the mad Hungarian ..."

From inside, Peter's basso voice replied, "As I live and breathe."

He stood in the barn's loft, six feet tall, muscular and trim, silver hair streaming to his shoulders. God of the Mountain, just as her young self had believed him to be. Mopping his face with his sleeve, he looked down. His crystal-blue eyes met hers, and he said, "God, I miss him."

"Me too."

He hoisted a sack over his shoulder, extinguished the light in the loft, and clumped toward the ladder, his gait uneven. As a child, she'd learned to judge how tired he was by the length of time it took his shrapnel-damaged right leg to catch up with his left. Tonight, the delay was long.

He tossed the sack into the bed of the rusty truck and, with both arms free, wrapped her in a hug. His bushy beard scribbled across her cheek. She felt her shoulders relax in the long-remembered comfort of Peter's protection.

When he stepped back, his eyes were shiny with unshed tears.

"How's Tina?" she asked.

"I don't think she's slept. Do you have any leads?"

What could she say? She couldn't tell him about the sheriff's file. Instead, she described the review of Fitz's legal files and the follow-up by Abbie's PI's. She added, "You mentioned Fitz was going to check out an old apple barn. Who would have a clear view of that barn?"

He paused to think. "You can see the barn from the old Norton place. Our newest jet-set neighbors bought it. Annika and Preston Vandermeis." He lifted a stack of crates and pushed them into the truck bed. "Annika's been a good friend to Tina. We'll introduce you."

Noli hoisted a pair of crates into the truck and asked, "And her husband?"

"Big-shot CEO, usually out of town."

From Peter's tone of voice, it was clear Preston Vandermeis, unlike his wife, wasn't anyone's friend. "Who else lives on Norton Road these days?"

"Ah!" Now Peter was smiling. "I've been meaning to tell you. A guy named Wolf Faber bought twenty acres south of the Vandermeis house. He claims to know you from New Harmony Commune."

"Sure, I remember. Roly-poly little guy, younger than me. He wasn't in the commune long. His father suffered horrific flashbacks." When Wolf, at age eight, had sneaked up behind his father to surprise him, his father had unconsciously reacted, flinging Wolf against a tree. Wolf'd spent weeks in the hospital with multiple fractures. When he'd been released, his mother had taken him and fled the commune.

"Wolf has been a tremendous help to us," Peter said. "He bought the land back in '04 and built a yurt, then went off to earn enough money to plant a vineyard. He's in demand as a vineyard consultant, so he's gone a fair amount."

"Was he around on Wednesday?"

"I don't think so." Peter reached into the truck cab and retrieved a thermos. "There's another possibility. Remember the abandoned farm across the valley? It's now the property of a dot-com mogul named Gary Varley, an asshole who blasts over here in his Mercedes every week, offering to buy us out." He grimaced, unscrewed the cap of the thermos, separated two plastic mugs nested within, and set them on the hood of the truck. Steam spiraled as he poured two coffees.

"Nectar of the gods, Peter." She drank the hot coffee, searing her tongue, while she considered the many changes in Andolini Valley. During her childhood, the mountains had been a haven for small landholders with alternative lifestyles—hippies, communes, marijuana growers, organic farms. A few small vineyards. But at some point, folks with money had realized the mountains were within commuting distance of Silicon Valley. Not only that, but much of the land was suitable for vineyards. Irresistible. Now, with the exception of the state park on the Hanaks' northern boundary, they were surrounded by large holdings and deep pockets.

She stole a glance at Peter, imagining how he was perceived by his new, glitzy neighbors. Hair down to his shoulders, bushy beard, moth-eaten shirts, ripped and patched jeans, scruffy boots. *Old, eccentric hippie*, they'd say. And they'd wonder how much longer he could hold on before selling out.

Peter turned two buckets over to make seats. She grabbed the thermos and sat down next to him. "Did Fitz mention he was representing a new labor union for vineyard workers?"

"Yep. Hopeless, if you ask me. But thin odds never stopped Fitz."

"Why hopeless?"

"Because honorable owners make sure the workers get paid. And the other guys aren't going to change."

"Cesar Chavez disagreed."

"You have a point."

She drained her cup and poured a refill. "What do the 'other guys' do?"

"When it's time to prune or harvest, they hire a labor contractor to bring in a team of undocumented men. When the job's done, they pay the contractor. No guarantee how much ends up in the hands of the workers."

"Workers who might have been promised anything. But they speak no English and have no recourse."

"Exactly. Also, working conditions are an issue: toilets, housing, number of hours worked in a day."

"Raul thinks one of the growers, or maybe a group of them, took out a contract on Fitz. How does that strike you?"

Peter's eyebrows rose. "Pretty far-fetched, given the suicide setup. My idea of a hit man is he shoots Fitz in the head and dumps his body." He sighed. "But what do I know? I probably got that idea from television." He limped to the barn door and looked out. "As soon as there's light, we should go up to the dome. Tina will have breakfast waiting."

"Did Fitz tell you he offered me a job?" Noli said.

"No, but I'm not surprised. What did you say?"

"I told him I'd consider it. I don't want to keep doing the work I've been doing. We were going to talk it over at dinner on Thursday. I would have said yes."

Peter tossed the dregs of his coffee onto the ground. "Well, much as Tina and I would love to have you come home, I'm not going to offer an opinion. You have to do what feels right for you." Sadness lay so heavy on his shoulders, he sagged beneath the weight.

"Peter, is there something else on your mind—besides Fitz? Is it Tina?"

Leaning against the barn door, Peter shook his head. "Tina's doing great. That is, she hasn't lost any ground since her legs went numb. It's you searching for Fitz's killer that worries me."

"I'm careful. Fitz did show me how, back in the day."

Peter's frown showed how unlikely he thought that was.

Then she remembered the '08 vintage. "Peter, what happened with last year's vintage?"

Slowly, Peter blew the air from his lungs, and his shoulders slumped even further. "Lost it all to vinegar. The year before, too."

Finally, the truth. "What happened?"

"Beats me. Wolf and Annika both tried to find an explanation. We think it must have been the barrels, so I've ordered new ones. They'll be delivered today."

Another expense. On top of two years with no product to sell.

Then she remembered the bottle of old Andolini wine Munch had sent with her as a gift for Peter. Should she get it now? If the wine was good, it might cheer him up.

But what if it wasn't?

CHAPTER FOURTEEN

At first light, Peter insisted he and Noli return to the dome. At their approach, Tina opened the new dome's sliding glass door and rolled onto the deck. Silver hair flowed over her shoulders as gracefully as ever, but her dark eyes were red-rimmed and sunken. Since Noli had last seen her, she'd lost so much weight she seemed like a child nestled in a grown-up's wheelchair, a chair which had previously fit her.

At Tina's side stood a golden retriever undoubtedly named Raz, as all the Hanaks' dogs had been. A quick calculation told Noli this was Raz the Seventh. More precisely, Count Haraszthy the Seventh, named in honor of the man long believed to have brought the first zinfandel vines to California.

Tina opened her arms, saying, "My dear, dear girl. What a homecoming you've had."

They hugged for a long minute, and Noli kissed her on the cheek. As she did so, she noticed Tina's necklace. It was fashioned from ceramic beads in shades of green and blue, and from the center hung a pendant with an image of a California poppy.

She smiled. "I can't believe you still have that necklace!"

Tina took her hand and squeezed. "I wear it all the time. Don't I, Peter?"

Peter nodded. "I wish I still had mine."

Noli doubted that, but her heart warmed nonetheless. When she was twelve years old, she'd made five ceramic necklaces for Christmas presents. For her stepmother's necklace, the pendant had shown a tiny Celtic harp. For her mother's grave, a heart. For her father's and Peter's, a zinfandel grape bunch. In the '80's, it wasn't unusual for men to wear beads. At some point, Peter's fell off and was lost. Her father was wearing his on the day he died.

Peter bent to kiss Tina. "How're you doing, sweetheart?"

Rather than answer the question, she said, "I hope you two are hungry." She swiveled her wheelchair and rolled into the dome.

Once inside, Tina commanded them to sit at the kitchen table, which she'd already set. Moving smoothly around her adapted kitchen, she pulled serving dishes from the oven and brought them to the table.

Astonished at how hungry she was, Noli downed a glass of fresh-squeezed orange juice and tackled a mushroom omelet. Tina seemed determined to avoid talking about Fitz and instead make the meal a warm welcome for Noli. She asked questions about Noli's life in Dublin. How many of her mother's relatives had she met? What kinds of cases had she been working on?

But in the end, there was no dodging Fitz's death. Peter began by asking Noli to repeat the small amount of information she had: Fitz and Pilar fighting, the newspaper report, the lack of strong suspects in Fitz's case files. Noli was about to ask Peter about the Veterans for Peace forum when the house phone rang.

Peter excused himself. "I need to answer—could be the barrel delivery." In less than a minute he returned, saying, "Sorry, I have to meet the truck. Will I see you this evening, Noli?"

She hesitated, not knowing what the day might bring. "I'll do my best. Can I check in with you later?"

Tina said, "Of course. Peter, there's a thermos of cocoa on the counter."

Peter kissed her and grabbed the thermos on his way out the door.

Tina sighed, then straightened her back and smiled at Noli. "You asked how early we could call on our neighbors. And you want to see the land Fitz was going to buy, right?"

"Yes. Sooner, the better."

"Let's go. By the time we get to the Vandermeis house, it'll be okay to knock on their door."

★ ★ ★

When Peter reached his winery, he found the delivery truck had already parked. At its rear, a man flung open the doors and extended a ramp. His eyes met Peter's with a level, open expression. "Russ Lankshaw," he said, with an unmistakable Australian twang. He was medium height and sandy-haired, dressed in jeans and a cotton twill work shirt. The ravines in his tanned face suggested a life spent outdoors. His handshake was strong.

"Peter Hanak. Always glad to meet an Aussie. What brings you to California?"

"Grandkids. Left the vineyards of Coonawarra to be near 'em. Clemworth Estate, know their cab?"

Peter nodded. "One of the best."

Lankshaw jutted a thumb to his chest. "Cellar master for twenty years."

"With that kind of experience, you shouldn't be driving a truck," Peter said.

"Helping out my son's friend, getting familiar with the wineries in the region."

Peter considered what he should say. Arnant needed a new cellar master, but he might not be a congenial boss. And there was Varley the Asshole, who might not have hired a cellar master yet. Deciding Lankshaw could evaluate Arnant and Varley for himself, he said, "You might want to talk to Daniel Arnant, director of the winery you passed coming in."

"Big Victorian mansion?"

"Right. Andolini Winery. They just lost their cellar master. And across the valley, there's a new winery going in. Owner's name is Gary Varley."

"Much obliged."

Peter opened the double doors on the winery's north side and flipped a switch. A line of low-wattage bulbs hung from the ceiling, illuminating the cavernous barrel room, a concrete-walled and windowless space where his wine spent the crucial first months. Tiered, scalloped steel racks ran the length of the room, each scallop ready to hold a new wooden barrel.

Pulling a dolly loaded with four barrels, Lankshaw crossed the threshold and paused. "Where do you want 'em?"

Peter pointed to an empty area beyond the metal racks. "Just stack 'em there."

Lankshaw raised his voice to carry over the drumming of the dolly's wheels. "I hear you lost two years' vintages."

"You heard right."

"You're certain the wine you used to top off wasn't contaminated?"

Peter knew why Lankshaw was asking. The most likely opportunity for contamination of wine in a barrel came when the winemaker opened the barrel's bunghole and poured in wine to replace the amount that had evaporated. If the wine used to top off the barrels contained vinegar bacteria, the contamination would ruin the entire barrel.

He answered, "I'm positive. Had it tested."

Lankshaw nodded thoughtfully. He walked the length of the room, sniffing the air, looking at the ceiling, scuffing the floor.

"Ever have leaks in here?"

"Never."

"Ever have *acetobacter aceti* contamination before?"

"No."

"Sulfate level too low?"

"No different from the years before."

"New yeast?"

"Nope. Same one we've used for a decade."

"I don't suppose you kept the bad barrels?"

"Sold 'em, along with the vinegar, to a condiment company in San Jose."

Lankshaw nodded. "Probably for the best."

Peter grabbed his hand truck and together they unloaded the remaining barrels. When they'd finished, Lankshaw asked, "You keepin' your doors locked?"

"If I'm away for more than a day."

"If I was you, I'd start lockin'. Maybe someone out there doesn't like you."

"You mean sabotage?" Peter laughed. "Why bother? We aren't even a whisker on the face of the wine market."

"You won a gold medal, didn't you?"

"Yes, but—"

"Maybe someone wants you out of the runnin'."

"That's crazy."

As they exited, Lankshaw craned his head and pointed to the exterior wall above the doors. Morning light, beaming through gaps in the trees, illuminated a spray-painted message that, although faded, was easy to read.

Die Camalfucking traiter

Peter exhaled slowly, blowing air through his pursed lips. Acetone hadn't removed as much of the painted letters as he'd hoped. It had been difficult, trying to scrub while perched on a ladder. If the damn kids had settled for a message at ground level, cleaning it off would have been a hell of lot easier. To Lankshaw, he said, "It's just kids. As you see, they can't even spell."

Lankshaw clapped a friendly hand on Peter's shoulder. "Your call, mate. I'm just sayin'…"

"Yes, point taken."

Lankshaw returned to the cellar and evaluated it again, floor to ceiling. He pointed to a half-open door at the back. "More barrels in there?"

"Racked bottles. Seeing how they age."

"Zinfandel? No one ages zinfandel."

Weary and impatient, Peter said, "An experiment." He took a step toward the cellar exit, showing he was anxious to get on with his day.

Lankshaw pulled a business card from his pocket and wrote a number on the back. "My cell. If you have trouble with *these* barrels, call me."

CHAPTER FIFTEEN

Saturday, 8:30 a.m.

Tina led the way west on Andolini Road. She propelled her chair by hand and rolled slowly over the bumps and potholes.

Where the road emerged from the redwoods, the Hanaks' newer zinfandel vineyard spread downhill to the edge of the ravine holding Andolini Creek. Noli wasn't sure exactly how big the vineyard was, but it spread over several acres, rolling across undulating ridges and depressions.

In contrast to the lush vineyard on her left, the ground on her right was a dry, uphill slope of rocky, unplanted ground: a fire break between the vineyard and Loma Buena State Park's dense forest.

As Tina zigged around a particularly large pothole, Noli noticed Tina's hands were coated with dust. Adopting what she hoped was a casual tone—Tina did not, as a rule, appreciate offers of assistance—Noli said, "The dust on this road is pretty bad. Mind if I push for a while?"

Tina shook the dirt from her hands. "Good idea."

The morning sun was warm, the air rich with ripening grapes. Rows of trellised vines glimmered red and gold as a breeze rustled the zinfandel leaves. Deep-purple grape clusters hung heavy, awaiting harvest.

Tina said, "Quick detour. I want to show you something."
She pointed to the uphill side of the road, where a red metal
locker stood on six tall legs. It was the size of a refrigerator
lying on its side.

Noli positioned Tina's chair in front of the locker. Tina
pulled a knob, and a door swung open. Inside were coils of
hose of the gauge found on fire engines. "It's fed by a new
water tank further up the slope," Tina said. "Finally, we have
firefighting capacity. It wouldn't save us from a crown fire off
the park, but we could hold off a smaller fire until the county
fire trucks come."

"That's wonderful," Noli said, recalling the many times
the Hanaks had evacuated under threat from wildfires in the
park. She thought of the Hanaks' most valuable vineyard, the
one north of the domes. "What about Old Marco's Hill?"

Tina shook her head. "We'd have to write it off." She
closed the locker door.

Beyond the vineyard, Andolini Road mounted a ridge
and narrowed to a single track overlooking Andolini Creek.
Peering over the edge, Noli spotted a trickle of water some
forty feet below. Noting that the edge of the road was crumbling, she steered Tina's chair toward the center and asked,
"Do you visit Annika often?"

"Yes. More often she comes to me, though."

"Does the propane truck still drive through here?"

"Once a month," Tina answered. "Sounds like you're
worried about the road caving in."

"Well, that cliff edge does look pretty dicey."

"Hasn't caved for years," Tina said.

Noli did a quick tally of the hazards Tina and Peter
accepted as the price of living their dream: forest fires, earthquakes, drought, road collapses, and vintage failures. Tina
couldn't have stuck it out all these years if something as
minor as a dicey road would scare her off.

The road veered ninety degrees to the north. The vista was transformed. A long-neglected apple orchard stood on the slope below, and the musky aroma of rotting apples filled the air. In the distance she could see a weathered old barn. To the west, beyond the orchard, stood the white-walled Queen Anne house that was now the home of Annika and Preston Vandermeis.

The figure of a woman appeared in the distance, coming up the road in front of them.

Tina waved, calling, "Good morning!"

The woman waved back, striding rapidly toward them. She was slender as a ballerina, dressed for work in jeans and a stained T-shirt. A blue kerchief mostly covered her hair and accented her high cheekbones and golden-brown eyes. No makeup on her clear skin and narrow lips. She stopped in front of them and smiled at Noli. "Hi! I'm Annika Vandermeis. You must be Noli." Annika spoke with a strong Bostonian accent.

"Glad to meet you," Noli said. "We were about to knock on your door."

"Oh?" Annika shifted her gaze to Tina. "Were you hoping for some of Preston's scones?"

Tina mustered a smile. "Not today, thanks. Noli would like to ask you a question."

Looking puzzled, Annika returned her attention to Noli.

Deciding to plunge ahead without ceremony, Noli said, "I was hoping you might have seen John Fitzpatrick—your new neighbor—last Wednesday when he was here to check out the apple barn."

"Wednesday?" Annika appeared to search her memory for several moments before she answered. "Yes! Fitz came over and asked to borrow a hard hat. Which we have plenty of, what with the winery construction. I volunteered to go with him—he was going into that old barn—but he told me not to worry."

"Was he alone?" Noli asked.

"I didn't see anyone else."

"Do you recall the time?"

"Um, no. But Preston left at a quarter to nine, and it wasn't too long after."

"Did you notice when Fitz left?"

"Is it important?" Annika asked, with a hint of impatience. Noli took a step toward her. "Yes, very."

"Hmmm, okay. Let me think. UPS came late morning. The Woody was still there. But it was gone when I came out to gather apples." She inclined her head toward the old orchard.

"Could you estimate what time that was? When you came out of your house?"

"You know, I don't watch the clock much," Annika said. "Life here is pretty much unscheduled, right, Tina?" Open-handed, she looked at Tina for support.

In a gentle voice, Tina said, "Have you heard what happened to Fitz, Annika?"

Annika looked blank.

Tina continued, "They found his body in Cruces Cove Thursday morning."

"Oh!" Annika's hand flew to her mouth. She gulped, blinked, then reached out a hand to touch Tina's shoulder. "I'm so sorry! He's been such a good friend to you and Peter."

Tina said, "Yes, he has."

Annika looked back and forth between the two of them. "Pardon me for saying this, but he wasn't young. You don't think ..." Looking uncomfortable, she didn't complete the sentence.

"That he died of natural causes?" Noli said, finishing for her. "No, we don't."

Annika reached out to Tina again, her fingers lingering on Tina's shoulder. "What happened?"

"The police think he killed himself," Tina answered. Her eyes were shiny. "We're trying to find out as much as we can about Wednesday, because that's the day he died."

Noli said, "So, could you estimate what time it was when you found that Fitz had left?"

Annika thought for a moment, then said, "Probably one thirty, or a little later."

Concluding she'd gotten all the information Annika had to offer, Noli said, "I want to have a quick look at that barn. Would you two like to wait here?"

Tina said she hadn't been near the barn in over a decade, and Annika said she had always been curious but hadn't wanted to trespass on the Hanaks' property. So, as a threesome, they continued down the road.

The old apple barn stood about forty yards uphill from the road. Tall and straight, apparently undamaged by earthquakes or storms, the barn was constructed of solid redwood siding, redwood roof shingles, and, most likely, redwood beams. Behind the barn, a limestone shelf rose as tall as a four-story building, marking the boundary of Loma Buena State Park. Noli wondered how Fitz had felt about the prospect of hikers in the park watching him from on high. Maybe after decades of living on a boat, cheek by jowl with other boat owners, the barn felt private by comparison.

Thickets of manzanita and poison oak covered the slope. A wide path from the road had been cleared, presumably by Fitz, but bristly stubble from the felled plants lay so thick, there was no possibility of pushing Tina's wheelchair up the hill.

Annika said, "You look. I'll just stay here with Tina."

Noli took care not to twist her ankle on the stubble, which was still green and stiff. She guessed Fitz had cleared it very recently, perhaps on Wednesday morning. In addition to the path, he'd cleared a swath roughly two yards wide along the front of the barn. She peered around the barn's corner and saw that he'd continued clearing all the way to the back. Returning to the front, she found a sliding door, much like on the Hanaks' storage barn. The door's hook-and-eye latch was secured by a shiny padlock. There was only one window—four panes of old, wavy glass, caked with dirt. Peering in, she could see old farm machinery, bedsprings, and vintage furniture piled to the rafters.

Back at the road, after Noli described what she'd seen, Tina said, "You can understand why Peter and I never got around to clearing it out."

"Do you have a key to the padlock?" Noli asked.

"We never locked it, so that lock must be Fitz's," Tina said. "I wonder why?"

"Liability. When a lawyer looks at that barn, he sees an 'attractive nuisance'," Noli said. "Fitz was many things— among them, a damn good lawyer."

Noli's cell pinged. Surprised, she pulled it from her pocket and checked the screen. A text from a friend on vacation; no need to respond. But now she knew there was cell service near the barn. Perhaps Fitz had been here, on his property, when he'd left the morning message for Peter. Had he simply wanted to talk about clearing the junk from the barn?

Turning, Noli took in the view that would have belonged to Fitz and Pilar. Stunning. In the foreground, the apple orchard, decrepit but picturesque. Beyond, the green ridges of the Santa Cruz Mountains.

The home of their nearest neighbors, the Vandermeis estate, was off to the west, where Andolini Road ended and Norton Road joined at a right angle. The Vandermeises had quadrupled the size of the original Norton farmhouse, retaining its Queen Anne style. Behind their house stood a half-finished, barn-like building, probably their new winery.

Across a bridge and down Norton Road, a redwood-shingled yurt perched on a ridge: Wolf Faber's home.

Noli said, "Now that I see the view from here, I can understand why Fitz wanted to convert the barn to a home. How old is it?"

"I don't know," Tina said. "Marco Andolini won an award at the 1920 State Fair for his apple cider, so the orchard and barn must go way back."

Noli pictured Fitz, his arm around Pilar, standing there and planning their life together. A drenching sadness washed over the scene. Would Pilar want to live here without Fitz?

"Noli." Annika's voice seemed to come from far away, pulling her back to the present. "I understand you grew up on a commune. Is it nearby?"

Uncertain how long she had been on a mind walk, Noli summoned a smile. "Yes. it's about four miles west of here." She glanced at Tina and saw tears rolling down her cheeks. Had she, too, been thinking of Fitz?

"What was it like?" Annika continued. "I mean, it just sounds so exotic." Her golden eyes were wide with interest.

The commune was the last thing Noli wanted to discuss at that moment, but she figured Annika was trying to help by shifting Tina's attention away from Fitz. Squelching a sigh, she offered Annika the description she'd polished over the years: "From a kid's perspective, it was hard work, similar to living on a family farm in the nineteenth century. We kids couldn't wait to leave and join the modern world of televisions and radios, not to mention wear clothes that weren't secondhand."

Tina looked up and smiled. Noli continued: "But in retrospect, there's a lot I'm grateful for. I learned how to grow a vegetable garden, milk a goat, and build a dome. I knew my work was important, so I felt valued, strong, and self-reliant."

In New York, Dublin, Paris, and Milan, these few sentences effectively redirected conversation away from her childhood to contemporary urban issues: the urban garden movement, the best farmer's markets, or the challenges of raising children in the city, where their connection to nature depended upon the quality of summer camps. But Annika was not to be diverted. "That sounds so wholesome, practically Amish." She chuckled. "Ask anyone on the East Coast, and they'll tell you California communes meant sex, drugs, rock and roll."

"There were lots of communes," Noli replied. "I'm sure some were like that. But New Harmony was a place for healing. All the fathers were Vietnam vets."

A sudden growl of massive engines echoed down the valley. Looking southeast, in the direction of the noise, Noli could see what she hadn't noticed earlier: on the ridge across the valley from the Hanaks' place, earth-moving equipment crawled across a mountainside, molding and terracing the earth. At the top of the slope sat a breathtaking glass-and-steel mansion. Gesturing toward it, Noli asked, "Is that the Varley place?"

Annika answered, "Yes."

The entire west face of Varley's house was floor-to-ceiling glass. The occupants could see the apple barn and every square inch of land Fitz had planned to buy. For that matter, the construction crew had a clear view, too. She debated whether she should question them before heading into Santa Cruz to meet with Luz and Munch.

Not today. If it became important to get a better estimate of Fitz's time of departure, she'd follow up with Varley and his crew.

Tina asked, "Noli, do you remember how much your father loved the orchard?"

Noli came up blank. "Sorry, I only remember the vineyard."

"The grapes were most important. But your dad urged us to revitalize the apple orchard and start pressing cider again. He insisted we could make a handsome profit. But the vineyard was all we could handle. I'd often find him poking around, checking the condition of the trees."

She did remember how much her father had loved cider.

Annika chimed in, "I've collected bushels of cooking apples out there. I was sorry John Fitzpatrick was going to dig up those trees—" She turned to Noli, her face tensing. "I'm sorry. I didn't mean—"

"Of course," Noli said. "Don't worry."

Annika bent to hug Tina. "Would you like to make apple-sauce with me? Maybe Wednesday?"

"I'd like that. Ten o'clock?"

"Perfect. You're invited too, Noli."

"Thanks. I'll have to take a rain check. If any details come to mind about last Wednesday, please let us know."

Annika, her voice now tinged with regret, said, "I loaned him the hard hat. I'm afraid that was all."

"I understand. But sometimes people remember things later, a detail that didn't seem important at first."

"Okay. I'll try." To Tina, Annika said, "I'm so sorry about Fitz. Let me know if there's anything I can do." Then she reached out to Noli, placing a hand on her arm. "Noli, I'm so glad you're here." Then, with a "Bye for now," Annika turned and walked away.

Tina and Noli watched Annika's graceful form stride down the road. Tina shook her head, saying, "Making apple-sauce! She's just trying to cheer me up. I told her I've taken next week off work."

"It'll do you good to spend time with a friend."

"Maybe." Tina's voice was hollow.

CHAPTER SIXTEEN

Saturday, 11:30 a.m.

Luz entered the law offices' conference room and, sniffing the musty air, opened the windows. Her eyes burned from lack of sleep. Her chest felt hollow. Two days had passed since Fitz was killed, and what did they know? Almost nothing.

She circled the U-shaped conference table, pushing the chairs into place. She'd decided to come in before the noon meeting with Munch and Noli Cooper to set up a situation room the way Fitz would have wanted it. And she'd asked Fitz's computer and research consultant, Irv Shoenstein, to join them.

She assumed Noli would run the meeting. Fine. They'd see what she could do.

Munch liked her. Fitz, apparently, had been ready to hand over his practice to her. How could they trust someone who'd walked away for a decade? Was it because they'd known Noli since she was a kid?

The good news was, she didn't work for Noli. She would decide for herself what direction to go.

At the open end of the table stood three whiteboards. She approached the first board and wrote *Timeline* on the top. So far, they knew very little about Fitz's last day of life, but, as a result of her work that morning, she had two additions to share with the team.

WEDNESDAY SEPT 23

- *Morning: Fitz went to mountain property near Hanak Vineyard?*

- *Cruces Cove: 6 p.m. Fitz seen "sleeping" with straw hat over face*

THURSDAY SEPT 24

- *Morning: 9:15 Young woman reported Fitz's body with 911 call from Safeway*

She allowed herself a small feeling of satisfaction. Her trip to Safeway that morning had yielded a description of the woman who'd found Fitz's body. And later, at Cruces Cove, she'd found a young couple who'd seen Fitz's body on Wednesday night.

Moving to the second board, she wrote *Suspects* at the top.

- *Vineyard Owners Assn—motive: block union of vineyard workers*

- *Four angry men culled from old case files—motive: revenge*

Her spirits sank. The suspect list didn't show much promise. But maybe Abbie's PI's would find something on one of the angry men.

She moved on to the third board and wrote *Evidence*. All the evidence they had came from the sheriff's case file, evidence they were not supposed to have. Other lawyers in the building had keys to the conference room; what if another lawyer came in and read the board?

Deciding she would cover the evidence board with butcher paper at the end of the day, she wrote:

- *Suicide note on Mortal Zin: Writing does not match Fitz's.*

- *Picnic stuff on blanket: Two empty wrappers from Señor Tico's, empty tequila bottle, empty tortilla chips pkg, cooler containing Cokes and beer. Suggests Fitz had company.*

- *Wallet contents include ID, credit cards, and $275. Robbery not the motive.*

- *Empty plastic pill container in pocket, unlabeled; source of barbiturate?*

- *Cell phone missing.*

- *No signs of injury on body.*

Munch walked in and took a chair.

"Any luck at the harbor today?" she asked.

Munch shook his head. He still hadn't found anyone who'd seen Fitz on Wednesday. His brow furrowed in concentration as he read what Luz had written on the whiteboard.

A knock on the conference room door. In stepped Irv Shoenstein. Irv was Luz's age, late twenties, of medium height and blessed with golden-brown skin that seemed to radiate a gentle light. He rocked a resplendent, light-brown Afro that added six inches to his height. His tight, stringy build suggested long distance running, which was, in fact, his favorite pastime. His hazel eyes met hers as he asked, "Bring in the equipment?"

"Sure."

Irv waved to Munch before turning around and heading back to his truck.

When Irv returned with his boxes of equipment, she cleared her throat. Trying to sound matter of fact, she said, "Irv, Munch, we've had help from someone in the sheriff's office. We don't know who. Our anonymous benefactor has given us a copy of their file on Fitz." Nodding at Irv's wide-eyed surprise, she continued, "I know, amazing, right? I'll bring it in so you two can have a look."

As she walked down the hall, she felt a moment of unease. Should she have shared the sheriff's file with two more people? Then she thought, *If we can't trust Munch and Irv, who can we trust?*

Noli Cooper arrived, apologizing for being late. She was wearing jeans and an old work shirt—she was a commune kid, right? But the clothes were spotless, the boots carefully oiled. If she was trying to fit in, she wasn't fooling anyone.

Noli greeted Luz and Munch, then turned to the man who was a stranger to her. Irv introduced himself. "Irv Shoenstein. Fitz's computer and research guy."

"Good to meet you," Noli said, taking in his computer-geek uniform: T-shirt, jeans, Birkenstock sandals. The T-shirt displayed a picture of the *Star Wars* robot R2D2 with the caption, *Hacking the Universe.*

"We always bring Irv in when we need a situation room," Luz explained.

Pointing to his top-of-the-line iMac, Irv said, "Fitz talked the landlord into installing high speed Ethernet connections in here. Room for two more workstations if we need them." Explaining that he often brought in a cot when he had to work through the night, he said, "Basically, I hold down the fort, answer phones, crank out research. Twenty-four-seven, if needed."

Noli looked at Munch, who nodded his approval. Turning to Luz, she said, "The two of you have worked cases together with Fitz?"

Luz answered, "Most of last year."

Irv said, "I'll do anything I can to help you find his killer."

Noli shook hands with him. "Glad to have your help."

Checking his watch, Irv said, "I leave in an hour for another appointment, but after today, I'm all yours."

Noli walked toward a chair, then stopped in her tracks. Her eyes were locked on the photos from the sheriff's evidence file, displayed on the table.

CHAPTER SEVENTEEN

Noli settled into a chair beside Munch. She forced herself to breathe deeply while waiting for Luz and Irv to take seats. She wanted to lash out at Luz, tell her that if the person who'd brought them the file lost their job and career, she, Luz, would be the person to blame. But the harm was done.

In carefully controlled tones, looking at Munch, then Irv, she said, "I see Luz has brought you up to date on the sheriff's case file."

"I'll need more time with it later," Irv stated.

Noli continued, "I'm sure you understand that everything in the file is confidential. If you reveal *anything* in that file to a person outside this room, you're jeopardizing the career of the person who put his—or her—job on the line for Fitz."

Solemn expressions on both their faces, Munch and Irv nodded.

Not risking a look at Luz, Noli took a moment to scan the whiteboards, then said, "Luz, thank you for getting us started. I can fill in some of the timeline." She walked to the Timeline whiteboard and uncapped a marker. "At eight a.m., Fitz had rolls and coffee with the Hanaks at their house. At nine a.m., he left them and drove to the property he was buying, a three-minute drive. We don't know when he left that property, only that he was gone by one thirty in the afternoon." She described their witness, a woman named Annika, owner of land adjacent to Fitz's. Annika had loaned Fitz a hard hat.

"Why did he need one?" Luz asked.

"He wanted to inspect a wonderful old barn on the property," Noli answered. Pointing to Luz's entry on the board, she said, "I see you found a witness who was at the Cove last Wednesday evening?"

Luz answered, "A young couple. They arrived around six p.m. Wednesday to watch the sunset."

"I don't remember a straw hat in the evidence photos, do you?"

"No. Maybe the wind carried it away."

"They were quite certain there was no one with him?"

"That's what they said."

Noli pointed to the next board entry. "You have a description of the 911 caller?"

Luz consulted a small notepad. "The Safeway manager described her as young, maybe even a teenager. My height, wearing baggy jeans and multiple sweatshirts. Short black hair, mostly hidden by a baseball cap under a hoodie. Eye color hidden behind yellow sunglasses. Dressed in jeans and a blue sweatshirt. When I was at the cove, I watched for anyone near to that description. No luck."

Noli walked to the next board. "Anything new regarding the suspects?"

"Nothing yet," Luz said. "Tonight, Raul hopes to get more information from a vineyard owner who's a friend."

Turning to Munch, Noli said, "I've been thinking about the blowback Peter and Fitz got after their TV programs with vets from Iraq and Afghanistan." To bring everyone up to date, she summarized what she'd learned from the coverage in the newspaper, then described the graffiti at the Hanaks' dome. "Both Peter and Fitz received threats on their lives, right, Munch?"

Munch wrote his answer and passed it to Irv. In a clear tenor voice, Irv read aloud, "'They wouldn't talk about it.

But I'm sure they did. After those programs, I saw guys pick fights with Fitz at the Pelican. Happened more than once.'"

Noli wrote *Angry vets* on the Suspects list.

Munch shook his head, then wrote again. Irv read, "'Not vets. I recognized three or four of the guys, and none of them served.'"

"Three or four men who might be suspects?" Noli asked.

Munch thought for several beats, then wrote, *Hotheads. Like to brag about the guns they own. Not smart enough to pull off what happened to Fitz.*

Erasing her previous entry, Noli said, "Okay, for now I'll write 'blowback from TV programs'. Let's find out whether the other vets who participated have been threatened."

"I'll find them for you," Irv said. "Top priority?"

She considered. What information was most urgent? "Yes, but call Veterans for Peace. Tell them what we need and why, see if they'll help by doing the phoning for us. If they'll help, you can focus on Fitz's phone records. I assume you can hack his cell provider?"

"Piece of cake." Irv checked his watch. "I have to leave now, but I'll start tonight."

As Irv closed the door behind him, Luz said, "There's another angle we should consider. What about that land Fitz was going to buy? It's for a vineyard, right?"

"That was his plan," Noli answered.

"So it's really valuable?"

After considering for a moment, Noli answered, "I really don't know."

"Fitz used to talk about the Hanaks' vineyard, how special it is," Luz said.

"That's true," Noli said. "What are you thinking?"

"That someone wants the land he was going to buy," Luz said. "They want it bad enough to kill him."

Noli thought this was unlikely, but she said, "It's worth following up." She wrote *Someone who wants Fitz's land* on the Suspects board. "I'll see the Hanaks tonight. I'll ask if good land for zinfandel vineyards is hard to find." She pushed away from the table, saying, "Tomorrow, at the regatta, we have our best shot at finding someone who saw Fitz sail out of the harbor on Wednesday. Could we three meet at the harbor at eleven o'clock? I know the regatta doesn't start until one, but if we start early, we can talk to folks as they arrive."

Munch wrote, *I have to cover the store by myself tomorrow. If you need me, I'll close up and join you. Otherwise, come see me after.*

When Munch had closed the door behind himself, Noli turned to Luz. "We need to talk."

CHAPTER EIGHTEEN

Night was descending by the time Noli pulled into the Hanaks' driveway. Because the airline still had not located her suitcase, she'd stopped at the mall to buy a basic set of clothes and a warm jacket. Wearily, she gathered the shopping bags from the back seat. Beneath them lay Munch's gift wine for Peter—it had been riding in the car all day.

Not good.

How could she have forgotten? With luck, the foggy air had kept it cool. Hoping the wine would be an exciting discovery, not a bottle of vinegar, she reminded herself to retrieve it in time for dinner.

Inside the old dome, heat radiated from the wood stove. Once again, Peter had set a fire. Warmed as much by gratitude as by the stove, she stepped into the bathroom to clean up for dinner. As she washed, she reviewed her talk with Luz.

Not great.

When they sat down together, Luz opened with, "Let's be clear. I don't work for you."

Noli responded that she hoped for a partnership. She understood she was a stranger to Luz, but she hoped to earn her trust. For now, could they agree to share information with one another?

They worked out the nuts and bolts of sharing Fitz's office and agreed to keep the sheriff's file in Fitz's office safe. Luz would get the safe key copied so they both had access to it. About Luz's unilateral decision to share the file with Munch and Irv, nothing was said.

There was one fleeting moment when Noli thought she and Luz might connect more deeply. She said, "You know, I keep expecting Fitz to walk through that door. I look up, he isn't there, and it feels like a knife stabbing my heart again."

Luz nodded. "I can't believe he's gone. Sitting at his desk ... occupying the space where he *ought to be* ... it's the hardest thing I've ever done." While speaking, Luz's eyes grew shiny. But she wiped her face with her sleeve, set her jaw, and announced she had to leave. Her parting words had been, "I'll meet with the team. But I call my own shots."

Cradling the gift wine, Noli climbed the stairs to the deck, resolving that Tina and Peter would have her full attention tonight.

Through the glass she could see Tina busy in the kitchen, and Peter uncorking a bottle of wine. A behemoth of a man appeared behind Tina—bald but not old, with a round face and dimpled cheeks. When he leaned in to say something to Tina, the sadness in her face seemed to lessen for just a moment.

Noli slid the door open, calling, "Hello!" The aromas of roasted garlic, onion, sausage, and red sauce caused her stomach to growl.

Peter came to her and gave her a hug. "We have a surprise for you. Remember Wolf Faber?"

There weren't many people tall enough to make her feel small, but Wolf had at least five inches on her. "I would have known you anywhere," he said, as his hand enveloped hers.

"I would *not* have recognized you, Wolf! What a pleasure to see you again." His warm, brown eyes, which had seemed strikingly sad when he was a child, now twinkled with mischief. She wanted to ask him what his life had been like after leaving the commune, but that would have to wait for another time. "Peter tells me you've been a tremendous help to him."

Wolf beamed. "Not as much help as he has been to me, I assure you. My yurt would have collapsed on my head if Peter hadn't given me a crash course—pun intended—on construction."

Tina rolled toward them in her chair, a basket of garlic bread in her lap. "I thought we'd eat early, if that's okay with you, Noli?" The corners of her lips tried to form a smile.

"Perfect," Noli answered. "I sort of skipped lunch, and the aromas filling this dome lead me to think we might be having your special lasagna. Am I right?"

Tina's face broke into a real smile. "You are."

At this point everyone was looking with interest at the large package wedged beneath Noli's left arm. Grasping it with both hands, she extended it to Peter, saying, "Munch sent you a gift."

Puzzled, Peter grasped the package and immediately registered the shape of the Styrofoam box. "Wine? From Munch?" He extracted the bottle. "Andolini '82? Is this a joke?"

"Not at all. He had two bottles, and he and Fitz drank one. According to Munch, Fitz rated it two points above terrific."

Curious, Wolf moved to Peter's side. "Has it been riding in your car?" he asked.

"Yes, I'm sorry. Munch gave it to me the day before yesterday. But the car has never been parked in the sun."

Speaking to Wolf, Peter said, "Will two days' rest be sufficient? We could open it Monday if you'll be back for Tina's birthday."

"Wouldn't miss it!" Wolf replied.

At the table, they took the seats Tina assigned them: Wolf across from Noli, Peter and Tina at the head and foot. After Peter filled their glasses with his '04 vintage zinfandel, Wolf said, "A toast to Fitz, at play in the vineyards of heaven."

Wolf's toast, which Noli guessed had been intended to console his hosts, seemed only to remind Peter and Tina of their loss. They both cut into their lasagna, eating slowly. Noli and Wolf followed suit. Across the room, a clock ticked. Wolf caught her eye and said, "So Fitz was murdered, but the Sheriff's Department is calling it suicide?"

"Yes, that's about it." Noli forked another bite of lasagna.

"And you're looking into it?"

"With help from Munch Gutterson and Fitz's PI, Luz Alvarado," she answered, biting into a slice of garlic bread. In spite of everything, she was truly hungry.

"Any suspects?"

She met his gaze. "Not really. A few leads, but I don't feel like we're on the right track yet."

"Motives?" he asked.

"Good question." Then, uncertain whether Tina would want her to continue, she said, "Perhaps we can talk after this wonderful dinner?"

Tina placed a hand on Noli's arm, saying, "There's nothing more important. Any ideas you've come up with, we want to hear. Don't we, Peter?"

Peter nodded. "Absolutely. Tell us what you're thinking."

Noli considered where to start. "After the TV programs you and Fitz hosted with guys who'd come back from fighting in Iraq and Afghanistan, there was a lot of blowback. Letters to the paper, threats to the TV station. Both you and Fitz received threats, didn't you?"

Peter was clearly caught off guard. He cleared his throat, looked at Tina—who looked startled—then at Noli. "That was ages ago. And the answer is no. No one threatened me. I'm sure Fitz would have told me if he'd had any serious problems."

Certain he was lying to reassure Tina, Noli chided herself for not waiting until she had him alone. She glanced at Wolf and saw that he was watching Peter intently, a strange expression on his face. Discomfort, for sure, but something else too. Did he also know Peter was lying?

She decided to drop the subject and talk with Peter later, privately. Wolf, too. From the corner of her eye, she could see that Tina had teared up. Noli took another bite of lasagna and said, "Tina, I'd put your lasagna up against Italy's best."

"I'll pretend to believe your outrageous flattery, you sweet girl," Tina said. Then, pushing away from the table, she said, "Please excuse me."

They all watched as Tina rolled away, circling behind the wooden screen that separated their "bedroom" from the rest of the dome's first floor. Noli wondered what else Tina was pretending to believe. That the graffiti threats were harmless?

There was an awkward silence while the three of them focused on their food. Outdoors, an owl hooted. A squirrel skittered across the roof. Wolf raised his wine glass to the light and twirled it, watching the "legs" it formed on the sides of the curved glass, then said, "Peter, the balance is excellent. You blended the grapes from Old Marco's Hill with the new vineyard's grapes?"

"Yes."

"What ratio?"

"Four new to one old."

Wolf nodded thoughtfully.

Wondering if she understood their exchange, Noli asked, "Haven't you always blended the grapes from Old Marco's Hill with those from the new vineyard? I seem to remember Old Marco's are too tannic to make good wine on their own."

Peter answered, "It isn't just the tannin, but that's right. I tried for several years to ferment Old Marco's Hill alone, but never succeeded. Drove me crazy, 'cause I'm sure that Dino did—you remember Tina's brother?"

"Sure." Dino had been beloved by all the commune kids because he always took time to play with them. He died in a motorcycle accident when Noli was eight, her first encounter with death. Only ten days later, her mother died suddenly of a cerebral aneurism. Thus, in a weird way, the two of them were linked forever in her memory.

Peter continued, "Dino made wine with crazy old Paolina Andolini for years, and I'm sure they only used the grapes from Old Marco's Hill. But he and Paolina took their secret to the grave." He paused to glance in the direction of the bedroom.

Noli thought perhaps she should go to Tina. Catching Peter's attention, she mimed with her fingers leaving the table and walking to the bedroom.

Peter shook his head, an emphatic no, then refilled their wine glasses.

Noli sipped the rich wine, trying to recall the stories she'd heard about Paolina Andolini. Paolina was the granddaughter of Marco, the man who cleared the redwood stumps, built a mansion, and planted vineyards on this mountainside in the nineteenth century. By the time Tina and Peter bought the land from Paolina and built their first dome in the 1970s, Paolina would already have been ancient. And how did Dino come into the picture?

She was about to ask when Wolf said, "How long did Dino make wine with Paolina?"

Peter's gnarled fingers pulled on his beard. "I'd say, from about 1979 'til he died in '84. We can double check with Tina."

Wolf continued, "And you didn't own Old Marco's Hill until Paolina Andolini left it to you when she died, right?"

"To Tina, really. Tina took care of Paolina for two years while she was failing. Not just nursing, either. Paolina dictated her autobiography to Tina." Then Peter slapped the side of his head, saying, "I'm so sorry, Wolf. I totally forgot you wanted to read it. We'll ask Tina for it when she comes back."

Thinking this was a good opportunity to ask about the value of land in the area, Noli said, "This afternoon, Luz asked an interesting question. She wondered whether the land Fitz was going to buy was so valuable that someone would kill him in order to buy the land from you."

Peter gave a rueful laugh. "There's land for sale all over these mountains."

But Wolf took the question seriously. "With all due respect, Peter, you don't know that they have the same terroir."

"Yeah." Peter turned to Noli. "Wolf has some grandiose notions about the potential of our vineyards. He's got me experimenting with the grapes from Old Marco's Hill, thinks he can figure out Dino's secret." As much as his words made light of Wolf's ideas, there was hope and respect in his voice.

CHAPTER NINETEEN

When all the dishes were washed, Noli led Wolf to the old dome, pleased she would be able to question him in private. Wolf knelt to rekindle the fire in the wood stove while she found two wine glasses and pulled a chair over to the couch to serve as a coffee table.

Pouring wine from the unfinished bottle Peter had sent with them, Wolf said, "This place is like a second home to me. While I was building my yurt, Peter and Tina let me stay here. You too, right? You lived here while you were in high school?"

"Long story," Noli said, wondering how much Peter had told him. She felt the slow throb of a headache coming on and considered dashing back to ask Tina for aspirin. Instead, she continued, "Do you remember Gwen, my stepmother?"

Wolf closed his eyes, summoning a distant memory. "Slender, long red hair. Played a harp?"

"Right. It turns out Gwen suffers from schizophrenia, which got worse while I was growing up. My dad and a few very dear women in the commune looked out for her. The night Dad died, she had a serious break with reality. She set fire to our dome. I barely got her out alive, and we both were badly burned. When we were released from the hospital, Gwen was sent to a residential clinic. The Hanaks arranged for me to live with them."

Wolf waited for her to continue. When she didn't, he asked, "It was the Loma Prieta quake that killed your dad?"

"Yeah. He was hiking back from visiting Peter, got caught in a landslide." Immediately, Fitz's message played in her mind. *Noli, call me. It's about your father.* Was it possible he was still alive? She felt a spark of hope, but quickly dismissed it. He never would have abandoned her or Gwen. It must be something about his life, something important. Maybe about his service as a medic in Vietnam? He'd never opened up about his time in Vietnam—at least, not with her.

She realized Wolf was looking at her, expecting a response, and she had no idea what he'd said. "Sorry! I went on a mind walk for a moment there."

In his face there was so much kindness and understanding, she wondered what losses *he* might have endured, beyond what she had witnessed in the commune. She wanted to ask, yet her headache was mounting, and a crushing weariness threatened to overcome her. She reached out to touch his hand, saying, "I'm at a disadvantage here. Peter's clearly told you a lot about my life, but I know nothing of yours, except that you're now a consultant for vineyard owners. I'm about to crash from jet lag, so maybe we could talk in the morning?"

"Tomorrow I leave early for Sonoma and Sacramento. I'll be back in time for Tina's party Monday evening. We'll catch up then."

"Definitely. Before you go, a couple of questions?"

He smiled. "Fire away." He raised the wine bottle, asking, "Refill?"

"Not for me, thanks." Choosing her words carefully, she began, "When Peter denied receiving threats after the TV programs, you looked like you disagreed."

Wolf gave her a rueful smile. "Remind me never to play poker with you. Have you seen the Hanaks' winery?"

"No, haven't been down there yet."

"On the front, above the doors, there's graffiti saying, 'Die camel-fucking traitor.' It's misspelled, but the intent is clear. Peter claims it was just a teenage prank, but when I asked whether he knew who the teenagers were, he changed the subject."

"Do you know when the graffiti appeared?"

"Yeah, last March. Right after their TV program. And there was a smaller one in 2007, on the winery door where it was easier to scrub off. That one just said, 'Traitor.'"

Noli said, "On their deck, where it can be seen from the living room, there's the remains of another one. It says, 'Die Traitor.' It didn't look very old to me."

Wolf's eyes narrowed. "So maybe they're still being harassed. Did Peter tell you about the '07 and '08 vintages?"

"Turned to vinegar in the aging barrels."

"Yeah. Do you know how easy it would be for someone to make that happen?"

"You mean sabotage the barrels?"

"Exactly. All you have to do is open the bung and pour in a few drops of vinegar. It would only take a few minutes to ruin every barrel."

"It's quite a jump from graffiti to expertly ruining a year's vintage, don't you think?"

"Yeah, it is. But I've seen how careful Peter is, and it makes me wonder how two vintages in a row—*all* the barrels—could have gone bad."

Noli nodded. "You're saying someone is trying to ruin Peter."

Wolf looked grim. "I know it sounds far-fetched. But yes, that's what my gut is telling me."

"Duly noted. Last question: Peter dismissed the idea that their land is special. You disagreed."

"It's complicated, and we can go into it when I get back. For now, just think about the amazing soil here, how it was created over a couple of thousand years by giant redwoods. Then consider that the parcel Fitz was going to buy has excellent southern exposure. Add to that, the Hanaks have already proven the land produces a superior zinfandel. So, it's valuable. Not unique, of course. There's similar terroir up around the Russian River."

"Not worth killing for?" Noli asked.

CHAPTER TWENTY

Midnight

Raul Espinoza, labor organizer, was beginning to despair of ever getting Carl Hoskins III, member of the vineyard owners' bargaining team, to talk about Fitz's death. The more they drank, the more Carl driveled on about divorce from his third wife.

"I loved her," Carl repeated.

"I know you did, *hermano*. Let's go out on the deck."

Raul stood and gently pulled on Carl's arm, coaxing him out of his chair, praying he could still walk. Obediently, Carl rose and staggered through the doorway. Raul guided him past comfortable reclining chairs to a cement bench, saying, "We can see the stars better from here."

Carl dropped to the bench and threw his shoulders and head back, looking straight up. " Shtars."

Raul decided to make his play. "I gotta serious problem. I need your help, bro."

"Shpeak to me, dude."

"My good friend Fitz got killed."

"True."

"He was my very good friend. Like you."

Carl nodded sadly.

"If someone killed you—"

Carl swung his head around in alarm.

"I'm just saying 'if'. Like in a movie, okay?"

"Movie?" Carl closed his eyes.

Certain Carl was about to pass out, Raul raised his voice. "In a movie, someone hurts you, I find him and hurt him, like he hurt you. Right, man? Are you with me?"

"You go...hurt him."

"That's what friends do, right?"

"Friends. Yesh."

"So I have a problem. Someone hurt my friend Fitz, but I don't know who."

"Bashtard."

"I want to find that man, *hermano*."

Carl swung a wobbly fist through the air, showing how he would punch.

Raul leaned in. "*You* know who hated Fitz, *hermano*. Tell me."

Carl said nothing.

In a loud whisper, Raul said, "You can tell me. I always keep secrets, remember?"

Carl opened one eye. "Trusht you."

"Tell me. Who wanted Fitz dead?"

Carl waved a hand, dismissively. "Losh of people."

"I need names."

"Pash... Pasolini. Gasquet. Shwanson." Carl yawned. "Varley. Ooooh yah, ol' Gary says, 'Someone owtta get rid of tha' fucking lawyer!'"

CHAPTER TWENTY-ONE

Sunday, 5:45 a.m.

Luz woke to the sound of a car. Eduardo was home.

She lit the bedside lamp and swiveled her feet to the rough plywood floor of her sleeping porch. Her clammy T-shirt turned frigid in a split second; she peeled it off, longing for a hot shower.

No time for that.

She pulled a fresh cotton winding cloth from her dresser and wound it around her torso, starting at her waist, around and around, working higher until her breasts were bound and her waist thickened, then tied the ends behind her back. A fresh T-shirt, then black cotton pants with a drawstring waist, a white cotton *gi*, and a long belt of black cloth.

She peered between the slats of the bamboo shades that gave her sleeping porch some privacy. Fog lay thick on the ground, but she could make out Eduardo's new Mustang in the driveway, blocking her Corolla. Again.

She closed the porch door softly. Luis, her little brother, had the ears of a bat and had a hard time getting back to sleep if awakened. Crossing the cold cement driveway to Eduardo's garage-studio, she knocked on his door.

A woman's voice filtered through the door, eerily distorted by an answering machine. *Eduardo, mi caro.*

She knocked louder. Footsteps approached.

"Eduardo, it's me. Open up."

He did. Her handsome-as-a-model brother stood barefoot, dressed only in boxer shorts. "*Hola*, Lucita. You're up early."

She gave him a passing embrace, stepped inside, and waited while he switched the answering machine to off.

"Again, you've blocked my car. My class starts at seven."

He braced into a karate pose, mocking readiness for a fight, then blew her a kiss. He pulled his keys from the pocket of a leather jacket.

"Wait, Edo." Luz realized her fists were clenched. Taking a slow, deep breath, counting to five, she forced her hands to relax. "What I want to tell you is, Fitz didn't write the suicide note. All his writing slants. In the note, the writing's straight up and down."

"It was written on a mirror, Lucita. You can't—"

Luz cut him off. "We have leads. We need your help."

"Lucita, get clear on this: Rinzler is a very powerful man. He's worked Santa Cruz County for thirty years, and his tentacles reach every little valley. You cross over the line, and he'll make sure you lose your PI license. And he'll get me fired. I won't be able to pay for this house. We'll go back to *Sal si Puedes*. You want that?"

CHAPTER TWENTY-TWO

Sunday, 7:15 a.m.

The triangular windows of the old dome glowed with gray, foggy light. Rolling over in bed, Noli grabbed her cell from the bed table. She'd slept for nine hours, but the headache still pounded in her temples. She needed whatever painkiller Tina could offer. And she needed to catch Peter before she left for the harbor.

She climbed from bed, wrapped a wool shirt over her pajamas, and descended the spiral stairs. She stopped at the kitchen sink to drink a pint of water in case dehydration was contributing to the headache. When she opened the front door, cold, damp air enveloped her, but she plunged ahead. She was two steps from the new dome when she heard Tina's voice shout, "No, I will not *drop it*, Peter! I know you're mourning Fitz. But get a grip!"

Noli froze. The sliding glass door to the new dome was partly open, and she could see Peter's silhouetted back just inside the door.

Tina continued, her voice softer now. "We're *broke*, Peter. Either we find an investor, or we sell Fitz's land. Daniel Arnant and Gary Varley both made good offers. Do you want to sell to them?"

"You know I don't."

"Then, for the love of God, go to Daniel's party. He's handing you access to a room full of potential investors."

"Don't you wonder *why?*"

"No, I don't. He's a decent guy who's trying to help us."

"I don't believe it. Why don't *you* go? You've seen me at parties: Open mouth, insert foot."

"*Look at me, Peter.* I'm in a wheelchair!"

"It doesn't—"

"Investors require confidence in their investments. Does an invalid give them the right impression?"

"Don't hand me that. You're no invalid. They'll know it the minute you open your mouth. You're—"

"It doesn't work that way, Peter. They want to see a strong, capable man who knows his business. Even if I were on my feet—"

Embarrassed to be eavesdropping, Noli slipped quietly into the old dome, shutting the door soundlessly.

★ ★ ★

After Peter stomped out the door, Tina made herself a pot of mint tea. Time to pull herself together.

Just five days ago she'd believed a new life was beginning for herself and Peter. With Fitz and Pilar as neighbors, it was all going to work out.

Now, what?

She thought of Paolina—"Crazy Old Lady Andolini"— warning her, "This mountain will curse your children and your dreams."

Tina hadn't believed in jinxes, or curses either, even after her miscarriages. She'd believed the sad history of the Andolini family was just one among dozens of shattered dreams in the Santa Cruz Mountains. But now? Fate, fortune, or simple bad luck had torpedoed every dream she'd brought to Loma Buena Mountain.

Now, unless they found an investor, Hanak Winery would become a tiny footnote in zinfandel history. And their commitment to a world-class wine? A quixotic notion, soon to be erased by whichever large winery bought them out.

Did it matter?

Not to her, not the wine itself. But the dream, yes. It had been Dino's, then Peter's. They'd worked so hard, given their hearts and souls to this vineyard. It was too late for Dino, but not for Peter.

Ever since she'd seen the word "suicide" in the newspaper account of Fitz's death, Dino had been haunting her in a way he hadn't for many years. Had Dino meant to die on that night? Maybe. He'd raced his motorcycle through the Santa Cruz Mountains every day after his release from the VA hospital, tempting death to reach out and take him. Maybe it was a miracle he'd lasted as long as he did.

Dino, the lost babies, the wheelchair, now Fitz. And always, the uncertainty of multiple sclerosis.

She felt like MS toyed with her. It was the cat, she the mouse. It tore her apart, one muscle at a time, never letting her know when the end was coming. The first time her legs went numb, feeling returned in six months. The second time, the numbness stayed, and she started taking an antidepressant. Then, after a year with no further attacks, she accepted life in a wheelchair and threw the pills away.

This morning, she'd give anything for those pills.

All night she'd lain awake, straining to hear the next catastrophe approaching. Yet it was going to be a beautiful morning. The fog was lifting, and a breeze from the west filled the house with the perfume of ripe grapes, a scent that used to make Peter giddy with anticipation. But this morning, his face haggard with grief and exhaustion, he'd turned to her and said, "Who will carry on? Why are we doing this?"

She stared out the window in the direction of the winery, looking back through time to August 4, 1979, the day the winery was built. Dino's and Peter's friends, all vets, had shown up for the "barn raising." She took breaks from cooking to watch them—

"Tina?"

Noli stood just inside the sliding door, looking at her as if she'd called her name more than once.

"Hello, dear. This morning I'm lost in old times. Have some tea with me?"

"Love to. But first I need about a pound of aspirin."

Tina opened a kitchen drawer, selected a bottle, and set it down with a glass of water. "Have a seat. I'll brew a pot of Earl Grey."

When she and Noli were settled with their tea and muffins, Noli asked, "What were you thinking about?"

"Last night, talking about Dino and old Paolina, it took me back. Just now I was remembering the day the winery was built. A barn raising, done in a single day by Peter, Dino, and a group of vets they knew. I was scared it would be a disaster; drugs and alcohol ruled their lives back then. I fixed lunch as an excuse to go down and check on them. Peter was kneeling on roof joists, nailing sheets of plywood. Dino was climbing a two-story ladder, a big canvas sack of shingles slung across his shoulders. They were laughing, talking about getting more hands on the job by recruiting the vets who were still living in caves in the state park.

"I could feel the manic undercurrent of rage each man carried inside. Each used his drug of choice. Hash and gin for Dino. Vicodin for Peter. The guy operating the table saw guzzled a six-pack, then switched to grass. I wanted to shout at them, make them stop before it was too late.

"Then Fitz arrived. He made a joke about saving the beer and joints till later, and they should 'cut out the pills, 'cause Tina's only a nurse forgodsake, who-the-fuck is going to sew you up?'

"The guys all laughed, got back to work, sobered up. Somehow Fitz kept the lid on, kept morale high, made it fun, the way a natural leader keeps his men on task."

Fitz. Tina paused to let the pain wash through her again. Then she summoned a smile for Noli, and said, "That afternoon, a mustard-colored VW van rolled up the hill. The doors flew open. Your mom and dad and you stood there, amazed to see a building growing right before your eyes. Do you remember?"

Noli didn't.

"Well, you were pretty young. Maybe four? I remember your dad saying, 'How does it feel to live in paradise?'"

This is the beginning, she had thought. *The pain within these men will melt away into this mountain. We will have children. We will grow grapes and make wonderful wine. We will be a family.*

Tina shut her mind's door on the memories and realized Noli had taken her hand.

"I want to hear every story you can remember," Noli said. "Every single one, okay? We'll have lots of time now that I'm back."

She squeezed Noli's hand, thinking *yes.*

"Before I head down to the harbor," Noli said, "I'd like to ask you a question. Have any of your neighbors—or anyone else, for that matter—offered to buy you out?"

"All three of the neighbors, multiple times. I don't know about other offers. Why?"

Noli shook her head. "I'm not sure. Just trying to get a feel for the Andolini Valley, the way things are now. So much has changed."

Tina suspected Noli wasn't being completely honest, but she let it go. "Peter should be back soon. He'll give you more detail on the offers."

"I'm interested in the neighbors," Noli said. "Tell me about them."

"Well, you've met Annika already. Her husband—"

A polite tap at the glass doors cut their conversation short.

Tina looked up, and seeing the man standing there, suppressed a sigh. She liked Daniel Arnant, but this morning she didn't have the energy for company.

She waved Daniel in. He had to duck slightly to avoid hitting his head on the doorframe. "Daniel, this is our goddaughter, Noli Cooper."

As they shook hands, Noli said, "Pleasure to meet you. You've done wonders with the old Andolini Estate."

Daniel Arnant was thin, with the kind of over-large features that would be an asset on the stage. A pink Polo shirt flattered his rosy coloring and strawberry-blond hair. He turned to Tina and handed her a large bouquet of chrysanthemums and lilies, saying, "I heard about your friend Fitz. I'm so sorry."

"Thank you, Daniel. You're very kind."

"I hope I haven't come too early. I'd hoped to catch Peter."

"You're just in time to join us for tea. Peter should be back in a few minutes."

Daniel said, "I don't want to impose."

"Nonsense." Tina summoned a warm smile and pointed to the table. "Have a seat. You've lucked into my very best muffins."

Daniel joined Noli at the table, saying, "Did you feel the quake this morning?"

Noli said, "No, what time did it hit?"

"Around five o'clock," Daniel said. "Then a couple of aftershocks."

"I'm surprised I slept through it," Noli said. "Little quakes used to be just a fact of life. But after the Loma Prieta, I'm a little jumpy when the earth moves under me."

Tina thought "a little jumpy" glossed over a level of PTSD that had taken Noli many years to overcome. She poured a cup of tea for Daniel. "Is the cave remodel going to be ready for your big celebration?"

"It's finished," Daniel said. "We're already decorating for the party, which is why I wanted to check in with Peter. He promised to bring six bottles of his '04 for the harvest dinner."

Tina said, "He's looking forward to it, Daniel." *A lie. But only a small one.*

"Sure you won't join us?" Daniel asked her.

"Maybe next year." Changing the topic, she said, "Noli's very interested in the work you've been doing. How about filling her in while I make us a fresh pot?"

Daniel turned to Noli. "Are you familiar with the Andolini Estate?"

Noli said, "As a kid, I explored every inch of it. And, I hasten to add, neither Tina nor Peter knew I was there. But you know how kids are. The old buildings were a combination ghost house and playground. I think I know the cave you're—"

There was a forceful knock on the sliding door. They all turned to see a middle-aged man slide the door open and step through.

Gary Varley. Tina stifled a sigh and introduced him to Noli as "our neighbor to the south." It was the first time he'd dropped by in the daytime. Seeing him clearly, she noticed he was going soft around the middle and wondered how old he was. Mid-fifties? His dirty-blond hair was buzzed short. His pale-blue eyes darted around the room. "I'm looking for Peter."

She could guess why Varley had come: He'd heard about Fitz's death and wanted to buy the unused acreage Fitz had been about to buy. She imagined Annika's husband knocking on the door next, and had the overwhelming sensation that vultures were gathering to fight over the remains of Hanak Winery and Vineyards. Taking care to speak in an even tone, she said, "He'll be back any minute, Gary. Why don't you join us?"

"I can't stay. Tell Peter I'll call him." Turning on his heel, Varley exited and gave the sliding door a shove behind him. It didn't close.

Daniel rose, slid the door shut, and said, "I shouldn't be keeping you. I'll just—"

"If you have the time, please stay," Tina said. "Noli would enjoy hearing about your cave remodel." She took a deep breath, trying to push away her gloom.

Daniel rejoined Noli at the table, saying, "You were about to tell me about your childhood explorations in the Andolini cave..."

Half listening to Noli, half listening for the sound of Peter's return, Tina measured loose tea into the teapot and filled the pot with boiling water. She set the teapot on a towel in her lap and rolled her chair back to her guests. "We'll let this steep for a few minutes," she said, wrapping the fingers of her right hand around the teapot's handle. She lifted it toward the table.

Her fingers gave way.

The teapot fell, crashing into shards on the tiled floor.

Hot tea flew in all directions.

CHAPTER
TWENTY-THREE

Deeply upset and struggling to regain his equilibrium, Peter climbed to the top of Old Marco's Hill. Slowly, he surveyed the Andolini Valley. This was his sanctuary and his life's work. He wasn't going to let it go.

In his mind's eye, he pictured Tina on the day in 1973 when he'd been discharged from the VA hospital. Still wearing her nurse's uniform, she drove him to the Andolini mansion to meet Paolina. Then they walked up Andolini Road to the redwood grove. "We'll build our dome here," she said. And further up the road, pointing to the wild, sunlit flank of Loma Buena Mountain, she said, "Perfect place for our vineyard."

Before they'd even built shelter for themselves, they'd planted the vineyard. Old Ms. Andolini had given them zinfandel cuttings. His fingertips still recalled how delicately he'd parted the fertile earth and inserted the tiny vines. Tina had wept, blessing each one with all the love and hope they'd held for their new life.

And now, after thirty-six years, it spread before him. One of the best vineyards in California. Green, gold, and purple. The perfume of ripe grapes rose from the valley floor, whispering the promise of a great vintage.

He hated fighting with Tina.

And he knew she was right. He needed to find an investor if they were going to avoid bankruptcy.

Bad luck? Or his mistake?

For two years running—'05 and '06— Hanak Zinfandel claimed gold medals in the *San Francisco Chronicle*'s Wine Competition. Wine critics phoned, wanting to visit. Hanak Winery was poised for fame.

But in '07, everything changed. He'd been topping off the barrels, adding wine to fill the space created by evaporation while the wine aged. Just routine maintenance and an opportunity to taste. Routine.

But not this time.

The second he pulled the plug from the first barrel, he knew he was in trouble. The sharp stench of vinegar, acetic acid, filled his nose. A winemaker's nightmare. The '07 barrels were lost. All of them. He didn't know how it had happened.

For Tina's sake, he'd done his best to pretend he wasn't worried. He told her they'd recover. The '08 would be their best vintage ever. And it was—until it, too, turned to vinegar.

What would happen now? This new crop was extraordinary, the best ever. A cool summer had allowed the grapes' sugar to develop slowly, fostering the complexity of flavor required for a great wine. Maybe, if he was careful, he could figure out what had gone wrong. Maybe he could save their reputation.

He took a deep breath and massaged his rigid neck muscles. He lifted his gaze to the horizon, where a strip of blue marked the Pacific Ocean surging into Monterey Bay. When he was a child, the ocean was, to him, no more than a wash of pale blue ink on the *Child's Map of the World* his grandfather spread on the floor of their frigid Chicago tenement. His *nagyapa* would trace their journey in reverse, from Chicago back to Ellis Island; then east across the blue Atlantic; across European countries colored pink, green, and yellow; to Hungary, where he had been born.

Huddled next to their only radiator, Nagyapa tried to warm him with tales of summer sunshine and fragrant vineyards, tales of their village before the Communists took it, before they escaped in a hay wagon with nothing but their lives. Nagyapa told him of the Bükk Mountains, where early spring painted the vineyards with bright green shoots and tender pink blossoms. As he spoke, the old man's hands wove magic in the air, tending remembered vines, counting buds, pruning branches. "Two buds only, you cut the others. Not too much fruit, Pieter. Much fruit, no flavor." With a flat hand, Nagyapa contoured the air, showing Peter the mountainside stored in his memory. "Here, the land slopes east, so I trim the leaves to welcome the sun. Over here, the vines are sick; I pull them out. The roots, Pieter, the roots! You know how long? Three meters, even four!"

When their lesson ended, Nagyapa grasped Peter's shoulder and confided, "Making wine is to love a beautiful woman. Waking up, you think, 'Today I will lose her.' Every harvest, I am crazy. Crazy for worry."

Then Nagyapa laughed. "Born to love the vine?" Before Peter could answer, he thumped Peter's chest, saying, "It is my prayer for you. May you give it your life!"

With his grandfather's ghost at his side, Peter rose and made his way back to the domes.

CHAPTER TWENTY-FOUR

Sunday 11 a.m.

Noli parked near the harbor, still worried about Tina. The tea had been near boiling, but Tina's feet were not badly burned—quick application of ice to the affected skin had prevented serious injury. Nor had anyone else been hurt, although Daniel Arnant's Gucci loafers might need some touching up. Peter had not returned, nor had he answered his cell. She hadn't wanted to leave Tina alone. But after Daniel Arnant departed, Tina had been adamant about needing time alone.

What bothered Tina the most was the loss of the teapot. It had won a prize for Gwen Cooper, Noli's stepmother, the year before the Loma Prieta quake. In an effort to console Tina, Noli promised to find a replacement as soon as she could visit Gwen's pottery studio. She was pretty sure Gwen still worked with clay during the intervals she was well enough to live at home.

Her cell pinged, pulling her out of her thoughts. A text from Luz. *Parked on west side. Start canvassing here?*

Noli responded, *Yes. Meet you top of harbor 1 p.m.*

As the harbormaster had predicted, good weather had attracted a large number of sailors. Some were lounging on their boats, sharing food and drinks with friends. Others were preparing to sail, removing sail covers, checking sheets and cleats.

On P Dock she spotted two Columbia 32's, their masts standing taller than those of the surrounding vessels. On one, a straight-backed, gray-haired woman and a teenage boy were preparing to sail. The woman wore pressed khaki trousers, a blue-and-white striped shirt, a red sweater and topsiders. Dressed for Connecticut rather than California.

The boy hopped from the boat to the dock and jogged to the locked gate, opening it for two compatriots carrying grocery bags. Noli slipped through behind the boys. As she approached the boat, she called, "Ahoy, *Clarion!*"

The woman looked up.

Noli said, "May I speak with you for a moment? My name is Nollaig Cooper."

"Yes?"

"I'm a friend of John Fitzpatrick—nicknamed Fitz—who owns the sloop *Mortal Zin* on C Dock. Do you know him?"

The woman frowned and stared at the water. Irritation? Sadness? Memory loss? After several moments, she called to the teenager, who was carrying bench pads up through the hatch. "Jerry, take care of the sail covers?" She stepped onto the dock, and said, "I'm Janet Greenway."

Noli offered her hand, but the woman's arms stayed at her side. A stalwart member of the old women-don't-shake-hands school of manners?

"My condolences," the woman continued. "We did not know Mr. Fitzpatrick well, but my husband—Roger is an attorney—admired his commitment to assisting the poor."

Wife of a lawyer. Okay, do this by the book. "I, too, am an attorney, Mrs. Greenway. As you may know, the police believe Mr. Fitzpatrick committed suicide. However, the evidence is inconclusive. I believe they are mistaken, and I—"

Janet Greenway interrupted with a raised hand. "You want to know if I saw him?"

"Yes."

"My husband and I sailed the regatta last Wednesday. Just before the first buoy—do you know the regatta course?"

Noli nodded. "A triangle."

"We were one of the last boats to tack around the first buoy, so naturally we were focused on the boats ahead of us. But Roger happened to look back after we'd come 'round, and he called me to take a look. The *Mortal Zin,* at least a hundred yards behind us, was heading west-northwest. Mr. Fitzpatrick was standing on the port deck, working the rigging. Such a beautiful sloop! We enjoyed seeing it under sail."

"Do you know what time that was, Mrs. Greenway?"

"Not precisely. But I did look at my watch when we left the harbor. One thirty. I would estimate we made the first buoy twenty-five minutes after that, so approximately two o'clock."

"You said Mr. Fitzpatrick was standing on deck. Are you certain it was him?"

"Yes. His appearance was quite distinctive—Greek sailor's hat, beard, blue windbreaker."

"Was there anyone else on board?"

"Yes. At the wheel there was a small person, maybe a boy. He wore a baseball cap and a black windbreaker with the hood pulled up."

"You say 'small.' How could you tell?"

"His head barely topped the wheel."

Noli made a mental note to measure the height of the *Mortal Zin's* wheel. Too many years had passed to remember with certainty, but she thought the boy would be nearly five feet tall. "What about body type? Fat, average, thin?"

"Thin as a stick."

Probably not the teenager who called 911 the next day. "Was there a third person on deck?"

"Not that we saw. But we didn't watch very long."

"Thank you for your help." Noli pulled a card from her pocket. "If you think of anything else, any detail at all, I'd appreciate a call."

Janet Greenway stared at the card. "You're from Dublin?"

"I'll be staying in Santa Cruz until this investigation is complete. My cell number is on the back."

Janet Greenway returned the card. "I want no further involvement. I've told you everything I saw." She turned, clambered onto her boat, and disappeared through the hatch.

By one o'clock, Noli had spoken to every available sailor on the east side of the harbor without finding anyone who could corroborate Mrs. Greenway's story. She walked to the top of the harbor, where Luz had promised to meet her. Several spectators had settled onto benches in the area, but Luz wasn't one of them.

She scanned the westside docks, thinking she might spot Luz. Of the nearby vessels, only two were preparing to sail. People were visible on both boats. No sign of Luz. What if she'd been detained further down the harbor? Both boats could sail before their crews had been questioned, so she'd better talk to them now.

At H Dock there was a Columbia 36—the *Cruzin for Fun*. In the cockpit, three T-shirted young men huddled around a girl whose back alone was enough to stop traffic. Glistening black hair cascaded over the back strap of her sports bra and down a sleek bare back.

Those guys weren't going anywhere soon.

At G Dock she hailed a Catalina 320, where a three-man crew was preparing to sail. "Hello, *Evening Dream*! Hello!"

The crew looked up. A sandy-haired, fifty-ish man climbed onto the dock and jogged to the gate. When they were face to face, the gate's mesh between them, he said, "Yes?"

"My name is Nollaig Cooper. Are you captain of the *Evening Dream?*"

He tipped his baseball cap and broke into a smile, showing a full set of small, very white teeth. "Jack Johnston. How can I help you?"

"I realize you're probably getting ready for the race."

He nodded.

"I'll be brief. I was a close friend of John Fitzpatrick, who lived on the *Mortal Zin* on C Dock."

"I heard about his suicide. I'm terribly sorry."

"I'm looking for people who were here, in the harbor, last Wednesday—"

He interrupted. "Are you part of the same investigating team as that young woman?" He pointed to the *Cruzin for Fun.* "She was here just a few minutes ago, asking about Fitz."

She was?

Seeing Noli's confusion, he said, "Well, I'm not surprised Fitz has so many lovely women upset. He was a terrific guy. Sorry I can't help you. I wasn't here last Wednesday."

"Thank you for your time. Good luck in the regatta."

He tipped his cap again and walked away.

Was Rinzler investigating after all?

No, not Rinzler. Who, then?

Given the number of individuals and groups Fitz had helped during his long career, would it be surprising if someone else had hired a PI to investigate his death? Absolutely not.

Whoever it was, she needed to meet her. Ideally, they could coordinate and share information.

The gate to *Cruzin*'s dock was propped open. As she approached, no one on the boat even glanced in her direction. The girl tossed her head, and a musical laugh filled the air. The young men stared at her as though God had just invented women and she was the first off the assembly line.

"Excuse me?" Noli said.

Three male heads jerked away from their reverie to regard the source of interruption. The girl turned slowly.

Holy shit. It's Luz.

Luz said, "*Amigos*, this is Noli Cooper, the lawyer I told you about."

"Hey, come aboard!" said a broad-shouldered man with Celtic tattoos on his biceps and a shaved head.

"Wanna beer?" offered a wiry, blond, spiky-haired man.

The two men seated on either side of Luz were glued in place. Opposite them sat a stocky man with gelled black hair. His turned-up nose and baby-blue eyes were offset by metal studs in his eyebrows, lip, and tongue. Offering Noli a reluctant smile, Mr. Face Metal patted the cushion next to him.

She climbed aboard, shooting Luz a *what's up?* look.

Luz just smiled.

"No beer, thanks," Noli said.

After Luz introduced each young man, she said, "These *hombres* crewed for Fitz sometimes. They were not here last Wednesday. But all of them, they know Cruces Cove very well."

Noli said to Luz, "Have you asked about the 911 caller?"

"Not yet." Luz repeated the Safeway manager's description of the girl who used his phone. "Have you seen anyone like that, maybe out at the Cove?"

Face Metal and Tattoo Guy glanced at one other, then looked away. Spiky Blond said, "We might. Have to check."

"How soon can you do that?" Noli asked.

Spiky Blond answered, "We, um, might know by tomorrow."

Luz gave him her card. "Call me anytime, day or night. We have to find her."

He took the card solemnly, like a knight accepting his lady's banner.

"One more question," Noli said. She repeated Mrs. Greenway's story. "Does the thin guy—maybe a boy—in a black windbreaker sound like anyone you've seen around the harbor?"

After taking several seconds for consideration, all three shook their heads. Spiky Blond said, "We'll keep it in mind, though."

Luz stood, saying, "It's been a pleasure meeting you." She smiled at each of the men in turn. "*Hasta luego.*"

Noli followed Luz onto the dock. When they passed through the gate, Luz pulled a huge T-shirt from her shoulder bag and slipped it on, effectively hiding her figure. Then she tied her hair into a tight bun and jammed a baseball cap on her head. "It sounds like a friend of theirs has the 911 girl," she said.

"I agree," Noli said. "Let's hope we hear from them, and that the girl knows something. Where are you parked?"

Pointing to the west, Luz said, "At a friend's house on Fourth Street."

"I'll walk with you."

As they walked down the west side of the harbor, Noli described her interaction with Mrs. Greenway. "All in all, not a very reliable description," she concluded. "On a different matter, I followed up on your question about the value of the land Fitz was buying from the Hanaks. An expert, who's a friend of theirs, thinks the Hanaks' land might be the best for zinfandel in all of California. But Fitz was just buying three acres. And there is similar vineyard land available north of San Francisco. So it just doesn't seem like enough to warrant murder.

"But I've been thinking there could be a larger tie-in," Noli continued. "Imagine the value of the Hanaks' entire property, maybe twenty acres, which includes a five-acre, hundred-year-old vineyard. Nothing like it for sale anywhere. What if the Hanaks' entire property is the target? I told you about the graffiti death threats, right? I thought the threats were tied to the TV programs, but what if someone is trying to scare the Hanaks into selling by spraying death threats on their buildings *and* by killing Fitz?"

Luz said, "Why the Hanaks, if there's comparable land available elsewhere?"

"Good question. It isn't clear to me exactly how unusual their old vineyard is. I'll get a better picture tomorrow night, when I can talk with the expert again. What I know so far is all three of the Hanaks' neighbors have offered to buy them out. It's worth looking into the background of each, see what we find. I'll ask Peter if there have been other offers."

Luz said, "I'll leave that to you. I'm headed back to the office. I'll see what Irv has come up with, and I want to spend some more time on the sheriff's case file."

"I'll let Munch know what we've learned, then I'll meet you there."

As she headed for Munch's store, Noli felt encouraged. *It's starting to feel like we're partners.*

★ ★ ★

An hour later, Noli left Munch, who promised to pursue the lead Mrs. Greenway gave them. "Slender as a stick in a black windbreaker" wasn't much to go on, but it might spark a memory for one of the guys who frequented the harbor.

Munch entrusted her with a new surprise for Peter: another bottle of old Andolini wine, 1981 vintage this time. She knew that Peter, and especially Wolf, would be pleased to have a second bottle, though exactly how that was going to enlighten them, she wasn't sure.

She put the key in the ignition but waited to start the engine. She closed her eyes and tried to imagine the sequence of events leading to Fitz's death on Wednesday afternoon. When had Black Windbreaker joined Fitz? At the harbor, or earlier? Was Black Windbreaker someone Fitz knew, someone who called Wednesday morning with the suggestion of going sailing? Or was he a stranger who'd been waiting in the harbor, hoping Fitz would show up so he could volunteer to crew for him? Was he the killer, or had the killer been waiting in Cruces Cove?

And when had the killer written the suicide note on the mirror in the head? Before they rowed ashore for their deadly picnic? Or had he rowed back to the boat after Fitz passed out?

Either way, he would have left the cove after Fitz was unconscious. There were only three options, and the first was very unlikely: He had an accomplice who knew the rocky hazards of Cruces Cove so well that he could steer a getaway boat to the beach and pick him up. Second, and much more likely, the accomplice drove him away in a car. But if the killer had no accomplice, there was a third option: the county bus.

Grabbing her cell, she pulled up the Santa Cruz Metro website. Route 40 showed weekday stops at Cruces Cove at ten a.m., one p.m., five p.m., seven forty-five p.m., and eleven fifteen p.m. Assuming the *Mortal Zin* hadn't arrived at the cove earlier than two p.m., the killer had had three choices.

CHAPTER TWENTY-FIVE

Grateful to have the house to herself, Tina gazed through the living room window, watching a northern flicker drill the bark of a nearby redwood. Last night's conversation had brought back so many memories of her brother. Dino returned from Vietnam with severe PTSD symptoms and was unable to live in society. He and a small group of other vets camped in Loma Buena State Park, sleeping in caves, sustained by monthly food deliveries from their families. Eventually, Peter pitched a tent for him beside their winery. Miraculously, Dino became fascinated with winemaking and asked Paolina to teach him. They became inseparable.

But Paolina was losing touch with reality by then. And Dino bought into her paranoia, believing someone was "out to steal Paolina's secret." What that secret was, Dino never said.

Then Dino crashed his motorcycle, and time caught up with Paolina.

What would Dino be like today, had he lived? Peter had believed Dino possessed a gift. "Dino has *the nose*. Either you're born with it, or you're not." The nose: that delicate sense of smell that guides every step of crafting a great vintage. She'd had enough of that ability to help Peter in the early years, but nothing like Dino. What if Dino—

A tap on the window.

Annika was standing on the deck, holding a thick manuscript.

I need to ask Peter to make an enormous Do Not Disturb sign I can post outside the dome!

Tina motioned Annika around to the kitchen and met her at the sliding door. Annika stepped inside, saying, "Hi! I thought I'd get this back to you before Preston and I head out. Sorry I kept it so long." She wore an ankle-length silk dress patterned with gauzy flowers, along with a matching jacket. Diamond earrings sparkled when she moved, and another diamond dangled from a gold chain around her neck.

"Time for a cup of tea?" Tina offered, trying to be welcoming. *If I drink any more tea today, I will float out of the dome.*

"No tea. But we can chat until Preston's ready." Annika pointed to Tina's bare feet, which were splotched with red where the tea had burned her. "What happened?"

"Dropped a teapot—my favorite one," Tina said. "But my feet will heal."

Annika set the manuscript on the dining table. "Better keep this away from the food. Have you considered publishing it?"

"Heavens, no," Tina said. "How many people would be interested in the story of the Andolini family? I just need to edit the manuscript, then I'll offer it to the UC Santa Cruz Library for their local history collection."

"So it's factual?"

"Who knows? It's oral history, meaning it's Paolina Andolini's story of her family. As you saw, I fact-checked whatever I could. On her good days, her memory proved to be quite accurate."

Annika settled onto a chair and smoothed her dress. "Why did you agree to write it? Did she pay you?"

"No. History was my first love, not medicine. When Paolina Andolini knew she was dying and a worthless nephew was set to inherit her estate, she wanted to preserve the story of her family." *And I'd just had my third miscarriage.* "I convinced her to let me record her. I probably have a couple of hundred hours of interview with her on audiotape." *And transcribing those tapes gave me a purpose.*

"Any sane publisher would jump on this manuscript," Annika said. "Classic California, right? Dirt-poor Sicilian kid works his way across the oceans, jumps ship for the California gold rush, finds enough gold to buy some logged-over land, and becomes one of the most important vintners of nineteenth-century California."

Tina couldn't help smiling. "Care to be my agent?"

Annika laughed. "I wouldn't know how. But you've got a hell of a story there. Even a doomed romance. Paolina's great-aunt and the Haraszthy boy! Wasn't Haraszthy Senior the one who first brought zinfandel vines to California?"

"That's a myth, propagated by his son. Widely believed until recently."

Annika laughed. "Okay. Are you going to keep me in suspense?"

"You really want to know?" Tina teased.

"Yes, goddammit."

"Zinfandel was brought to California as a table grape by a rich Bostonian who settled in San Francisco in the 1840s. Back then, it was all the rage for wealthy folks to grow grapes in hothouses to serve at the table and impress their friends. Zinfandel was one of his favorites. He wasn't even thinking about wine, can you imagine?"

Annika said, "Where did he get it from? Zinfandel doesn't exist in Europe."

"Intriguing, isn't it? There's research—"

A car's horn beeped twice. "Oh, that'll be Preston," Annika said. "Gotta go."

Alone again, Tina ran her longing hands over the manuscript.

CHAPTER TWENTY-SIX

The Santa Cruz bus transit center lay in the heart of downtown. Along a broad, curved driveway, signs marked the boarding spots for each route. The Route 40 bus wasn't due for an hour.

Across the driveway, opposite the business office, stood the Santa Cruz Coffee Roasting Brew Bar, an open-front caffeine dispensary from which the aroma of fresh-ground coffee wafted. Two men wearing drivers' uniforms leaned against a tree, sipping and chatting. Both were mid-twenties, Anglo, with unremarkable faces. One had buzz-cut red hair, and the other wore his black hair long, tied in a bun at the nape of his neck.

Noli crossed the driveway and approached them. "Excuse me. I'm looking for the drivers on Route 40 last Wednesday night. Can you help me?"

"Why?" asked Buzz Cut.

"You police?" asked Long Hair.

"I'm a friend of the man who was murdered in Cruces Cove last Wednesday."

Buzz Cut shook his head. "Sorry, lady, but that guy offed himself."

Long Hair elbowed his friend. "For fuck's sake, Joe! She's his friend." To Noli, he said, "Sorry for your loss. But we can't give out information."

"I'd just like to—"

"No can do." Long Hair dismissed her by turning his back, resuming his talk with his friend.

She walked the looping driveway, scanning the area. No more uniforms in sight, but three out-of-service buses were parked in a fenced-in lot behind the depot. Where were the drivers?

She walked to Front Street, looking for nearby cafés and restaurants. The building across the street, which she remembered as a popular muffin shop, was now a yoga studio. Just a few yards up, a miniature red surfboard hung at eye level, advertising Surfrider Café. In front, a sandwich board listed the day's specials: Tofurky Sandwich & Green Algae Smoothie.

Welcome to Santa Cruz.

The café was jammed. In the back, two women in Metro uniforms were counting change for their bill. One, a slender brunette, mid-thirties, heavy makeup. The other, middle-aged, bleached-blond, tanned skin tough as leather. A cigarette belonged in the corner of her mouth, but you couldn't smoke in a California restaurant.

"Excuse me. I'm looking for the drivers on Route 40 last Wednesday night. Can you help me?"

"Ask the scheduler," said the brunette, pulling a compact from her purse.

"Headquarters won't open till tomorrow," Noli said. "I can't afford to lose a day."

"You police?" the blonde asked. The name on her pocket: Emma Stanton.

"No," said Noli. "I'm a friend of the man who died in Cruces Cove last Wednesday."

Emma sized her up for a few seconds, then said, "Since 9-11, the scheduler don't talk to no one 'cept police." To the brunette, she said, "That twenty includes the tip, Linda. See ya tomorrow."

Brunette nodded and applied a new layer of lipstick.

Emma said, "Walk with me." She led Noli into the bus parking area. "I got five minutes before I pull out. What's your story?"

"I'm investigating the death of John Fitzpatrick, known as Fitz. The police say he committed suicide. I think they're wrong. His murderer may have left Cruces Cove on one of the Wednesday evening buses. Here's my card."

Emma studied the card. "Dublin?"

"Yeah, but I grew up here."

"My husband got knifed on the pier in '98."

"That's awful. I'm so sorry."

"Yeah. Police didn't give a shit." Emma studied her face, as though deciding whether to trust her. "Stay where you are." She unlocked the bus door, climbed into the driver's seat, and rifled through papers on a clipboard. "The afternoon shift was Marilyn Grover. Nightshift, Morrie Slighter."

"Are they driving the same shifts today?"

"Should be."

"And the shifts change when?"

"Six in the morning, two in the afternoon, ten at night. Breaks come different times on different routes. Can't help you with that."

"Thank you."

"Good luck." Emma closed the bus door and revved the engine.

Noli watched the bus roll away, thinking it was worth trying to catch both bus drivers today. If they had nothing to offer, so be it, but at least she would know.

Noli's thoughts turned to checking in with Tina.

It was Peter who answered. He sounded tired. She told him about Black Windbreaker Person. The description rang no bells with Peter, but he promised to ask around. He asked, "Will you be home for dinner?"

She explained why she might be downtown until late, waiting for the bus drivers, relieved that she could share this part of the investigation with him. "Peter, about the graffiti—how recent are they?"

"Why on earth do you—"

"They're threats, Peter."

"I'm telling you, it's nothing to take seriously!"

Her desire to break down Peter's denial was at war with her sense that he needed denial in order to get out of bed each morning. Reluctantly, she replied, "Whatever you say."

"I have two favors to ask," Peter said. "First, would you go to Daniel Arnant's harvest party with me Tuesday night? Tina's not up to it. There will be lots of deep pockets there, and Daniel's giving me an opportunity to serve our wine at dinner."

"Okay, but if I'm going to represent you, I'd better get a good briefing before we go."

"No problem. Second favor, would you have dinner with Tina on Wednesday? I'm driving to King City to pick up a load of grapes, won't be back until late, and I don't want her to be alone. She's arranged to spend the day making apple-sauce with Annika, so the daytime is covered. Ordinarily I wouldn't ask, but the way things are now—"

Thinking Peter was right to be concerned, she said, "Of course! And Peter, some good news. Munch got another bottle of the old Andolini zinfandel. I'll bring it home tonight."

"Wolf'll be pleased," Peter said. "We'll taste one and save the other for analysis."

Next she called Luz, but her call went straight to voicemail. After leaving a message, she slid her phone into her back pocket. She had another hour to kill before the No. 40 bus came through the station. Deciding the best way to clear her head would be to exercise, she headed off for a run on the beach.

Back at the station an hour later, her headache was gone. She ordered a double espresso and a bottle of water. She'd finished the coffee by the time a bus rolled into the driveway, its marquee reading, *40 Davenport/North Coast Beaches*. A tall Black woman in a driver's uniform climbed out and scanned the station. Noli hailed her. The woman strode across the turnaround, Kikuyu braids swinging in curtains on either side of her face. "You the PI?"

"You the driver of Number 40 last Wednesday?"

The driver smiled. "Emma said you were investigating a murder."

"A friend of mine died in Cruces Cove last Wednesday night. I think it was murder, but the sheriff doesn't give a damn. In my view, the killer could've taken your bus back into town. Do you recall anyone boarding at Cruces Cove that night?"

"Good thing you're asking about the Cove, and not the stops in town. Out there, 'cept in summer, I don't get but a few passengers on weekday evenings. Can't swear it was Wednesday, but I'm pretty sure. On the seven forty-five stop. One guy, in jeans and a black windbreaker, knit cap low on his forehead. Dirty, like he was homeless. Made an impression 'cause he had on dark glasses even though it was dark out, you know? Lotsa druggies do that. Sometimes they freak on the bus, so I always keep an eye on 'em."

"You're sure it was a man?"

The driver paused to consider, then nodded. "Pretty sure. Walked like a man, you know?"

"Can you describe him?"

"Skinny. Kinda bent over. Could have been tall as you. Hard to tell when I'm sitting down."

"Did you see him get off?"

"Yeah, he rode all the way down here."

CHAPTER TWENTY-SEVEN

L uz sat behind Fitz's desk. Raul Espinoza sat across from her, his grim smile not reaching his bloodshot eyes.

"Bad night, Raul?" Luz said.

"It took *five* hours to get Carl Hoskins drunk enough to talk." He paused to sip from a water bottle. "Gave me three names—three growers who wanted Fitz dead. This morning, I put in some calls. There's a guy, name of Varley, made his fortune manufacturing electronics. Over the past decade, three reporters who've tried to investigate his company in Taiwan have turned up dead in brothels over there."

Luz let out an appreciative whistle.

"Luz, I've been on the phone all morning, talking with union leaders and reporters familiar with the scene in Taiwan. If Varley's behind those murders, we need proof. We've got this crazy idea to run past you. But no pressure, okay?"

Luz nodded.

"If you're willing to go undercover as the emergency replacement for Varley's housekeeper, she'll claim a family emergency in Mexico. She's the cousin of a steward for the local Teamsters Union. She'll leave for one week. In that time, you could get access to his computer—"

Luz interrupted. "Surely, his computer can be hacked. We have an expert—"

Raul interrupted, "Varley's in the computer business, so we have to assume he's got good protection." He paused, then added, "Besides, you can't be sure the information we need is even in his computer. He works from home, so you can look through his files. And you can charm him, get him to confide in you."

"Let me think." She walked to the window and looked out, just to break away from Raul's earnest gaze. She recalled that Fitz had had confidence in Raul. If Raul's sources were to be believed, Varley was a prime suspect.

Turning back to Raul, she said, "When?"

Smiling broadly, Raul spread both hands on the table. "Tuesday? I still have to work out the details."

"If Señora Navarro will stay with my family, I'll be ready."

Raul beamed at her. "Excellent. I'll call tonight with the details. You've worked undercover before, right?"

"Yes," Luz lied.

It was a small lie. She'd been a maid for real, and she knew this: No one noticed a maid.

CHAPTER TWENTY-EIGHT

When Noli finally reached Fitz's office, Luz was gone. She sank into Fitz's desk chair, exhausted. Four days had passed since Fitz's murder, and they still had nowhere near enough evidence to force the sheriff to reopen the case. Battling a swelling sense of incompetence, she entered the conference room and switched the lights on. Irv had left, promising a full report in the morning. The mostly blank whiteboards taunted her. Seizing a marker, she added *7:45 Black Windbreaker boards bus at Cove* to the Timeline board for Wednesday, the day Fitz died.

She turned to the Suspect board. The clues were few.

All three of the Hanaks' neighbors had offered to buy them out. The Hanaks' finances were so precarious, they might be forced to sell to the highest bidder now that Fitz was out of the picture. Yes, the three-acre plot could be sold alone, but Peter was dead set against it.

Interestingly, the Hanaks were in financial trouble only because they'd lost two consecutive vintages. Wolf thought these losses were highly suspect. Was it crazy to connect sabotage of the Hanaks' winery and the murder of Fitz? A plot spanning nearly three years?

She wrote, *Unknown person—Motive: wishes to purchase the Hanaks' land*

Feeling her energy waning, she scanned the boards one last time, then turned out the lights and returned to Fitz's office. It was nearly midnight. The twisting mountain drive to the Hanaks' domes was not one to attempt when exhausted.

She raided two candy bars from Fitz's file drawers, then collapsed at his desk to take a short nap, resting her head on her arms.

A dream followed:

Fitz appeared, sad eyes, gray beard, Greek sailor's cap.

"Hello, Scout."

She tried to answer. Her lips moved, but no sound emerged.

He pulled a cigarette from his pocket and held it between his thumb and forefinger. The cigarette lengthened, becoming a long white envelope. He struck a match and set the envelope on fire, saying, "Never mind, Scout."

She reached for the envelope, but Fitz stepped back, shaking his head. He faded away.

The burning envelope hung in the air.

She grabbed it and burnt her fingers.

Startled awake, she checked her fingers. No burns.

Stumbling to the bathroom, she splashed cold water on her face.

A white envelope.

Suddenly she understood. She scanned the room, looking for the Hanaks' copy of Sullivan's book on zinfandel. She'd slipped Fitz's letter, the one Abbie had given her, into the book, intending to take both with her when she left on Friday evening. Then the arrival of the sheriff's file had put it out of her mind.

Sullivan's book still rested on the corner of Fitz's desk. She opened the envelope. Inside, a letter. Dated October 11, 1999, almost exactly a decade ago.

Dear Scout,

How strange, writing a letter for you to read when I am dead! I don't feel old, but my luck will run out someday. When it does, I'm asking you to take over.

But who knows what your life will be? Perhaps you'll have roots in a place far from here, and work that makes you happy. If that is the case, I have a different request: Choose someone to replace me.

I've arranged funding for a foundation that will pay my replacement a decent salary. Abbie Wheeldon will give you the details.

You have been as dear to me as any daughter could have been. My wish is that you have everything a good life can offer.

With love, Fitz

CHAPTER TWENTY-NINE

Luz slid a rusty saltine can off the top of the refrigerator, saying to her ten-year-old brother, "Get your jacket and get moving, Luis. You'll miss the bus." By the time she'd dug two quarters from the tin can, Luis was ready. She gave him the money and zipped his backpack.

"Lucita?" He was looking up at her, his wide eyes so like their long-dead mother's, it still broke her heart.

"Come on, out you go!"

"Will you lose your job, now Mr. Fitz is dead?"

"Yes. But I'll find a new one. Don't worry, okay?"

She urged him out of the kitchen and into the living room. In a cushioned recliner, softly framed by morning light, a gray-haired man watched the television news. Luis dashed across the room to give him a kiss on the cheek. "*Hasta luego, Papá.*"

Half of their father's face smiled; the other half, paralyzed by stroke, did not. The man shaped his mouth into words Luz recognized as "Be a good boy." Luis nodded and headed for the door Luz was holding open. "I want to go to Mr. Fitz's funeral, Lucita. Even if it's on a school day."

She put her arms around him and hugged him close. "*Claro.* We'll go together, you and me." He broke away and ran down the street.

Closing the door, she turned to her father. "*¿Papá, como vas? ¿Has comido?*"

He nodded and pointed to an empty plate and cup on a tray. She kissed his cheek and took the tray.

Magda emerged from the bedroom, a skinny tomboy, dressed in a loose T-shirt and jeans. Though only sixteen, she was taller than Luz and possessed a dignity that made her seem much older.

Magda's hazel eyes glowed with compassion. She dropped her book bag on the table and came to Luz, wrapping her in a consoling embrace. "You prayed for Mr. Fitz, no?"

"You do the praying, little sister. I'll find his killer."

Magda nodded. "God has taken him to heaven, Lucita. He was a very good man."

Luz answered simply, "Yes, he was." Gently, she pulled away. "*¡Date prisa, Magda!* The bus won't wait."

Magda opened the front door, nearly colliding with a short, plump, gray-haired woman dressed in faded pink sweats. "*¡Perdón, Señora Navarro!*" she said, and paused to hold the door. Señora Navarro shuffled into the living room, carrying a large shopping bag, from which two knitting needles protruded.

"*Bienvenido, Señora Navarro,*" said Luz. "How are you today?"

Señora Navarro answered, "*Bien,*" and headed for her usual spot, a sagging upholstered chair next to Papa, where they would spend the morning engrossed in their favorite *telenovelas*.

Luz took a seat facing them. "*Papá,* with your permission, I wish to ask *Señora* Navarro whether she can stay here with you and the children for one week, starting tomorrow. I have an important—" Her cell rang, and she checked the screen. "Will you excuse me?" She carried the cell into the kitchen and closed the door.

A man's voice. "Is this Luz Alvarado?"

"Yes. And you are?"

"Clay Offord. We met at the harbor yesterday? You gave me your card?"

"Yes, I remember."

"I have a friend. Sort of. Hangs out at Cruces Cove sometimes? He might have some information about the girl you're looking for."

"He knows the woman who called 911?"

"Yeah. Thing is, he wants to know if there's a reward. Like, for helping the investigation."

Luz had to decide quickly. She had no money to offer. Maybe Noli and Abbie? "I might be able to arrange something. Depends on how helpful he is. When can he talk?"

"Just a minute." A muted discussion, as though Offord had covered his phone with his hand. "This afternoon. Two o'clock. He'll call you."

★ ★ ★

When Noli opened the door to Fitz's office, Luz was seated at Fitz's desk, holding the office phone tight to her ear, nodding. Finally she said, "Good. Call me when you have something."

When she hung up, she gestured for Noli to take a chair. "I have some news." She gave a quick summary of Raul's report on Varley, both the suspicious deaths of the investigative reporters and his declaration that someone should "get rid of" Fitz.

"Did Raul mention that Varley built a mansion on land very near Fitz's?" Noli said.

Luz's expression hardened. "No."

Noli described the view across the Andolini Valley from the old apple barn toward Varley's mansion, then told her about the buyout offers from Varley. "No doubt he wants that land. Still, it's hard to believe someone would murder for it."

Luz shrugged. "If Raul's information is correct, he hasn't stopped at murder."

"You say 'if.' You don't trust Raul?"

Luz seemed to debate with herself before she answered. "Raul's emotions control his brain. But yes, I think this is a solid lead."

"Then let's ask Irv to focus on Varley right now. Is he here?"

"He's here. I already asked him to." Checking her watch, Luz said, "It's a good beach day. I'll work Cruces Cove until two o'clock—that's when Clay's friend is supposed to call. I'll leave the reward up to you." She headed for the door.

Noli felt that something was off between them. Ever since she'd walked into the office, Luz had avoided looking her in the eye.

CHAPTER THIRTY

Monday, 1 p.m.

Noli carried a bag of take-out burritos into the conference room. Irv made a fresh pot of coffee. When he poured her a mugful, he offered to add a splash of half-and-half from a private supply he kept in the office refrigerator. "Easier on the stomach, right?"

"You're a prince. Thank you."

They unwrapped their *carne asada* burritos and enjoyed a few bites in companionable silence. Irv asked, "Any luck with the PIs Abbie hired?"

Abbie's PIs had come in that morning to meet with Noli. The results were important, but disappointing. Bottom line, none of the four potential suspects she and Abbie had culled from Fitz's case files should be considered any further. One was dead, another in prison. Of the remaining two, one had moved to the East Coast and was employed there—his alibi was solid. The last one lived in Seattle and had recently undergone a hip replacement.

After Noli gave Irv a summary of her meeting, she said, "Anything from your contact at Veterans for Peace?"

"Yeah, talked with him this morning. He says the vets who appeared on the TV shows did get harassed. Three of them got the kind of graffiti you saw at Peter Hanak's place.

Two were heckled during a darts competition at a bar near the esplanade. But it all died down quickly. No threats the guys took seriously, no graffiti in recent months."

Another dead end.

"Okay. Where are we with Fitz's phone records?"

Irv put his burrito down. "Fitz had no incoming calls on Wednesday. He placed one call on Wednesday morning: the call to Peter Hanak."

"Right. Peter played the message for me. Fitz asked him to call as soon as he got home."

Nodding toward an arm of the conference table that was covered with papers and files, Irv said, "I'm working on identifying each of the incoming and outgoing numbers for the days previous to his death. Luz printed out Fitz's contact directory for me, and brought in his open case files. So far, I've gone back as far as the previous Sunday." He shook his head. "There's not a single call we can't identify a reason for. Each call seems reasonable in length and timing. You can scan the master list to see if you disagree."

"That's great work, Irv. Unless something comes up to make us look at those calls through a different lens, we'll consider it done."

She paused to consider what it meant, that there were no unidentified calls. How had Fitz's killer arranged to meet him? Again she imagined Black Windbreaker waiting in the harbor, asking to join Fitz on the *Mortal Zin.*

Irv's voice broke into her thoughts. "Here's some basic information on the Hanaks' neighbors," he said, handing her a clipped set of papers. "I was just getting started. Luz filled me in on Raul's report on Varley. She said I should focus on Varley right now—do you agree?"

Irv looked distinctly uncomfortable. Noli figured she, too, would be uncomfortable in his shoes. He was reporting to two different bosses. One boss he knew well and had worked with before. The other boss had appeared four days ago like a prodigal daughter, claiming Fitz had left everything to her.

"I agree with Luz. Varley's our top priority now," Noli said.

The door opened. Luz stepped into the room, and before Noli could ask, she shook her head. She hadn't found any witnesses at the cove.

"There's a burrito waiting for you," Noli said, holding up the paper bag. "*Carne asada.*"

Luz accepted the bag. "Thanks, I'll eat it later." She pulled her cell from her jeans' back pocket. Checked the time. "It's almost two o'clock. When Clay's friend calls, I'll set it on speaker. Noli, do you want to talk to him? He'll ask about the money."

"Sure." Noli took a chair next to her.

Luz took long draughts from her water bottle. At two o'clock sharp, her cell rang.

"This is Luz Alvarado."

"This is Clay's friend."

Luz said, "Nollaig Cooper, my partner, is here with me."

"Clay says there's a reward for information about the dead guy they found in Cruces Cove."

Noli responded, "No official reward. But if you can help us, we'll make it worth your time."

"Yeah, well, she saw his body."

"Let us talk to her," Noli said.

"No dice."

"When did she find him?"

"Just after dawn."

"Where?"

"South end of the cove, covered with gulls."

Noli could feel her heart beat faster. "Tell us something we don't know."

"The guy was alive on Wednesday afternoon. Anchored his sailboat out beyond the cove and rowed in."

"Was anyone with him?"

"Just a minute." All the sound was silenced. After a long minute, he returned. "A thin boy."

"Describe him."

"Couldn't see 'im good. Too far away."

"What was he wearing?"

Again a silent pause, then, "A black windbreaker and jeans."

"When did the boy leave the cove?"

"She doesn't know. Fog came in."

"Was she in the cove all night?"

"You gonna pay her for this?"

"Answer all my questions, she gets three hundred dollars."

Silence. He must have muted his phone. One minute passed, two minutes. "Yeah, she slept there."

"Okay, what about the parking lot that night? Was it empty?"

Another long silence, then, "She checked. It was empty."

Luz held up a finger to indicate she wanted to speak, then asked, "Does she have a dog?"

"None of your business."

Luz persisted. "If she wants to be paid, we need an answer."

A pause. "Yes on the dog."

"What kind of dog?" Luz asked.

The man said, "That's all, lady. Clay's meetin' you in the harbor, four o'clock, to pick up the cash. You better be there."

"Where in the harbor?" Luz asked.

"Señor Tico's Burritos." He hung up.

Luz blew out a long breath and handed the phone to Irv. The caller hadn't blocked his phone number, so Irv might be able to trace it.

"What do you think?" Noli asked.

"I believe him," Luz said. "Here, I want to show you something." Luz pulled a plastic file from her backpack and opened it, withdrawing a photograph. "Crystal Langley, a runaway from Fresno. Mother's an addict. Her aunt hired Fitz to look for her, said there was good reason to think she'd come to Santa Cruz. Fitz assigned the case to me. Crystal has a German shepherd."

"You think she could be the girl in the cove?"

"The dog footprints in the photos are big, so that fits. And sleeping on the beach is dangerous, something a kid from the Valley might be dumb enough to try."

Noli said. "Does she fit the Safeway manager's description?"

"The height is right. The manager said the 911 girl's hair was black, but Crystal could have dyed her hair."

"Show the photo to Clay. Odds are he's seen the girl at his friend's house."

"Good idea," Luz said. "You'll get the money?"

"Yes."

Irv looked up from his computer, saying, "No luck on the phone. He used a burner."

CHAPTER THIRTY-ONE

P eter followed the aromas of clove, rosemary, and thyme into the kitchen. Tina was humming to herself while preparing *osso bucco*, her favorite dish, which was fitting, since it was her birthday. For the first time in days, she seemed happy.

She was so intent on cooking, she hadn't heard him come in. He was about to speak when Wolf Faber burst from the mudroom door singing, "Happy birthday to you!"

Wolf carried a pink pastry box, which he placed in Tina's lap, saying, "Sachertorte from Gayle's Bakery."

"Oh, bliss!" Tina said. "How are you? How's Ryan?"

There was a brief pause before Wolf answered, "We're good."

"Tell Ryan it's been too long since he came to dinner, will you?" Tina said.

"I will. Now, how can I help?"

"Plate the appetizers?" She pointed to a cluster of containers and platters on the counter.

Wolf grinned. "My specialty."

While Peter set the table, he watched Wolf from the corner of his eye, marveling at how deftly Wolf's enormous hands sliced and arranged cheeses, olives, and vegetables, creating a swirl of color on each platter.

The mudroom door opened again. Annika stepped inside, singing, "Happy birthday to you, Happy birthday to you—" Tina shot Peter a look, her face tense. Annika had not been invited.

Annika bent to kiss Tina's cheek. Annika had, Peter thought, made an effort to blend in, wearing jeans and a plaid shirt. Her jewelry was limited to dangling emerald earrings. But if the emeralds were real, which they undoubtably were, then the earrings alone could be a down payment on a new winery. He felt an upsurge of dark resentment and tensed, working hard to suppress it.

Annika turned to Wolf, saying, "Wolf, I was about to call you. Preston's *finally* agreed to hire Ryan as our consultant. I apologize for the delay. You know what they say, 'It's hard to consider anyone under thirty an expert.'"

Wolf looked her in the eye, his expression strained. "No one on the face of this Earth, no matter their age, knows more than Ryan about zinfandel clones."

Favoring him with a dazzling smile, Annika said, "Right. I have copies of our soil analyses ready. Could he evaluate them this week?"

Wolf hesitated. "He's kind of buried right now, completing his master's thesis. I'll ask him to call you."

Annika's smile dimmed. "Just so we're first in line when they announce the best clones. It's soon, right?"

"October twentieth," Wolf replied.

Annika turned to Tina, pulled a small box from her shirt pocket, and placed it in Tina's lap. "Happy sixtieth, Tina."

Tina lifted the box. "Thank you. But you really shouldn't have."

"Nonsense! This is an important milestone."

Inside the box lay two teardrop-shaped pearls suspended from tiny silver chains. Tina removed her beaded earrings and fastened the gift earrings in place. The pearls were lustrous, a perfect echo of the silver hair piled on her head. She looked quite pleased.

But she was pretending, right? How many times had she told him she had no interest in jewelry? Her wedding ring was a simple silver band, all they could afford at the time. She'd never asked him to replace it.

Feeling at sea, he retrieved two bottles of chardonnay from the refrigerator and opened one. He was filling four glasses when Noli stepped into the room.

"Happy birthday, Tina!" Noli kissed Tina, then set a bag from Bookshop Santa Cruz on the counter beside her. "Hope you haven't already read these. But if you have, they promised you could exchange them."

Tina peered into the bag. "Wonderful! These will get me through the winter. Thank you!"

Annika showed no sign of departing. Peter considered asking her point-blank to leave, but he was pretty sure Tina wouldn't like that, so he pulled a fifth wine glass from the cabinet and filled it. "Okay, everyone, time to sample these appetizers."

As soon as they were seated, Annika turned to Noli and said, "You might not want to talk about it while we're having a party, but just tell us quickly, how's the investigation going?"

Noli gave Tina an apologetic look before she said, "Briefly, we have a 'person of interest.' Maybe the description will bring someone to mind, someone you've seen with Fitz when he's been out at the apple barn? This person is very thin and was seen wearing jeans and a black windbreaker. Maybe taller than average, although we aren't sure about that."

"Man or woman?" Annika asked.

"Witnesses are leaning toward a man or a boy."

Annika shook her head. "That's awfully vague." She took a sip of wine. "I haven't seen anyone like that, but I'll certainly let you know if I do. Have you asked Daniel and Gary?"

"Not yet," Noli replied. "Now, tell me Annika, you have an interesting accent. Did you grow up in Boston?"

Annika blinked and shifted in her chair, obviously taken aback at the abrupt change in topic. But she got the message.

"When I was little, yes. My stepfather was an Episcopal minister, so we moved around the country with his postings." She gave a mischievous grin, then, adopting a Southern drawl, "I could tell y'all some hair-raisin' stories about livin' in South Carolina—"

She was interrupted by several forceful knocks on the front door. Wondering what more could happen to complicate the evening, Peter walked through the mudroom and opened the door only a few inches at first. Then he swung it wide, saying, "Hello, Preston."

A basso voice boomed, "Is my wife here?"

"She is. Come in."

The man who stepped into the dome was slightly shorter than Peter and meticulously groomed, wearing a gray bespoke suit and a crisp blue shirt that set off his wavy black hair and silvering temples. He was slight of build but had an athletic spring in his step. The irises of his eyes were so dark, they appeared black in the low light of the dome. When they fastened on Annika seated at the table, Peter was reminded of a hawk sighting its prey. Preston's slightly hooked, narrow nose added to the illusion. "Annika, my dear, time to go home."

Annika stood immediately. "You're back early, Preston." A hint of accusation colored her voice. Then she said to Tina, "See you Wednesday? Applesauce?"

"Wouldn't miss it," Tina answered.

Annika joined her husband. He put his arm around her waist, steering her toward the door, then stopped. Looking over his shoulder to Peter, he said, "Say the word and I'll take that apple orchard off your hands. Whatever that other fellow was offering, plus twenty percent."

"It's not for sale, Preston."

"Let me know if you change your mind."

As Peter was closing the door behind them, Annika called out, "Wolf, don't forget to have Ryan call me!"

CHAPTER THIRTY-TWO

After dinner, Peter and Wolf carried Tina to the couch. Noli brought the two bottles of wine Munch had sent as gifts and laid them on their sides on the coffee table, cushioned by a towel. She'd watched Tina carefully all through dinner, ready to make excuses and leave at any sign Tina was exhausted. But the dinner had buoyed her spirits. She'd even eaten a generous slice of Sachertorte, much to Wolf's delight.

Peter said, "Okay, Wolf, it's time we found out whether Fitz was off his rocker when he raved about this wine."

Wolf raised one bottle. "1982 Andolini Zinfandel." He held the bottle above a candle so its contents were backlit. A streak of sediment lay along one side. "You've taken good care of this." With a flourish, he removed the foil seal from the cork. Slowly, expertly, he removed the cork and sniffed it. "Not rotten, good sign."

He poured a small amount of wine into each glass, rotating the bottle as he poured to prevent the sediment from leaving the bottle.

Noli felt the group's energy rising around her. What if the wine was good? Or great!

Just as Wolf reached for a glass, there was a knock at the front door. Alarmed, Tina looked at Peter, who shook his head. Sighing deeply, he excused himself and opened the door.

"Hello, Gary. What can I do for you?"

From where she sat, Noli could see Varley rise on his toes to peer over Peter's shoulder. Noting the group gathered inside, Varley asked, "Could I have a quick word? In private?"

Peter nodded and stepped outside but did not fully close the door behind him.

Varley's voice carried into the dome. "Whatever offers you get on that land your friend was going to buy, I'll beat that offer by twenty-five percent. I mean it."

"It's not for sale, Gary."

A pause. Varley said in a frosty voice, "My misunderstanding." Footsteps receded. A powerful engine revved and roared away.

Peter returned. "I swear to God, anyone else knocks on that door tonight, they can just cool their heels until morning."

Wolf lifted his glass. He inhaled across a sip of wine, then moved the wine slowly around his mouth. As he swallowed, his eyebrows rose and his eyes widened. He sipped again. Swallowed. Said nothing.

Noli thought, *The wine is dreadful, and he wants to let Peter and Tina down gently.*

Tina's eyes grew shiny, and Noli knew she'd drawn the same conclusion.

When Wolf finally spoke, his voice was soft with wonder. "Only once in my life have I tasted wine this good."

Now all eyes were on Peter. His hand trembling, he raised his glass and sipped. His cheeks bellowed as he moved the wine around his tongue. He swallowed. He took a second sip, then set his glass down. All excitement drained from his face. "It's too good. Someone's scamming Munch."

Her face stricken, Tina reached out to Peter, her hand grasping his.

Wolf's eyebrows rose. "An expensive scam, don't you think? There are plenty of old, empty Andolini bottles kicking around. Arnant has a slew of them. But the wine in this bottle would cost thousands." He turned to Noli. "What did Munch pay?"

"He wouldn't say." Noli lifted her glass, inhaled aromas of spice and plum. She took a sip. It was full-bodied but also elegant. Understated. She thought she tasted the same terroir that Peter's award-winning wine contained, but she knew her palate couldn't make the fine distinctions that Wolf's or Peter's could. Still, while working in Europe, she'd had some experience with fine wine. Memories flooded in, a leisurely dinner on the patio of a Tuscan restaurant... A man she'd thought she was in love with ...

Wolf's voice pulled her from her memories. "Dino made this wine, right?"

Tina pointed to a framed black-and-white photograph hanging on the wall. A thin young man and a very old woman stood shoulder to shoulder, looking straight ahead, their expressions solemn and intense. "Yes, although Paolina Andolini was still very hands-on at that time." She turned to Peter. "We were complete novices then. Was Dino's wine this good? Would we have known?"

Peter shrugged. "I was still on painkillers, in addition to being inexperienced." He paused to think. "Dino put plenty of wine on the table, and I have a clear memory of the bottles. They didn't have labels, just the year marked on a piece of tape."

"Not unusual," Wolf said. "Small family wineries often save money that way. They know they're going to drink the wine themselves, so they just mark the varietal and year." He raised the bottle so they could all see the label. "What's intriguing about this bottle is that they used the Andolini label on the front but omitted the back label. Both are required to offer wine for sale." He tasted the wine again, his eyes growing wide with delight. "It just gets better!" He settled back into his chair. "All right. I can think of one explanation. Sort of. Whoever crafted this wine obviously crafted it to age for many years. Maybe they didn't know whether they'd still be around when it was ready to drink. How would they ensure that a person who found the bottles in the future would know what they've found?"

"Label each bottle," Tina answered.

Wolf nodded. "And they had no intention of selling it, so forget the back label."

Slowly, appreciatively, they all sipped until their glasses were empty.

Setting his glass down, Wolf said, "Let me be very clear. This discovery, this *aged* zinfandel, is a game changer for Hanak winery. You have the only original Andolini vines, right?"

Peter, his jaw clenched, answered, "Only for a few more days."

"You're thinking about the cuttings you donated to the Zinfandel Clone Project?" Wolf said.

"Yeah."

Peter looked so deflated, Noli had to ask, "Would someone please fill me in?"

Wolf said, "How much do you know about zinfandel, Noli?"

She laughed. "That Peter and Tina make a great zinfandel, and I love to drink it."

Wolf smiled. "Okay. Here's the first thing you need to understand: Zinfandel is unique among wine varietals grown in California. All the others—like cabernet, pinot noir, chardonnay, sauvignon blanc—have long histories in Europe. If you want to plant those varietals, we can give you advice on the best clones for your terroir —"

"Wait, you said 'clones'?"

Wolf grimaced. "It's confusing. I wish they'd come up with a different term, but we're stuck with it. In wine talk, 'clone' has the *opposite* meaning from all the cloning that's in the popular press. To clone a sheep, you create a genetically *identical* copy of an individual. But with grape vines, each clone of a varietal is slightly *different*, genetically, from another clone. Not a huge difference—that would make it a different varietal."

Peter joined in, saying, "A slight genetic difference can have a huge effect. For example, one clone's grapes might have more tannin than another's. Or it might ripen earlier. Or it might be resistant to certain diseases."

Nodding, Wolf continued, "For example, there are over four hundred known clones of pinot noir. Imagine you want to grow pinot noir in a vineyard that includes a sunny hillside with rocky, dry soil and a west slope with rich soil. You'd select two different clones, one to match each terroir."

"Okay, I get it," Noli said. "Selecting the right clone is crucial for a successful vineyard. And you're saying that for zinfandel, we don't know much about its clones?"

"Nada. In 1995, the Zinfandel Clone Project was founded at Cal Poly Sacramento. They asked the old zinfandel vineyards in Northern California to give them cuttings from their vines so they could find out how many different clones of zinfandel exist and what their characteristics are."

"Their research began almost fifteen years ago," Noli said. "Don't they already have results?"

"This kind of research takes a long time. The vines need four years to mature before you can get much fruit, and if you're going to study the quality of the wine made from that fruit, you need a lot of vines to work with because you have to try different yeasts and other variations in the fermenting process. Meanwhile, back in the field, you'll be looking at terroir, finding out which clones do well in different types of terroir common in California."

Tina cut in to say, "Wolf's friend Ryan is part of the research team at the Project."

"He, like everyone else involved, is sworn to secrecy. But in just three weeks, their findings will be announced."

There was pride in Wolf's voice, but it seemed to Noli there was also a touch of sadness. She asked, "And the clones will be for sale then?"

"That's right," Wolf answered.

Now she understood Peter's distress. The vines on Old Marco's Hill might be very special, but anyone who wished could soon duplicate them.

Wolf poured a last taste of the old wine for each person. "Peter, I wouldn't assume the Project has discovered the aging potential of the grapes from your vines. And even if they have, how many vineyards have your terroir to work with?"

Peter still looked downcast. "Any vineyard in Northern California where the soil was created by a redwood forest and there's southern exposure."

"Okay, I'd agree similar locations *could* exist. But your terroir might be more unusual than you think. In any case, you have a tremendous head start on anyone planting now. The vines on Old Marco's Hill are how old?"

Peter looked at Tina, who said, "We're not sure. More than a hundred years, certainly. Paolina told a story about the vines being a gift from a man who jilted her aunt, which would place them well into the late nineteenth century."

"And your other vineyard?" Wolf asked.

"Planted in the '70s," Peter said.

"With cuttings from another of Paolina's vineyard's, one that doesn't exist anymore?"

"Right," Peter said. "When she died, the nephew who inherited the estate just let the vineyards go to weeds and die. Arnant had to replant them all."

"And just to confirm, the Zinfandel Clone Project took cuttings from both your vineyards?"

"No, just Old Marco's Hill," Peter answered. "Look, Wolf, couldn't you sound out Ryan ahead of time? Ask him how much they know about our clone?"

"I guess this is the right time for me to tell you: Ryan and I have broken up." He shook his head slowly. "More accurately, Ryan has ended our relationship."

Tina said, "Oh, Wolf! I'm so sorry!"

Wolf managed a sad smile. "Broken hearts mend, or so I'm told. Look, Peter, I'd like to take the second bottle of '82 Andolini up to the Project and talk with Ryan, see who he'd recommend to examine it. It's possible that analysis of the wine could tell us more about how it was made."

"Sure. That'd be helpful."

Wolf stood, saying, "Time for me to head home. I'll be up north for a couple of days. If you're ready to harvest on Thursday, I'll be here."

"I appreciate that," Peter said. "There's rain forecast for the weekend, so we'll harvest Friday at the latest."

Wolf clasped Peter's shoulder. "I'll say it again: I think you should be very encouraged by this '82 Andolini. When I get back, we can talk some more."

Noli said, "Time for me to get some sleep." She bid Peter and Tina goodnight, then followed Wolf out the door. The autumn air was chilly, dense with the perfume of redwoods and ripe grapes. To the east, a gentle glow above the trees signaled a quarter moon on the rise. "Can I keep you company partway home?" she asked Wolf. "I have some questions."

"Sure. Grab a flashlight."

As they walked, Wolf said, "I'm glad you're home, Noli. Tina and Peter have had a rough couple of years. And now, losing Fitz, they're on the ropes."

Noli asked, "What do you really think about the '82 Andolini?"

"Exactly what I said. It's sensational. It seems the Hanaks have a unique clone, matched with very special terroir. Possibly *two* unique clones—one in Old Marco's vineyard, the other in their younger vineyard. I guarantee, no one in the California wine world has ever heard of zinfandel aging like the wine we just drank."

The quarter moon cleared the treetops and illuminated their path, turning the dusty road into a silver lane. Noli switched off her flashlight.

"Wolf, I still don't have a grasp on this business of clones. Where does a clone come from?"

"Every once in a while, when a plant reproduces, like when a grape vine produces a bud for a shoot, there's a spontaneous change in a gene. Most of these changes don't have a noticeable effect. But once in a while, eureka! A crucial new characteristic appears, and you have a significant new clone.

"For hundreds—probably thousands—of years, the way it worked was, a farmer would notice he had a vine that was behaving differently from the others. Perhaps the vine thrived during a drought, when its neighbor vines were dying. Or its grapes made better wine. So he takes cuttings from the improved vine and grows them, then more cuttings, and soon he has a vineyard filled with the new clone. His neighbors see how much better his vineyard is performing, and they ask for cuttings. Word travels. More clones appear over time. Eventually there's a body of local knowledge about which cuttings match which kind of soil."

"Does this mean that when Marco Andolini planted his vineyard, he somehow got ahold of a clone no one else had?"

"Good question. Maybe other vineyards had the same clone back in the nineteenth century, but they've been replaced. Or the clone was a perfect match for the terroir here, but died out in other locations."

They'd arrived at the Hanaks' younger vineyard. Wolf said, "Wait a second." He reached into the nearest vine, twisted his grip, and offered Noli a cluster of grapes nestled in his palm. "Taste one."

She pulled one grape free of its stem and popped it into her mouth. Wolf followed suit. In her mouth, an explosion of flavor, sweet and tart together—plum, raspberry, and just a hint of black pepper. She said, "It's no surprise the nineteenth-century millionaires loved to serve zinfandel grapes to their guests."

Wolf's jaw was closed, muscles moving the grape around, sampling it in different taste regions. The corners of his eyes wrinkled in delight. "This could be Peter's best vintage ever. August was unusually foggy and cool, so the grapes have ripened slowly."

"Slow is better?" Noli asked.

"Yes. Greater complexity of flavor develops before the sugar rises to the point where you have to harvest."

As they continued down the road, Wolf said, "You know, the first time I tasted the grapes on Old Marco's Hill, I knew they were special. Peter agreed to set aside some of those grapes for an experiment. Instead of following standard procedure—which would mean sterilizing the harvested grapes, then adding a commercial yeast for fermentation—we let the grapes ferment using yeast that grows naturally in the vineyard. It's called 'fermentation with field yeast.' Very risky, and no commercial winery would dare try it today. But in Marco's day, it was much more common.

"Our experiment has been coming along nicely. And now that I've tasted the wine Marco's granddaughter crafted, I'm convinced we're on the right track. We're going to replicate the old Andolini wine we just tasted. Of course, it'll take a few decades." He chuckled. "Right now, we need to do two things," he continued. "First, find out whether the Zinfandel Clone Project is about to sell the Hanaks' clone. I didn't want to promise Peter I could do this, but I'm going to try to persuade Ryan to help us. Secondly, find out who sold the old Andolini wine to Munch. Would you follow up and talk to his source? And for heaven's sake, find out if more bottles exist!"

"Munch is a night owl, so I can probably catch him tonight. You're thinking that someone who knew how great the Andolini wine was could be sabotaging the Hanaks, hoping to buy their land?"

"Look, I live in the wine world. On a weekly basis, I talk with deep-pocket folks who will spend unimaginable amounts of money to own a world-class vineyard. It's not a stretch to think one of them would stop at nothing if they knew the potential of Old Marco's Hill."

CHAPTER THIRTY-THREE

B y the time Noli arrived at the office, Munch had already
sent a report via email.

*The old Andolini wine came from Whitman "Goose"
Gossen. He recently inherited a mansion in the mountains, about four miles from the Hanaks. Huge wine
cellar, hundreds of bottles.*

*Mansion built in 1883 by his mother's grandfather, Elijah
William Norton, black sheep of Boston family. Elijah's
brother, Jeremiah Norton, built the house on Norton
Road near the Hanaks. Elijah started a lumber company,
got very wealthy. His love of wine was passed down to
Goose's mom. But Goose himself is not interested. He's
selling everything in cellar. No more Andolini wine there.*

She forwarded Munch's report to Wolf. Now they knew
where the bottles of Andolini zinfandel had been aging. With
his brother living right on the edge of the Andolini estate,
it wouldn't have taken Elijah long to connect with Paolina
Andolini.

What Munch's report did not address: Had Goose's
mother known the Andolini wine was aging far beyond
conventional expectations for zinfandel? That it was

extraordinary? If so, had she told friends, and were any of them still alive?

By return email, she asked Munch to find out.

Although she'd left the office door open, there was a polite knock.

Irv stepped in. "Got a minute?"

"Have a seat."

Irv passed her a folded note. "Luz wanted to be sure you got this."

Noli opened the note.

When I met with Clay Offord, I showed him the photo of Crystal and emphasized that she's only fifteen. He said he'd try to get a look at the 911 girl when he delivered the reward money.

Irv cleared his throat. "There's more."

"About the 911 girl?"

Irv looked both determined and uncomfortable. "About Luz. She's decided to go undercover as a maid in Varley's house."

"She *what?*"

"Today. She should be there already. Raul set it up. Once he heard that Varley had actually said someone should get rid of Fitz, Raul went hyper. Luz plans to get access to Varley's office. And, um, when Varley's out of the house, I'm going to hack his computer."

"*You* are going in?"

"Yeah."

Struggling for composure, Noli said, "When Luz can speak privately, we'll talk this over. You'll be breaking the law. And if you are caught, what if he's the bad actor Raul thinks he is? We can't assume he will turn you and Luz over to the police rather than handling it himself."

Irv looked abashed. "Wise words."

She was furious with Luz for jumping into such a dangerous situation. And hurt that Luz hadn't trusted her enough to even ask for her opinion. And at a loss to think how they could protect her.

Noli and Irv worked side by side all morning. At regular intervals, they called Luz's cell. She never answered. Finally Noli left a message asking Luz to please hold off entering Varley's home. Could they please discuss how to keep her safe?

That afternoon, while she shopped for a cocktail dress, she checked her phone often, but there was no response from Luz. As she drove back to the mountains to keep her promise to Peter, she pictured Luz in Varley's mansion, waiting for a chance to rifle through Varley's files. Had Luz ever gone undercover before? What would Varley do if he caught her?

CHAPTER THIRTY-FOUR

Tuesday, 2 p.m.

When Varley's house came into view, Luz slowed to familiarize herself with the layout. Built of concrete and glass, it was shaped like a giant V, its arms opening toward the driveway. The main entrance, marked by bronze-plated double doors, was reached by a winding path through the Japanese garden within the arms of the V.

To the far right of the house stood a detached six-car garage; to the left, a small paved parking lot. Beyond the parking lot, a bridge led to a second ridge. At the ridgetop, a beehive of workers hammered siding on a new building. The slope below was infested with earth-moving equipment. Trucks dumped topsoil, which bulldozers shaped as fast as it fell.

Luz parked and checked her face in the rearview mirror. By applying thick foundation, she'd given her skin a sallow hue. Around her eyes she'd blended a purple tint, making them look tired and sunken. Her hair was pulled into a tight bun and hidden beneath a kerchief. Satisfied that her makeup looked natural even in strong light, she closed her eyes and slowed her breathing. Though she would never have admitted it to Raul or Noli, she was frightened. Varley was the kind of man who, if they were correct, caused enemies to disappear. Confronting him in an office downtown would be one thing;

snooping in his house in the middle of nowhere was something else.

She pulled a suitcase from the trunk and followed a discreet sign saying *Service Entrance* to the left arm of the V. At the door there was a button marked *Ring for Delivery.* Luz rang.

In less than a minute, Consuela Salvo opened the door. She was barely five feet tall, with a soft, round body supported on birdlike legs. Raul had said Consuela was forty-five, but she looked sixty. Her mostly white hair was pulled severely into a bun. Fleshy folds swallowed her eyes, and her lips were a thin, nervous line.

"*Bienvenida.*" Consuela gave her a brief embrace, then motioned her inside a long hallway. On the right, windows looked onto the Japanese garden; on the left stood a series of doors. Consuela led her through the first door into a pleasant living room, where Mixteca rugs decorated the floors and a deeply cushioned maroon couch faced a large, flat-screen television.

"This is my apartment. You will stay here," Consuela said.

Photographs covered the walls, portraits of the elderly parents, aunts, and uncles she fed, the nieces and nephews whose school fees she paid—all in Mexico.

Consuela looked Luz over, her eyes coming to rest on the Beach Inn crest above the pocket of her blouse. "Is good idea, the uniform. *El Señor* Varley agreed to have you because of your experience." In the ruin of her face, two brown eyes still shone clear and bright.

Luz took her hand and squeezed it. "Thank you, Consuela. I promise, whatever happens, Varley won't blame you."

The corner of Consuela's right eye began to twitch. "We will see. Come, *El Señor's* plans have changed. He wants to meet you as soon as possible."

At the end of the hall, a swinging door opened into a kitchen resembling a hospital operating room. "Later, I show you cooking. Breakfast and lunch only. He is gone for dinner now, looking for next wife. Come."

Consuela pushed through a second swinging door and ushered Luz past a dining table with seats for twelve, and from there to the great room. It could have been the lobby of an expensive hotel—marble floor, leather and chrome furniture, large bronze sculptures, bright oil paintings. At the apex of the V, the room thrust out, offering an unobstructed view to the west.

Quickly Luz oriented herself, visualizing the Google maps she had studied. To the north of the house was a steep valley. On the far side of that valley was a redwood grove where Noli's friends, the Hanaks, lived. If things went so wrong that she could not reach her car, she could escape across the valley to the Hanaks.

She told herself she was fully prepared, had considered every eventuality. But the truth was she felt profoundly out of place. She'd never been in such an opulent house, and the wealth and power it represented was alarming. "Consuela, you know Varley better than anyone. Would he have someone killed if they got in his way?"

"*Claro*. If I did not think so, you would not be here." Consuela trailed a finger along the top of each chair, table, and sofa as she hurried past. "He is a strange man, *El Señor* Varley. To me, he is very good. He pay twice what I earn before, and when I am sick, he hire help, no question. He treat me with respect. But always, I do what he say." She lifted her finger to the light. "Dust make him *loco*. Two times a day, dust this room."

She opened a set of chrome-and-black-glass French doors, leading to the second arm of the V. Along the terrazzo hallway, she gestured to doors on the left. "His bedroom. Separate bedroom for wife. Many nights, he not sleep. Walk around. Take pills." She paused, placed a hand on Luz's elbow, looked her in the eye. "I tell him, ten o'clock I go to bed. You do same. Lock door. No answer if he knock."

Luz told herself she could handle this. If Varley tried to attack her, she could floor him. But it wasn't that simple, was it? She needed to keep Varley happy until Irv had a chance to hack his computer. And just as important, she needed to manage him in a way that didn't create a problem for Consuela. Had she made a mistake in coming here?

Luz took a deep breath and held it, willing her tightening chest to relax.

At the end of the hall, they passed through another set of French doors into a room full of color: forest-green carpet, Asian rugs of gold, crimson, and blue. Rosewood furniture.

"This, I like," Luz said.

"Is my favorite. When first I come work for *El Señor* in Los Altos house, his wife was Mary. Mary decorate this."

Luz scanned the room. A massive cockpit-style desk supporting multiple computer screens occupied a third of the room. A conference table for eight was tucked into a bookcase-lined corner. The remaining space was dedicated to a comfortable couch and glass coffee table. One wall was entirely windows; an enormous photograph that might be a Google Earth map was tacked to redwood paneling near the bookcases.

A carved mahogany door flew open, its inside handle slamming against the wall. A man, face flushed, jaw clenched, strode into the room. Luz was surprised to see how ordinary he appeared. Middle-aged, well-muscled but going soft, washed-out blue eyes, short-cropped pale hair. He was dressed in Silicon Valley's uniform: T-shirt, jeans, and tennis shoes. He was halfway to his desk before he noticed them.

"Señor Varley, this is Alma Martinez, who will be your maid while I am gone," Consuela said. Consuela's voice quavered, and Luz hoped Varley didn't notice.

His pale eyes moved slowly over Luz's padded body and disguised face. Luz felt her heart race. His cool look of appraisal suggested she was nothing more than a slave at auction, a commodity whose usefulness he was weighing. Could he see what she had hidden beneath makeup and winding cloth?

Varley sat in the desk chair, leaving them standing. He opened a folder. "I checked your references. The inn was sorry to lose you, and Professor Gleason gives you high praise indeed."

Inwardly, Luz relaxed just a little. Clearly Irving had been convincing as "Professor Gleason, retired professor of mathematics." After Varley had called him to check the reference, Irv had called her, saying, "Be careful, Luz. All Varley really wanted to know was what you look like."

"Do you cook?" Varley asked.

"Yes, Mr. Varley," she answered, laying on a heavy Mexican accent. "I make simple, healthy food." Consuela had warned her that Varley was a "health nut." As long as she could put together cereal, fruit smoothies, and salads, he'd be satisfied.

"You'll do." He tossed her file into the trash basket. "I'll pay you when Consuela returns. There may be a bonus, based on your performance."

"I will do my best, Mr. Varley."

"Good. Consuela, see that my dry cleaning goes to town before you leave."

Varley swiveled away from them, pulled a keyboard into position, punched a few keys, and stared at the monitor.

Consuela headed for the door.

Luz said, "About the books, Señor Varley?"

"What?" Sounding annoyed, Varley didn't turn from the monitor.

"Professor Gleason trained me to clean the dust from his books, a special cleaning every three months. If you wish, I can do this for you while Consuela is gone."

Varley glanced her way, his lips curving slightly, as though he intended to smile. "Excellent. I'll be gone Thursday evening. That should give you enough time."

CHAPTER THIRTY-FIVE

Tuesday, 3 p.m.

"Please sit down," Ryan said. "You're making me nervous."

"Sorry." Wolf stopped pacing and sat. While Ryan focused on his computer, Wolf surveyed Ryan's room in the finished attic of an old farmhouse near Sacramento. The only furnishings were a battered brown couch, a mattress on the floor, a crammed bookcase, and a table with a computer, where Ryan now sat. Wall decorations featured posters of U2 and Sinéad O'Connor. The only unusual-for-a-student feature was a well-stocked wine rack occupying one corner. Nothing had changed since Wolf's last visit, yet it felt alien to him.

Ryan said, "You have to see this."

Wolf positioned a chair next to Ryan, near enough to see the monitor, far enough to avoid accidental contact.

Ryan's thick, red-gold eyebrows knit into a single concentrated line as he pointed to a spot on the screen. "This chart shows outcomes for each contribution to the Project. The Hanaks contributed cuttings in '95. In '99, after the cuttings in the vineyard had matured into budded vines, a new test for GLR virus—grapevine leafroll—was developed. Using that new test, forty percent of the Project's vines were found to be infected. All infected vines were pulled out and destroyed."

Stunned, Wolf stared at the on-screen display. "You're saying the Hanaks' vines were ripped out?"

"Yep. It looks totally legitimate. But then, there's this." Ryan scrolled to a new page and pointed to the last sentence. *Early results suggest strong similarity to Fresno 3. No further collection efforts made.* "Similarity to Fresno 3? Impossible. The Fresno 3 clone does well in the hot, dry climate of California's Central Valley. It requires irrigation. Sugar develops slowly, fruit is low in tannin and acid. They use it to make jug wine." Ryan pushed away from the desk. "Fresno 3 is as different from the Hanaks' clone as it could possibly be."

"An honest mistake?" Wolf asked.

"*Very* unlikely." Ryan spun away on his wheeled desk chair. "Damn! I wasn't around then, so I can't say. Maybe a student botched the labeling." He ran his hand through his hair. "Look, I'm going to break my confidentiality oath—but only to you, okay? This goes no further until the results are public."

"Right."

"*None* of our clones behave like the Hanaks' old vines. Not one."

"No shit." Wolf locked eyes with Ryan. "Thanks for telling me."

Ryan nodded.

Wolf said, "Then we have two choices: student error, or someone knew the Hanaks had a very special clone and elected to keep that clone for themselves."

Ryan sighed. "I can't work out how anyone would know the Hanaks' clone was worth stealing."

"We're working on that," Wolf said. He brought Ryan up to date on Goose Gossen's mother's wine cellar. "Gossen's mother probably knew what she had. And, wine lover that she was, she probably had friends who knew. Some might still be alive. And there might be other old cellars we don't know about yet—"

Ryan interrupted, "I should have said this before: I'll get that bottle you brought me to the chemical analysis guys this afternoon."

"Thanks. Look, I know this is asking a lot, but I need the names of everyone working on the Project when the Hanaks' clones were pulled."

"No fucking way!" Ryan stomped to the window and stood with his back to Wolf, his hands clenched into fists.

Wolf waited. After a minute passed, he said, "I can imagine how difficult this is for you. But wouldn't it be best for the Project if we found out what really happened?"

Ryan checked his watch. "I have an appointment with my thesis adviser in just a few minutes. Wait for me, okay?"

Wolf agreed.

Two hours later, Ryan returned. "On my walk across campus, all I could think about was the disappearance of the Hanaks' clone. You're right. We need to find out what happened. But I can't jeopardize the Project. I'll find the students who worked on the Project in the '90s, but only on the condition that you keep this between us. I don't want rumors impugning the integrity of our research."

"You mean, beyond what we already know is wrong?"

"I *mean*, nobody hears about this until I can tell my professor what we've found. It's only fair."

"We have to tell Noli. This could be linked to the Hanaks' troubles and maybe even to the murder of Fitz."

"Not yet."

"Then when?"

"Goddammit, Wolf! I don't know. Maybe when we have a better idea what happened."

"If I'm right, we'll have solid evidence as soon as we track down the culprit. He'll have a vineyard full of vines matching the ones on Old Marco's Hill."

Ryan grimaced. "Even if you found that vineyard, you'd still have to prove it began with stolen cuttings."

"I'll find a way," Wolf said.

Ryan sighed. "When you contact the students, what will you say?"

Wolf's answer was ready. "I'll say I'm a journalism grad student who's working on a website that will go live on the day the Project's results are announced. One part of the website will be devoted to all the folks who've worked on the Project over the years and will include their photos and stories."

"Christ, that's perfect. Did you think that up just now?"

Wolf smiled. "Too many detective novels. Now, if you can just—"

"I know, I know." Ryan turned to his computer. In less than a minute, he'd found what he was looking for. "Grab a pencil and paper. I don't want to print this. Ready? The supervising grad student in 1999 was Oliver Wickam. Other grad students: Jim Sanchez, Guy Forman and Kim Rolford. A work-study assistant named Allison Giannopoulos is listed, in addition to 'volunteer assistance from students in viticulture and enology'. The volunteers would be undergraduates, not likely to be our culprit."

"You're assuming the faculty weren't involved?"

"Fuck, yes. I *know* them, Wolf!"

"Sorry. Just asking."

As Ryan's fingers danced over the keyboard, the computer screen flashed from page to page so rapidly, Wolf couldn't keep track. "I can't find Sanchez, Forman, or Rolford. I'll ask around, see if anyone knows them. We'll start with Wickam. He's a well-known consultant based in Napa. And I know of an Allison Giannopoulos. She's a vet here in Sacramento. My housemates take their cats to her."

Wolf smiled. "How many Allison Giannopouloses could there be?"

CHAPTER THIRTY-SIX

Tuesday, 5 p.m.

After an afternoon's cram course with Peter on the track record of Hanak Winery, the wine market, and investment possibilities, Noli felt ready to represent Hanak Winery at Arnant's party. Dressed in a new black cocktail dress and low heels, she watched as Peter lifted a half-case of wine from his truck. "Ready?" he said.

"As I'll ever be." She led the way to the Andolini Tasting Room. Gentle spotlights accented its Victorian gingerbread and gabled roof. Glass doors filled the space where carriage doors once swung. Within, the party was well underway.

Noli reminded herself of her second objective for that night. In addition to finding potential investors for the Hanaks, she wanted to learn as much as she could about Daniel Arnant.

Arnant greeted them at the door and took her hand, saying, "How lovely you are!" Slender as a professional model, dressed in a black silk shirt and beige linen suit which complemented his reddish-blond hair, Daniel was strikingly handsome. His face crinkled into a warm smile. She searched his eyes, looking for a hint of duplicity, but saw none.

Turning to Peter, Arnant asked, "This is the '04?"

"Six bottles."

"Wonderful. I'll have them opened immediately." He called to one of the waiters, "Greg, give us a hand."

After entrusting Peter's wine to the waiter, Arnant said, "I haven't had a chance to thank you for sending Russ Lankshaw to me. Men with his level of experience are hard to find."

Peter nodded an acknowledgement, and Arnant stepped away to greet arriving guests.

Noli said, "We'll have a better chance of talking to all the guests before dinner if we split up." Although he looked reluctant, Peter agreed and headed to an adjoining room.

Wanting to keep a clear head, she requested a glass of water, then set out to mingle. Arnant's guests were an international crowd. She passed a laughing man whose loud "*Mais, oui!*" was countered with "*Ce n'est pas possible!*" She joined a group of women dressed in exquisite saris, quickly learning that two of them were wives of partners in Andolini Winery. To her surprise, over the next hour and a half, she got a strong sense of political infighting amongst the Andolini partners.

At last, seeing no one with whom she had not spoken, she joined Peter and suggested they step onto the deck to compare notes.

"I found three possible investors," she told him. "They'll call tomorrow to set up appointments."

Peter actually smiled. "I met two fellows who seemed genuinely interested. Maybe this'll work out."

"After talking with several wives of Andolini partners, I'd say Daniel's staging a takeover. Has he talked with you about the changes he wants to make?"

"Yeah, it's been a struggle for him. He was only a junior member of the law practice that bought Andolini, and it took years for him to convince them to put him in charge. The original partnership didn't care about quality. They were all about profit, so Andolini mainly sells white zinfandel."

Noli had observed a few of the guests drinking the distinctly pink version of zinfandel called "white zinfandel." Although she'd never tasted it herself, she was aware it was regarded with disdain by wine lovers and often called "alcoholic soda pop." "I've forgotten why white zinfandel is more profitable," she said. "Something about higher production, more grapes per vine?"

"Yeah, they allow each vine to produce as many grape clusters as it can, because no one expects depth of flavor in white zin. I limit our vines to two clusters per shoot. They get six tons of grapes per acre while I get one and a half."

"Quadruple the yield? That explains a lot."

"And the second reason white zinfandel is more profitable is they don't age it. The wine is sold as soon as it's bottled, so they get their money within months after the harvest."

"So Daniel would like to take Andolini in the direction of fine wine, and that means less profit, at least for a few years. What will his next move be?"

Peter considered for several moments and sighed. "In his shoes, I'd take advantage of the Zinfandel Clone Project. Find a top-notch match between the Andolini terroir and the clones they offer, replant as quickly as possible over the coming years."

"And you think he'll end up planting the clone from Old Marco's Hill?"

"Yeah, I do."

A discreet bell sounded, alerting Andolini partners and their guests to leave the harvest party and move on to their exclusive dinner. Noli claimed her coat and walked out in the company of a woman she hadn't seen since law school and who was now a partner in Andolini Winery. They joined a procession moving toward a rose-entwined arbor. From there, a sandstone staircase looped gracefully down the mountainside. Recessed lighting marked every step, and fairy lights twined through nearby trees and bushes. A fountain splashed and tumbled alongside the staircase.

"When I was a kid, I played in the weeds and tumbled-down buildings on this hillside," Noli told her. "What a transformation!"

Her former classmate, a compact and athletic blonde, led the way. At the bottom of the stairs, beneath heat lamps, the guests congregated on a tiled patio the size of a large living room. An elegant bamboo screen blocked the entrance to the cave. Noli spotted Peter talking with two of the young guests. Very promising.

Just beyond the patio, on a service road, stood a van labeled *Chez Patrice*, a hive around which buzzed a swarm of waiters. Smoke rose from an impressive barbecue grill, and two men in tall white chef's hats wielded tongs and spatulas, rapidly moving sliced vegetables over the flames. Garlic, basil, onions, and peppers perfumed the air.

Noli and her friend lingered on the stairs. "Improving the cave was Daniel's idea?" Noli asked.

"Actually, no. Last year, one of Daniel's new investors, Sedge Green, toured Bordeaux and fell in love with their cellar caves. When he returned, he showed a zillion photos of romantic dinners in wine caves to our partners, *et voilà*! They all agreed, and Sedge put up half a million dollars to 'improve' our cave."

Noting a sarcastic edge to her voice, Noli said, "You were against it?"

"I was initially. Why invest in space to age fine wine if we aren't making any? But Daniel decided to support the idea, so I backed off. Now I think he was anticipating getting the support he needed from the new partners, including Sedge, and in a few years he'll make wine worthy of aging, so this is a step in the right direction." She chuckled. "Or, it could be a guy thing—you know, cave envy."

A soft chime sounded.

Daniel, standing in front of the screen, announced, "Ladies and gentlemen, dinner is served!" He stepped aside. Two waiters folded the screen and carried it away.

A gasp of surprise rose from the guests.

"Daniel's really outdone himself," Noli's friend whispered.

Like a passageway into a fairy tale, the entrance glowed with golden light from large sconces enclosing electric candles. A royal-red carpet led to a long chamber where a banquet table was set with white linen. Electric candelabra graced the center of the table, leaving the surrounding space mysteriously dark. On the table, silver utensils glimmered beside gold-rimmed plates. Crystal wine glasses, eight per setting, shimmered.

With expressions of delight, the guests filtered along the table, examining engraved place cards. Peter took a seat, and she was pleased two of the prospects she'd found were seated just opposite him.

Arnant called to Noli from the head of the table, indicating a chair to his left. He held the chair for her, and as she took her seat, the elegant woman seated on Arnant's right nodded to her, saying, "I'm Claudia."

Claudia was so famous, even Noli recognized her: Claudia Donatto, wine critic, contributing editor for *Vin Extraordinaire*. Claudia was Girl Wonder of the wine world, the first female wine critic to be taken seriously, descendant of a pioneering wine family in the Napa Valley.

Arnant proved to be a skillful host, introducing Noli to the others at their end of the table, then opening the conversation by asking about her experiences with Irish law. She responded with two humorous anecdotes, which led to wide-ranging discussion among all the lawyers regarding the challenges of advising clients on international deals.

Noli was about to ask Arnant about long-range plans for the Andolini winery when a forty-ish red-haired man left his seat at the middle of the table and came to Arnant's elbow. Bracing one hand on the table, he leaned in, saying, "Great spread, Daniel! Say, tomorrow I'm heading to Monterey early. Conditions are supposed to be great for diving. Thought you might like to come along, since you've missed the last two Wednesdays."

While Claudia looked daggers at him, Arnant focused on his friend. "Can't tomorrow, Eliot. We'll catch up soon, right?"

As the man returned to his seat, Arnant gave Claudia a sheepish smile. Apparently unmollified, Claudia excused herself and walked out of the cave. With a forced smile, Arnant excused himself and followed.

From his girlfriend's reaction, Noli guessed Daniel Arnant hadn't been where he'd said he was on the previous Wednesday, the day Fitz died. He was tall and thin. Could he have been mistaken for a "boy" when dressed in a loose windbreaker? Noli tried to picture him in a black windbreaker, hood pulled forward to hide his face. He was certainly thin, but "thin as a stick"?

She turned to the man on her left. "Have you been an Andolini partner for very long, James?"

James had difficulty focusing his watery blue eyes. "I fucking created this partnership." His pronunciation was slow and precise, as though he was drunk but had had plenty of practice hiding it.

"Then congratulations are in order," she said. "You've transformed a wreck into a place of beauty."

James set his glass down, giving her his full attention. "How old are you?"

Not the response she'd expected. "Thirty-four. And you?"
"Forty-eight," he answered. His interest had obviously
flagged. Too old for him? Too young? "Same as Daniel fucking Arnant. I thought we might have met you when we were
kids." Then, looking alarmed by his possible insult, he said,
"I mean, you look way too young. But these days, with surgery and all ... Anyway, Daniel's grandmother was friends
with the old lady who ran this place, and sometimes we'd
come with her to visit. The old lady, we called her Miss
Andolini, she liked kids. Never had any of her own. She made
zabaglione and almond biscotti for us, spoiled us rotten." He
looked away, lost in memories.

Before Noli could form her next question, Claudia
returned and greeted them all with a forced smile. Arnant
followed, also smiling but obviously tense. He signaled to the
waiters. They cleared rapidly and returned with tiny bowls
of lemon sorbet—a palate cleanser, they explained, offering
the alternative of a piece of French bread for serious wine
connoisseurs.

When the next course, roast duck in a raspber-
ry-and-black-pepper sauce, had been served, Daniel rose
and waited for the attention of his guests before speaking.
"The wine you are about to taste is Hanak Zinfandel, 2004
vintage, expertly crafted by our neighbor to the west, Peter
Hanak." Nodding to Peter, he said, "Peter, please stand up."

Awkwardly, Peter rose from his chair, nodded briefly to
left and right.

Arnant continued, "Peter's wine is a sublime expression
of Santa Cruz Mountain terroir." He raised his glass in a
toast, then sipped from it.

Surprised, the Andolini partners and their guests reached
for their wine goblets. Noli looked down the table at Peter.
He caught her eye and winked.

Worried that the wine she'd already consumed was fogging her mind, Noli took only a perfunctory sip and set her glass down. She watched Claudia, the wine critic, as she carefully inhaled and evaluated the aroma of Peter's zinfandel. Claudia took a sip and moved it slowly over her tongue. It was a half-minute before she swallowed. She said, "Remarkable. I've never tasted anything like it. Unique terroir?"

How could she not be familiar with Peter's wine? He won a gold medal in the Chronicle's *wine competition in 2004, as well as lesser prizes in earlier years. Was she faking to set Arnant up?*

Daniel answered slowly, shooting a meaningful look at James. "Possibly. The grapes come from a ridge just to the west of us that was originally in the Andolini estate."

James said, "Why don't we buy him out?" His tone was belligerent.

Daniel shot Noli an apologetic look before answering. "As a matter of fact, I've raised that possibility with Peter. He's not interested."

"Just a matter of price, surely."

An icy look escaped Arnant's eyes before he took a deep breath and let his face settle into a pleasant mask. "I believe winemaking means more to Peter than money, James."

"Let him keep making his bloody wine, then. Just acquire the—"

"You won't *make a profit* on his wine, James. At least, not until our reputation has changed."

James scowled but decided to let the matter rest. He sawed off another bite of duck and chewed loudly.

What Arnant had said wasn't quite true; Peter did make a profit on his wine. But nothing like the profit Arnant's buddies were making on white zinfandel.

Claudia picked up the ball so gracefully, Noli suspected she had been briefed ahead of time. "James, you may already have the ability to make a zinfandel like this." She paused for effect, smiling warmly. "If I were you, I'd get terroir analysis on all the Andolini fields as quickly as possible."

She waited for a response. When none came, Arnant said, "Great idea, Claudia. Then we'll be ready to take advantage of the research results from the Zinfandel Clone Project. James, did I mention that the Project will be releasing zin clones next month?"

If Arnant thought he could hook James' interest, he was mistaken. Pointedly ignoring Arnant, James said to Noli, "Will you be sending the rest of that duck back to the kitchen?"

Noli traded her half-empty plate for his bare one, thinking Arnant was wasting his time if he thought he could win that man's vote. James was as crude as he was avaricious.

Arnant turned his attention to his dinner, radiating the pleasure he was deriving from the pairing of duck with Peter's wine. The man on Claudia's right, another partner, said, "Daniel, are we insured for this folly? What if there's an earthquake?"

Daniel stared at him, silent for a few seconds while the muscles in his jaw twitched. "You may remember, John, we had three different geologists evaluate this cave. And it survived the Loma Prieta quake in '89 in perfect condition. But yes, we have appropriate insurance."

John harrumphed and pointedly turned away.

Struggling to sound casual, Noli asked, "Did you find any old bottles of wine when you started the remodel?"

Arnant said, "No wine. But it wouldn't have been any good. You have to remember that the Andolinis only made zinfandel. You can't expect zinfandel to age for thirty years."

CHAPTER THIRTY-SEVEN

Tuesday, 11 p.m.

W hen Peter began to snore, Tina pulled herself along the transfer board from bed into her wheelchair. She wasn't going to sleep any time soon. She might as well make good on her promise to Wolf and examine Paolina Andolini's oral history for clues as to the provenance of Marco Andolini's zinfandel vines. She set the manuscript on a table next to a small reading lamp, pulled reading glasses from a side pouch on the wheelchair, and began.

Paolina had been enthralled with the notion that she'd descended from Sicilian aristocracy, a story handed down by Marco. According to Marco, his father had fought in the 1848 Sicilian revolution, losing everything because he "fought for freedom, just like George Washington." If the revolution had succeeded, Marco never would have ventured to the California gold fields in hopes of restoring his fortune.

Then there were stories of the hardships Marco had endured in the gold fields. How he had left the mines when he had enough gold to buy land. He'd purchased a hundred acres of logged-over Loma Buena mountainside at a bargain price. He'd cleared the land of cabin-sized redwood stumps using a team of oxen, doing all the work himself so he had enough money to buy passage for his wife and children. Later came enough money to build a mansion for them.

Often Paolina's tales of her ancestors' struggles were so vivid, so detailed, it was as though she herself had witnessed them. Which made the details suspect. But the most difficult problem in understanding her narrative lay in Paolina's inability to stick to a single time period. She would jump from describing her grandmother's voyage from Sicily to describing a cruise she herself had taken in the Caribbean. The grapevines Marco planted in the nineteenth century were confused with the ones his son had replanted after Prohibition. But one part of the vineyard stories was clearly true: The Andolini family had succeeded in hiding Old Marco's Hill, where the vines had been planted by Marco himself, from Prohibition inspectors.

Tina searched through the manuscript, scanning until she found the story of Paolina's aunt.

My Aunt Cosima was madly in love with this Hungarian fellow. His name was Arpad. He made champagne, can you imagine? They fell in love and planned to marry, but it came to a tragic end. Arpad's father was a very important man in California, and he insisted Arpad break the engagement to Cosima and marry the daughter of one of his business partners. Else the boy would be disowned.

So Arpad broke his engagement with Cosima. I guess Arpad didn't have much backbone, 'cause if he'd married Cosima, they could have had half of Grandpa's land, which would have been enough, don't you think? Anyway, Grandpa threatened to kill Arpad, but Cosima said no, and not two months later, she died of a broken heart. Arpad felt so bad, he brought Grandpa a wagon filled with special grapevines from Europe. Then he ripped off his shirt and handed Grandpa a hunting knife, crying, Take your revenge! *I suppose he was drunk, don't you? Anyway, Grandpa refused, on account of Cosima's love for him. Instead, he said,* "Help me plant the vines." *So they did.*

Now everyone calls it Old Marco's Hill. Mama said it ought to be named Cosima's Hill, but no one listened to her. There aren't any other vines like those in all of California, 'cause they weren't torn out during Prohibition.

Tina stopped reading, removed her glasses, and rubbed her eyes. In the morning, she'd send Wolf an email. Now they knew *who* had brought the vines to Old Marco's Hill. The Arpad in Paolina's story had to be the son of Agoston Haraszthy, the Hungarian entrepreneur whose leadership in the young California wine industry was so well acknowledged that he was called "The Father of California Wine."

All those years ago, when she'd been recording Paolina's story, the name Arpad wouldn't have meant anything to her.

She tried to estimate the year of Cosima's tragic death, when Arpad brought the vines. She rolled her chair to the kitchen counter, where Noli had left the copy of Sullivan's book on zinfandel history she'd retrieved from Fitz's office. If she remembered correctly, Agoston Haraszthy had personally imported an enormous selection of European grapevines, sometime around the Civil War.

CHAPTER THIRTY-EIGHT

When Noli awoke, her first thought was that Daniel Arnant's harvest party had given them hope. Peter now had potential investors. All he needed was an outstanding '09 vintage!

As she showered, Noli considered Arnant himself. He'd grown up nearby; his family had known Paolina. How much did he remember about Paolina's wine? Should he be at the top of their list of suspects?

Stepping outside, she paused to breathe the morning air. Shafts of sunlight radiated through the redwood canopy, warming the domes. Nearby, a Townsend's warbler trilled its four-note question over and over, and a downy woodpecker accompanied it with a steady *rat-a-tat-tat*. A soft breeze from the west carried the heavy scent of ripe grapes. She recognized the scent's intensity: It was time to harvest. In the old days, Fitz would be pulling up to the domes right now, all fired up, promising to get the old Zambelli crusher running smoothly.

She helped Tina and Peter make breakfast. They worked in silence. No doubt Peter and Tina were feeling Fitz's absence as strongly as she was.

Peter broke the silence. "It's a perfect morning. We should eat on the deck." After scrubbing the outdoor table, he brought Tina an extra blanket and loaned Noli a plaid wool overshirt. Once they were settled, he said, "I want to apologize to you both. Tina, you were right about going to Arnant's party. Noli, thanks for spending your evening holding my hand."

Tina smiled and caressed his cheek. For a moment, they looked into each other's eyes. Noli thought the love that had pulled them through decades of hard times was as strong as ever. They would make it through Fitz's death.

As they ate, Peter said, "Sam Gaither's helping me bring home two truckloads of grapes from a heritage vineyard in King City. With the extra grapes, we'll have more wine to sell. We'll climb out of our financial hole."

Noli understood the subtext: Peter was betting everything on the new barrels. Betting that the infection that had ruined his last two harvests was a problem of the past. She bit her tongue, thinking of the risk. He was spending money he didn't have to buy the additional grapes. If the fermentation failed again, they'd be even deeper in debt.

"About last night," Noli said. "It was useful. I sat between Daniel Arnant and an Andolini board member who was his childhood friend. Did you know Arnant grew up near here? As a kid, he knew Paolina Andolini."

"He never mentioned it to me," Tina said.

"Me neither," said Peter.

"Which means Daniel's family probably knew how well Paolina's wine was aging," Noli said. "As an adult, he might well remember that fact. Did you ever discuss yours and Wolf's experiments on aging the wine from Old Marco's Hill with him?"

"No," Peter said. "Not with anyone."

"Are you thinking Daniel's been after our land all this time?" Tina asked, her voice shaking.

"I'm not thinking anything yet," Noli answered. "Near as I can tell, he's been a good friend to you. But Wolf thinks we should look at anyone who might have known the potential of Old Marco's Hill, and I agree with him."

Tina didn't look convinced.

Noli continued, "Think back to when Paolina was alive. Do you remember her having friends?"

Tina answered quickly. "She'd outlived them all. That's why Dino's friendship was so important to her."

"Did she mention families who had been important friends when she was younger?"

Tina blew out a breath. "It was such a long time ago." She paused to think. "The Nortons were her closest neighbors, but I don't think she liked them much. I seem to recall they were teetotalers. Off the top of my head, I can't recall anyone else. I'll look at her autobiography again, see who she mentioned."

Peter said, "I've got to hit the road in just a few minutes. FYI, I've called around this morning. All our regulars have promised to come help harvest on Friday morning. I'll have time to work on the crusher tomorrow." He gathered up the plates and forks. "With any luck, Sam and I should be back here pressing grapes by about eight o'clock. Don't save dinner for us—we'll get something on the road."

When Peter's truck had disappeared down the mountain, Tina turned to Noli. "I didn't want to tell Peter until I'm certain. But I think I've traced the clone on Old Marco's Hill. I emailed my theory to Wolf, so let's see what he thinks."

"Have you heard from him since he left?" Noli asked.

"No," Tina said. "Have you?"

"Not a word, but he promised to be back for the harvest. You're spending the day with Annika, making applesauce?"

"Right," Tina said, with little enthusiasm.

Noli thought it was just as well that Tina wouldn't be spending the day alone with her memories. "Don't forget, I'm bringing dinner," she said.

She stayed long enough to see Tina roll safely down the road to Annika's house, Raz trotting at her side.

CHAPTER THIRTY-NINE

Wolf drove out of Sacramento, heading toward Healdsburg for his appointment with Oliver Wickam. He hoped he could get Wickam, the former grad student in charge of the Zinfandel Clone Project, to admit to covering up the theft of the Hanaks' clone.

Their appointment wasn't until four p.m., so rather than taking Highway 101, the fastest way north, he planned to detour through Sonoma and stop at the historic Buena Vista Winery, the second oldest winery in California, founded by Agoston Haraszthy. Wolf was convinced by Tina's research: The Hanaks' clone had been personally selected by Agoston Haraszthy, Arpad's father. Now he wanted to know more. At the home and winery of the old robber baron, he hoped to find records documenting the tragic outcome of his visionary trip to Europe. Ideally, he would nail down the location in Europe that the Hanaks' clone had come from.

In 1861, Haraszthy had personally crisscrossed the continent to collect vine cuttings and bring them back to California for systematic testing in different California terroir. He'd returned with more than one hundred thousand cuttings from three hundred and fifty varietals. He'd used his own funds in hopes the California legislature would cover his costs when he returned. This, they refused, and the history books seemed to concur that most of the cuttings rotted in a warehouse. But what if one of the varietals he'd collected was zinfandel? Perhaps a sensational clone from his family's hereditary estates near the Dalmatian Coast?

And what if a few cuttings from that clone had been given to Marco Andolini? In this way, Old Marco's Hill might have been planted with a clone that was now unique in California. Perhaps in the entire world!

Upon reaching the Buena Vista Winery, Agoston Haraszthy's home, Wolf found the historic building closed. Kicking himself for failure to call ahead, he sighed and climbed out of his truck. The old winery was beautiful. Two stories tall, fashioned from cut-stone blocks, very European in feel. Covered with ivy. He circled to the front door and wasn't surprised to find a sign saying *Closed for Renovation.* Damn. He'd especially wanted to see the hand-dug limestone caves Haraszthy had insisted upon for aging his wine. One had been dedicated to champagne, made by Agoston's son, Arpad, who'd studied champagne-making in France.

Resigning himself to returning another day, Wolf drove on toward Healdsburg, replaying his early-morning interview with Allison Giannopoulos. She'd agreed to give him ten minutes before her first appointment. Dressed in a white lab coat and jeans, she admitted him with obvious reluctance.

"Thanks for seeing me," Wolf said. "As I said, we're on a very tight deadline."

"The Zinfandel Clone Project is ancient history for me," Allison said. She had acne-pocked olive skin and a halo of black curly hair. Her narrow lips were not smiling. "I don't know what I can tell you that others won't recall in more detail."

Wolf forged ahead. "I'm looking for colorful stories about the early days of the Project, human-interest stories to add to the website. I was hoping you could tell us about a crisis time for the Project. The records show you were working with Oliver Wickam in 1999. That's when many vines were found to have GLR and had to be pulled, correct?"

Her expression slid from unfriendly to wary. "Yes, I was an undergraduate assistant to Ollie—no one called him Oliver."

"It must have been a very discouraging time. Was morale low?"

"I was just a lowly work-study student. I drove the truck, carried a bucket and shears, clipped what I was told to clip. Why aren't you asking the Project directors these questions?"

"Oh, I am!" Wolf said, giving her his best smile. "But you know how it is—the guys on top don't always know the most interesting stories."

"I don't have any stories."

Feigning a lapse in memory, Wolf consulted a notepad. "Right. Well, maybe you remember the only donation site in Santa Cruz County? Hanak Vineyard, owned by Peter and Tina Hanak? Were the owners helpful? What was it like to tell them they had infected vines?" Again he smiled at her.

"I really don't remember." Her eyes slid away. "Look, you're wasting your time and mine. Talk to Ollie."

"He's next on my list," Wolf said, adopting a jovial tone. "How long did you work with him?"

"Just two quarters. Decided to become a vet, switched majors."

"Any lab work? Or were you strictly in the field?"

"I worked in the lab too."

"Any stories there? It was early days in genetic analysis of clones, wasn't it?"

"Why are you asking?"

"Just trying to picture it."

"Ask the experts. Now, if you'll excuse me, I have sick animals to look after." She stood and exited through a door labeled *Hospital*.

Wolf felt certain Giannopoulos was stonewalling. But why? Maybe she was covering up a mistake she herself had made in the lab. Maybe Wickam, her supervisor, had never known about her error, and now she was afraid of being exposed.

On the other hand, maybe she'd been Wickam's accomplice. Or maybe Wickam wasn't the villain, and she was protecting someone else?

Or—and he had to be honest about this—maybe he was imagining a conspiracy that never existed. The mix-up could have been an honest accident, and no one even knew it had happened.

He needed to focus on the coming encounter with Oliver Wickam. Although Wickam had agreed to an interview on very short notice, he'd sounded wary. He'd insisted on meeting in downtown Healdsburg for lunch, supposedly for Wolf's convenience. "It's so difficult to find my house. Some of last night's dinner guests still haven't shown up." The joke fell flat, maybe because Wickam's voice was tense as a violin string.

Wolf suspected Wickam wanted to keep him away from his vineyard. Why? Maybe he was operating a profitable marijuana farm in the midst of his vines. But given how evasive Allison Giannopoulos had been, Wolf figured the plants Wickam was hiding weren't for smoking.

As he traversed the quaint town of Healdsburg, he remembered the many happy weekends he and Ryan had spent here. Healdsburg was poised at the confluence of three of the world's best wine appellations—Dry Creek Valley, Alexander Valley, and Russian River Valley. A wine lover's paradise. He sighed.

As he pulled into the parking lot of The Bean Affair, his cell rang. It was Ryan, calling as though he knew Wolf was thinking of him. "Thought I'd let you know I've tracked down the other three grad students from the Project," Ryan said. "Forman's working in Australia right now. Rolford died in 2000. Sanchez has a winery in Chile. I've emailed Forman and Sanchez, asking what they remember about the samples from Santa Cruz County." He hesitated, then continued, "Unless Forman or Sanchez took cuttings out of the country with them—which is very unlikely—it's Wickam we need to focus on."

"Right. I'm about to interview him. Anything on his finances?"

"Wickam has three partners: two women and an investment fund. That's as far as I got."

"Forward the names to Irv and we'll see what he comes up with," Wolf said.

They rang off.

At the entrance to the coffee shop, he was hailed by a painfully thin man in jeans, T-shirt, and leather jacket. "Are you Wolf Faber?"

Wolf offered his hand, saying, "I am. Thanks for meeting me."

Wickam was prematurely bald. His eyes sat close together above a ski-jump nose, and his voice was high and squeaky, reminiscent of a boy at puberty. When he smiled, his chinless face lit up. "Hope you're hungry! The crepes are to die for."

After they ordered, Wolf said, "I hear you're greatly in demand as a consultant."

"I've backed off on consulting," Wickam replied. "I have plenty to do, managing the vineyard and making wine." He paused, scanning the room, foot tapping nervously. "Our pinot noir vines are ten years old now and bearing well. Four Friends Noir is our label. Do you know it?"

Wolf nodded. "Of course. Out of my price range, I'm afraid." He stared into Wickam's eyes and realized the pupils were dilated. He was high on something. Cocaine? Meth? Had he "backed off" on consulting because he was no longer reliable?

"I hope to have my own vineyard someday," Wolf said. "From your label, I'm guessing you put together a partnership?"

"That's right."

"Any advice?"

Wickam snorted. "Find rich men—or women—who want the panache of having their own wine label and will leave you alone to run the operation."

"I was afraid you were going to say that."

Wickam grinned. "Put the word out, you'll find 'em." He shifted in his seat. "But first, you've gotta establish yourself as a winemaker. Find a label that's not doing well and bring their quality up."

Their food arrived. Wolf enjoyed several bites of chicken pesto crepe before he realized Wickam was ignoring his food and looking around the café as though searching for a friend. Wolf cleared his throat to get Wickam's attention, then said, "I'm curious to know why you chose to work with pinot noir after all the time you invested in studying zinfandel."

Grinning, Wickam rubbed his right thumb against index and middle fingers. "Money, my friend. I get two, three times the price for a bottle of noir as for a bottle of zin of equal quality."

"Right." Wolf pretended to consult his notes. "Like I told you on the phone, I'm collecting stories about the early stages of the Zinfandel Clone Project, sort of an informal history. When we announce the Project's results, we'll upload these stories onto our website, sort of a human-interest facet to the research. I know you were central in the early years, so I'd like your remembrances."

"Sure thing."

"Mind if I record you on my phone?" Wolf asked. "I'll email you any quotes we want to use so you can verify them."

"Fine."

After several unthreatening questions about the collection of cuttings from heritage zinfandel vineyards, Wolf asked, "How about the GLR testing in 1999. Near disaster, right? You had to burn forty percent of the vines?"

"Hell of a time. We found clean replacements for most of them. That was the fun part for me, traveling around the state to collect new samples."

"Any stories for me? Interesting winemaking families? Surprising locations?"

For the next half-hour, Wickam held forth as though he'd just been waiting for an audience. Whether he had a great memory or was a gifted fabricator, Wolf wasn't certain. No mention of the Hanaks or the Andolini Estate.

Wolf said, "I noticed that one collection site was in Santa Cruz County. But that county's never mentioned in the Project's reports."

Wickam blinked, looked down at his empty coffee cup. "Yeah, that was a big waste of time. Nice owners, though. I remember them. The guy'd been shot up in Vietnam, still had a limp."

"Why was it a waste of time?"

"Theirs was a clone we already had. I forget which one."

Wolf nodded, working hard to contain his excitement. *Please, God, let my phone recorder be working.* Here it was, confirmation that the Hanaks' clone had been mishandled. But was it intentional? After a strategic pause, he said, "You've really brought the early days to life. Were you also involved in the lab?"

Ollie shook his head. "To be honest with you, man, I'm a total klutz in the lab. Had to choose the right girlfriend, know what I mean?" He winked.

"You don't happen to recall any of your girlfriends' names? It would be a great angle for the website if we could talk with a couple of them."

Ollie opened his hands, palms up. "Ancient history."

A homely guy with drug jitters had so many girlfriends, he couldn't recall their names? How likely was that? Wolf made a show of putting away his cell phone. "It's been an honor to talk with you."

They stood and shook hands. Dropping a tip on the table, Wolf turned as if to leave, then turned back to Wickam, saying, "Oh, I almost forgot. Word has it you raise the best German shepherds in Northern California. I'd like to—"

Wickam stared at him, wide eyed. "You pulling my chain, man?"

"No, I'd like to buy a puppy."

"No shit. Who told you I had dogs?"

"I don't recall. I've talked to so many people—"

"Well, someone's fuckin' with you. I *hate* dogs."

CHAPTER FORTY

When she parked her car in front of the domes, Noli took a moment to prepare herself. Today marked the one-week anniversary of Fitz's murder. Tina would ask how the investigation was going. What could she say? Officially, they'd made no progress since Sunday, when they'd learned about Black Windbreaker Person.

No progress, but not for lack of effort. This afternoon, she and Munch had covered the harbor again, just in case a witness returned for the Wednesday regatta. No luck. Meanwhile, Luz remained in danger, waiting for the opportunity to look at Varley's files. Irv burned along on his computer, digging out information on Varley. He and Luz were consumed by Raul's theory that Varley had Fitz murdered to block formation of the new vineyard workers' union.

Alternatively, there was Wolf's conspiracy theory, which had seemed ridiculously far-fetched at first. But was it more believable now? Wolf was convinced the Hanaks had a uniquely valuable clone, a zinfandel that aged like a fine cabernet.

A motive for murder? She still had a hard time believing it. But sabotage? Yes, that was plausible. She'd made a list of every friend of Goose Gossen's mother and begun following the families. And she'd dug up some very interesting background on Daniel Arnant. But discussing this would only distress Tina.

Grabbing a carry-out bag filled with dinner from Gayle's Bakery and Rosticceria, she exited the car and climbed the steps to the new dome. Calling "Tina, I'm here!" she slipped through the sliding door and set dinner on the kitchen counter. The enticing aroma of lemon chicken wafted from the carry-out, reminding her she'd skipped lunch. "Tina?"

No answer.

She checked the bedroom. Empty, as was the bathroom. Puzzled, she walked out to the deck and checked the old dome.

No Tina. No wheelchair.

Maybe she'd forgotten their dinner date and gone off with a friend?

Raz came barreling through the dog door and skidded to a seated position at her feet. The dog rolled her eyes to the box of dog treats on the counter and waited, tongue hanging from the side of her mouth.

Noli gave her two treats. "That's all, girl. You'll get dinner soon."

The phone rang.

"Hello. Hanak residence."

"This is Annika Vandermeis. Noli?"

"Hi, Annika. Is Tina with you?"

A long pause. "No. I'm calling because I just found her glasses."

"What time did she leave you?"

"About three thirty," Annika said. "Maybe she's with Daniel. She wanted to talk with him about something. Was she expecting you?"

"Yes, but she might have forgotten."

"Probably silly to worry," Annika said.

"After everything that's happened, we'd be crazy *not* to worry. Let's check along the road, just in case."

Grabbing one of Peter's coats as she ran out the door, Noli called, "Raz! Come!" Enthusiastically, the dog ran ahead of her.

The sun had dropped below the horizon, leaving little light or warmth on the mountainside. A stiff breeze had risen, and it whipped the heat from her body. She buttoned the coat as she ran.

Shouting, "Tina!" she zigzagged from side to side on the road, checking for any sign of Tina's wheelchair.

Thinking it was a game, Raz ran in delighted circles around her. A scrub jay cried out, then crows added raw shrieks. Noli's mind filled with images of Tina lying on the ground, cold, hurt, helpless.

"Tina!"

Only the crows answered.

Racing the growing darkness, Noli moved on, cursing herself for leaving her cell behind, hoping Annika would bring flashlights. She passed the vineyard and moved more slowly along the cliff. Spotting a crumbled edge on its rim, she dropped to her hands and knees, peering over the edge into a tapestry of shadows.

"Tina? Are you there, Tina?"

Raz barked, then scooted herself forward until her head hung over the cliff's edge. She whimpered.

"Noli!" Annika's voice.

"Over here!"

A strong beam of light bobbed up the road as Annika arrived. Holding onto a battery-operated lantern, she handed a flashlight to Noli.

"Shine the light there," Noli said, pointing to the base of the cliff.

As they swept their light beams across the shrubbery below, they spotted a sock-covered foot and a bare shin.

Annika cried out, "No!"

A mangled wheelchair lay by the foot, like a loyal dog unwilling to leave its injured master. At the top of the leg, Noli could see bits of blue patchwork, the material of Tina's favorite jacket.

"Tina, can you hear me? It's Noli."

Silence. Even the crows were quiet.

Without warning, Raz leapt over the edge, scrambled down the slope and pushed through the brush to Tina's side.

Noli pushed hard against rising panic. If Tina was still alive, every second counted. "Annika, run to the Hanaks' house. Call 911. Wait for them, so you can guide them here."

Without a word, Annika raced away.

Noli aimed a light beam down the face of the cliff. She estimated it was at least seventy feet to the bottom. The first ten were a straight drop, but then came a gentler slope and a slide of loose soil.

"Tina, I'm coming down."

She held the flashlight tight to her chest with her right hand. The drop was fast. Rocks, embedded in the softer soil of the cliffside, ripped into the backs of her legs. Then her left foot slammed into a boulder, twisting her sideways and sending lightning bolts of pain through her leg.

At the bottom, seconds passed before she could breathe into the pain. Slowly she pulled herself upright, testing the leg. More pain, but it held her weight.

"Tina? It's Noli. I'm going to get you out of here."

Still no answer.

She attacked the bushes encasing Tina. As soon as she reached Tina's feet, she eased the sock down from one ankle and pressed a finger inside. A pulse.

Tina lay on her stomach, her face half in the dirt. Raz had worked her way through the brush to Tina's head, where she lay licking Tina's forehead. Tina's skirt had been ripped aside, and her right leg was bent at an unnatural angle. Broken, but no bones protruded from her skin. No sign of serious bleeding. However, the crucial question was, had branches punctured her abdomen or chest?

"Tina, it's Noli. The paramedics are coming. While we're waiting, I'm going to clear this brush away. It'll make a lot of noise, so don't be scared."

The branches encasing Tina's torso were covered with the bright red and orange leaves of poison oak. But that wasn't important right now. Noli slammed her foot into the poison-oak branches until they snapped, then tossed them out of the way. As she worked, she talked to Tina. "I'm clearing the brush, Tina. Help is on the way."

Noli stripped off Peter's coat and laid it over Tina, tucking the sides around her. "Tina, you're going to feel my fingers on your neck. Don't be afraid." She found the carotid artery. The pulse was thin and irregular.

She wanted to pull Tina out of the brush and hold her until the paramedics came. But she couldn't risk moving her for fear of aggravating a hidden puncture wound. Instead, she sat down beside her, holding her battered right hand, talking to her continuously.

Waiting, waiting, waiting.

CHAPTER FORTY-ONE

"This is the best I can do," said the hospital's social worker, offering Noli a used but clean pair of men's jeans, a plaid work shirt, and white socks.

"Thank you. I'll return them, I promise."

The gray-haired woman nodded and left the curtained-off cubicle where Noli had been scrubbed and injected with prednisone. She dressed and wriggled her feet into her shoes, which were encased in pale blue surgical shoe covers until they could be cleaned of poison-oak resin.

She followed signs to the family waiting room. There, Peter sat with his head in his hands. Next to him sat Sam Gaither, Peter's friend ever since they'd served together in Vietnam. Sam had followed Peter to King City with a second truck to fill with the carignan and syrah grapes Peter blended with his zinfandel.

It seemed to Noli that Sam hadn't changed in all the years she'd known him. A short, wiry man, with strongly muscled arms, he'd always hidden behind a bushy beard, an unruly mustache, and a wild corona of curly hair that fell to his shoulders. Even in her earliest memories, his hair and beard were gray.

Peter roused and rose stiffly to his feet, looking like a monster from a B horror film. His face, beard, and neck were streaked with black grease and motor oil—he'd had to pull over in Salinas to repair an oil leak in his aged truck. His clothes were blotched with grape stains that looked too much like blood.

"Are you all right?" he asked.

"I'm fine," Noli said. "Got a major shot of prednisone, so I won't be sleeping for the foreseeable future. Any word on Tina?"

"Not yet."

Sam stood behind Peter as though preparing to catch him when he fell. Looking into Peter's weary eyes, she thought Sam had reason. Pulling gently on Peter's arm, she led him back to his chair. "We need food and coffee. Wait for me."

Sam said, "I'll go with you." When they'd put a corridor between themselves and Peter, he said, "Peter's blaming himself. Normally he checks Tina's chair every morning, but with everything that's been happening—" Sam wiped his eyes with his sleeve. "He's pretty sure the last time he looked at the brakes was Friday night, and they were fine. The tires were new."

"Has she ever had trouble before?"

"Peter says not. I'll look at the chair in the morning, but I doubt we'll learn anything. From what Annika said, it's pretty smashed up."

Noli had only a vague impression of the wheelchair—all her attention had been focused on Tina. If Annika were still at the hospital, this would be a good time to question her. "Did Annika go home?"

"Yeah. Peter insisted. She promised to buy a new wheelchair first thing in the morning, so it'll be ready for Tina when she comes home."

When she comes home.

When Tina's surgeon finally came to the waiting room, it was nearly midnight. Circles of exhaustion ringed his wide brown eyes. Tina had been in the operating room for six hours.

"Your wife is in stable condition, which is all I can tell you right now. In a situation like hers, where trauma to the skull has bruised the brain, the brain swells. We had to open her skull to make way for the swelling. We'll keep her in an induced coma, see how she progresses. We won't know anything more for twenty-four hours at the very least, so I suggest you go home and get some sleep. We'll take good care of her."

Peter shook his head no and started to speak, but the weary doctor cut him off. "Rest now, so you can be here for her later."

Sam put a hand on Peter's shoulder. "Come on, I'll follow you home. You need to wash up, man! The way you look, you'll scare her to death when she does come around."

The word "death" rang out through the quiet waiting room.

Quickly Noli said, "Sam's right. I'll stay until you get back."

Grimacing as he straightened his right leg, Peter turned to Sam. "Do you need your truck tomorrow?" Which seemed an odd question. Then Noli realized Sam's truck, like Peter's, was full of grapes.

"I'll stay with you tonight," Sam said. "In the morning, we'll crush the grapes before you head to the hospital." Sam's purple-stained hand squeezed Peter's shoulder.

Peter turned to Noli. "Have you checked the forecast?"

Weather had been the last thing on her mind. She pulled her cell from her pocket. "Rain predicted to start tomorrow, possibly as early as one p.m."

Immediately Sam said, "I'll bring our construction crew. You'll need to call your neighbors and friends in the morning. With Noli's help, we'll bring in the harvest."

Peter shook his head. "That old crusher is a temperamental son of a bitch, Sam. Without Fitz or me to run it—"

Noli interrupted. "I can handle the crusher, Peter. I've done it before, remember?"

CHAPTER FORTY-TWO

On a visit to the tasting room of Four Friends Winery the previous evening, Wolf had formed a mental map of the property, noting terrain that would be hidden from visitors' view. The vineyards extended over sixty-seven acres of rolling hills; much, but not all, of the vineyard was visible from the Mission Revival house, winery, and tasting room perched on one of the hills.

He didn't expect Wickam to be peering out his window in the middle of the night, but he was nonetheless relieved when fog settled among the hills, leaving the hilltops open to moonlight but providing excellent cover for someone who kept to the valleys. Fog was the very attribute that made the Russian River Valley such great terroir; grapes ripened slowly here, their flavor developing fully before their sugar became too high.

The stone walls were easy to climb. As he dropped to the ground inside, he smiled, congratulating himself on his *Columbo* ploy, telling Wickam he wanted to "buy a puppy." If Wickam had owned dogs, this would have been far more complicated.

He worked his way along the southern fence, using his flashlight only when he entered fog pockets so dense he couldn't see the ground. Here, the grapes had been harvested, but he could tell by the shape of the leaves that he was in the midst of pinot noir vines. Besides, all the vines here were trellised; if Wickam were truly replicating Old Marco's Hill, his stolen vines would look like baby versions of the goblet-shaped vines on Old Marco's Hill.

Zigzagging from east to west for nearly an hour, he estimated he'd covered the thirty acres south of Wickam's house without finding a single head-trained vine. Using the eastern fence as a guide, he made his way north, checking each hill as he went. Well north of the Four Friends Winery, he emerged from the fog onto a hilltop and took a moment to orient himself. Only the northwest corner of the estate remained as a likely location for the stolen vines.

He heard a new sound, a chatter moving rapidly in his direction. He flicked his flashlight on. When the beam hit three black bandit masks, the raccoons veered away.

His heart thumped against his chest. Feeling silly for allowing raccoons to frighten him, he climbed the next hill.

Trellised vines only. House still dark.

Descending into the mist, he thought he heard a scratching sound, then tiny thumps. Rats or mice? He'd never really considered what animals might be nighttime denizens of vineyards. Curious, he turned the flashlight beam in the direction of the sounds.

A black-and-white-striped tail lifted.

He turned to run, but it was too late. The spray enveloped him, sweet for a split second, then noxious. Holding his breath, squeezing his burning eyes shut, he stumbled away, uncertain how far he needed to go to convince the little beast he wasn't a threat.

No wonder the raccoons had been running.

Gagging, he stripped the balaclava from his head, ripped off his sweatshirt, crumpled to the ground, and vomited, trying his best to retch silently. The night was still, not even the slightest breeze. He listened for a rustle of leaves that might warn him the skunk was attacking but heard nothing.

Did skunks attack?

He considered his options. Leave now?

No point. At this hour, there wasn't anywhere he could buy ingredients for a de-skunking scrub.

His hat and jacket were saturated. Should he leave them behind? No, if Wickam found them, he'd be suspicious.

He settled on turning the sweatshirt inside out and rolling the balaclava inside it, then tucking the bundle under his arm. Mercifully, he was no longer gagging. Slowly he moved north and west, stopping frequently to listen for the skunk. A second encounter might be more than he could handle.

Half an hour later, he found what he was looking for: petite, goblet-shaped vines on slopes not visible from the house. The tight grape clusters had not yet been harvested, and the five-lobe shape of their leaves left no doubt: zinfandel.

Got you, bastard.

Chilled to the bone, he nonetheless moved slowly and systematically, collecting samples and securing them in plastic bags.

CHAPTER FORTY-THREE

I n the hospital's admittance documents, Peter had listed Noli as his and Tina's daughter, a ruse which allowed her to be admitted to the ICU. Now she sat at Tina's bedside, feeling the truth beneath the lie: Tina had, indeed, been a mother to her.

Noli took Tina's hand and surveyed the damage to her body. Her right leg was in a cast, left leg and both arms lightly bandaged. But the real issue was her brain, quietly swelling through an open skull covered with mummy-like bandages. Noli feared that, no matter the impact of the drugs they'd given her, Tina must sense she was fighting for her life.

There was also good news. None of the poison-oak branches had punctured her abdomen, and her spine had not been damaged.

A nurse entered and checked Tina's IV. As she walked away, she said, "If you see any movement in her limbs, call me immediately. Meanwhile, talk to her. Tell her soothing, happy stories. Nothing upsetting."

Not so simple. She'll be worried about Peter.

"Hi, Tina. It's Noli. I'm staying with you while Peter showers. He'll be here soon. Sam and I are taking care of the harvest. Everything is covered. You and Peter can rest."

Noli closed her eyes and searched her memory for upbeat stories. "I have such happy memories of cooking with you.

I wasn't a very good student, was I? But you never gave up. Remember your birthday dinner, when I wanted to surprise you with risotto? I used brown rice instead of white, and it came out like pellets of plastic in mushroom sauce?"

She stayed with the cooking motif, every silly story she could recall. But she couldn't control her racing thoughts. Over and over, in her mind's eye, she watched Tina tumble over the cliff in her wheelchair.

Why? Did the ground crumble beneath the chair's wheels? Did she roll too near to the edge?

She repositioned her chair and took Tina's hand again. Suddenly she remembered her father singing to her when she was sick. She could hear his voice, reminding her of folk songs she hadn't heard in decades. Softly, she began to sing.

Are you going to Scarborough Fair?

Parsley, sage, rosemary, and thyme

She continued, verse after verse, as though her father were singing through her, while another part of her brain recalled Fitz's note on the door: *Noli, call me. It's about your father.*

If Fitz had discovered important new information about her father, wouldn't he have told Peter over coffee that morning?

When she finished "Scarborough Fair," she segued into "There But for Fortune," then remembered how much Tina loved "Alice's Restaurant." The songs came easily, and the hours passed.

Peter arrived at four o'clock in the morning, grumbling that Sam had forced him to lie down and rest first.

Noli rose stiffly, shaking circulation back into her legs. Nodding toward the curtains, she said, "Before I go, could I ask you a couple of questions?"

Peter whispered to Tina, "Be right back, sweetheart," and followed Noli to the waiting room.

"When Fitz dropped by for coffee on Wednesday morning, did he say anything about my father?"

Peter's brow scrunched. "No, I'd remember that. You're thinking of the note he left you?"

CHAPTER FORTY-FOUR

Thursday, 5 a.m.

When Noli reached the domes, she shed the clothes the hospital had loaned her and donned work clothes for the harvest. Then she grabbed a flashlight and strode down the path to the winery. Raz raced ahead, ecstatic to have an adventure.

She felt a surge of anxiety. She had to bring this harvest in. This was the turning point for the Hanaks. Without a good '09 vintage, they'd have no chance of convincing investors to come aboard.

They were going to be short-handed. How many of the friends who'd planned to help the next day would be able to change their plans and come immediately?

Peter's and Sam's trucks were backed up to the side of the winery, still loaded with crates of grapes from King City. As soon as possible, she needed to teach someone to operate the crusher so that those grapes were processed and out of the way when grapes started arriving from the Hanaks' vineyards.

She played the flashlight beam across the winery wall. In the morning damp, the graffiti looked fresh:

Die Camalfucking traiter

But it was old news, right?

Right.

Rubbing her hands together for warmth, she opened the door to the fermenting room and played the flashlight beam from wall to wall. The scent of crushed grapes lingered in the cool, damp air like a ghost of last year's failed vintage. On the cement floor, a triple row of six enormous plastic vats awaited the fruit of that day's labor. Someday—someday!— Peter would have a proper new winery with stainless-steel fermenting vats.

Now, check the crusher. Old but well cared-for, the Zambelli crusher-destemmer perched on a cement pad halfway up the slope on the east side of the winery. So ugly! It resembled a barrel-shaped barbecue equipped with a large, rectangular funnel on top.

Soon they'd be pitchforking grape bunches into that funnel. The machine would whirl and grind, separating stems from grapes, and out of the barrel would stream *must*—a mushy slop of crushed fruit and bits of stem. A large hose would carry the must through a hatch in the winery wall and spout it into the fermenting bins. By placing the Zambelli up the hillside, Peter used gravity to help pump the must into the bins.

It had always been Peter and Fitz who managed the crush and, her assurances to Peter aside, she wasn't at all certain she could keep the Zambelli running smoothly. She said a silent prayer to the universe that Wolf knew more about the damn machine than she did.

Everything was set.

She was wired on prednisone, but still craved a cup of coffee. There should be enough time for a quick dash back to the domes. She started up the path, thinking how unglamorous the hard work of making wine was. When wine lovers sipped from their wine glasses, did they ever pause to consider how their wine had been produced? Perhaps they pictured an enormous wooden tub in which barefoot peasants stomped, crushing the new harvest while drinking liberally of the previous one. And they'd be singing, accompanied by at least one accordion. The Romance of the Grape!

A smile creased her chilled face, and she wondered if she were losing it. Today was do or die for the Hanaks, and she needed to keep calm. Manic energy from the prednisone buzzed her brain and throbbed in her arms and legs, just as the emergency-room doctor had warned her.

Emergency room. Tina.

Peter had promised to call if there was any change. But Tina was in a drug-induced coma. Nothing would change until the doctors tried to bring her out of the coma. Nothing... unless she died.

The sound of tires crunching through gravel caught Noli's attention. She raced back to the winery and stepped inside to flip a switch. Floodlights turned night into day as a blue van pulled up.

Sam Gaither sprang from the van, greeted her with a hug, then introduced the men and women exiting the van, the crew from his small construction company. There were six men and two women, ranging in age from twentysomething to fiftysomething. Noli felt a surge of hope. If even a few of Peter's friends were able to join them, they could get the job done—if the rain held off.

Sam said, "Folks, there's a storm coming in, maybe as soon as this afternoon. We need to start as soon as it's light and work fast. But there's time enough for coffee and doughnuts while we wait for dawn." He set up a large pastry box and a two-gallon coffee dispenser on the van's tailgate. Watching his crew gather around, Noli noticed high-tech artificial legs on two of the men.

When Sam brought her a cup of coffee, she asked, "Are all your crew vets?"

"Yeah."

"Is that how you got started after the war, by doing construction?"

Sam didn't answer right away. She remembered that, as a small child, she'd been afraid of him. He was touchy, often silent, and sometimes took offense in ways she couldn't predict. When she'd asked her father why Sam wasn't married, he'd answered, "War hurts people in ways you can't see on the outside." She'd nodded sagely, concluding Sam was missing his male parts. Not until she was much older had she understood the damage of war could be invisibly lodged in a man's soul.

Over time, Sam had won her trust, becoming a favorite uncle. Ironic, often funny, always ready for a weekend camping trip. Then she remembered. When Sam had returned from Vietnam, he'd lived in the state park with Dino. One year, maybe two. Not the right time for this conversation.

He was staring at the crusher, at the spot where Fitz would ordinarily be standing. His face was heavy with grief. Like Peter and Munch, he'd served with Fitz.

"Sam, are you game to operate the crusher?"

"Sure, if you'll show me how."

Sam backed his truck up to the crusher's platform so the stack of grape crates was within easy reach. Grabbing a pitchfork, Noli climbed onto the platform, Sam by her side. She flipped the Zambelli's *on* switch and listened carefully to the rolling grind of its metal teeth before saying, "Watch me. The key is to keep the rhythm slow and steady." She dug the pitchfork into a pile of grapes and lifted it above the Zambelli's funnel, turning it slowly so the grape bunches didn't all fall at the same time. Again and again, six repetitions, steady and unhurried. She looked at Sam, who nodded. "If you go faster, it'll jam."

"Let me try," he said. He repeated what he'd seen, mimicking her speed perfectly. She gave him a thumbs-up, and he set to work.

Relieved, she climbed down and rubbed her arms and shoulders, trying to warm and loosen her muscles. Three minutes of pitchforking grapes into the Zambelli reminded her how little she used her upper body. If she were the only one who could relieve Sam when he needed a break, they were in trouble. Where the hell was Wolf? Surely he'd heard the weather forecast?

She ducked into the fermenting room to check that the must was flowing. A black hose, four inches in diameter, snaked through a hatch in the east wall and dropped into a fermenting vat. From the end of the hose spewed rich purple must. She tried to estimate how long it would take for that vat to fill, at which point she would have to move the hose to the next vat. Fifteen minutes, maybe twenty.

One thing left to do. She scanned the room and spotted what she needed: waterproof cards and marker pens. On a card she wrote, *King City Carignan* and the date, then slid it into a holder on the side of the vat that was filling.

As she stepped outside, a man's voice shouted above the noise of the crusher. "Noli! Here!"

She turned to see Wolf standing some ten feet away, waving at her.

CHAPTER FORTY-FIVE

"Man, you are a welcome sight!" Noli started toward him, but he held out a hand to stop her.

"I've been skunked."

"Where have you been?" The words were out of her mouth before she had time to think. "Sorry. I'm on edge. You heard the forecast? Rain this afternoon."

Wolf pointed to Sam feeding the crusher. "Where's Peter?"

Shit. There was so much to fill him in on, and no time to spare. "Tina had an accident. She's in the hospital, and Peter's with her. I'll fill you in later. Take over from Sam?"

His face clouded with concern. "Is Tina okay?"

"We don't know. Her wheelchair went over the cliff on her way back from Annika's. She hit her head. She's in an induced coma, at least until tomorrow."

"Jesus." Wolf shook his head, trying to take in the news. "I'll run the crusher, no problem. But let me tell you what I've found."

Turning to check the crusher, seeing that the refuse bin beneath it was overflowing with stems, she said, "Can't it wait?"

Wolf followed her gaze. "You dump the stems. I'll swap out the empty crates so Sam doesn't have to stop feeding the crusher. Then give me ten minutes. I guarantee you want to hear this."

She nodded assent and strode up the slope to the crusher. Beneath it, broken grape stems—the refuse left over after the machine pulled the grapes free—spewed into a plastic crate. She pulled the overfilled crate out and pushed an empty crate into its place.

Now the hard part. The filled crate was heavy, and she had to carry it down the slope and dump it into a trailer. She lifted carefully, bending her knees to get power from her legs, but still her shoulder muscles screamed. Resolving to enroll in a gym as soon as possible, she struggled downhill and tipped the crate over the side of a trailer, listening to the satisfying *thunk* of heavy stems hitting its wooden floor. When the trailer was full, it would be hauled out to the vineyard, where the stems would be strewn over the ground as compost.

Wolf led her up the path toward the domes, away from the noise of the crusher. Without remembering his earlier warning, she closed the gap between them. Not until she was close enough to touch him did her nose catch a whiff of rotten eggs.

He stopped at a fallen tree, turned, and was startled to find her so close.

Reading his expression, she said, "It isn't that bad."

He gave her a rueful smile. "Glad to hear it. Ryan scrubbed me till my skin nearly came off." He sat on the log and gestured for her to sit beside him. "Listen, Ryan's helping me on the condition that no one knows what we've found until he's got everything confirmed and has taken it to his adviser. But I told him I absolutely had to tell *you*."

"All right."

His brows knit as he looked at her more closely. "You're all scraped up."

"Tina landed in a huge patch of poison oak. I cleared the oak so the paramedics could reach her. And now I'm wired on prednisone."

"Shouldn't you be resting?"

She shook her head. "Even if we weren't harvesting, I couldn't sit still. Prednisone's like drinking twenty cups of coffee."

"Be careful, then. You shouldn't be operating equipment today."

"Now that you're here, I won't have to."

Wolf's brow furrowed as he described the evidence Ryan found, and why they thought the Hanaks' clone had been stolen.

"So that means—"

"Wait! There's more. I spent last night in Four Friends' pinot noir vineyard, which is run by a guy named Oliver Wickam. He was a grad student at the Zinfandel Clone Project when the Hanaks' vines disappeared. And amongst his pinot vines, I found a couple of acres of head-trained zinfandel vines. I took samples. Today Ryan will be comparing them to the Hanaks' clone."

"You think that Wickam stole the Hanaks' vines and has been growing and replicating them?"

"Yes."

"But we have no proof."

"Also true."

Noli considered for a moment, then asked, "Where did Wickam's money come from? Unless he's independently wealthy, he needed investors to set up a vineyard and winery. I recognize the Four Friends label—it's excellent pinot."

"Four Friends is a partnership; Wickam is the managing partner. Three additional partners are listed, and Ryan gave the names to Irv yesterday. Whether Wickam's investors know about the zinfandel clone is another question."

"How can we prove he stole the clone from the Project?" Noli asked.

Wolf shook his head. "Ryan's thinking about that. It'd be up to the Project's director to decide whether to take Wickam to court. The problem is, Wickam could destroy the evidence before we could get legal access to Four Friends' vineyard."

"And before he destroyed the vines, he could store some cuttings with an accomplice somewhere, even plant a new vineyard under someone else's name, and we couldn't prove a thing," Noli said.

"That sums it up."

★ ★ ★

Returning to the warmth of the old dome, Noli poured herself a cup of coffee and ate two doughnuts before she dialed Irv on the landline. When he answered, he sounded excited.

"I've been looking into Arnant," Irv said. "He didn't just grow up here. He's got a strong background in wine. His grandmother's maiden name was Gautier, matching a well-regarded vineyard near Saint Emilion. And guess what? He was a high-school exchange student there. He was a chemistry major in college, and he wrote a couple of articles about French vineyards for a travel magazine before he graduated. In one of those articles, he talks about *his family's vineyards* near Saint Emilion. But then he went to law school, and we don't find another connection to wine until his law partnership bought Andolini."

"I wonder if his grandmother was Paolina's friend. And if she taught her grandson about wine."

"Bingo," said Irv. "Why don't you ask him?"

"I will." Noli's thoughts turned to Daniel's harvest dinner. His support for Peter. His efforts to convince his partners to improve Andolini's wine. Was it just a waiting game, keeping himself in position to grab Old Marco's Hill when the time was right?

Irv interrupted her thoughts with, "Wolf asked us to look into the managing partner of Four Friends Winery. Is he around?"

"He's running the crusher. I'll pass it on."

"Got something to write with?"

She opened the cabinet drawer beneath the landline, fished out a pen and scrap paper. "Ready."

"Four Friends is owned by a limited partnership of four entities. Oliver Wickam; Mary Ellen Foremaken, who turns out to be his sister; Allison Giannopoulos; and a private equity firm called Cal Vin. Manager of Cal Vin is Maria Norton. Haven't cracked the investor list yet."

Norton? Not an unusual name, but if she were descended from the Nortons who knew Paolina... "See what you can find on Maria Norton, will you? Where'd she grow up, who were her parents? If it's her husband's name, same questions about him."

"One more item of interest," Irv said. "The home office of Cal Vin is in the same Cupertino building as Varley's company headquarters."

"That's intriguing. I wonder if he's an investor with Cal Vin."

"We'll find out."

"Top priority, Irv." That would prove a link between Varley and the man who stole Hanak's clone from the research project. But she couldn't share that information with Irv.

It dawned on her that the work Irv had reported was more than he could conceivably have done by himself, even if he'd pulled an all-nighter. "Hey, Irv, I know you're a genius. But what you've brought me is more than any one person could track down in less than twenty-four hours."

"I had help from The Wizards. My hacking crew." Then, anticipating her next question, he added, "No worries. We worked for Fitz. Sworn to secrecy, always."

Thinking she couldn't afford to question Irv's methods at this point, she said, "I'll call you around six, okay?"

"Uh, maybe tomorrow?" He cleared his throat. Suddenly sounding nervous, he said, "Luz called. Varley's going out on a dinner date tonight. I'm going to hack his computers."

★ ★ ★

1 p.m.

The storm was closing in, turning day to night. Noli stepped into the winery and turned the floodlights on. As she headed back to the crusher to confer with Wolf, the first wave of rain swept across the tarp roof they'd created to protect the Zambelli. She signaled Wolf to stop feeding the crusher, then cut the power. As the machine ground to a halt, Sam roared up on an ATV, pulling a trailer loaded with crates of harvested grapes.

She asked Sam, "Where are we with the harvest?"

"Old Marco's Hill is finished. Only sixty, maybe seventy percent of the main vineyard."

Could they save the unharvested grapes? She knew that zinfandel grape clusters were among the tightest of any of the grape varietals. That meant when a cluster got wet, mildew could blossom in its interior in mere hours. She turned to Wolf. "What do we do?"

Wolf didn't hesitate. "We'll try to save the rest. Stop crushing, for now. All hands work to harvest the remaining grapes. Then we'll crush them first to head off the mildew. No promises, but it could work."

CHAPTER FORTY-SIX

Thursday, 5 p.m.

Irv Shoenstein stowed his car in a brushy turnout on the road to Varley's mansion. He hauled his equipment case from the trunk, tucked it under his poncho, and trudged through the pouring rain to Varley's driveway. Luz had mapped a route to Varley's office that would avoid detection by the security cameras. Hard enough in good weather; as it was, he found himself sliding uphill and down, through mud and brush, around the far edge of the property. A final dash across open ground brought him to a door on the east arm of the mansion.

Luz was waiting for him. "Good job. I watched the cameras. Even if Varley decides to examine the recording, he won't see you." She handed him towels and a steaming cup of coffee.

"How much time do we have?" he asked.

"Varley's on a date. Early movie, then dinner. Any woman in her right mind would cut out before dessert, so don't count on working past seven thirty."

Irv let out a long whistle. "That might not be enough. It'll depend on what kind of security he's got."

"Do what you can, and leave enough time to cover your tracks." She didn't want to take any chances that might result in trouble for Consuela.

"Right," Irv said. He seated himself in front of Varley's computer and began pulling devices and cables from his briefcase.

"I think his passwords are in that notebook." Luz pointed to a black pocket-sized notebook on the desktop.

Irv opened it and scanned a couple of pages. "Yes." With his phone, he snapped photos of each page.

Luz climbed the library ladder and emptied half a shelf of books into a sack, then carried them down and stacked them on the conference table. *Santa Cruz Remembered, The History of Highway 17, Santa Cruz Trails.* The titles were a surprise; she hadn't expected Varley to care about local history.

She tested one book, running her finger over the top, and found a satisfying layer of dust. Odd that Varley didn't let Consuela touch his books, as nutty as he was about dust everywhere else in the house. In any case, the heavy dust gave her a good excuse for progressing slowly.

"Varley's just as paranoid in cyberspace as he is at home," Irv said. "I can get you his email and copy his hard drives, but I don't know about setting up real-time surveillance."

"Copy his email first. Raul wants it ASAP."

Over the next hour, Luz climbed the ladder again and again, listening for a chime that would indicate a vehicle passing through the gates.

"Varley's got three email accounts, all copied," Irv announced. "Now the hard drives. You should check the file drawers for additional hard drives."

"Right."

There were only four file drawers. Varley hadn't locked them. In a bottom drawer, she found a laptop, a cell phone, and two external hard drives. These she handed to Irv, who whistled. "Wanna bet the good stuff is on these?"

By eight o'clock, feeling they were operating on borrowed time, Luz cast an anxious eye at Irv, who was still working full speed. She had dusted and replaced several shelves' worth of books and stacked the library table with more books. To Varley's eye, it should be clear that the cleaning project would require more time.

She had photographed the tabs of all the files in the file drawers; it appeared they all dealt either with his house, his new winery, or with personal issues like insurance and car-repair records. When Raul reviewed them, he could tell her if any of the files should be opened and copied. She'd found Varley's business checkbook and snapped photos of every page. The register went only back to June, but that might be enough. Would you pay an assassin with a check? Sure. There'd be a legitimate-looking title for the guy's "business."

Thinking that if Varley's date had ditched him after dinner, he could be home any moment, she said, "Wind it down, Irv."

"Almost through with the laptop. Still have two hard drives to go."

"He could walk through that door any minute."

"I can't work any faster, Luz."

The gate alarm chimed. She ran to the desk.

Irv looked at the monitor and said, "Holy shit! That's an Aston Martin DB5." Stunned with admiration, he didn't move.

"It's him!" Luz said. "Shut it down!"

"But—"

"You have ninety seconds! My apartment. Go!" She threw his tools and cables into his canvas bag.

"But he'll know—"

"Leave it to me. Stay put unless you hear me scream, understand?"

With his laptop in one hand and sack in the other, Irv ran.

Always have a Plan B; that's what Fitz had taught her.

She hid the camera among her cleaning rags, then yanked the dust scarf from her head. She unpinned her hair and, with a shake of her head, sent it cascading over her shoulders. She removed the fake glasses and, with a wet rag, wiped the thick foundation from her face. She removed her apron and unbuttoned the top of her blouse, enough to give Varley an eyeful. After Varley had left for the evening, she'd removed the cotton wrapping that hid her figure in case Plan B had to be put in place.

She'd no sooner remounted the ladder than the outside door flew open, and Varley stomped in. "Christ on a stick, what a fuck-up." He stripped off his sopping leather jacket and dropped it on the floor, then kicked his wet loafers halfway across the room. "Fucking shoes are wrecked. Throw 'em in the garbage." He had yet to look at her.

"Señor Varley, I may bring something?" she said, stepping down from the ladder and picking up his shoes. "There is wine. Or perhaps whiskey?"

"Just go a—" He looked up. Blinked. Studied her with the bleary-eyed confusion of someone who knew he'd drunk too much to trust what he saw. "Coffee. I need coffee. You too. Two cups."

"Yes, Señor Varley."

In the kitchen, she pressed the switch on the electric kettle, ground a handful of decaf coffee beans, and set a paper filter in the Melita drip pot. Surely he was too drunk to notice it was decaf? She added a small measure of regular grounds to strengthen the taste.

On the counter stood a bottle of red wine from which Varley had drunk a single glassful before leaving for his date. She added it to the tray, along with a clean wine glass.

When she reentered Varley's office, he was slumped in his desk chair, cell phone glued to his ear. Without pausing, she carried the tray to his desk and set it in front of him.

Ignoring her, Varley spoke into the phone. "Fuck, Wickam, quit sniveling. Exactly what did he say?"

Quickly, Luz poured a cup of coffee and added cream. If he reached for the computer, she'd "accidentally" tip the cup onto the keyboard as she handed it to him.

"Pull your pathetic head out of your ass. They can't prove anything." He dropped into his swivel chair and picked up a pen. "Shit, you're telling me this *now*?" Varley reached for his computer's *on* button, changed his mind, and scribbled on a yellow pad.

Luz lifted the brimming cup, ready to launch it.

Varley waved her away. "Anything else I should know?"

Luz hesitated, pretending his signal hadn't been clear.

"Tomorrow." Varley ended the call. He reached for his computer's power button.

"Señor?"

He looked at her. His lips twisted from a snarl to a slimy smile. "Ah, Alma. What a sly little fox you are, hiding behind those big glasses. Bring the coffee, join me." He pointed to the coffee table. His words were still slurred, but the phone call had pumped him awake.

He slid onto a couch. She bent from the waist, slowly arranging mugs of coffee, pots of cream and sugar, spoons, napkins, wine bottle, and goblet on the table while he stared. She filled his wine glass. He ignored it. She picked up the creamed coffee and held it out to him. "Señor Varley, you like cream, no?"

Varley accepted the cup and sipped. "You're a real sweetheart, know that? I could use someone like you to look after me."

"Oh, Señor, Consuela know so much more. I—"

"Aw, don't worry. I'd never fire Consuela. I mean, I could use you both. Plenty to do here, and the old gal's not getting any younger."

"I am honored, Señor, but I—"

"Just think about it, okay? Right now, we're going to get

to know each other a little better." He stood, unsteady on his feet, and gallantly pulled an armchair up to the coffee table, opposite the couch. "You sit down. Rest." He glanced at the clock. "Shit, you're gonna have to charge me overtime." Pause. "Just a joke. I mean, I appreciate how late you've been working. Now, time for a reward." He handed her the goblet of red wine. She put it down.

"Thank you, Señor, but the red wine does not agree with me. Please, you should enjoy." She pushed the glass to his side of the table.

"Don't you worry your pretty little head. I got somethin' better." He staggered to his desk, opened a drawer, and pulled out a cut-glass bottle and two brandy snifters. "Bet you never tasted anything like this." He unstoppered the bottle and tilted it. An amber liquid cascaded into one snifter, then the other. "Cognac, the king of spirits. You'll like it."

She raised her snifter, hoping to encourage him. "¡Salud!" The more Varley drank, the better her chances.

Varley clinked his snifter with hers. "May your beauty never fade!"

Luz sipped carefully. "¡Maravilloso! Like nothing I taste before."

Varley took a substantial slug, then set his snifter down. "Very, very expensive. So, tell me about yourself. How long have you been working as a maid?"

"Seven years, Señor."

"You live with your family?"

"Sí, Señor. Mi Papá, two brothers, one sister."

"Your mother?"

"She die many years ago."

"I'm sorry."

She nodded and pretended to sip more cognac, hoping Varley would also drink. But he focused on her, surveying her body, her face, her hair.

"You're very beautiful, you know. A girl like you could go far." He knit his brows into a serious expression and—*¡gracias a Dios!*—picked up his snifter, drank it down, and poured himself more. "Did you go to school?"

"I have two years of high school, Señor Varley. I wish to go to college, but after my mother die, this is not possible."

Smiling and snapping his fingers, Varley said, "I knew it. A smart, ambitious girl." He drank more cognac, then patted the couch next to him. "Come sit over here and tell me about school."

She dropped her eyes in embarrassment. "You are an educated man. This cannot be of interest to someone like you."

Varley's chest swelled. "We'll see 'bout that," he slurred. "Come on over here."

She looked up at him through her long eyelashes. And burst into tears.

Between her fingers, she watched Varley. At first, he seemed too startled to speak. Then he extended a hand across the coffee table and squeezed her knee gently, saying, "Now, whas the problem? I'll... make it better."

Luz looked up. "Señor Varley, you are so kind. I must be honest. There is a reason I am here. Consuela does not know this, so do not be angry with her."

Varley's eyes narrowed. "Reason?"

"A bad man is looking for me. To kill me. I hide here to protect my family."

Retrieving his hand, Varley tried to straighten into a dignified posture. Again patting the couch beside himself, he said, "Tell me."

She moved to the couch. He poured himself a new round of cognac, splashed more into her snifter, and pushed it toward her. "You just take a big ol' drink of that." She took one swallow, watching his eyes. Yes, he was drunk. But in the pale blue of his irises were chips of emerald green she'd never noticed before. Marks of greed. And duplicity. Her mother had warned her of *coyotl,* the shape-shifter coyote who took the appearance of a man. He stopped at nothing to get what he wanted.

For the first time, she was afraid.

Varley quaffed his cognac in a single gulp and refilled his snifter. "Why's this guy wanna hurt you?"

"I am witness. I saw him kill a man."

"And why'd he do that?"

"I do not know. He is—how you say? For the *jefe*, he is the gun man," Luz said.

"The enforcer."

"I do not know this word."

"He kills anyone his ... *jefe*... tells him to," Varley explained.

Luz sobbed. "*Sí.* There is no hope for me."

Varley grasped her hand. She could tell he was having difficulty focusing on her face. Another hit of cognac might lay him out. He said, "I have friends... acquaintances, you might say. I'll take care of this... problem." His speech grew more slurred, and now he seemed to have difficulty finding words. "Just tell me... who this guy is. Where we... you know... can find him."

Luz sniffled. "You can do that?"

"Bet... your sweet pa... pa... patootie."

She kicked herself for not planning how she could trap Varley into revealing his hit man. For now, all she could do was evade his advances without offending him. Tomorrow, she would think of something.

A long, long story might put him to sleep. "It started when I was only ten years old," she began. "We lived in Watsonville. My mother was very sick, and we did not know why..."

CHAPTER FORTY-SEVEN

All through the drizzly night, Sam, Wolf, and Noli had taken turns operating the Zambelli. Now, Noli insisted they stop and fuel up.

Sam headed for the new dome, calling behind him that he would cook breakfast. Wolf asked for use of the landline, so he could check in with Ryan. Noli headed for the old dome, planning to lie down for however many minutes she could grab. There wasn't a single muscle in her body that didn't hurt. She managed to haul herself up the spiral stairs and collapse on the bed, where she closed her eyes and listened. Steller's jays screeched at one another. A woodpecker hammered on a distant snag. And beneath these sounds: silence. A deep, soothing silence. She tried to relax. Her thoughts went to Tina. Was it today the doctors would take her off sedation? No. At least one day more.

Lying down had been a mistake. She was never going to relax. She shifted her legs over the side of the bed. Large patches on her legs and arms were starting to itch—not a good sign. Her legs stuck out straight, as if she was a doll without joints. Leaning forward, she ignored the objection of her shoulder muscles and massaged her calves and thighs. Ultimately, she descended the spiral staircase on her butt, thumping down one step at a time.

All her senses were on hyperalert, as though a predator lurked in the brush, just out of sight. She told herself it was the expected impact of the prednisone. She'd get over it. At the same time, she felt weirdly elated. For the first time in years, she felt she was where she belonged. Yesterday she'd pushed her body to the limit; most, if not all, of the harvest had been saved.

She thought of Fitz's letter, asking her to take over his practice. It was meaningful work, work she'd be proud of. And she was good at it. Maybe Luz would stay on. Luz had the makings of a good investigator, if they could just inject her with a bit of caution. Fitz had hired Luz, and he'd had a way of seeing right to the core of a person.

Thinking of Fitz, sadness returned. Murdered just when he was about to live a new dream with Pilar. Planting a vineyard. Transforming an old barn into a home.

She walked in circles inside the dome, windmilling her arms. The crush wasn't finished, and she couldn't afford to let her muscles seize up. Slowly, an idea took shape, an idea of a home for herself. When Pilar returned from Mexico, they could meet and talk about Pilar's plans. If Pilar did not want to live in the Andolini Valley without Fitz, maybe Noli herself could buy the barn. Then the Hanaks would have some of the money they needed, and she could have a home of her own. The thought of remodeling the barn was exciting. And she'd be nearby to help Peter and Tina.

She could swing it, financially. The sale of her Dublin condo would more than cover the cost, leaving enough money saved for five years of Gwen's residential treatment. The possibilities filled her with new energy. She grabbed her jacket and crossed the deck to the new dome. Wolf sat alone at the table, eating hungrily.

She served herself a stack of pancakes. "Where's Sam?"

"He had to leave," Wolf replied. "Something went wrong at his construction site in Gilroy." Wolf paused to refill his coffee mug. "Listen, there's important news from Ryan. His lab friends confirmed that Wickam's zinfandel vines at the Four Friends Vineyards and Winery are identical to the Hanaks' clone on Old Marco's Hill."

"So, it's official. Wickam's a thief. Can we prove it?"

Wolf looked worried. "I haven't figured that out yet. Meanwhile, Ryan's deeply upset. He's thinking the entire research project is compromised, and he's worried he'll have to throw out his dissertation and start over."

"Do you agree?"

"No. Near as I can tell, the theft and cover-up were limited to the Hanaks' clone. Ryan's getting up the courage to tell his advisor, who is also the director of the Zinfandel Clone Project. He wants me to go with him."

"When?"

"I told him I couldn't come until tomorrow. I won't leave until we finish the crush. And I want to get the fermenting started. Can you manage on your own tomorrow evening?"

CHAPTER FORTY-EIGHT

For Noli, Friday passed in an exhausted blur while she worked side by side with Wolf. Peter had come and gone, staying only as long as it took him to shower, change clothes, and listen to Wolf's report on the harvest. There was no news on Tina, who remained in a coma.

Today, as he prepared to leave, Wolf gave Noli a tour of the fermenting vats, repeating instructions on how each vat was to be handled. He handed her the key to a padlock he'd installed on the winery door. "Keep it locked, Noli. I'm serious. Given what happened to the last two vintages, we can't take any chances. Call if you have questions."

She watched Wolf's truck vanish down the driveway, headed for Sacramento. She hoped he and Ryan, perhaps with help from the research project's director, would come up with a way to charge Oliver Wickam with a crime.

She had a plan for the afternoon, but first she should check with Irv. He'd had thirty-six hours to dive into whatever data he'd been able to copy at Varley's office.

He answered on the first ring.

"Hi Irv. Any news?"

"Not yet. We have the contents of Varley's desktop, laptop, one of two external hard drives, and photos of the weird map on his wall. This morning I've been trying to hack the records for an extra cell we found in his file cabinets, but I haven't broken through yet."

"How's Luz?"

"She's a fucking genius, you know? Varley came home while we were still working. He made a play for her. She just told him some endless story while he got so drunk, he fell asleep. Gave me a chance to cover my tracks before I left."

Thinking the story ploy wasn't likely to work again, Noli asked, "How much longer is she going to be there?"

Sounding uncertain, Irv said, "Didn't she commit to a week?"

Three more nights. Well, unless Varley drugged her, Luz could take him down if she needed to. Noli couldn't help smiling, imagining Varley flying through the air and landing flat on his back as Luz flipped him. On the other hand, three days and nights was a long time to deflect someone bent on seduction. Or rape.

"Could you use an extra pair of hands?" she asked.

"No, we're fully staffed. Raul's taken time off from work to help me. I think he's feeling guilty about sending Luz into the lion's den. And Munch is here. Plus, I've got help from two of my Wizards."

"All right. I'll check back in the morning."

She knew what she wanted to do. She had six hours before the fermenting vats had to be tended again. The thought of leaving the property in the meanwhile made her nervous, but truly, with the winery locked up, there shouldn't be any problems. She gathered a few items into a backpack: water bottle, rain slicker, and the bamboo handle to Tina's treasured Gwendolyn Cooper teapot, the one which had slipped from her fingers and smashed. When Tina came home—and she *would* come home!—there would be a new teapot under that handle, a teapot she would find today in Gwen's workshop.

All day, in the back of her mind, she'd been mulling over Fitz's last day of life. Something had happened that Wednesday morning, before he left the mountain to go sailing, that had caused him to think of her father. Something so significant, he left her a message. What was it? Thanks to Irv's hack of Fitz's phone records, they knew he hadn't received a phone call that morning, so that wasn't the answer. Was there something here on the mountain? Today she intended to retrace Fitz's steps more carefully.

And she was going to visit her father. She wasn't superstitious, didn't believe in communication from beyond death. She just wanted to talk to him.

Last, but not least, she intended to go into the old barn. As unlikely as it seemed, perhaps the link to her father lay there. Tina said he'd loved the old apple orchard, had wanted to save it. Maybe he'd left something in the cider barn. Besides, if the barn was to be her new home, it was time to look inside. She sorted through the keys she'd taken from Fitz's Woody and pocketed the only three which could possibly belong to the barn's padlock.

Even under a gray sky, the vineyard was beautiful, the tattered leaves still arrayed in red and gold, now sparkling with raindrops. The storm had filled the ruts and potholes of Andolini Road with puddles; avoiding the puddles meant clomping through mud that gripped her boots at every step.

Beyond the vineyard came the cliff where Tina had fallen; Noli resisted the urge to peer over the edge. Turning onto Norton Road, she passed the Vandermeis home, which seemed even larger than it had at a distance. Were they planning to start a family? Or would they host "country weekends" for Preston's business acquaintances? Annika certainly wasn't the type to run a bed-and-breakfast.

Farther south, she spied Wolf's yurt. A generation after Peter and Tina brought their dream to the Andolini Valley, Wolf was bringing his. She wondered when he would have enough savings to plant a vineyard of his own.

Just before a bridge over the arroyo, a small green sign saying *Mt. Charlie Trail Access* pointed to a footpath that skirted the Vandermeis property. A wooden fence separated the path from their land—the fence was eight feet high, obviously new. Noli peered through a gap between the boards—the Vandermeis land was cleared and leveled, ready for vines. Annika and Preston had lived there nearly three years. Why had they waited so long to plant? Perhaps they planned to wait for the results of the Zinfandel Clone Project. Or they'd spent so much money remodeling and building a winery, they couldn't afford to plant a vineyard at the same time.

She could see the half-built winery, where roofers were hammering shingles. The winery was even bigger than their mansion, so they must have big plans for their debut on the California wine scene.

She came to the end of the Vandermeis fence and plunged into a mixed-growth forest, passing a small wooden boundary sign announcing, *Loma Buena State Park*. A few more steps brought her to Mt. Charlie Trail. Pushing on, relieved to have the trail to herself, her mind eased into something like a meditation. Her muscles warmed, and her body found the rhythm of her youthful cross-country walks with her father. She was lifted out of time. From the corner of her eye, she imagined her father moving alongside in easy companionship. This was their time together, their escape from Gwen's unpredictable moods. They discussed her classes, her boyfriends, his teaching, their favorite books, conflicts in the commune. Only two topics were avoided: Gwen's mental health and her father's experiences in the Vietnam War. Because he had been raised a Quaker, his status as a conscientious objector had been accepted. But he had been sent to Vietnam nonetheless, trained as a medic rather than a soldier.

Once, when a veteran in the commune committed suicide, her father had talked about the "injury to one's soul" that killing another human being might inflict. She often wondered whether, under fire, he had shouldered a rifle and killed enemy soldiers to save his injured comrades. But to ask would have been to cross a line she saw as clearly as if it were painted on the ground in front of her.

When she reached a sharp dogleg in the trail, she stopped. A trail marker pointed to the right, saying *Bay to Beach Trail, 7.8 miles.* However, straight ahead, barely discernible in twenty years of overgrowth, lay the remains of the old trail her father had followed the day of the Loma Prieta earthquake. That trail that would take her to his grave.

At first it was slow going, plowing through undergrowth, but then she came to open, rocky ground. She strode along, trying to ignore a mounting anxiety that set her stomach roiling. She tripped over a tree root, lost her balance, and fell face down in the dirt. The dust-and-resin scent blasted her mind, overwhelming it with memories. Flashlight beams crisscrossed the darkness. Rescue workers with teams of bloodhounds raced across the ravaged landscape. She scrambled over fallen trees and loose boulders, trying to keep up. Aftershocks threatened to pull the earth from beneath their feet. Terrifying howls issued from dogs every time they picked up a scent. Confusion, darkness, searchlights. Despair.

She scrambled to her feet, dragged her mind back to the present, and brushed the soil from her face.

Walking slowly now, choosing her footing, she approached a landslide that began high on the mountain and flowed as far as the eye could see. A historical marker read:

Mud Slide, 23.7 acres

Loma Prieta Earthquake

October 17, 1989

On the edge of the slide, nearly obscured by brush, a sandstone shelf offered a natural resting place. She scrambled up and surveyed the slide. In the months after the quake, it had resembled a mound of ripped and diseased flesh. Now it hosted new life. Grasses, parched golden-brown over the summer, disguised the churn of clay and limestone beneath. Here and there, madrone and oak saplings hinted at the beginnings of a new forest.

She couldn't help wondering where her father's body lay. How far down the mountain had the wall of cascading earth carried him? Had he died quickly, or had the enveloping earth cocooned him, suffocating him slowly?

She closed her eyes and opened her heart, imagining she could feel his presence. The midday sun was warm on her head and shoulders. Brush birds resumed their chatter.

I'm in trouble, Dad. Tina's in a coma. Peter's breaking down. Someone's trying to ruin them. Fitz is dead—murdered—and I don't know why. Fitz wanted to tell me something about you, but he never got the chance. What is it, Dad? What do I need to know?

CHAPTER FORTY-NINE

Returning from the commune, Noli stayed on the new trail. The visit to her father's grave had been a comfort, but she felt no need to return there. No answers to her questions had echoed from beyond, but she felt calmer. Ready for whatever was coming.

In her backpack she carried a perfect new teapot for Tina.

When she reached the old barn, she pulled three of Fitz's keys from her pocket. The first one she tried opened the padlock. Expecting the door's hardware to be rusty and difficult to slide, she grabbed the handle and pushed with all her strength, nearly falling on her face when the door slid easily.

One step inside, then she paused to allow her eyes to adjust to the dimness inside the barn. Her nose sounded the alarm.

Skunk!

She stepped back, her eyes searching the dim interior for a white-striped, pissed-off little critter. But as her vision adjusted, she saw only old farm equipment and broken furniture.

She sniffed again. Recalling the lingering scent on Wolf, she thought the sweet edge of skunk spray was missing. This was only sulfur and ammonia.

Cleaning fluids? Fertilizer? If no one had entered the barn in many years, why would either of those products still be around?

Looking more closely, she saw no boxes, cans, or sacks.

The barn floor was dirt. A narrow aisle led along the front wall, so she followed it, examining the piled junk as she went. Was there something here of significance to her father? A photo album? A memento, the importance of which was obvious to Fitz but lost to her?

If so, she was stumped. There were bedframes and bedsprings. Sideboards and credenzas too beat-up to qualify as valuable antiques. A white-enameled wood stove. Two old horse-drawn carts and a buggy.

She continued down the west wall, where a cleared corridor ran to the back of the barn. Realizing her examination of the junk pile was made possible by light from above, she craned her neck for a view of the ceiling. High in the back wall, below the apex of the roof, there was a large square opening that encased a four-paned window. One pane was missing, allowing fresh air into the barn.

As she drew closer to the rear, the odor of ammonia grew stronger.

Ten feet from the rear wall, the piles of junk ended abruptly, revealing a makeshift kitchen. Two parallel counters, constructed of old doors supported on trestles, ran the width of the barn's rear wall. Had this been Marco Andolini's cider factory?

Maybe. But now the facility had been outfitted for a more nefarious purpose. A propane-fueled cooktop sat on one counter, surrounded by pots, funnels, blenders, aluminum foil, glass beakers, spoons, and kitchen scales. On the other counter and on the floor sat containers labeled acetone, mineral spirits, isopropyl alcohol, Iso-HEET, fertilizer, battery acid, and more. Six powerful battery-operated lamps hung from regularly spaced framing nails above the counters. A blackout curtain hung from the loft and traversed the side of the kitchen facing the front of the barn.

A methamphetamine laboratory.

The plip-plop of a drip pulled her to the far end of the lab, where she found a sink and water faucet old enough to have been installed when the barn was still a cider factory. The water probably came from a spring; availability of water would explain why the barn had been built in that location.

Beyond the sink, low on the back wall, there was a hasp. She knelt to get a better look and spotted hinges. Someone had sawed through the wall and studs, creating a half-door that swung inward. On the ground beside the door rested a battery-operated fan.

A fan to disperse chemical fumes. When the lab was in operation, the heated chemicals would release dangerous gases. By placing the fan in front of the "back door," the lab operators brought in fresh air and sent the heated, poisonous air up toward the gaping window-hole. And if they were operating at night, they could open the sliding door enough to increase circulation without alerting anyone who happened to pass by.

All the lab's power came from batteries. The stoves used propane. No generators were required, so their work would be relatively quiet. If they worked at night, their chances of getting caught were minimal, for no one walked the dirt road at night. Nor would hikers be watching from the park's cliff trail up above. But wasn't the danger of explosion extreme when they worked with open flames?

She pulled out her phone and took photos of the lab and the storage containers. Then, as she exited the barn, she looked more closely at the front window. A rolled-up blackout shade had been mounted above it. A further precaution against light escaping. But if they did work at night, wouldn't some of the light escape from the high windows in the back wall, and play on the cliff behind? Wouldn't the Vandermeises notice?

And how did the lab workers bring in their supplies and send out their finished product? If there had been unfamiliar vehicles coming to the barn, especially at night, they would have passed either the Hanaks or the Vandermeises. Wouldn't someone have noticed?

On the other hand, it was a small-time operation. Maybe the operators came and went by foot, using Mt. Charlie Trail or the paths in the state park.

Returning to the front of the barn, she closed and locked the sliding door, feeling deeply disappointed. She'd hoped to find a connection to her father. Instead, she'd found a new problem for Peter and Tina.

Walking around the barn to the back, she could see a narrow path of beaten-down weeds leading in a more-or-less straight line toward the state park's cliff. No poison oak, so, raising her bare arms to protect them from scratches, she followed the path almost to the cliff. There, the trail veered away to the left and ran west for a considerable distance, maybe fifty yards, parallel to the base of the cliff.

From her childhood days of playing at the Hanaks', she knew there was a way into the state park at the end of the cliff. Had the meth lab operators carried their supplies—and their product—in and out through the park? There was a public parking lot not too far off Mt. Charlie Trail access, maybe a half-mile's walk. She could imagine them carrying meth out in backpacks, looking like hikers.

Fitz's call to Peter on Wednesday morning was now explained. The discovery of a meth lab on the Hanaks' land was a delicate situation. By law, the Hanaks were liable for a drug lab on their property, even if they had no knowledge of it.

The last thing Peter needed right now was another problem. She decided that, since Fitz had scared the lab operators away, she'd wait to tell Peter until Tina recovered.

Returning to Andolini Road, she looked across the valley to Varley's imposing mansion. On an impulse, she dialed Luz's number. After one ring, she was sent to voicemail. "Luz, hope you are okay. Remember, you can leave anytime. Be safe, please."

6 p.m.

When Noli reached the domes, she shed her hiking clothes and stepped into a pair of Peter's stained denim overalls. Discovery of the meth lab was deeply worrying, and she struggled to push it out of her mind. At this moment, all her energy needed to be focused on the winery. The success of Peter's '09 vintage was on her shoulders. She would get this right.

Entering the winery, she took a deep breath of the damp, fruity atmosphere and surveyed the vats. She worked her hands into Peter's stiff, purple-stained gloves, reviewing Wolf's instructions.

Every four to six hours, a hard shell of grape skins and stems called a "cap" formed atop the must. The cap—a product of the fermenting process—had to be pressed until it was fully submerged. Otherwise, the cap would become so dense, it would cut off fermentation in the must below. Potential disaster. It was very, very difficult to restart fermentation when this happened.

She grasped the pressing pole, a long wooden dowel attached to a disk of heavy wire mesh, and lifted the mesh over the rim of the first vat. Positioning the wire mesh atop the cap, she took a deep breath, tightened her grip on the dowel, and pushed with the full weight of her body. Her feet nearly lifted off the ground.

At first, there was no movement.

Then, slowly, juice bubbled up at the edges of the cap.

She summoned all her strength and pushed harder. Trickles of juice flowed from the edges onto the cap. She continued, pressing with all her might. Slowly, slowly, the cap sank into the must. When the cap hit bottom, she hauled the wire mesh out, leaned the pole against the railing and shook her trembling arms.

She became aware of the exhaust fan, placed low in the north wall. *Whirr-screech-whirr. Whirr-screech-whirr.* The "screech" part was louder than it had been yesterday. If the fan broke, the concentration of carbon dioxide in the winery's air, a byproduct of grape fermentation, could become life-threatening. There were open windows high in the adjacent wall, but they could not provide sufficient circulation to move the heavy carbon dioxide out of the winery. Peter must have made a backup plan for ventilation if the old fan gave out, and she made a mental note to ask him next time they talked.

She moved on to the next vat. Three more, then her shoulder muscles cramped in full rebellion. She paced while circling her arms. Back and forth. Back and forth. She read the index cards that displayed crucial information on each vat: the varietal, its source, the day it was crushed, the day it was sterilized, the day yeast was added and the type of yeast. She made a game of shouting the first line of each card as she passed.

"Hanak Zinfandel, Lower Vineyard!"

"King City Zinfandel!"

"Zinfandel, Old Marco's Hill!" That card had no entry under "Yeast" and was marked with a red star. It and its two neighbors were the vats Peter had been most concerned about. They were his and Wolf's big experiment, their attempt to replicate the wine Paolina Andolini had made, a zinfandel that would age successfully for decades. Unlike the other vats, where the must had been sterilized and then inoculated with a commercial yeast, these vats were fermenting on "field yeast," the yeast that flourished naturally on Old Marco's Hill. She leaned over the vat and inhaled. The aroma was redolent of ripe grapes. The surface was bubbling with released carbon dioxide. It was fermenting well.

She checked the other unsterilized vats; they also were doing well. She'd have a good report for Peter on their next call.

CHAPTER FIFTY

Sunday 7 a.m.

Having finished the early round of pressing caps, Noli locked the winery. Raz danced and barked, urging her up the path to the domes. Someone had arrived, and Noli hoped it was Sam.

Coming down to the winery at midnight to press the caps, even with Raz by her side, had been daunting. She'd imagined someone knocking her over the head and poisoning the fermenting vats while she was out cold. This, she told herself, was ridiculous. Besides, if anyone had been lurking in the shadows, Raz would have sounded the alarm.

Still, she would be glad for a helping hand.

Raz surged ahead. When she reached the domes, it was Peter who awaited her. His face was ashen.

"Tina?"

"No change," he said. "The doctors remain hopeful. Where are Wolf and Sam?"

She explained and reassured him she was handling the vats by herself. No problem.

"I don't like that you're alone," he said.

"Everything's under control," she insisted. "The winery's securely locked. I'm locking the domes at night. No sign of trouble." *No new graffiti. No attack on the winery. In the old barn, however...* "Wolf says you'll have a great vintage. So no worries here. When you bring Tina home, we'll have the biggest celebration ever."

Peter looked like he wanted to believe her. "A quick shower, a change of clothes, and I'm off."

She was peeling her borrowed overalls off her weary body when the landline rang.

"Noli? It's Irv. We have something you should see."

On her way to Fitz's office, Noli stopped to pick up sandwiches and drinks. As she entered the conference room, Irv proclaimed, "You're a goddess!" He and Raul each liberated an Italian meatball sandwich. She carried the last one to the far end of the conference table, where Munch was seated behind a computer monitor. She forced a smile to mask her alarm at his appearance. In just one week, he'd become an old man. Skin hung loosely on his cheekbones, and his tan seemed like a bad dye job. He gave her a smile and scribbled *Tina?*

"Stable. The doctors plan to wake her up tomorrow."

Irv said, "It's just the three of us now. I lost the Wizards to a previous commitment. Nonetheless, we've hit gold."

"Tell me you've found a smoking gun," she pleaded.

His effervescence dimmed for a moment, but recovered quickly. "Not exactly. But have a look at this." He handed her a printout. "Email from Oliver Wickam to Varley. Two days ago." It was a long email. Irv had highlighted one section in yellow:

Bottom line, the wine isn't behaving the way we hoped. No chance the wine is going to age well. I'm checking the terroir characteristics—maybe we missed something. Double check the yeast Hanak is using. Double check for possible blended additions from lower vineyard or elsewhere.

A conspiracy. Wolf had been right all along. Probably Varley planned to fill his own vineyard with the stolen clone, pretending he'd bought it from the Zinfandel Clone Project.

She reread the text, considering the implications. Wickam was having no luck with the clone. That would be a huge reassurance to Peter.

Secondly, it was clear they knew Andolini wine had aged spectacularly. How did Wickam and Varley know? Had Varley, like Arnant, grown up near the Andolini estate? Or had he or Wickam encountered a bottle of aged Andolini wine many years ago? However it happened, they had known early enough to plan the theft of the Hanak / Andolini vines from the Project.

"Email this to Wolf. Is there any mention of Fitz? Or hints that they're sabotaging the Hanaks?"

"Negative on both," Irv said. "But look at this. No doubt, Varley is Wickam's paymaster." He pointed to a chart he'd sketched out on butcher paper and taped to the wall. The partnership that owned Four Friends Vineyard and Winery was delineated there.

Oliver Wickam owned a twenty-percent share. Mary Ellen Foremaken, Wickam's sister, held ten percent. Allison Giannopoulos—the vet who'd worked with Wickam on the Zinfandel Clone Project when she was an undergraduate—held five percent.

That left a sixty-five-percent controlling interest in the hands of Cal Vin, a private equity firm. And somehow Irv had cracked the protective shell around that firm. Gary Varley was the primary investor. No surprise. More interesting was the fund's manager. Her name was Maria Norton. Irv had drawn a star next to her name.

Noli pointed to the star. "Is she related to the Nortons who lived next to the Andolini estate?"

"She's the granddaughter of the last Nortons to live there. She's our missing link. Wanna bet she heard about the aged Andolini wine from her grandparents? But there's more. Guess who was married to Gary Varley in the early '90s?"

"Maria. So they planned the theft together."

"Sure looks that way," Irv said. He waited while she studied the chart.

Noli took a photo of the chart with her phone, then said, "Great work, Irv. Anything else?"

"Yeah, check this out." He unfolded a taped, multipage reproduction of a Google map. "This is on the wall of Varley's office."

It was a satellite map of the Andolini Valley. Using various colors of marking pen, Varley had outlined the boundaries of each property: Andolini, Hanak, Vandermeis, Varley. Each property was subdivided in irregular polygons; each polygon was labeled with a set of symbols.

"Do the symbols mean anything to you?" Irv asked.

"No. We should send this to Wolf," Noli said. "But if I had to guess, I'd say they were soil analyses. I think Varley has surreptitiously collected all the data he needs to turn the Andolini Valley into his personal empire of vineyards."

Raul, who'd been looking over her shoulder, cleared his throat. "I have a request."

Noli turned to him.

"There's a hard drive at Varley's that Irv didn't have time to copy," Raul began. "It was labeled VTek LLC. That's Varley's company operating in Taiwan. It might have evidence linking Varley to the deaths of the reporters investigating his company. Or, better yet, it might explain the reason why those reporters were after him. Varley's going out this afternoon, probably just for three hours. Not enough time for Luz to bring the drive here, and it's too dangerous for Irv to sneak back into Varley's house. But Luz says she can bring the hard drive to the Hanaks' for Irv to copy. Can you be there?"

Turning to Irv, Noli asked, "Do you think this is a good idea?"

"I do," Irv said. "Low risk. Potentially, a big payoff."

"Not low risk for Luz," Noli said.

"Her idea," Irv countered.

Seeing no risk for the Hanaks, Noli exhaled a long breath and said, "What time?"

"Two o'clock," Raul answered.

"Then let's get moving," Noli said. "Anything else for me?"

"Yeah. It isn't pretty." Irv scrolled through a set of emails. "What's the name of the Hanaks' neighbors who bought the old Norton place?"

"Annika and Preston Vandermeis."

"Thought so. Take a look at this."

In an email addressed to Varley from "Your kitten around the corner," a woman's nude photo was accompanied by sexual proposals so graphic as to be almost comical.

"Is that Annika?" Irv asked.

"It is." Noli found herself feeling sorry for Annika. How desperate would a woman have to be to proposition a man like Varley?

Running a hand through his afro, Irv said, "What does she see in that jerk?"

After a moment's consideration, Noli offered, "Proximity. And who knows? Maybe Varley can be charming when it matters? He's rich enough to give her jewelry, which she seems to like. And having an affair is a sort of revenge on her uber-controlling husband."

Irv shook his head in wonder. "Through her, Varley's got a pipeline of information on Peter's every move."

Would Annika be protective of Peter's secrets for Tina's sake? Her friendship with Tina appeared to be authentic. Or was Annika completely in thrall to Varley?

CHAPTER FIFTY-ONE

"Where can I get a good view of Varley's driveway?" Luz asked. She was dressed in a maid's uniform, and her makeup rendered her unrecognizable. Once again, Noli marveled at Luz's talent for disguise.

"Follow me," Noli said.

"One moment. Can I leave this bag by the door?" Luz pointed to a sack of groceries she'd carried in, no explanation offered.

"Sure."

Leaving Irv at work at the Hanaks' kitchen table, copying the disk drive Luz brought, they stepped onto the deck. Taking in the two domes, Luz asked, "You grew up here?"

"When I was orphaned at fourteen, the Hanaks brought me to live with them there, in the old dome. The new dome was built a couple of years ago when multiple sclerosis crippled Tina Hanak's legs."

"Before that, the commune?"

"That's right. New Harmony. It's a few miles west of here."

Luz studied the two structures for a few moments. Perhaps she'd never seen geodesic domes before? Then she said, "Which way?"

Noli led her to the redwood bench atop Old Marco's Hill. The view across Andolini Valley offered a clear view of Varley's garage and parking area.

Luz sat and raised her binoculars. "Where's the land Fitz was buying?"

"Not visible from here. It's west of that ridge."

Scanning the valley, Luz said, "You know, Fitz loved the ocean so much, it surprised me when he said he was moving to the mountains. But now I understand. It's heaven up here."

Taking a seat beside Luz, Noli said, "Fitz would never want you to get hurt, right?"

Luz kept scanning, said nothing.

Noli tried a different approach. "Irv told me Varley tried to seduce you."

"He was stupid drunk."

"What happened the next day?"

"Nothing."

"Seriously?"

"Yes."

"I don't believe you."

Luz lowered her binoculars and turned to Noli. "That night, Varley came home before Irv had covered his tracks in the office. I had to distract him, so I removed my disguise. Fortunately, he was very drunk. So the next morning, when I greeted him looking like this"—she waved a hand across her face and padded body—"he probably thought he'd just imagined I was an attractive woman. Or he didn't remember anything from the night before. Whatever. He just blinked, shook his head, and told me what he wanted for breakfast."

Deciding she wasn't going to change Luz's mind, Noli took a deep breath and pointed out the Hanaks' red firehose locker. "Luz, if you have to escape on foot, aim for that red metal box. You'll find the easiest crossing through the arroyo that way."

"Good to know."

Noli rose and excused herself. She was five steps away when Luz shouted, "*Mierde*! Shit, shit, shit!"

Five sedans, led by Varley's Aston Martin, halted in unison in front of the mansion.

Dashing back to the domes, they found Irv was still working.

"How much longer?" Luz demanded.

Alarmed, Irv said, "Twenty minutes. What's happened?"

"Varley's back," Luz said. "Go ahead. Finish." She strode out the door.

His face ashen, Irv watched Luz leave. "What's she going to do?"

Noli's stomach clenched. "I don't know." She stepped outside, where Luz was pacing the deck. "Luz, can I help?"

Luz paused, shot her a look both stricken and angry. "No." She resumed pacing.

Exactly twenty minutes later, Irv called, "Finished."

Luz swept into the dome, lifted her bag of groceries, dumped the contents onto the counter, placed the disk drive in the bottom of bag and reloaded the groceries. Irv's distress was obvious. She placed a hand on his shoulder, saying, "It will be fine."

With arms wrapped around the grocery sack, she departed.

CHAPTER FIFTY-TWO

Sunday, 4 p.m.

Noli hobbled from the winery to the new dome, a gash in her thigh bleeding through the rip in her borrowed overalls. She located Tina's medical kit, stripped naked, climbed into the shower, soaped the injured thigh, and let the water flush it clean.

Should the wound be closed with stitches? Yes. But if she kept it clean, it would heal without them. There would be a scar, but one more scar hardly mattered.

She bandaged her thigh and borrowed a pair of shorts from Peter's closet. On the floor lay the pair of Peter's overalls she'd been wearing, ripped and bloody. She'd have to replace them, but that was a small price to pay. Of this she was certain: the protection of the denim had saved her a trip to the emergency room.

When she'd encountered a cap she couldn't budge, she'd jammed portable wooden stairs up against the vat and climbed up to get more leverage. She hadn't noticed the top step was split. Her shoe caught on the protruding wood, and as she fell, the stairs' splintered edge had ripped across her leg.

Lack of focus, that was the real problem. She was so damn worried about Luz, she could hardly concentrate on the wine vats. Luz had promised to text Irv as soon as she'd safely restored Varley's hard drive to its drawer. When would that be? Midnight? Tomorrow? Meanwhile, what if Varley looked and it was gone?

Forcing herself to deal with the problem at hand, Noli limped back to the old dome to finish dressing. Time to get back to the winery and finish pressing the caps. But if she didn't rest for a few minutes, she would drop. On the deck, she settled into a chair, closed her eyes, and listened to a lonesome bird. Raz nuzzled close, licked her hand in consolation, and curled up at her feet.

Her thoughts turned to the revelation of Annika's affair with Varley. Annika's sex life was her own business, but if Varley was using her to get privileged information on Peter's wine making, then they needed to know whether she was a willing accomplice or an unwitting dupe. Noli resolved to confront Annika as soon as she was done at the winery.

Raz's ears pricked up. Seconds later, Noli heard the rev of an engine as a vehicle charged up the hill and into the Hanaks' parking area. A steel-gray Range Rover lurched to a halt, and Preston Vandermeis stepped out. As he ascended the stairs, he called, "Is Annika here?" His suit was rumpled, tie loose. Purple circles beneath his dark eyes.

Raz stood and gave a low, warning growl. Noli grabbed the dog's collar, saying, "Whoa, girl. It's okay." To Preston, she said, "No. I haven't seen her."

Without waiting for an invitation, he dropped into the chair next to her. "Her car's at home, but I can't find her." He stared into space for a moment, then seemed to collect himself. Offering a hand to shake, he said, "You're the Hanaks' goddaughter, Noli, right?"

She shook his hand. "That's me."

"Annika told me what happened to Tina," he said. "How's she doing?"

"She's in a coma. We'll know more in a day or two."

"What a shitty accident." Preston rested his head against the chair and closed his eyes. The predatory-hawk energy he'd seemed to emit when he had come to the door of the Hanaks' dome, commanding Annika to come home, was utterly absent. Instead, here was a profoundly tired middle-aged man, who seemed somewhat at a loss.

When he didn't speak again, she wondered if he'd fallen asleep. After what must have been at least five minutes, he opened his eyes, shook his head, and said, "Sorry. Long flight from Taiwan." He took in her bandaged thigh and burn-scarred calves. "Are you all right?"

"Little accident in the winery. I'm fine." Realizing she had an opportunity to question him, she said, "Can I offer you some coffee?"

"That would be great. Thank you." His worn face broke into a smile.

Now she could see how handsome he must have been when young. Had Annika fallen for a charming man who, once they were married, showed himself to be an abusive, controlling bastard? Or was their relationship different from what Tina had assumed?

Preston followed Noli through the sliding doors into the kitchen.

She said, "It seems your business requires a lot of travel."

"I'm director of a start-up. We manufacture hard drives and other tech parts, in both Thailand and Taiwan. We hope to go public soon. Then I'll retire and be home with Annika." He ran a hand through his hair. "She doesn't... do well alone. I was so glad she found a friend in Tina."

While Noli filled the kettle and spooned coffee into the Melita drip funnel, he examined every detail of the dome. "Most efficient living space I've ever seen. Love the simplicity."

He sounded sincere. How did that fit with the mansion he called home? Was the remodel solely Annika's ambition?

He continued, "I really like living here. Annika seems happy, finally. Has she told you how many times we've moved? Baltimore, Austin, Phoenix. Me? I can work from anywhere. All I want is for her to be happy. Now she's crazy for wine making, learning everything we need to know. People don't realize it, but she's really smart." He paused, as though waiting for confirmation.

Noli turned to meet his gaze. "A wife who's beautiful and smart. You're a lucky man."

"I am."

Preston answered quickly, but his face betrayed uncertainty. And something else she couldn't identify. Did he suspect Annika's affair with Varley? Was her infidelity a pattern?

Noli poured boiling water over the coffee grounds, considering her next question. *Now she's crazy for wine making.* Was Annika nothing but a spoiled dilettante, dabbling in one hobby after another, moving her husband all over the country?

"So the wine business was Annika's idea?" she asked.

"Oh, yes," Preston said. "We were living in Phoenix, surrounded by desert. One evening we were drinking a good bottle of zinfandel, and she said, 'You know, we could make our own wine. Plant a vineyard and build a winery. We'll do it together. It would be a great adventure!' I agreed, and within a week we'd bought the Norton place. She enrolled in online courses in oenology—no problem, since she has a strong background in organic chemistry." Preston sighed. "As soon as I retire, I'll be her vineyard manager."

Noli poured two cups of coffee and offered him milk and sugar, which he declined. Nodding toward the door, she asked, "Outside?"

"Great idea." He politely slid the door open and waited for her to pass through.

She was puzzled by Preston and Annika's relationship. Was theirs a passive-aggressive dance as in, "I have sex with someone else, we fight, then we kiss and make up until the next time?" Or was theirs an open marriage? Was Preston the abusive and controlling husband Tina thought he was?

They reclaimed their deck chairs. Noli was considering how to broach the subject of Gary Varley when Preston asked, "Do you live here, or are you just visiting?"

"I've come back after working in Europe for several years."

"Well, I hope you'll stay. Annika likes you a lot."

Really? She doesn't know me. Uncertain how to respond, she took a long drink from her coffee mug.

Preston continued, "The thing is, it's hard for her to make friends. She isn't—" He broke off. Drank coffee. Stared into the distance. Whether he was just appreciating the scenery or was lost in thought, she couldn't discern. Finally, he took a deep breath and set his mug on the deck. "Thank you. Time for me to get going." His eyes met hers only for a moment, then he moved away, descending the stairs two at a time. At the bottom, he paused and turned back. "You know there's a new storm coming in?"

"When?"

"Around seven."

"Thanks for letting me know."

Noli remained on the deck for several minutes, reviewing what Preston had said. Finally she phoned Irv. "Can you free up one of your team to do some background on another neighbor of the Hanaks?"

"What do you need?"

"Preston and Annika Vandermeis." She spelled the last name and gave him their current address, as well as the name of Preston's company. "Moved here three or four years ago from Phoenix. Previously they lived in Austin. Before that, Baltimore. Annika says she's from Boston. I want to know what they were doing before they got here."

CHAPTER FIFTY-THREE

The eight men and three women gathered around Varley's dining table showed no signs of departing. Their fingers traced lines on charts and raced across their laptop keyboards as they compiled and compared their findings.

Luz served a steady stream of refreshments: coffee, soft drinks, wine, beer, and snacks. No hard spirits. From the bits of conversation she caught, she concluded there was a time-limited contract under consideration; hence, the Sunday meeting.

She was in the kitchen, replenishing a cheese tray, when Varley strode in, saying, "I've ordered pizzas. Here's for the delivery boy." He tossed two fifty-dollar bills on the counter. Spotting the sack of groceries, he said, "Anything good?" and spilled the contents onto a chopping block. "Barbeque, my favorite." He ripped the bag of chips open as he strode back to the dining room.

Luz swallowed hard, calming her racing heart. Since when was Varley interested in a bag of groceries? *No importa.* She had stowed the hard drive in the cleaning cart at first opportunity. But what if Varley needed that drive for his current meeting? She could feign innocence, let him think it had been misplaced, and hope he couldn't imagine his lowly maid absconding with it.

But how could she restore the drive to the drawer where it belonged? Varley often spent the evening in his office. Sometimes, he fell asleep there. And when he did finally retire to his bedroom, he often was not—according to Consuela—asleep.

A middle-of-the-night foray to his office was too risky.

She paced. By the time the pizza cartons were empty, she had a plan.

CHAPTER FIFTY-FOUR

When Noli reentered the winery to finish tending the vats, she realized that in her rush to tend to her injured leg, she'd left the door unlocked. Stepping inside, she was reassured to find it looked exactly as she'd left it. The pressing pole was still half-submerged in a vat of must from Old Marco's Hill. Moving carefully, deliberately, she retrieved the pole and checked the next vat. She was shivering. It had been a mistake not to change out of Peter's shorts, but she was damned if she was hiking back to the domes before this job was done. Already the delay meant the caps were much more difficult to submerge.

She moved down the line. At the end, on the right, was a vat of carignan from King City. It looked different from the others, but then, it was a different variety of grape. She bent to examine it. No bubbles. No lumpy, foaming cap of grape skins and stems. She checked its card. It had been sterilized and inoculated with commercial yeast, but it wasn't fermenting.

Why?

She remembered Fitz and Peter agonizing over vats in which fermentation had stopped. Restarting it was tricky. And what had caused it to halt? Was there something in the air that would infect the other vats?

From a nearby shelf, she grabbed a tasting cup, swirled it in the carignan vat, then lifted a sample. The juice tasted slightly alcoholic, meaning some fermentation had occurred. She tasted again, more slowly this time, inhaling as she sipped. Lingering around the edges of the carignan's rich aroma was a faint petroleum smell. Not vinegar, so maybe the problem wasn't Peter's nemesis, *acetobacter aceti,* the bacteria that had turned the last two years' harvest to vinegar.

Thinking it must be a different sort of bacteria, she imagined contagion spreading from that vat until, one by one, it would infect every vat, terminating fermentation. A disaster that would bankrupt Peter and Tina.

Someone would know what to do. By tomorrow, when Peter called, she would be able to report, honestly, that everything was *fine.* She climbed a set of rickety stairs to Peter's office. Next to the landline, he had posted a sheet of winery-related contacts. Annika was top of the list.

When Annika's home number didn't answer, she dialed the cell. No luck. She left a message.

She tried Wolf, who didn't answer either. She left a message explaining the problem and asked for a call back.

That left Daniel Arnant and, through him, Russ Lankshaw. Three numbers were listed for Daniel: winery, office, and home. She tried the office first, then the home phone. No answer. The winery number rang and rang. When a young female voice finally answered, Noli could hear happy conversation in the background.

"This is Noli Cooper at the Hanak Winery. I need advice on an urgent problem. I'm trying to reach Mr. Arnant."

"Mr. Arnant is not available. May I take a message?"

"How do I reach Russ Lankshaw?"

"I'm sorry. Russ left hours ago."

"Do you have his cell?"

"I'm not at liberty to give out his private information."

"Then please, get an urgent message to Mr. Arnant. He can reach me at this number." She recited the Hanaks' number.

The only other name on Peter's call list was Sam, and Sam knew very little about wine making. The only chance for immediate help was Arnant. What if he had plans for the evening? What if he didn't get her message until tomorrow?

She would take a sample to Andolini Winery and track him down.

From Peter's tiny laboratory, she grabbed a sterile bottle with a screw-on top and carried it to the carignan vat, where she filled it with a few ounces of the non-fermenting must. She raced to her car. Overhead, clouds were gathering. The storm Preston Vandermeis had alerted her to was coming, but it didn't matter now—all the grapes were safe in their vats.

When she reached her rental car, its headlights shone like faint yellow eyes in the darkness. With a sinking heart, she remembered she'd turned them on the previous night while driving home from a grocery run. Apparently, she'd left them on. She climbed in and tried the ignition. A faint grinding sound on the first turn, then nothing.

Okay, not too far to walk. Grabbing a flashlight to guide her way home after dark, she jogged down the road to Arnant's office. In the Andolini Winery parking lot, a thirty-something man climbed out of a Jaguar and bounded across the lot to intercept her. "Could you show me the new cave? Is it finished?"

"Sorry," she replied. "I don't work here."

He stared at her grape-stained overshirt, then at the jar of purple liquid in her hand, a puzzled look on his face.

She said, "Why don't you ask one of the servers in the Tasting Room?"

"Uh, sure. Thanks."

She hurried to the Andolini mansion. Above the entrance, a sign announced *Andolini Vineyards and Winery* and underneath, in only slightly smaller letters, *International Headquarters*.

A *Closed* sign hung just to the right of the door. However, the door was unlocked. She entered a softly lit foyer graced with an empty receptionist's desk. Beyond, double doors opened into what must have been the front parlor. Two fringe-shaded floor lamps cast a gentle light over Victorian furnishings: blue Oriental carpet, green velvet curtains, and a love seat and four chairs in walnut and red damask. The walls featured sepia-toned photographs of the Andolini Estate in the late nineteenth century. On the far side of the parlor was a door labeled *Daniel Arnant, President*. It was slightly ajar. From behind it leaked the sound of conversation.

She would wait, but not for long.

CHAPTER FIFTY-FIVE

Pushing a cart filled with cleaning supplies and dragging a vacuum behind her, Luz exited the kitchen just as Varley bid goodbye to the last of his workers. "Señor Varley, please, I finish books in your office now. Then you no have to do business at dining table again."

Varley smiled, saying, "Great idea, Alma. Just try to keep the noise down."

Walking several paces behind, she followed him down the hall. Watched as he entered his bedroom and closed the door. Moved the cart into the office. Closed the door.

The un-dusted books waited on the conference table. She flipped the *on* switch for the small vacuum and set to work. Periodically, she stopped and listened. Explosions and gunshots from the movie Varley was watching carried through the wall. Could anyone fall asleep in front of such chaos?

She worked slowly. But when all the books had been cleaned and replaced on their shelves, she could still hear movie-set shouts and gunfire.

She had no further excuse for being in Varley's office.

Pulling the hard drive from its nest in the rag bag, she slid it into her apron pocket, grabbed a duster, and headed for Varley's desk.

The door opened. "You about done in here, Alma?"

Turning to face Varley, she prayed the outline of the hard disk wasn't shouting at him from her pocket. Waving the duster in the direction of his massive desk, she said in a weary voice, "*Sí*, I have only to dust over there."

CHAPTER FIFTY-SIX

Noli sat on the edge of the love seat, careful to keep her stained overshirt from touching the upholstery. Time passed. Her mind swirled with images of potential disaster in the winery: all the vats going bad, a swampy smell filling the air. Her anxiety climbed, her hard-used arms and legs knotted up, and the poison-oak burns screamed.

Finally, she decided to knock on the office door. She took two steps across the room. Stopped. A girlish voice said, "Taste it."

The unmistakable sound of liquid pouring, a short silence, then Arnant's voice. "Paolina's wine. My grandmother always said Andolini would make wine history. I'm ready to prove she was correct."

In a soothing voice, the girl-woman said, "All you need to do is replant."

In that instant, Noli recognized the voice: Annika.

"With the right clone," Arnant replied. "How can I—"

"Not a problem," Annika said, sweetly. "I have a source."

"I might not have the right terroir."

"I think you do," Annika cooed. "Besides, the Hanaks can't hold on much longer, can they?"

"Look, I don't want—"

His sentence was cut off. By a kiss? Annika said, "By rights, this is all yours. I'll take you to the cave on Wednesday. You can see for yourself."

"Not while it belongs to the Hanaks, darling. We'll have to wait."

"But it isn't theirs! It's in the state park, but surely it was part of the Andolini Estate originally. You can fight to get it back."

Murmurs of affection, then Arnant said, "You've given me leverage I could only have dreamed of." More murmurs, furniture scraping the floor.

Damn. Surely he would close the door if he—

She tiptoed back to the foyer, hoping they'd decide Arnant's house was a more comfortable venue for sex. When they came out, she'd pretend she'd just walked in.

Arnant's office door clicked shut. Then the metal-on-metal sound of a latch being fastened.

Now what? Pound on his door? Scream for help?

Frozen in indecision, she scanned the room for inspiration. If there was a fire alarm box, she would break it. Then she noticed six bottles of wine on a sideboard. She moved closer and flipped her flashlight on briefly, shielding its beam so only the bottles were illuminated. They bore the same label as the bottles of Andolini Munch had bought for Peter. 1982. And, like Munch's gift bottles, they had no back label.

She tiptoed through the front door, steaming with frustration, and stepped off the porch into a steady drizzle. Where had Arnant found *six* bottles of 1982 Andolini zinfandel? No, seven, because obviously they were drinking from one.

As for Annika, what was she playing at? *I have a source.* Did she know about the Hanak clone that Wickam had stolen and Varley planned to plant? Was she promising to put Arnant in touch with Wickam? Or did she think Varley would sell cuttings of the stolen clone to Arnant?

Good luck with that.

And then there was Annika's cold-blooded assessment of the Hanaks' chances of holding on. Clearly, her friendship with Tina was a charade.

As for the cave that was "in the state park," Noli was pretty sure she knew where to find it.

Oblivious to the rain, she plodded down the road, following the beam of her flashlight. When she reached the winery, she inspected every vat. Only two looked as though they'd stopped fermenting.

The caps on one row of vats remained to be pressed. Looking at the pressing pole and down the line of vats, she thought she'd rest for just a moment. She pushed a stool against the wall and sat down, supporting her back on the rough redwood planks. The rain drumming on the winery's metal roof soothed her to sleep.

CHAPTER FIFTY-SEVEN

Sunday, 10 p.m.

Before she opened her eyes, Noli smelled fire. She heard it snapping and cracking. A heavy weight pressed her, binding her arms. She screamed, "Fire! Help! Fire!"

"Noli, you're safe. Look at me."

She opened her eyes. Sam knelt beside her. Searching the space behind him, she recognized the Hanaks' dome. In the fireplace, a fire roared, much too close. On top of her lay a stack of blankets and comforters.

"Is it the fire?" he asked.

"Too close," she whispered, her energy spent.

He pushed the couch—and her—across the room as though they were weightless. "Far enough?"

"Yes. Thanks."

"Sorry to scare you. I should have remembered."

Safe. Sleep now.

"Oh, no, you don't!" He pulled her into a sitting position, tucking the blankets around her shoulders. "You have to eat before you sleep. Look at me, Noli." He offered her a glass of pale gold liquid. "Can you hold this?"

She reached for it with two hands, expecting a chilly glass, but it was warm.

"Sorry to give it to you warm, but the last thing you need right now is a cold drink."

Her hands were shaky, but she managed to lift the glass to her lips, catching the sweet aroma of apple juice. She swallowed and felt the warmth spread through the frozen center of her body. Then her stomach knotted, squeezed, and sent waves of nausea up her throat. She lowered the glass and waited.

He dragged a chair over to sit beside her. The fire lit half of his face, leaving the rest in shadow. Even so, she could tell he was very pale. "Keep drinking," he said. "Small sips."

When the nausea backed off, she took another sip. Sam's dark eyes never left her face. "I found you in the winery. Hypothermia. You could have died."

Hypothermia. First-Aid for Backpackers *says...*

"Noli?" Sam's hands wrapped around hers, holding the glass steady.

With his help, she sipped more of the juice, then leaned back to rest. "I don't know what happened," she whispered. "I was tired. I remember sitting down—"

"How did your clothes get so wet?"

"Walked to Andolini Winery, looking for Daniel Arnant."

He started to say something, thought better of it.

She felt embarrassed, as though she'd been a careless child. "Sam, one of the vats stopped fermenting. I needed help."

"Which vat?"

She closed her eyes, picturing the inside of the winery. "South side. End of the row."

"We'll deal with it. Rest now. I'll be right back."

She looked down at her arms. They were covered with flannel sleeves she didn't recognize. Of course, Sam had removed her wet clothes. Her cheeks flushed with embarrassment. She tried to tell herself it didn't matter; he was like an uncle to her. He was probably more embarrassed than she was.

He reappeared, carrying a tray loaded with food and two steaming mugs. He resumed his position next to her, tray on his lap, and handed her a mug.

The aroma of hot chocolate set her stomach rumbling. Then came a memory from the deep past: She was sitting by the fire with her father. Gwen offered them each a cup of steaming cocoa, chocolate scent radiating with her smile as she teased her husband. "Cooper," she said—she always called him by his last name—"Cooper, you two are going to catch pneumonia." Gwen had laughed as she gathered Noli into the warmth of her arms.

It was good to recall the days when Gwen had been young and happy.

"You're trying to do too much," Sam said, his voice fierce. "And you got blindsided by this storm. Thirty-degree temperature drop in less than two hours."

Rain slammed against the window. He waved a hand toward the sound. "That's what you were up against." He leaned forward. "When you came back to the winery to finish pressing the caps, did you close the winery door behind you?"

Trying to remember felt like swimming through mush. She'd been in Arnant's waiting room. Then she'd left. It was raining. She'd run down the road. Then—yes, she'd raced for the shelter of the winery. She'd opened the door, entered. Surely she'd closed it behind her.

"Yes. Why?"

"When I got there, it was wide open."

"Maybe it didn't latch, and the wind blew it open."

"Maybe. Or maybe you weren't the only person there."

Her brain tried to focus. The winery was poorly lit. Many dark corners and places to hide. She hadn't expected anyone, so she hadn't looked. "I was so shaken by the bad vat. Everything else went out of my head."

Sam nodded and handed her a plateful of food. "Eat."

It was enough to feed two linebackers. Sausage, lasagna, quiche, bacon, and toast. "Sam, put it in the fridge. I'll eat soon. I promise."

He shook his head. "You're exhausted, in the true meaning of the word, so you don't feel any hunger. Try eating two bites."

The lasagna had no taste, but she forced herself to swallow. Sam watched her intently. She said, "What? Are you waiting for a green light on my forehead to light up, indicating that lasagna has entered my bloodstream?"

"Yes." He didn't laugh.

One more bite. "That's all I can manage."

Sam took the tray back to the kitchen. When he returned, he said, "How many times do you think Tina has made the trip to Annika's and back in her wheelchair?"

"Lots."

"Has she ever had an accident before?"

"None that Peter spoke of. He wonders if the brakes failed."

"No way. He keeps that chair in prime condition. No racing car gets more attention. Someone either sabotaged her chair or pushed her from behind. Someone she never got a look at."

Sam's eyes bore into hers as he continued. "Too many bad things are happening. We're supposed to believe it was an accident that Peter's '07 and '08 vintages turned to vinegar? No way. The graffiti? Tina's crash? Now a vat has stopped fermenting? I think it's sabotage, and the person who did it was planning to do more. He was either in the winery when you returned from Arnant's or he came back. He saw you sleeping and left the winery door open on purpose, hoping you'd die from hypothermia. Just another accident."

Sam rose to his feet, paced to the fireplace, his fists clenched. He kicked the hearth, saying, "I fucking hate this."

Peter had often refused to take Sam's worries seriously. And Sam had, in fact, been a sucker for many conspiracy theories in the past. But this time? What if he was right?

Minutes passed. Sam didn't move, didn't talk. Noli pushed the blankets aside, wrapped herself in the sheet, limped to him, and put her hand on his shoulder. "Sam?"

He wiped his face with his sleeve. When he turned to her, she could see he'd been crying. He took a deep breath. "Don't you go and die, you hear me?"

"I won't. Scout's honor."

He didn't smile. "From now on, you lock every door, got it?"

"Yes."

"And from now on, we leave the winery's floodlights on all night. Tomorrow I'm buying motion-triggered cameras to monitor the winery entrance." He paused. "But don't tell Peter—he might rip them down."

"Agreed."

He kissed her forehead. "I'm going to press the caps. You rest."

When he opened the door, a cold wind blew through the house.

CHAPTER FIFTY-EIGHT

Monday 5:30 a.m.

When Noli woke again, the storm was still raging. Morning or night? The windows were black.

She rolled onto her back. Someone had placed her clothes, washed and folded, on a chair by the bed. She called, "Hello, Sam?"

"Here."

When she slid from the bed, she saw the poison-oak sores on her legs and arms, which had been oozing, had been wrapped with bandages, and the dressing on her thigh was fresh. With trembling arms, she dressed.

She hobbled around the wooden screen that divided the bedroom from the rest of the dome. Sam stood at the kitchen counter. At his elbow, a bottle of Bowmore whisky, nearly empty. She'd never seen Sam drink alcohol of any kind.

Gesturing to the table, he said, "Sit." It was an order, not a suggestion. "You have a message from Irv. He said, 'The hard drive is back in place. Luz is okay.' Does that make sense to you?"

"Yeah. Thanks." She'd completely forgotten about Luz.

She sat with her back to the fire. The table was set for breakfast: cream, cereal, yogurt, a bowl of fresh raspberries, and two bowls and spoons.

She gave his arm a squeeze. "Thank you for everything, Sam. Where did you learn to dress wounds so beautifully?"

"Your father taught me." Bringing his whisky bottle and a glass, he sat in the chair opposite. He said, "What happened that night, the fire in your dome?"

Surprised by his question, she said, "I've never exactly remembered."

He sipped whisky, then asked, "Gwen freaked out and started a bonfire?"

"That's what I believe."

Sam shook his head. "What a fucked-up world. A woman like that, an angel, and the fates screw her head until she doesn't know the devil from the good guys."

Uncertain how to respond, she spooned yogurt and berries onto her cereal and ate, watching Sam in brief glimpses. Hearing Gwen described as an "angel" always threw her, but she'd heard it often enough, always from men her father's age.

He tossed back the rest of the whisky in his glass and reached for the bottle.

"What's wrong, Sam?"

"What isn't?" he said. He refilled his glass, took a swig, then looked her in the eye. "Gwen's insane. Fitz, murdered. Peter, sabotaged. Tina might die. *You* nearly died. And—"

"Wait a minute. You never told me why you came back here last night."

"I'm paranoid, remember?" His voice was bitter. He brought the glass to his lips but set it down without drinking. "Call it a hunch. I was afraid for you."

Saved by a hunch.

Minutes passed while she crunched cereal, watching Sam as he watched the fire. Then, with a deep sigh, he turned back to her. "Fermentation has stopped in three more vats: two zinfandel from the lower vineyard and one syrah from King City."

Disaster.

She thought of Peter waiting by Tina's bedside, not knowing whether she would live, while he lost another year's work. Struggling to understand, she asked, "Are the bad vats next to one another?"

"Yes."

"So it's contagious?"

"Damned if I know. I called Russ Lankshaw to come have a look. He took samples up to Arnant's lab."

"How long will it take to analyze them?"

"Who knows? He'll call when he's got an answer." Sam pushed aside a yellow pad and pen to make room for a cereal bowl.

"What are you writing?" Noli asked.

"Not important."

"Can I see?"

He shrugged, pushed the tablet across the table to her.

THE UNCOUNTED CASUALTIES OF WAR

"Bill's dead."

That's what his best friend told us as we gathered for the weekly meeting of our PTSD support group. "He got drunk, drove his car off a cliff near Felton."

Over the coming year, more vets will try to kill themselves. Many will succeed. Some use guns. Others drive into trees, over cliffs, off bridges. Many more self-medicate with alcohol and drugs until their bodies give out.

All are casualties of war, but they will not be counted.

"You write well, Sam. Is this a guest editorial?"

"Maybe."

"You knew Bill?"

"Oh, yeah. Spitting image of me forty years ago. Enlisted to fight in Iraq. Believed he was saving the Iraqi people." He reached for his glass, changed his mind. "Know what the worst part is?"

"Tell me."

"We could have prevented this. Me, Fitz, Sam, Peter, Munch. Everyone who came home from Vietnam. Shoulda camped in front of Bush's White House and refused to leave until people came to their senses. Weapons of mass destruction, my ass! 'Bring democracy to the Iraqi people'? Give me a break. We *knew* what was going to happen."

Something thudded on the roof, rolled, crashed onto the deck.

He retrieved the writing pad and stared at it blearily. "Know what my commanding officer told me the night before we shipped home?"

"Tell me."

"Whatever you do, don't tell anyone you were in Vietnam."

She reached for his right fist and squeezed it with both hands, picturing him as a twenty-year-old boy forbidden to speak of the horrors he had witnessed. That boy had dutifully packed his kit and disappeared into Loma Buena State Park, living in a cave for nearly two years, knowing only the distant and silent company of others, who, like himself, had chosen to be hermits in the forest rather than swallow the hypocrisy of the citizens who had sent them to war.

Another thump on the roof.

She slid her half-full mug of coffee into his hand and wrapped his fingers around it. "Do you have to go to work?"

He shook his head.

"Tell me about Vietnam, Sam."

His hand shook as he lifted her mug, slopping coffee onto the table. He managed to drink the remaining coffee, then set the mug down. His eyes held a world of stories untold.

"Bad idea," he said. "I could—"

"Please."

Mumbling something resembling "goddamn it," he walked to the kitchen, poured a fresh cup of coffee, and returned, never meeting her eyes. He stirred cream into his mug, chugged the entire contents. Finally, raising his bleary eyes to hers, he said, "All right. You know the story of Lieutenant Unocello's court-martial?"

Her blank look must have been answer enough.

"Okay, from the beginning. Take Peter, a Hungarian refugee, so grateful to America, so proud of what it stands for. Ditto for my brother and me, sons of Russian Jewish refugees. We didn't wait to be drafted. Enlisted right out of high school. Wanted to defend democracy from 'the relentless advance of Communism in Southeast Asia'." He sipped some coffee.

"When Peter and I get to 'Nam, we're eighteen-year-old grunts. The first thing you learn is you can't tell who's the enemy. If a guy's shooting at you, you understand that. But go into a village? An old man, a woman, even a child might hand you a basket of fruit with a hand grenade in it. Do they hate you? Maybe. More likely, a Viet Cong is watching from the jungle with a gun to Grandma's head. You don't know. You're *never* gonna know, because you do not understand the first fucking thing about these people or their war.

"It's *Alice in Wonderland* gone bad. You shoot when your commander tells you to shoot; back at base, you get drunk and stoned so you don't have to think about what you've done. You want to keep your buddies alive. That's all there is.

"Now, Peter, he has a special experience. His platoon is ordered to take a Cong village. He's assigned to protect a reporter who wants to come along. The reporter, he twists his ankle, bad, going in, so Peter hangs back to help him.

"Up ahead, when the platoon takes the village, they find American prisoners. Skin-and-bone grunts stuck in cages so small, they can't stand up or lie down. They're sitting in their own shit. The lieutenant goes berserk, orders his men to kill everyone in the village. He starts blasting with his own M16. The guys are sick with rage, and several start shooting.

"Now, they know damn well every Cong soldier's long gone. So who are they killing? Women, old men, children." He stood up and paced. "Peter and his reporter arrive just in time to see it happen. While the grunts free the guys in the cages and strap them onto litters, the sergeant puts a knife to the reporter's throat and tells him, 'You never saw this, understand?'

"Back at base, they all get drunk. 'This didn't happen,' they say. 'This is a crazy fucking war.'

"Next sortie, they walk into a trap. Peter's damn near killed, shot all to hell, so he gets shipped home. Final touch is soon as he's been pieced together and is learning to walk again, he's court-martialed, along with the whole platoon and their commander, Lieutenant Frank Unocello. We find out later the brass tried to suppress the reporter's account of the massacre, but *The New York Times* spread it on page one.

"The reporter must have identified Peter as his helper, 'cause suddenly the charges against Peter are dropped, and he's subpoenaed as a witness instead. What's the right thing to do? He could refuse to testify, for which he'd get locked in a brig until hell freezes over—"

Standing just inside the door, rain cascading from his slicker, Peter cut in, saying, "Or he could say, 'It's true. My platoon, *my brothers for whom I would have died*, were gunning down women, children, and old men."

Peter walked toward them, his face carved in stone. His eyes met hers. "But I told a different truth: Unocello was losing his mind long before he gave that order. He harangued us every night about the need to increase our 'body count,' while he fingered a chain of enemy ears like a rosary. We had already reported him to the captain, who told us we were a bunch of pussies.

"I told the court-martial that Unocello's superior officers were responsible. They'd left an officer in command when they knew him to be unfit for duty."

He unzipped his slicker, tossed it on the floor, and took a chair at the table. She filled a mug with coffee, passed it to him. He took a long draught. Then, wearily, he continued, "I could have saved my breath. None of the brass got so much as a reprimand."

"And Unocello?" she asked.

"Two years, a slap on the wrist. But he hung himself in the brig during the first week."

Peter stared at Sam for a long minute, then turned back to Noli. "None of the grunts—the guys who killed a hundred and seventy-three civilians—were prosecuted. But here's where the story takes a special twist. There were several soldiers who tried to stop the killing. One tackled Unocello. Several others tried to shield women and children. After they testified at the court-martial, they received death threats. Their cars were vandalized. Dead animals appeared on their doorsteps—"

Sam stood abruptly, saying, "I'm going to press the caps." On his way to the door, he picked up Peter's slicker and shrugged it on.

As the door closed behind him, she said, "He's drunk. Should I stop him?"

"He'll be all right," Peter replied. He got up from the table and opened the refrigerator door. Selected a carton of eggs and loaf of bread, started cooking.

She closed her eyes, imagining the village, the soldiers finding their comrades in cages, the rage, the machine guns firing—

Thump. Clang.

Alarmed, pulled back to the present, she pushed herself to her feet, searching for the source of the noise. On the floor, a frying pan lay face down. Raw eggs oozed across the tiles. Peter stood immobile, staring down at the mess. Tears ran down his cheeks. She went to him and wrapped her arms around him. "I'm so sorry."

"Ancient history," he said, stepping away. "Don't know why the hell Sam had to dredge it up."

"I asked him."

Peter shook his head and bent to the floor. Righting the pan, he tried, with a spatula, to scrape the eggs back in.

She took the pan and spatula from him and, after gently backing him into a chair, cleaned the floor. Softly, she said, "Sam described the massacre like he'd been there."

"He was."

"He tried to stop them, didn't he?" she asked.

"Yeah."

And when he got home, he went to live in the forest. "Fitz too?"

"Yeah."

A kaleidoscope of childhood memories shifted and settled into a new array. "Was my father there?"

"He was our medic," Peter answered, and hobbled off to the bathroom.

She cracked the remaining eggs, added a package of bacon, and set about preparing breakfast while her thoughts swirled. Was the massacre the reason her father had never talked about Vietnam? The reason that Peter, Sam, and Fitz never spoke of the war? What had it been like to come home to anti-war demonstrations and be treated like pariahs rather than patriots? Worse, to know they'd been lied to by the leaders of the country they were so proud of?

When Sam came through the door, returning from the winery, he caught her eye and shook his head, as though to say, *Don't mention the fermentation problem.* Peter came to the table, and she served them eggs and bacon.

Sam said, "Peter, how's Tina doing?"

"Not good. No sign of the coma breaking."

"About her wheelchair—mind if I have a look?"

Peter said, "I'd be grateful."

Sam continued, "Before she gets home, we should tighten up the ramp going down from the deck." He sounded perfectly lucid, which, after the amount of whisky he'd put away, seemed miraculous. Between bites of egg, he bantered with Peter, listing repairs Tina would appreciate when she returned. Little by little, Peter's jaw muscles relaxed.

When Tina gets home.

Noli let the two of them make plans while she cleaned up, her thoughts returning to the apple barn's meth lab, another secret she was keeping from Peter. Was this the time to tell him?

Someone pounded on the front door.

Sam flashed a panicked look at Noli and said, "I'll get it."

Realizing it could be Russ Lankshaw and that Sam wanted to protect Peter, she said, "You two rest. I'll—"

But Peter cut her off, saying, "I'm leaving anyway."

And so, as a committee of three, they opened the door. Russ Lankshaw stood there in his rain gear. "I've got an answer for you," he said.

Peter asked, "Answer to what?"

After they'd brought Peter up to speed on the problem with four vats, Russ stated, "Someone added potassium sorbate to those vats. Simple and effective."

A moment of stunned silence.

Peter blew out a breath. "Those fucking kids."

"The graffiti kids did this?" Noli asked.

"Who else?" he answered. Peter's dark-circled eyes settled on Sam. "Will you install a better lock on that door today?"

"Right away," Sam answered. "I've got a big hasp and padlock in the truck."

Peter nodded, turned, and walked out.

Dumbfounded, Russ looked at Sam. They both turned to Noli for an explanation.

She said, "I think he can't bear to worry about anything but Tina."

CHAPTER FIFTY-NINE

S am departed, saying he had to check in with his construction crew. Peter set off for the hospital. Noli was about to return to the winery when the landline rang.

"Hi, Noli," Wolf began. He sounded weary but resolute. "This morning, Ryan and I met with his thesis advisor—who is also the director of the Zinfandel Clone Project—and told him everything we've learned. The professor talked with the university's administration. Upshot is we're meeting with a police detective tomorrow morning."

Her mind raced through the possible outcomes. She still doubted there was anything the detective could do beyond questioning Giannopoulos and Wickam. But if Giannopoulos broke down and was willing to testify against Wickam, then maybe they stood a chance.

"Is Ryan feeling okay about this?"

"He is. I have to go, but tell me, how's Tina?"

"Still in a coma."

"Damn. Peter?"

"With her day and night. If he loses her, I don't know how he'll go on. Look, a lot has happened since you left. We need your help."

"I'll get there as soon as I can."

They rang off, and she dialed Irv. "What's the news on the Vandermeises?"

Irv sighed. "Here's what I've got so far. Preston's company, LYX Devices, is legit. There're positive rumors in the tech world about them going public. He and Annika were married in 1991 in Boston. The wedding announcement says they met when she interned in his company. She has a B.S. in biology from Northeastern. In the announcement, her parents are listed as Mary and Michael Abernathy of Trenton, New Jersey, deceased.

"I verified the sequence of cities Preston told you they'd lived in: Baltimore, Austin, and Phoenix. What puzzles me is, they're all inconvenient for Preston's work. His partners are here in Cupertino. So, were those cities Annika's choice? And if so, why?"

Noli said, "No indication of previous involvement with the wine industry?"

"None that I saw. And those cities aren't exactly known for vineyards. Wish I had more to offer you, but all my helpers have deserted me."

"Good work, Irv. Now I need you to shift focus. I've got a possible lead on someone who would want to harm Fitz and Peter. The last name is spelled U-n-o-c-e-l-l-o. First name, Mark. He was court-martialed for ordering a massacre of women and children in a Vietnamese village. I don't have the exact date, but 1968 to 1970 should be close enough. Peter testified at his court-martial. Unocello committed suicide soon after he was convicted. Track the wife and kids, then the soldiers who did not testify against him. It was a big case, *New York Times* front-page coverage."

"I'm on it."

She placed the receiver back in its cradle. What was next? Interview Annika? Question Arnant about his bottles of

1982 Andolini? Would he claim they'd been discovered in the cave remodel? Or were they a gift from Annika, who had found them in the cave she was eager to show him?

The more she thought about it, the angrier she got. Annika had robbed Tina and Peter of Dino's legacy at the very time they needed it most.

She replayed the conversation between Arnant and Annika. Had there been any hint that she or Arnant were sabotaging the Hanaks?

No.

Suppose Annika had indeed ruined the Hanaks' '07 and '08 vintages and had tried to ruin this year's. Why? Was she in love with Arnant, and planning to jump ship from Preston—and Varley—as soon as Arnant was ready to replant?

And then there was the cave Annika had discovered. Annika claimed it was in the state park; Arnant thought it belonged to the Hanaks. The most likely place for territorial confusion was right at the base of the cliff behind the old barn. Did the trail from the back of the barn, through the weeds to the cliff, lead to a cave?

The phone rang.

"Noli, it's Peter. I was a jerk to walk off like that. I've called Sam. He's going to meet with me at five o'clock to go over some safety measures for the winery. Can you come stay with Tina while I meet with Sam?"

"Of course."

She checked the clock. There was plenty of time to confront Annika before heading to the hospital.

Not wanting to risk the rental car's undercarriage on the sodden road to Annika's, she donned a pair of tall boots and a warm coat, then headed down the road on foot. But as she drew near the Vandermeis mansion, she could see that both Preston's and Annika's cars were gone.

CHAPTER SIXTY

W hen the ICU's wall clock showed eight p.m., Noli began to worry. Peter had promised to return to the hospital by seven.

With a soft *shshshshsh*, a gray cuff encircling Tina's upper arm inflated, held, then deflated in a slow whoosh. Tina's slack expression was unchanged. The machines beeped and whirred. Rubber-soled footsteps squeaked back and forth outside the curtains. Somewhere nearby, a man was weeping.

When nine o'clock came, Noli stepped out of the ICU and called Peter. No answer. She tried Sam. No answer.

At ten o'clock, she tried them both again. No answer.

She stared at her cell as though it could give her more information. What should she do? Perhaps installing security cameras had been more complicated than expected? There was no cell reception at the winery, but there was a landline. No message—from either of them—by three hours past the promised meeting time?

Something had gone wrong.

She kissed Tina's forehead. "Tina, I have to leave now, but Peter's on his way. I love you."

Away from the city's lights, the night was pitch black. On Highway 17, southbound headlights whipped past, sometimes blinding her on the turns. It was a relief to reach the forested darkness of Bear Creek Road. A doe and her fawn leapt away from the headlights just as she reached the ostentatious Andolini sign and turned onto Andolini Road.

She'd passed the Andolini mansion and winery, both dark, and was within sight of the Hanaks' redwood grove when she spotted red flares a few yards up the road. She braked. Beyond the flares, a green-and-white County Sheriff's sedan blocked the road. Breaking into a cold sweat, she pushed the gear shift into park, killed the engine, and opened the car door. Suddenly she was blinded by a powerful beam of light.

"Come out slowly with your hands up!" a male voice boomed.

She stepped out of the car, arms raised.

The light beam jiggled slightly as two sets of footsteps moved closer.

Immediately she thought of the meth lab. Had the lab operators tipped off the sheriff, their revenge for being locked out? If so, the Hanaks' entire property would be undergoing a search.

Where was Peter?

She called out, "Officer, my name is Nollaig Cooper. I live a half-mile up this road at the home of Peter and Tina Hanak."

"Ma'am, we'll need to see your driver's license and car registration."

"My license is in my purse, in the car, Officer. The car is a rental."

The light beam moved to her right, illuminating the front of the car. A young, round-cheeked man in a deputy's uniform stepped to the passenger window of the car, drew his pistol, and waited.

Opening the driver's door, she extracted her license and the car-rental contract. She offered the documents to the source of the light beam.

The young deputy, his weapon holstered now, came around the car, took the documents from her, and walked toward the patrol car.

The voice behind the light said, "Just stay where you are."

Her thoughts turned to the worst outcome she could imagine: Peter had been arrested. What would the deputies do? Would she be arrested too? If she and Peter were in jail, who would be there for Tina? If only Abbie were in town! Acid climbed into her throat, and she swallowed hard.

The young deputy returned and handed her documents to her. The light beam shifted downward, and the officer holding the flashlight approached her. He was dark-haired and tall, his tanned face smooth.

"Ma'am, I'm sorry to inform you that there has been a serious incident at the Hanak property. Our orders are to seal off this road. Detective Rinzler is on his way. Please wait in your vehicle." With that, he and his partner returned to their squad car.

Back in the driver's seat, she tried to imagine why Rinzler would have been pulled into the investigation of a very small meth lab. It didn't make sense.

She heard a car engine, then a screech of brakes as a second green-and-white pulled up behind the first. When she saw Rinzler emerge, she slid out of her car and strode forward to meet him at the line of flares. Before he could speak, she said, "Detective Rinzler, what is going on here? Why is there is a barricade on this road?"

"I'll be the one asking questions, Ms. Cooper. What is your relationship to Peter and Tina Hanak?"

She could walk away without answering. But then she wouldn't know what had happened. Softening her voice, she said, "They are my godparents."

"When were you most recently on the Hanaks' property?"

"I was there all day today until approximately four p.m."

"Did you enter the winery before departing?"

The winery? "Yes."

"At what time?"

"Approximately one o'clock this afternoon."

"Did you see anything unusual, any sort of problem, in the winery at that time?"

Her mind raced, trying to guess the reason Rinzler's attention was on the winery. Had there been more graffiti? Sabotage of vats? Had Peter, not knowing he had an explosive legal problem hiding in his apple barn, called the sheriff to investigate the sabotage of his fermenting bins?

She said, "I saw nothing unusual at that time. But there have been a series of unexplained problems in the Hanaks' winery. You may have seen the threatening graffiti? I believe they are being sabotaged."

Rinzler's cold gray eyes focused on the oozing sores on her face, then looked away. "When did you last speak with Sam Gaither?"

Sam? Of course. He's implicated, because they know he was here. "He was here with me until mid-morning." Then, hoping to emphasize Sam's link to the winery rather than suspected drug trafficking, she said, "Sam and I have been tending the winery while Peter stays at the hospital with his wife. Yesterday we discovered four fermenting bins had been sabotaged."

The young deputy had moved to Detective Rinzler's side to take notes. Rinzler paused to let him catch up, then asked, "Ms. Cooper, has anyone else been helping at the winery?"

"Not recently. May I ask why this is of interest?"

Rinzler ignored her question. "We'll want the names of every person who has entered the winery. But first tell me, when did you last see Peter Hanak?"

"This afternoon, at his wife's bedside in Good Samaritan Hospital."

"Not since?"

"No. Can you please tell me what the situation is here, Detective Rinzler? I need to attend to the Hanaks' winery as soon as possible."

"I'm afraid that won't be possible. Access to the Hanaks' property is restricted until further notice."

"Have you spoken with Peter Hanak?" she asked. "I'm under the impression that—"

Rinzler interrupted. "Peter Hanak has been taken into custody on suspicion of murder and drug trafficking."

"Murder? You can't—"

"Ms. Cooper, I expect you to remain in Santa Cruz County until further notice."

CHAPTER SIXTY-ONE

The jail guard stared at the oozing sores on Noli's cheeks. "You got oaked pretty bad," he said, sympathetically. "My little girl can't get within a mile of the stuff." He closed the metal bars behind her.

At a beat-up table, Peter stared at her, a stunned expression on his haggard and unshaven face. His wrists and ankles were cuffed and chained to an eyebolt in the cement floor.

She took a seat opposite, trying not to wince as her slacks pulled on her leg bandages.

Shaking his head slowly, he said, "I told Abbie not to bring you into this."

"She asked me to fill in until she gets back tomorrow afternoon. If Rinzler gets wind of my being here, he'll boot me out, so we need to talk fast." She reached across the table to squeeze his hand, her fingertips registering the cold metal of his cuffs. "I stopped by the hospital to see Tina this morning. Her coma's not so deep now. Sometimes she mumbles for several minutes, like she's talking to someone. It's a good sign, the nurse says."

Peter's face lit up briefly, then tightened in an angry scowl. "I should be there." He looked down at his shackled feet. "This is a fucking nightmare."

"Peter, tell me exactly what happened yesterday. Every detail you can recall."

Reluctantly, he began. "When I got home, I went straight to the winery. I wanted to see the bad vats again and check on the others before I met with Sam. When I got to the winery, the fan was off and the ventilation flaps were down. I thought, what the hell?

"Then I remembered Sam said he might be able to bring a couple of helpers to install the security cameras, and I figured there was some kind of misunderstanding. So I opened the flaps and got the fan going. Went to the dome. Sam's truck was there, but no Sam. I thought he might have gone over to discuss security options with Russ Lankshaw. I called his cell, but he didn't answer. I screwed around until I figured the CO2 had aired out of the winery. When I walked in—" His voice broke.

"What did you see?""

Tears rolled down his cheeks. "You don't know?"

"In your own words, Peter. Tell me."

He swallowed hard. "Sam."

"Where was he?"

"On the floor of the winery, wedged between two vats. I tried CPR, but it was too late. If I'd only known when I first got there."

Unwillingly, she pictured Sam's body on the winery floor, his eyes open, sightless. She pushed the image away, struggling for control. Right now, everything depended on her ability to think clearly. "Peter, you can't blame yourself. Sam would have been dead before you drove up the driveway. It only takes what, a minute or two in carbon dioxide, before you lose consciousness?"

Peter nodded and tried to wipe his eyes with manacled fists. "Why would anyone want to kill him?"

"That's what we have to find out."

"There's more," Peter said. "There were bags of meth in his pockets."

Footsteps echoed along the hallway beyond the door, came near, walked away.

Peter continued, "Rinzler's team turned the winery inside out. They found meth in the shipping cartons."

Which explained why Peter was being held on charges of manufacturing and distributing meth.

Her heart sank. "Peter, this is my fault. I kept a secret from you." She told him the story of finding the meth lab in the old barn. "You were at the hospital with Tina. I thought we could wait to deal with it until Tina was out of danger." She took a deep breath. "I never imagined it would come to this. I'm so sorry."

Peter leaned his head forward to meet hers, and they sat, forehead to forehead, her hands encircling his. As the minutes passed, she processed the new information. The meth lab in the barn was a two-bit operation. The notion that whoever was running it would take revenge on Peter by sabotaging his wine vats and murdering Sam was ridiculous.

Pulling away from Peter, she said, "It's not like we're dealing with the Sinaloa cartel here. I could see the lab operator slashing your tires, or even setting fire to the winery or the apple barn, but murdering Sam? That's playing in another league altogether. It's personal, Peter. Who's out there who hates you so much, they want to frame you for murder?"

Peter had no answer.

Heavy footsteps came down the hall, and she was afraid her time was up. But the guard just peered at them through the bars. She smiled at him, and he walked away.

Needing to better understand Sam's death, she asked, "Any idea how Sam died?"

"For obvious reasons, Rinzler hasn't shared any details with me. Maybe the killers knocked him unconscious and planted the meth on him before they shut down the fan and closed the ventilation flaps to make it look like an accident.

"But it's also possible Sam walked right into a trap. He doesn't—didn't—know much about the winery. He wouldn't necessarily notice that the fan wasn't running and the flaps were closed. They could have shut down the fan, closed the flaps, and let the CO2 collect before he walked in.

"I blame myself. I only gave him a quick orientation to the vats so he could help you. It never occurred to me he didn't understand about the fan." Peter maneuvered his arm so he could wipe the tears from his face with the sleeve of his jumpsuit.

Again the guard walked up to the door, peeked, and walked away.

"In that scenario, the murderer had to get access after Sam died to plant the meth," Noli said.

"Wouldn't be difficult. Wear a mask, or even hold your breath, dash in and dash out."

Visualizing how Sam died, Noli felt grief swelling within her chest. She needed to change the subject, or she'd be sobbing in Peter's arms. She said, "Here's some good news. Daniel Arnant called me early this morning. He convinced Rinzler that your wine, since it's owned equally by Tina, shouldn't be forfeit while you're incarcerated. Rinzler's agreed to let Arnant's employees—meaning Russ Lankshaw—enter the winery and look after the fermenting vats—with your permission, of course."

"Arnant adores Tina. Makes sense he would try to save the wine for her."

Arnant's got more interest in your wine than you need to know right now. "So it's okay with you?"

"Yeah."

"Good. Don't lose heart. Abbie thinks we can get you out of here soon."

"Stay with Tina until I can get there. Please."

CHAPTER SIXTY-TWO

Irv popped a Kit Kat into his mouth and chewed angrily. Of all the times for the Wizards to be on assignment elsewhere! Raul had a job. Munch had a store. That left one person—him—to dig through the internet, pursuing thirty-five ex-soldiers, along with the family of Marco Unocello.

He erased the Suspects whiteboard and listed the soldiers who, along with Peter, Fitz, Sam, and Noli's father, had comprised Unocello's platoon. Then he listed the members of Unocello's family.

Wolf entered, surveyed the situation room, and said, "Last man standing?"

"Something like that," Irv replied. "You here to help?"

"Damn right." Wolf tipped his backpack upside down over a table, releasing wrapped sandwiches, apples, cookies, chocolate bars, and a pound of coffee.

Irv nodded. "I see you understand the situation. Noli briefed you?"

"She did."

"Here's what I have so far." He pointed to the board. "In the left column, the soldiers who followed Unocello's order to fire on civilians. On the right, the nine who tried to stop them. Of those nine, the seven underlined lived to testify against Unocello. That would include Sam, Peter, Fitz, and Noli's dad. And here's the reporter who broke the story. Now,

I'll cross out each one who's dead." Irv drew a line through all the names on the right. "Notice a pattern?"

"Everyone who testified against Unocello is dead except Peter."

"Bingo," Irv said. "Unlikely, don't you think?"

"Noli's dad died in the earthquake, nothing suspicious there," Wolf pointed out. "What about the others?"

"Nowadays, obits tend to omit cause of death. Can you look into it?"

"With pleasure," Wolf said.

Irv returned to his computer and focused on Marco Unocello's family. Three brothers. One had died, one was in his nineties and lived on the East Coast. The youngest of the three seemed to have dropped off the radar while living in San Francisco in the '70s. Was he still alive?

Then there was Unocello's immediate family. His wife remarried twice, changed her surname both times, died in Philadelphia in 2000. There were five kids: four daughters and a son. All had been adopted by the second husband and changed their surnames to Botero. The son, a businessman in New York, had died in 2002 of cancer. One of the daughters died at sixteen in a car accident. Of the remaining three daughters, he managed to track only one: married, living in Boston. Where were the other two? Social Security hadn't registered them as deceased; neither did they show employment. Did the surviving sister know?

He picked up his phone.

★ ★ ★

Tuesday, 3 p.m.

Determined to keep her promise to Peter, Noli headed to the hospital, prepared to stay the night. As she entered the

ICU, a nurse was replacing an empty IV bag, all the while talking to Tina in soft, conversational tones. When she finished, she turned to Noli. "You're the daughter?"

"I am," she lied.

"Step outside?"

"Of course." She followed the nurse through the curtained entry to Tina's cubicle, past a horseshoe-shaped nurses' station, and into a long, empty hallway.

"How is she?" Noli asked.

"Periods of restlessness, some mumbling. No response to people or verbal requests. However, the doctor's pleased with the reduction in her cerebral edema." She placed a hand on Noli's arm and led her further down the hall. "Will you be able to get her husband out of jail?"

"His lawyer is working on it."

"The sooner, the better. She knows he's gone—her vital signs have deteriorated since he left."

Returning to Tina's ICU cubicle, Noli pulled a chair close to the bed. "Hi, Tina. It's me, Noli." Tina's eyes remained closed, her mouth slack. "The new harvest is fermenting beautifully," Noli lied. "It'll be the best vintage ever." As she spoke, she watched Tina's face. Not even an eyelash fluttered.

While she pattered on about the new harvest, Noli's thoughts turned to Peter. Abbie hoped to get him released on bail, but what if she couldn't? Should she tell Tina that Peter was coming, even though he might not?

She leaned close to Tina's ear. Instead of false assurances, she said, "Peter really needs your help right now. He's in a tight spot. Come back to us as soon as you can, okay?"

The curtains parted. A nurse—not the one she'd seen before—came through, carrying a tray of equipment. "How is she? Any response?"

"Not that I could see."

348 | DIANE SCHAFFER

"I have to ask you to step out for a few minutes."

Tina began to mumble, so softly it was impossible to distinguish even one word in the flow of sound. Then her arms began to jerk, and her head rolled from side to side. One of the machines screeched alarm signals. The nurse pressed a button, silencing the alarm, and gripped the cast on Tina's right forearm, preventing her from ripping out the IV line.

The mumbling increased in volume, and Tina thrashed as though in a nightmare struggle. Was she reliving the terror of rolling over the cliff, of being unable to stop her wheelchair?

"Will she hurt herself?" Noli asked.

The nurse watched Tina's face intently. "Wait a bit."

Ten, twenty, forty seconds passed before Tina quieted.

"It's not unusual for head injury patients to exhibit involuntary movements and vocalizations," the nurse said. "I'll secure this arm to protect her IV."

When the nurse finished, she said, "If she starts moving again, buzz me." She pointed to the red call button on the console of Tina's bed.

"Right."

Worried she had upset Tina, Noli abandoned the idea of talking about Peter. Instead, she launched into a funny story she'd heard in Dublin. She'd barely begun when Tina began to mumble again.

Noli listened closely, and soon the flow of sound took shape. There were phrases. Pauses. Repeated sounds. From time to time, an emphatic statement.

"ell Peter...ell Peter...deeno...am noz...cello here!...cello here!...ell Peter...ell Peter..."

"...ell Peter"? Was Tina saying, "Tell Peter?"

Noli set her phone on Record, then pulled a notepad and pen from her purse.

CHAPTER SIXTY-THREE

Noli was reluctant to leave Tina. But it seemed more important to show Peter what Tina was trying to say. If he could make sense of it, they might have a new lead. She washed her face in the hospital's washroom, straightened her blouse, and drove back to the jail.

The moment he saw her, Peter asked, "How's Tina?"

She reached across the table to squeeze his hands. "Good news. She's trying to talk. Just mumbles so far, but I think she might be trying to tell you something."

She placed her notes on the table. "I recorded her speech on my phone. I also wrote it out, phonetically. Before we listen, let me show you what I've got." She pointed to one fragment. "'El Peter!' sounds like 'tell Peter!' Tina said that repeatedly and was very emphatic."

She waited for Peter to scan the page, then pointed to another line. "On this one, 'Am noz'? Sometimes there was a little bit of 's' in front of the 'am'. That would make it 'Sam', so I wrote in 'Sam knows.' Does that mean anything to you?"

"No, but it wouldn't surprise me if she's thinking about Sam. After Dino died, Sam kind of took Dino's place, a brother she nurtured and worried about."

"All right, maybe there's more we can decipher. Here for instance: 'mzandolini'. Did Tina call Paolina Andolini 'Mrs. Andolini'?"

That brought a rueful smile. "Not *Mrs.* It was *Ms.* Andolini."

"So, maybe Tina's remembering the years when she was nursing Paolina Andolini and you were helping Dino get the vineyard started?"

"Could be."

"What about the 'cello' word? Did someone play the cello?"

"Cello?" Peter thought it over. "No. Plenty of guitars and banjos, back in the day. And Gwen's harp, of course."

She set her phone on the table in front of him. "Okay, let's listen."

As they listened to Tina's struggling voice, she watched anger and sadness battle for control of Peter's face. When the recording finished, he said, "I think she's remembering Lieutenant Unocello."

"Why?"

"For Tina, it was a nightmare." He took a deep breath. "Unocello's court-martial and Dino's suicide nearly poisoned our early marriage." He crushed the paper into a ball. "Shit. Right now, she's lying there, reliving the worst time in our entire lives?"

He squeezed his eyes tight, but tears began to flow. "I was wrecked back then. Kept the vineyard going by day, got drunk every night. Tina was holding down two jobs: one at the hospital and one nursing Paolina Andolini. I don't know why she didn't throw me out."

"She believed in you."

"She made me get therapy. Probably saved my life. No, *definitely* saved my life." Tears streaked his cheeks. "We had so many good times after that. Why can't she think about those?"

Noli pulled the wadded paper from his hands and smoothed it onto the table. "Peter, did Unocello ever come here to visit you?"

"Hell, no. Why?"

"Look at this: 'no cello here!'"

Peter stared at the paper in silence.

A minute passed. Noli asked, "You're sure he's dead?"

"No doubt." Peter looked away, his jaw muscles throbbing with tension. "Look, her brain is in nightmare mode. Unocello, who was a very scary guy, has come here to get even." Peter slammed the table with his cuffed wrists. "*Fuck!*"

The door flew open and a guard came through, shouting, "Back away, Hanak! Now!"

When the guard saw Peter's tearstained face, he lowered his voice. "Get a grip, Hanak." Turning to Noli, he said, "Are you finished here, counselor?"

Looking to Peter, who nodded, she answered, "Yes." She pushed the transcription of Tina's mumbles into Peter's hands, saying, "Remember, Abbie expects to get you released this afternoon."

In the jail parking lot, she activated her cell. A message from Luz. *Consuela's return delayed.*

Shit! They needed Luz's help. And they needed to know she was out of danger. She texted back, *Stay safe.*

She was going to confront Annika, then Daniel Arnant. But first she was going to find that cave. She wasn't allowed onto the Hanaks' property to retrieve her clothes, so she'd have to buy jeans and a sweatshirt. Also a good flashlight.

Before heading to the mall, she checked in with Irv.

"Listen to this!" His excitement burst through the receiver. "First, about Unocello's platoon. All the soldiers, and the reporter who testified against Unocello, are dead—except for Peter. The soldiers who stood with Unocello, all but two are living. Second, I've traced four of Unocello's five kids, but one can't be found. I talked with his daughter in Boston this morning. She says her missing sister disappeared after high school and has never contacted the family since. I asked if she had photos of her sister. She's pretty sure she does, and she'll get back to us."

"Great work, Irv. Let me know right away when that photo arrives."

"Wait, there's more. Sometime around four o'clock this morning, while we were looking at the boards and drinking our umpteenth cup of coffee, Wolf said, 'Hey! Look at this!' He pointed to the locations of each of the dead soldiers and the reporter: Phoenix, Austin, Baltimore. The Vandermeises lived in those same cities at the time of each soldier's death."

"Please tell me the deaths were suspicious!"

"Sadly, no. Thus far, we've got one suicide, a heart attack, a car wreck, and anaphylactic shock from a bee sting."

A long silence passed while they considered the diverse fatalities. Finally, Noli said, "Fitz's death would have gone down as a suicide. Any of those deaths could in fact be murder. But my God! Could Annika really be a psychopathic killer?" Preston's statement flashed to mind. *People don't realize it, but she's really smart.*

CHAPTER SIXTY-FOUR

Peter wanted to embrace Tina, lift her from the hospital bed and carry her home. He would tell her stories of happiness and joy, break the spell of nightmares, make her want to come back to him.

"Mr. Hanak?" A gentle hand on his shoulder. "If you'd step outside? I'll call you when we're done."

The thought of releasing Tina's hand filled Peter with dread. "I'll stay out of your way. I need to be here."

"I'm sorry, Mr. Hanak. We won't be long."

Suddenly Tina jerked at the restraints on her arms and legs. Her face contorted. He kissed her, whispering, "Be still, my love. You'll hurt yourself."

She sighed and went limp. Then a torrent of sound. "Ann ah ello ello ello phto ello o'eece o'eece."

Unocello nightmares, again! His vision blurred with tears. Her eyes opened, watching him.

He kissed her hand, then her lips.

With great effort, in a strangled voice, she said, "An k-k-k-ka!"

Annika? He lowered his head until his ear was at her lips, then said, "Tell me."

Peter left the hospital on foot. A quarter-mile away, in a gas station mini market, he bought a pack of Camels and a

Bic lighter. Crossing the road, he squatted under a tree by a Highway 1 overpass, oblivious to the drone of traffic. He lit a cigarette and inhaled deeply, welcoming the burn inside, a pleasure long abandoned but not forgotten. The wind came from the south, warm and humid. Overhead, clouds.

He rolled up his left sleeve until it rounded his shoulder, exposing a tattoo that covered his biceps. He hadn't looked at it—really looked—for years. In the center stood a fence post capped with an Army helmet. Ammo belts crisscrossed the fence post. At the base, two well-worn boots. A banner engraved with the words, *Brothers in Arms*, encircled the fence post.

Every man in his platoon had acquired the same tattoo when they arrived in 'Nam. Their tribute to each other. A bond stronger than blood.

He flicked the ash from his cigarette and, grasping it awkwardly between his right thumb and forefinger, drove the burning tip into the tattoo. Unflinching, he held it there, inhaling the odor of burning flesh. In his mind's eye, he saw the pile of massacred bodies, Unocello dousing them with gasoline and lighting them on fire.

Time passed. The cigarette turned to ash.

He opened his eyes.

Was Annika the daughter of Unocello? Had she pushed Tina over the cliff? Killed Fitz and Sam? Had she been sabotaging the winery for years while pretending to be Tina's friend?

No evidence. No fucking evidence.

He walked to the Soquel overpass and stuck out his thumb. Half an hour later, he walked into a Verizon store in Capitola.

The clerk, an enthusiastic techie, responded to his questions by placing a black rectangle on the countertop. "Apple's newest. Best microphone, hands down."

CHAPTER SIXTY-FIVE

Noli approached Norton Road from the south, picking it up a mile below Wolf's property. She pulled the hood of her Salvation Army sweatshirt over her hair before sauntering past the Vandermeis home and up the slope to the old barn. The sheriff's crime-scene tape encircled the barn. She avoided crossing the tape by crashing through the weeds to reach the cliff in back.

Following the path west, along the cliff, she found her memory was correct: The cliff tapered rapidly, and a path branched off to the right, entering Loma Buena State Park. This provided the operators of the meth lab with a route from the park's public parking lot to the Hanaks' old barn without passing the Hanaks' or the Vandermeises' homes.

She moved on. Twenty yards farther, nearly obscured by weeds and brush, was an irregular oval shadow about three feet in diameter. She knelt and aimed her flashlight beam inside. Cool air met her face, carrying the stink of garbage. The cave floor lay twelve, maybe fifteen feet below. A ladder had been carved into the rock wall that dropped from the mouth.

Pulling back, she surveyed the position of the cave in comparison to the park boundary, and guessed the cave was on Hanak land, not in the park. If Annika had taken wine from it, she had stolen from the Hanaks.

With the flashlight in one hand, she turned her back to the entrance and slid her feet onto the ladder's first two rungs. She descended, testing each rung before she lowered her weight onto it.

The garbage stink grew stronger.

More confident now, she descended rapidly. The cave floor seemed near when her foot slipped on a crumbled rung. She fell, landing hard on her tailbone, smashing the phone in her rear pocket.

Scrambling to her feet, sore but unbroken, she aimed the flashlight to her right. There, immersed in a shallow pool of water, lay the source of the odor: plastic food containers, empty tuna cans, chip bags, soda bottles. The trash mound was crowned with an empty liter bottle of cheap vodka.

Rats or even raccoons would be attracted to the garbage. She pressed her back into the cold stone wall, the light centered on the trash, and from there she watched and listened.

No sound, not even the scurry of insects.

She swung the beam to her left. The cave opened into a room, perhaps thirty feet long and twelve feet wide. Tall enough for her to walk upright. A narrow wooden table and three battered chairs occupied the center. A propane lantern stood alone on the table.

The cave walls were lined with empty wooden wine racks. The ground beneath the racks was littered with shards of broken bottles. Wine had been stored there. How long ago?

With the toe of her shoe, she pulled a large fragment from the smaller bits of glass. Turning it over, she could see the label: *Andolini Zinfandel, 1981*. Another said *1980*, another *1982*. Like the bottles Munch had bought for Peter. Like the bottles in Arnant's parlor.

She searched through the broken glass, examining every label she could find. All were Andolini zinfandel, years 1978 through 1982. There were no labels from the backs of the wine bottles.

How many times had Peter and Tina said it? *Dino was just as paranoid as Old Lady Andolini.* Was Dino the one who'd brought wine here, who'd set up the racks and filled them with bottles he carried into the cave? Had Paolina Andolini known? Was there any wine left? Or had Annika cleared it out?

She wove the flashlight beam around the room, settling for a moment on the table. A blue ten-gallon plastic bottle— the kind made for office water dispensers—rested on the floor at the table's edge. A roll of plastic bags lay on a chair. White powder smudged the tabletop. She guessed the small-time meth dealer who'd used the apple barn had set up here to package his product.

She realized how vulnerable she was if he returned. She was unarmed, at the mercy of anyone at the cave's entrance. And she'd neglected to tell anyone where she was going.

Speeding up her survey, she examined the far wall, playing the light beam ahead of her. Past the wine racks lay a camp mattress topped with a pile of moth-eaten blankets and a tattered sleeping bag. Next to the bed, shelves had been carved into the limestone wall. Moldy paperbacks lay on the shelves, covered with dust.

The books looked too long abandoned to have been used by the meth dealer. She thought of Sam and the other vets who'd lived in Loma Buena State Park in the '70s and '80s. Brushing the dust from one cluster of books, she read a few of the titles: *Slaughterhouse-Five; The Denial of Death; Hell in a Very Small Place; Fields of Fire.* A serious reader, a vet, trying to make sense of what he'd gone through. Not Sam— he would have told Peter about the wine once he'd come back to the outside world.

She aimed the beam toward the shadows at the far end. The light caught on something familiar.

A dusty, gold-colored jacket hanging on a clothes rack.

CHAPTER SIXTY-SIX

Peter gave the taxi driver directions to Norton Road, then sat back to use his new phone. First, he called Noli. No answer. He texted, *Don't go near Annika until you hear from me.*

Next, he called Irv.

"Peter!" Irv exclaimed. "Are you out?"

"Yes, thanks to Noli and Abbie," he said. "Is Noli there?"

"No. She's with Tina."

"I just came from the hospital. She's not there. Listen, Tina's awake, and she told me Annika is Unocello's daughter. She saw a photo of Unocello in Annika's house."

"The missing Unocello daughter!" Irv shouted. "I told Noli about her."

His voice urgent, Peter said, "I'm on my way to get a confession from Annika, and I need you to—"

Wolf cut in, "Whoa, Peter! Before you assume Annika's the key, come over and let us bring you up to date. There's a lot more going on. Suspect number one is Varley, not Annika. He's been planning to steal the Andolini clone ever since the 1980s. He's been using Annika to watch your every move. He wants your vineyard, Peter, and he won't stop until he has it. *And* he doesn't hesitate to arrange assassinations."

Suddenly off balance, Peter considered. "I'm supposed to think it's a coincidence Unocello's daughter bought, out of all the vineyard land in California, the property next to mine?" Peter said. "That doesn't wash."

Wolf replied, "We assume she wants to hurt you, which makes her the perfect partner for Varley. Wait until we can—"

Irv cut in. "Peter, you should know we've been following up on the other men in your platoon who testified against Unocello. They're all dead."

Peter made up his mind. "I'm going to get a confession out of her, and I need your help recording what she says."

"It won't hold up in court," Irv said. "California law says—"

"We can still show it to the cops," Peter said. "Are you going to help?"

There was a long pause. Finally Irv said, "What do you need?"

The taxi reached Norton Road. "Hold on a sec." When he'd paid the driver, Peter moved off the road into a stand of trees. "Can your phone record a call?"

Irv said, "Of course."

"How long?"

"As long as you need."

Relieved and encouraged, Peter said, "Good. You've got my number?"

"Yeah. Here on the screen."

Peter looked up the road, estimating how long it would take him to reach Annika's home. "I'll hang up. Call me back in twenty minutes. When I answer, mute your phone, then record everything that comes after."

"Peter, let one of us come with—"

Peter cut the connection.

CHAPTER SIXTY-SEVEN

Noli approached the gold-colored jacket. Red-and-white bands decorated the neckline, wrists and hem. A red baseball cap perched above the neck. The letters "SF" appeared on the jacket's left chest and the cap. They belonged to a fan of the San Francisco football team, which was named The 49ers in honor of the 1849 California gold rush. Her father, a dedicated 49ers fan, had owned the same jacket and cap.

What kind of person threw garbage on the floor, slept on a scruffy pile of used bedding, yet went to the trouble of bringing a clothes rack into a cavern to hang his souvenir jacket and cap?

She moved closer and lowered the flashlight to peer under the cap.

In the space between the collar of the jacket and the cap, a skull leered, its empty eye sockets black as night.

A scream echoed from wall to wall. The sound set her heart pounding. Somewhere in the back of her mind, she knew the scream was her own.

She backed away, trying to make sense of what she saw. The jacket and cap were not on a clothes rack. They were supported by a skeleton. An elaborate Halloween trick?

The skeleton was tied to an old high-backed chair, giving the illusion that it was seated. Thigh bones stuck straight out from the bottom of the jacket, minus knee, shin, or foot bones. Extending from one jacket sleeve, the bones of a hand grasped a beer can.

She'd seen a skeleton years ago in high-school human biology. It had hung from a pole, every bone wired in place. "Otherwise, it would fall into a jumble of bones on the floor," the teacher had said.

She forced herself to imagine she was seeing that *plastic* high-school skeleton. Edging closer, she could see that this, too, was wired together. Someone had gone to a great deal of trouble to assemble a macabre display.

Extending an unwilling hand, she ran two fingers over the skull. The bone was rough and cool to the touch.

Her hand recoiled quickly.

Not plastic.

The 49ers cap was faded and dusty. The jacket was unbuttoned, revealing the rib cage. In precisely the spot where a living heart once beat, there hung a medallion set off by ceramic beads.

With trembling fingers, she lifted the medallion and ran her index finger across it. Cleared of dust, it revealed a cluster of purple grapes surrounded by golden leaves.

A zinfandel cluster at harvest time.

Her design.

The necklace she'd made for her father.

She wrapped her fingers around the medallion, her heart thundering in her ears.

Fitz's message: *It's about your father.*

The flashlight's beam swung wildly as she stumbled to a chair. She sat, folded her arms tightly across her chest, and wept. Once again, she was a girl waiting for her father to return. She had searched the mountainside for him that night, believing he would be found. She had continued searching long after that, knowing in her heart that he was dead.

Had he died here, in this cave? If so, why? Peter and Tina didn't know the cave existed. Had he discovered it himself, on the very afternoon the earthquake hit? Or had he been killed elsewhere, and his body hidden in the cave?

The flashlight battery was fading. Uncertain how much time had passed, she swept its weak beam across the table and spotted a box of matches beside the propane lantern. Her fingers were shaking so violently, it took many tries to strike the match and move its flame to the lantern wick. When at last she succeeded, a warm yellow light suffused the cave.

She forced herself to return to the skeleton and removed the cap. She held the lantern close to her father's skull. All the cranium bones, the jaw, even the teeth were undamaged. Swallowing hard, she pulled the jacket aside, examining the ribs and spine. No breaks, no marks of the kind she imagined a knife or bullet would make. Of course, fatal wounds wouldn't necessarily mark a bone.

Removing the jacket seemed too much like an invasion of privacy.

She knelt before him. Her first impression had been correct: There were only thigh bones. From the knees down to the toes, the bones were missing.

Why? Carried off by scavenging animals before anyone could turn her father into a sick work of art? Or had the "artist" lost interest before he finished?

She rose to her feet, unsteady, and searched the floor. No missing bones.

The back wall was a cascade of rocks and dirt. At the edge of the lantern light, something protruding from the rubble caught her eye: a broken stick, light gray, nearly white. Its broken end was sharply splintered, and its surface was slightly rough, like bone.

Dropping to her knees, she dug her fingers into the rubble, clawing until she freed it. A second, narrower bone lay beside the first.

The tibia and fibula of a human shin.

Her father's leg.

CHAPTER SIXTY-EIGHT

Annika was armed, Peter was certain. Unocello would have taught his kids to shoot as soon as they could walk.

But Annika'd passed up plenty of opportunities to kill him. Was Wolf right? Was the killer Varley, not Annika?

He'd soon know. It was time.

He rang the doorbell. A full minute passed before Annika opened the door.

"Peter? My God, I thought you were in jail! Come in." She led the way to the kitchen and pointed to a stool at the counter. "Coffee? Something stronger?"

"Just water, thanks."

She filled two glasses, then slid onto the stool beside him. "I've been so worried. How are you?"

Staring into her eyes, he saw nothing but friendly concern. "I'm okay. Out on bail. I'm not a flight risk with Tina in the hospital."

He took a sip of water. He really was thirsty, and he'd watched the water come straight from the faucet. "Right now, I need a friend."

"Sure. Preston's gone to Taiwan. But I'm here for you."

"Did you hear what happened in the winery?"

"The newspaper report was pretty sketchy. I know your friend Sam died there."

"Yes. And when I called the cops, they found meth packets on him and in my shipping boxes. So they claim I'm a drug trafficker. Possibly a murderer too—they're still working on that one."

She placed a hand on his arm. "I'm so sorry! How's Tina? When I tried to visit, they barred me. Only family allowed in the ICU."

"She's doing well. The doctors are taking her off sedation tomorrow, and her vitals are good." He wanted this to be true, so he had no trouble lying. "They think she'll wake up soon."

He thought a shadow passed through Annika's eyes before she smiled and said, "That's wonderful! What good news."

"I hope she'll remember what went wrong and sent her over the cliff, so we can keep it from happening again. She needs the freedom to wheel down Andolini Road and visit you."

Annika glanced out the window as though expecting Tina to arrive, then turned back to him, her golden eyes locking on his. "How can I help?"

"When Tina comes home, I'll have to tell her about Sam. I'm worried. Can she absorb another loss? Sam was like a brother. If they lock me up again, she'll need a friend."

"Of course. I assume Noli will be there too?"

Pretending to be uncertain, Peter said, "I'm not sure. Noli's completely obsessed with finding Fitz's killer."

Annika's forehead creased in concern as she said, "Does she have any leads?"

"Yep. She's ready to take her evidence to the police."

Annika offered a wooden smile. "Noli's brilliant. You must be proud of her."

"Very. About Sam—"

Annika cut in with, "I'm starving! Bet you are too!" She hopped off her stool and flashed him a big smile. "Excuse me while I get some appetizers."

Should he leave? Or play along? Before he could respond, she opened the pantry door, saying, "I'll just see what's on hand." A light switch clicked. "I'll find something extra special."

Peter heard a soft *swoosh* of a sealed door—freezer?—being opened. Half a minute passed, and she didn't reappear.

His gut knotted as he edged off his stool, ready to dive behind the counter.

Over the rustling sounds of packages she called, "Perfect! Curried prawns."

She emerged with a wine bottle in one hand, bags and jars jumbled in the crook of her arm. "I'm not much of a cook—nothing like Tina—but I serve some mean hors d'oeuvres. Here." She handed him the wine and a fancy cork extractor. "You do the honors." She sounded like a sparkling sorority girl hosting a party.

He checked the foil wrapper at the cork. No sign of tampering.

"Peachy Canyon Zin. Terrific black pepper," she said. "It'll stand up to the curried prawns." Her back to him now, she oiled a frying pan, filled it with frozen prawns, and added sauce from a jar. Rich curry scents filled the kitchen.

Exhaustion hit him. He braced himself against the counter. He'd imagined wearing down her defenses until she slipped up. But somehow she had taken control. Could he trust the food she offered? Or should he make an excuse and leave?

Circling the breakfast bar, he watched her preparations. He searched her face for any resemblance to Unocello and saw none. What if Tina was wrong? What if the concussion had jumbled her memories? Wolf had warned him: "*Before you assume Annika's the key—*"

Annika slid small white plates onto the bar. "Glasses in that cabinet." She nodded to her right.

Keeping one eye on her, he poured.

"How's the wine?" she asked, facing the stove.

"Waiting for you."

"Always the gentleman." She came to him. Her lips curled into a smile.

Peter raised his glass. "To Tina's recovery."

Annika chimed her glass against his. "May she come home soon."

He searched her face for any hint of duplicity. Saw none.

"Oh, the prawns!" She raced to the stove, pulled the skillet from the fire, and lifted the lid. "Whew! Perfect."

Opening two more jars from an under-the-counter refrigerator, she placed a dollop of green-brown paste and a dollop of white on little squares of Indian flat bread, then added a prawn to each.

If she was going to drug him, it'd be in that paste. "What's under the prawns?"

"The white is raita—yogurt, cucumber, and garlic. Beneath that, spiced dal—mashed lentils with spices." She picked one up, bit it in half and fanned her mouth. "Hot! Go on, try one."

A cautious man would leave now. But I'll stay until I get what I came for.

As he lifted one to his lips, her eyes never left it. No way to palm it; he would have to swallow. "It's good. Thanks."

She nodded. "My favorite. Preston hates them."

"To each his own, I guess." He sipped his wine, scanning the room. Had Tina really seen a photograph of Unocello? There was none in sight.

She finished her first glass of wine. Good. He refilled hers, topped his off.

Watching her closely, he reached for a second prawn. "I need to plan a memorial for Sam. Women are so much better at this kind of stuff. I thought maybe you could give me some ideas."

She seemed distracted, gazing out a window with a good view of the apple barn. He'd better get to the point.

"You and Sam got off to a bad start, I know that. Pull up a stool. I'll tell you his story." He reached for his wine glass.

His vision blurred. The glass moved to the left, then the right. His hand missed the stem, then knocked the goblet across the counter, shattering the glass, spilling wine.

"No worries." Annika wiped the shards and spilt wine with a towel and dumped it in the sink. With a stiff smile, she sat next to him. "Never mind Sam. Tell me your story, Peter. About Vietnam."

"Umm. Same story. Naive kids thought they'd save the world from Communism." The scenes spun. Morphed from one to another. Escape from Hungary. Chicago. *Nagyapa*. Grateful! Lucky to be in America...

He lost the thread.

She finished her wine and poured another.

Vietnam, that was the point! Enlisted. Shipped to Vietnam. Watching her closely, he said, "Our commanding officer was Frank Unocello." Annika's expression of polite interest didn't change. *Need to bear down harder.* "He was one sick motherfucker."

She left her stool and walked to the door, opened it, and looked out.

His head was swimming. Shit. He'd made a mistake, coming here when his brain wasn't rested. But he needed to know! "Who do you look like? Your mom or your dad?"

She returned to the counter. Leveling her golden eyes on him, she said. "My mother. But you know that already, don't you?"

"Do I know your mother?"

Her mouth curled into a cold smile. "We don't have to play this game anymore. Would you like to see a photograph of my parents? Perhaps it will jog your memory."

Before he could answer, she walked down a hallway.

Thinking he shouldn't let her out of sight, he stood.

The room spun.

He leaned heavily on the counter.

She returned with a framed photograph in her hands. She set it on the counter, facing him.

His eyes weren't working well, but he could make it out. A lovely blond woman—the image of Annika, but in a Jackie Kennedy-style helmet of lacquered hair—stood beside a soldier at ease. "Lieutenant Unocello and his wife," he said. "Tina saw this. That's why you tried to kill her."

She looked at him gravely. "Careless of me, leaving this photo out. Tina wasn't part of the plan. You see, I like Tina."

"What plan?"

In a singsong tone, as though reciting a nursery rhyme, she said, "Private Alan Morales. Private Elton Simpson. *Times* reporter Austin Rutherford. Private Reston L. Baker. Private John Fitzpatrick. Private Sam P. Gaither. Traitors, all of them."

Although he already knew the answer, he asked, "Are they all dead, Annika Unocello?"

She nodded solemnly, then held up one finger and pointed at him. "Almost."

CHAPTER SIXTY-NINE

Noli sat on the cave floor, weeping, her father's leg bones in her lap. When her gaze rose to the cascade of rubble from which she'd excavated his bones, she pictured him trapped there, dying slowly as the blood ran from his legs, calling for help until he was too weak to make a sound, while she had been searching the trail miles away.

How had he been trapped in the falling rocks in a near-horizontal position? Had there been wine storage racks deep in the cave, now cut off by the rock fall? Had he been there when the shaking began, and the collapse had trapped his legs as he raced for the cave's entrance? That would explain the fact that the rest of his body had apparently been unharmed.

How large had the room been before the quake? Did part of the room still stand open behind the rubble? Did racks of aged Andolini wine await discovery behind the collapse? Had that been where Paolina, and perhaps her father before her, aged racks of their special zinfandel? Or had it been Dino's secret?

Her heart climbed into her throat as she imagined what her father had seen: a cellar filled with aging wine. How excited he must have been, how eager to tell Peter of his discovery! When the ground began to shake, he would have gathered as many old bottles as he could carry, not worried about his own safety, for small quakes were a fact of life in California. And then, when he realized how bad it was going to be, had he tried to run?

The lantern's glow flickered, then faded away, leaving her in darkness. At the cave's entrance, twilight illuminated only the uppermost rungs of the ladder.

It would be night soon.

Slowly, her mind rose from the cave and reconnected with the world. Tina in the hospital. Peter in jail. No, Peter *out* of jail, back at Tina's bedside. Sam dead. Luz at Varley's, constantly in danger.

Annika.

I just loaned him a hard hat.

What a convincing liar Annika was.

Noli pictured Annika accompanying Fitz into the old barn, hard hats protecting both their heads. Finding the meth lab. Finding the trail from the back of the barn and following it to the cave's entrance. Exploring the cave. Finding the old Andolini wine.

Finding her father.

Noli, call me. It's about your father. Top priority. Fitz.

Annika must have asked Fitz to take her sailing that afternoon; after all, he couldn't do any work on the apple barn until the lab had been reported to the authorities, right?

She was having affairs with both Varley and Arnant. Had they helped her murder Fitz?

No. The 911 girl had seen only one person come ashore with Fitz. *Slender as a stick.* A small woman with a dancer's body, dressed as a boy.

Annika had kept the cave a secret from the Hanaks, but had told Arnant the night she brought him bottles of old Andolini wine. How much longer had she planned to keep spinning her web?

Slowly, Noli rose from the cave floor. With trembling fingers, she placed her father's leg bones at the base of the chair holding the rest of his skeleton.

Gently, she pulled the beer can free from his wired hand and threw it at the wall of the cave.

"Dad, I'm coming back for you."

CHAPTER SEVENTY

"**A**re they all dead, Annika?"

"Almost."

Wolf, Raul, and Irv listened in growing disbelief to Peter's conversation with Annika. When Peter stopped speaking, they heard a scrape and a thump. Then noises they couldn't identify.

When two minutes passed without the sound of Peter's voice, Wolf said, "I'm calling 911."

Irv nodded. He left the connection to Peter's phone open. They ran down the stairs as Wolf spoke with the 911 operator. "A man is under assault and may be dead. The address is 31 Norton Road, home of Annika and Preston Vandermeis... No, I am not at that location. I was on the phone with the victim when he was assaulted... I am at least three-quarters of an hour away... Yes, I will stay on the line. Yes, the victim is known to me. His name is Peter Hanak, that's spelled—"

Pointing to his Jeep, Irv said, "I'll drive."

Burning rubber, Irv zoomed onto Mission Street and commenced zigzagging through heavy traffic, leaving a trail of blaring horns. "If a cop stops us, all the better," he shouted.

Raul held Irv's phone, listening intently. "No conversation. No sounds at all," he reported.

Irv said, "Cut the connection. Call Noli."

Raul complied. "Noli's not picking up," he yelled. "Where is she?"

374 | DIANE SCHAFFER

Irv answered, "Don't know."

At the intersection with Highway 9, traffic came to a standstill.

Irv slammed his palms on the steering wheel. "*Fuck*! We need a goddamn tank!"

Updating the 911 operator, Wolf said, "Operator, we are caught in slow-moving traffic at the intersection of Mission Boulevard and Highway 9. How long before officers reach the scene?" He listened, then yelled, "That's too long! A man's life is at stake here!"

Irv said, "Raul, try Luz."

Luz's phone went to voicemail. Raul left a message. "Luz, call us immediately. Matter of life and death." He rang off and stared at the traffic ahead. "Farther up, we'll lose cell reception."

Irv said, "Call Luz again, leave a detailed message. Pray she listens soon. She's the only one close enough to help."

★ ★ ★

Luz felt her cell phone vibrate, but she ignored it.

El Señor Varley had been irate when she'd returned from her "grocery shopping trip" almost an hour late. Now, she would be an angel.

His guests, five men with whom he played poker, had arrived. She brought them six Pacifico beers and fresh guacamole. While she flirted with each *gringo* in turn, acting as though she had all the time in the world, her cell vibrated again. Returning to the kitchen, she saw that Wolf had texted, *Listen to my message NOW*. Quickly she finished dinner preparations and brought *taquitos de pollo* and jalapeño peppers stuffed with cheese to the poker table.

The men whistled and cheered.

Varley said, "Eat your hearts out, dudes."

Across from Varley sat a young man, maybe late twenties, blond. *Muy guapo*, and he knew it. He pushed back from the table, saying, "Sit on my lap, Alma. Bring me some luck."

Hands on her hips, she looked him over from head to foot, slowly. Then she shook her head. "It is true you need *something*, but luck will not help."

El guapo slid a look at his laughing compatriots, then returned to the table and raised a beer to salute her.

Flashing Luz an appreciative smile, Varley dealt the cards. Luz backed slowly to the kitchen door, raced to Consuela's apartment, locked the door, entered the bathroom, and again locked the door. With the cell pressed close to her ear, she listened to Wolf's message. Immediately, she pressed Call Back.

"Wolf, what is happening?"

"Where are you?" Wolf asked.

"At Varley's. Have you—"

"Listen!" Wolf filled her in on Annika's confession, and the subsequent silence on Peter's cell. "We're trying to get there, but we're blocked by a six-car crash on Highway 9."

"The sheriff—"

Wolf cut her off. "Tied up with a hostage situation in Bonnie Doon."

"Where's Noli?"

"No idea. Not answering her phone."

"What kind of car does Annika drive?" Luz asked.

"White Mercedes S-300 sedan," Wolf answered. "Also a black Ram truck."

She rang off, grabbed her backpack, and raced for the service entrance.

Holy Mother, even though I don't believe in you, pray for me.

CHAPTER SEVENTY-ONE

Noli climbed Old Marco's Hill and sank onto Peter's bench. With trembling hands, she tried to zip up her jacket. Couldn't grasp the pull tab. Shivering, she watched a full moon rise in the darkened sky. By moonlight, the gnarled vines of Old Marco's Hill resembled ancient crones, guardians of a mountainside where so many had lost their dreams.

Her father had died with the key to Peter's dream in his hands.

She would make certain he hadn't died in vain.

She would stop Annika. Expose Varley and Arnant.

She had to think, had to have a plan.

Should she find the deputy who was patrolling the Hanaks' land and ask him for help? To do what, arrest Annika? She had no evidence to show him.

Across the valley, the windows of Varley's mansion lit one by one against the failing light. Praying Luz was safe, she shifted her gaze down the valley to the Vandermeis estate, where Annika, no doubt, was planning her next move.

Suddenly a light appeared beyond the apple orchard.

A flame.

It rose, then exploded into a dozen small fires. A plume of smoke caught the wind and wheeled into a black shroud.

The apple orchard was on fire.

She pulled her cell from her back pocket. Tried to turn it on, but the screen had been shattered from her fall.

She raced down the path to the old dome. Yellow crime tape shimmered in the moonlight, blocking the door. She ripped the tape aside and tried the door handle.

Locked.

Grabbing a length of firewood, she positioned herself opposite a triangular window, stepped back as far as the deck railing would allow, turned her face away, and launched the log at the glass. The window burst, leaving jagged shards around the perimeter. She kicked them out and lunged through.

She punched 9-1-1 on the landline. "I'm reporting a fast-moving fire on upper Norton Road, headed for Loma Buena State Park." She tossed the receiver onto the counter, plucked a blanket from the couch, brought it to the sink, saturated it with water, threw it over her shoulder, and ran into the night.

Along Andolini Road, limestone dust shimmered in the moonlight. She sprinted toward the fire hose Tina had shown her. The wind shifted, enveloping her in smoke. She choked and stumbled.

Squinting, her eyes burning, she moved forward slowly, searching for the fire hose locker, finally spotting the dark rectangle. When she opened its door and groped for the nozzle, she realized she had no idea how to turn on the water. She ran her fingers over the underside of the locker, then circled to the back. A white PVC pipe, the connection to the water storage tank atop the ridge, came down the hillside and ended at the locker. But she couldn't find a lever, a handle, any moving part that would release the water.

She was losing time.

In the apple orchard, trees were igniting one by one.

Annika's fire hose was their only chance. Surely Annika was already fighting the fire. And maybe Annika knew how to release water into the Hanaks' hose.

She returned to the road, moving west, and plunged into the next wave of smoke. When she reached Norton Road, a woman's voice screamed, "Stop or I shoot!"

She skidded to a stop and peered in the direction of the voice. The apple barn glowed red with reflected fire. A slender figure in an oversized black windbreaker and a black baseball cap stood in the open barn door, a gasoline can at her feet. Firelight glinted on the squarish pistol she held. The gun was pointed at a body lying just inside the barn.

"Annika?"

"If you want to live, Noli Cooper, back up and get the hell out." Annika's girlish voice was gone, replaced and possessed by guttural hate.

Noli took a step forward, then another. "What's going on? Let me help."

Annika screamed. "*Get out!*"

Noli raised her hands. "I'm unarmed, Annika. Tell me what's going on."

Annika turned slightly. Firelight caught on her hair and cheekbones, leaving her eyes in skeletal darkness. She stepped sideways and kicked the body. A groan. "I don't think Peter has much to say to you right now. Bugger off before I change my mind."

Peter.

The wind shifted again. Smoke enveloped them. She pressed the blanket to her nose and willed her feet to run toward Annika.

But the smoke cleared as quickly as it had come. Just ten yards away now, Annika said, "One more step, I shoot. Makes no difference to me."

Noli's lungs burned, every breath an effort. *Think, god-damn it, think! Say something. Fire trucks are coming. Keep her talking.* "How about we sit down?" Noli folded her legs, sitting cross-legged. "You sit down, too. We can talk. I'm sure we can—"

"Fine. Stay and burn." Annika's gun never wavered from its aim on Peter while she flipped the cap on the gasoline can. She splashed gasoline at the side of the barn and over the weeds nearby.

"Jesus, Annika!"

Annika set the gas can down. Her free hand searched her pocket. Still holding the gun, she brought her hands together. A flame flickered—

She's going to—

Noli was on her feet and running for Peter.

Annika fired.

The dirt in front of Noli exploded, sending dirt into her eyes. She stopped, blinded.

"Next time I aim higher."

Noli blinked frantically. She could hear Annika move away from the barn and down the hill.

Then, just as her vision cleared, she saw Annika empty the gasoline can and strike another match. Flames leapt across the base of the hill as Annika backstepped down Norton Road. Reaching her black pickup, Annika climbed in, gunned the engine and backed down the road.

Surrounded by fire, praying that Peter was still alive, Noli wrapped herself tightly in the blanket. Pulling one corner over her face, she took a deep breath and plunged into the flames.

Her lungs screamed for breath, but she ignored them. Now she belonged to the flames. They gathered her in, as they had wished to do twenty years ago. Gwen's singsong echoed across the years:

"Angel light, bring me home. Angels sing—"

Gwen sits atop a mound of furniture, books, and firewood. She is dressed in her favorite emerald-green gown. In her hands, a box of long fireplace matches. She slides the box open and extracts a wand-like match.

"No, Gwen!"

Gwen strikes the match and drops it, singing louder now: "Angel light, bring me home. Chorus of angels—"

Flames devour the pile and leap onto Gwen's dress. Gwen welcomes them.

Gwen wants to die.

Noli leaps, scrambles to the top, pulls Gwen into her arms and away.

They are both on fire.

Noli stumbled against the barn wall. Her mind shocked back to the present. Move, move, move! She followed the wall to the open doorway, threw herself forward, stumbled again, fell.

In the distance, a tremendous crash. Metal twisting, breaking. Had the fire engine missed a turn and slammed into a tree? Had they just lost any hope of stopping the fire?

Fighting despair, she pulled herself to her feet and beat a blanket against her smoldering jeans and shoelaces. Searing pain lurked in the base of her brain, waiting to erupt.

She knelt beside Peter. "Peter, it's Noli. I'm getting you out of here!"

No answer. He lay on his side, eyes closed, wrists and ankles bound. She rolled him onto the blanket. She pulled.

He was limp, heavier than she thought possible. Slowly she worked her way across the interior of the barn to the corridor leading to the back. It was a calculated risk; she had to pull Peter to safety out the back of the barn before the fire reached the flammable chemicals in the meth lab. But there was no choice—if she pulled Peter through the fire in front of the barn, he would burn to death.

With all the strength she could muster, she dragged him down the aisle to the rear of the barn. Flames licked through the wall planks.

In the lab, she groped toward the hatch in the back wall. A coughing spasm brought her to her knees. She bent her head to inhale the clean air just above the floor. One breath, two. She filled her lungs a third time and ran her hands across the wall until she found the hatch and pulled it open. She dragged Peter as close to the hatch as possible, crawled through, grabbed the blanket, and, inch by inch, pulled him outside.

Now where?

The cave!

The fire had not yet cut them off.

Inch by inch, pulling the blanket over the stubble, she skidded Peter along the path to the cave. At the cave's entrance, she stopped, uncertain how to lower him to safety.

The smoke was thinner here. In the orange firelight she examined his face: eyes closed, mouth slack. She pressed two fingers to his carotid artery. Nothing. Her heart pounded in her ears, and the fire roared.

He's alive. I know he is. His pulse is weak and my fingers aren't trained for this.

Sirens. Two—no, three. Coming fast. Louder, louder.

She waited, watching flames encircle the barn.

Suddenly, with a deafening roar, the barn roof blasted into the sky on a fist of white light.

When her pain meds kicked in, Noli lowered her bandaged legs over the edge of the bed and maneuvered her bottom into a wheelchair. The doctors assured her she'd walk again, but only if she promised to use the chair until the burns healed.

Despite the meds, her head felt clear. The truth shall make you whole—or something like that.

Around her shoulders, she draped a soft robe, a gift from Tina and Peter. Though MS was relentless, Tina was recovering from her fall. The coming months would be difficult; they were all grieving the loss of Sam and Fitz. And the Andolini Valley had changed forever, bringing some challenging, but promising, opportunities.

Wolf had visited often—sometimes twice a day—and she hoped he would become the brother she'd never had. This morning he'd told her that Luz had been transferred to a room just down the hall. With luck, Luz was awake and able to talk.

She wheeled down the corridor, passing two, four, six rooms before finding the name plaque *Alvarado*. Inside, the near bed was empty, and a curtain enclosed the second. No sound. Was Luz asleep?

Noli leaned in and whispered, "Luz?"

"Come in."

Noli peeked around the curtain. Luz lay on her back, her left leg suspended in a cast. She had two blackened eyes. Her arms were abraded and bruised. Around her neck, a cervical collar. Noli's mind flashed back to the grinding, ear-splitting crash she'd heard while dragging Peter to the rear of the barn. At the time, she'd feared it was the sound of a fire truck smashing into a tree.

Luz was smiling.

Seated on a chair but sound asleep, her head cushioned on Luz's bed, was a slender teenage girl. On a bedside table, an enormous bouquet of fall flowers.

"No need to whisper," Luz said, nodding toward the sleeping girl. "Magda will wake when she's ready."

"Your sister?"

"Yep."

Noli rolled to Luz's side, imagining for the hundredth time what it must have been like for Luz to race her car toward Annika's truck, swerving at the last moment to block both lanes as Annika tried to accelerate past her. "I came to thank you for stopping Annika. What a price you've paid."

Luz didn't answer immediately. Finally, pain creasing her face, her eyes narrowed, she said, "She killed Fitz. I'd do it again."

Noli knew it was time to say what she'd come to say. "Luz, I'm going to take over Fitz's practice, like he asked me to. It will be difficult to fill his shoes. I need a partner, and I hope that will be you."

Her expression solemn, Luz said, "Let me think about it."

"Fair enough."

When the ensuing silence became awkward, Noli said, "If you're going to sideswipe any more trucks, we'll get you a Hummer."

That got a smile out of Luz. "Expense account for gas?" she said.

"No problem." Gesturing toward the bouquet on Luz's nightstand, Noli asked, "Boyfriend?"

"Client. Remember Crystal Langley, the runaway I was looking for?"

"Sure. Was she the girl who found Fitz's body?"

"Yeah. When Clay warned his buddy she was only fifteen, they got Crystal to call her aunt, her only stable relative. The aunt came and took her home. Sent me flowers."

"Your first case, solved. Congratulations!"

"If only Fitz was here to see it." Luz's eyes filled with tears. "I think about him all the time. If I'd been with him—"

"Luz, you could not have saved Fitz."

For a few moments they both watched Magda sleep. A gurney rolled down the hall. A family walked by, chatting happily.

Noli squeezed Luz's unbandaged hand and said, "Look, I apologize. I should've rocketed out of that cave and called you and Wolf ASAP."

"No way. If I had found what you found there, I'd have been on my knees."

"I was," Noli replied. "There's something else that bothers me. I was too close to the Hanaks to be objective. Sam suspected sabotage all along. Wolf, too. And a complete outsider, the Aussie cellar master, warned Peter about sabotage. But I let Peter stonewall me with his denial."

"You tried—"

"Not like I would have if he'd been a client."

Before Luz could comment, Abbie Wheeldon entered the room, holding two bouquets of flowers. "Thought I might find you two together." She lay one bouquet on Noli's lap. Spotting the bouquet on Luz's side table, she grinned. "Coals to Newcastle, I see." She lay the second bouquet at the foot of Luz's bed. "I wanted to tell you two in person. Annika Vandermeis—who will be in the hospital for many weeks to come—has been charged with attempted murder."

"Will the charges stick?" Noli asked.

"On attempting to kill Peter, odds are yes. Regarding the murders of Fitz and Sam, we'll have to see what evidence the sheriff's team uncovers. I'm sure you both understand that the recording of Peter's conversation with Annika—ingenious though it was—won't be admissible in court. But my sources tell me they found a large stash of secobarbital in Annika's closet; that's the barbiturate that, combined with tequila, killed Fitz. It's what she used to knock out Peter. And there's more. They found meth on her sneakers and jeans.

"With respect to the deaths of the other vets who testified against Annika's father, there's a damning discovery," Abbie continued. "They found a scrapbook Annika kept, detailing the movements of each man. She stalked them until they died. Their so-called 'accidental' deaths are being re-investigated."

"Was she involved in running the meth lab in the barn?" Noli asked.

"I can answer that," Luz said. "My brother, Eduardo, a member of the Inter-Agency Drug Task Force, told me what happened. The discovery of the operation at the Hanaks' barn helped the Task Force round up a large meth ring operating in three additional state parks. Eduardo interviewed each of the three guys operating at the Hanaks'; they all had the same story. They watched from the cliff above while Fitz, *along with Annika,* went into the barn that Wednesday morning. Fitz and Annika found the cave, too, so the operators knew they were totally busted. Fitz locked the barn before he left that morning. They saw Annika return to the cave, alone, and carry away all their product."

"I've been wondering how much of the sabotage of the Hanaks was down to Annika," Noli said. "Maybe that notebook will show how she ruined the '07 and '08 vintages."

"I'd put money on it," Abbie said. "Deriving pleasure from watching Peter suffer would fit her aberrant personality."

"And the graffiti?" Noli asked.

"Since it continued for the Hanaks long after it halted for all the other vets, my guess is Annika took advantage of what had already occurred and kept it going."

Noli considered the possible outcomes for Annika, feeling uneasy. "Preston will hire a top-notch lawyer. Insanity plea?"

"Might work." Abbie pulled a chair over to Luz's bedside and sat down. "Preston's an interesting guy. Even knowing what Annika has done, he still loves her. On the other hand, he's clear-eyed about the damage to Peter and Tina. He's gifting them the house and land he bought, did you know?"

In her mind's eye, Noli could see Peter choosing zinfandel clones for the Vandermeises' yet-to-be-planted acreage. And the mansion could become an inn, managed by Tina.

Abbie continued, "Right now, here's what's important: You two did one hell of a good job. You were within days of nailing Annika, but Peter went charging in and blew your case." Abbie raised a hand, as though to halt any objections. "Not that I blame him."

Abbie leveled her gaze on Luz, saying, "As for catching Annika, if you hadn't crashed into her truck, she'd be long gone. She had plane tickets to Brazil and a perfect fake passport."

Luz's face radiated satisfaction.

Noli asked, "Have they found Varley yet?"

"Not yet," Abbie answered. "After Giannopoulos turned state's evidence, Wickam crumbled, gave them Varley. But Varley has worse trouble than being nailed for the theft of the Hanaks' clone. Raul passed on information from Varley's hard drive to the CIA. Seems Varley's been manufacturing computer components in mainland China, labeling them with the brand of his Taiwanese company, and importing them. Wherever Varley is, we'll never see him in the US again—unless he's behind bars. I hear Wolf has a client who's interested in buying Varley's estate."

Luz asked, "What about the other neighbor who was scheming with Annika?"

"Daniel Arnant?" Abbie said. "He's testifying against Annika. And he resigned as director of Andolini winery, sold his shares, and moved to France."

"The Andolini Board offered Peter the directorship," Noli said.

Abbie looked pleased. "Will he take it?"

"Only if Wolf will work with him."

Noli and Wolf sat side by side on a redwood bench. At their feet lay a new graveyard, its perimeter marked by lines of fledgling redwoods. Behind them rose the forest of Loma Buena State Park. Before them, the Andolini Valley wound from east to west, its zinfandel vines alive with fresh buds.

Headstones marked the graves of three brothers-in-arms. Her father's headstone was inscribed, *Beloved Teacher.* Sam was buried next to her father. His headstone read, *Brother in Arms and in Peace.* The last grave was for Fitz. Pilar, Fitz's heartbroken fiancée, had chosen the perfect inscription, *Warrior for Justice.* Flowers and messages of gratitude graced all three.

The lowering sun glinted off three vehicles parked on the road below, ready to transport the mourners to a feast awaiting them at the domes. Munch helped Pilar into Fitz's classic Woody, which she had inherited. Luz and Abbie corralled Luz's sister and little brother, urging them into Abbie's venerable Volvo.

Bringing up the rear, Peter guided Tina's wheelchair down the path from the graveyard to his truck. They paused by the replanted apple orchard as a breeze caressed the tiny trees' pink-and-white blossoms, then swirled the black ash that still coated the burnt ground.

Wolf said, only half in jest, "You wasted perfect zinfandel terroir when you replanted that orchard."

"Not a waste," Noli answered. "The orchard meant a lot to my dad. In a few years, the taste of Cooper's Cider will knock your socks off."

"Can't wait!" Wolf chuckled. Then, serious again, he said, "Peter's eulogy was brilliant."

"He's received invitations to speak to veterans all across the country," Noli said. "He's lucky you're here to manage both the Hanak and Andolini vineyards."

Wolf ran a hand over his head, the weight of his coming responsibilities furrowing his brow. "I'm glad we have a few months to get organized. When Peter's '09 vintage wins every competition—which it will—this valley will be a madhouse." As if to savor the calm before the storm, he took a deep breath and leaned back.

Resting a hand on her father's headstone, Noli surveyed the sweep of the Andolini Valley, from the Andolini Estate, along Old Marco's Hill, past the Hanaks' second vineyard and the replanted apple orchard, all the way to the acreage that Preston Vandermeis had given to the Hanaks. Soon, the land across the valley, abandoned by Varley and purchased by a client of Wolf's, would also be under Wolf's management. Peter and Tina's dream was coming true, perhaps beyond their wildest imaginings.

She squeezed Wolf's arm. "I'm grateful you're back in my life."

"One question." Trailing a hand across the vista before them, he said, "I'm home now. Are you?"

THE END

AUTHOR'S NOTE

Mortal Zin is a work of fiction. All contemporary characters and the Andolini ancestors are imaginary. However, the historical character Agoston Haraszthy lived from 1812 to 1869. He was a robber-baron, polymath, and visionary, deservedly titled "the father of California viticulture." Only a small fraction of his larger-than-life escapades and accomplishments could be included in this novel. Whether he brought zinfandel vines to California, and if so, when, is disputed. For readers who would like to know more about the history of zinfandel, I heartily recommend the three sources listed below, all of them delightful reads.

The novel's "Zinfandel Clone Project" at the mythical Cal Poly Sacramento is based upon the very real Zinfandel Heritage Research Project at UC Davis. In 2009 the Project released nineteen clones to the public, and more have followed, greatly enriching the zinfandel vineyards of California.

The search for the origin of zinfandel in Europe is a terrific mystery story in itself. A clue discovered near the boot of Italy in 1967 led to an extensive search through ancient vineyards on the Dalmatian Coast and eventual discovery of crljenak kaštelanski, zin's ancestor, on a small island. For the full story, see the Wikipedia page for zinfandel.

If you're a zinfandel fan, consider joining ZAP (Zinfandel Advocates and Producers). Check out ZAP's information-packed website for events throughout the year: **zinfandel.org**

SOURCES

Darlington, David (2001) *Zinfandel: The History and Mystery of Zinfandel.* Da Capo Press. ISBN 9780306810299

McGinty, Brian (1998) *Strong Wine: The Life and Legend of Agoston Haraszthy.* Stanford University Press, 1998. ISBN 9780804731454

Sullivan, Charles L (2003) *Zinfandel: A History of a Grape and Its Wine.* (Volume 10) (California Studies in Food and Culture) ISBN 9780520239692

Enjoy more about
Mortal Zin
Meet the Author
Check out author appearances
Explore special features

ABOUT THE AUTHOR

Diane Schaffer, a Stanford PhD, is a retired professor and longtime resident of Santa Cruz County. *Mortal Zin*, her first mystery novel, is rooted in her summer work in a Santa Cruz zinfandel winery, where she became fascinated with the unique history of zinfandel, California's mystery grape. When she's not writing, she's hiking, river kayaking, or reading a good mystery novel. She now lives in Ashland, Oregon, with her husband.

ACKNOWLEDGEMENTS

This novel evolved over nearly twenty years, and many people helped along the way. For the initial inspiration, I thank Lynne and Michael Muccigrosso for so generously educating me on the workings of a small winery and for sharing their love of zinfandel. Also helpful in early development were Michael Bentzen, Julie Edwards and Susan Roper. Dr. Carole Meredith told me the story of discovering crljenak kaštelanski and encouraged me to learn about the Zinfandel Heritage Research Project.

For a decade I benefitted from the notes and encouragement of a wonderful group of women writers: Anne Batzer, Fayegail Bisaccia, Jan Boggia, Ellen Levine, Lois Langlois, Kathy Olsen, Ginger Rilling, Sharon Schaefer, Dolores Schleelen and Lois Schlegel. I'm indebted to readers of early drafts: Anne Batzer, Anne Chambers, Marea Claassen, Greg Conaway, Kiersta and Mark Gostnell, Lois Langlois, Marlaine Lockheed, Cory Ross, Blanca Tavera and Craig Schaffer. When the final rounds of editing came, Kiersta Gostnell, Julie Olsen Edwards, Anne Chambers and Bryan Frink provided invaluable assistance.

Many thanks to Book Passage's Mystery Writers' Conference for providing workshops on every aspect of writing that an aspiring mystery writer could wish for. In addition, their virtual seminars brought me excellent advice from Julia McNeal, Elizabeth K. Kracht, and Brooke Warner.

Invaluable editing insights came from Sibylline editors Julia Park Tracey, Suzy Vitello and Jennifer Safrey. Many, many thanks to Sibylline publisher Vicki DeArmon for shepherding Mortal Zin from manuscript to book-in-the-hand, and to artist Alicia Feltman for designing a perfect cover.

Last, but far from least: This book would never have come into being without the loving support and writing consultation of my husband, Bryan Frink.

MORTAL ZIN
BOOK CLUB QUESTIONS

1. When Noli decided to change her life, she might have gone in many different directions. Why did she return to the Hanaks? Why was the offer from Fitz appealing to her? How will discovering the truth about her father's death affect her?

2. When Noli first meets Luz, she expects Luz to trust her and want to work together. Luz feels differently. Why? What does Noli's assumption tell us about her? Do you think Luz will choose to work with Noli in the future?

3. After her mother's death, Luz assumed responsibility for raising two younger siblings and caring for her disabled father. But with the support of Señora Marquez, she managed to get an education and qualify for a private investigator's license. She could have become a police officer like her older brother and given the family a second, steady income. Was PI a better choice for her? Why or why not?

4. What do you think of Luz's decision to go undercover in Varley's home? When Irv joins her to copy Varley's computer files, does your feeling about this decision change? Would you have done the same?

5. When Noli discovers the amphetamine lab in the Hanaks' old barn, she decides not to tell Peter about it until Tina comes out of her coma. Do you agree with her decision? What might have happened if she had told him?

6. Like Noli's father, Peter, Sam, Munch and Fitz, many war veterans do not discuss their war experiences with anyone who has not been to war. What reasons might they have? Do you think this is a mistake? Why or why not? Do you know anyone who has been in the Vietnam, Afghan or Middle Eastern wars? If so, have they discussed their experiences with you?

7. In reading Mortal Zin, what did you learn about vineyards, winemaking, and the zinfandel grape? Have you ever visited a winery? If so, did it resemble the Hanaks' small, hands-on operation? Do you enjoy red wines? If so, which ones do you prefer? Are you interested in trying different styles of zinfandel?

8. As the story progressed, who did you think wrote the graffiti and sabotaged the winery? Why did Peter refuse to believe the graffiti were anything more than teenage vandalism? What does that tell you about Peter?

9. Mortal Zin introduces three communities established in the 1970's and now threatened by social change: communes, small farms/vineyards, and the yacht harbor with its live-in boat owners. Why would individuals choose to live in one of these? Would one be attractive to you? Why or why not?

Sibylline
PRESS

Sibylline Press is proud to publish the brilliant work of women authors over 50. We are a woman-owned publishing company and, like our authors, represent women of a certain age.

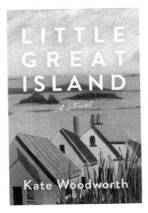

Little Great Island: A Novel
BY KATE WOODWORTH

FICTION
Trade Paper, 356 pages (5.315 x 8.465) | $21
ISBN: 9781960573902
Also available as an ebook and audiobook

When Mari McGavin flees with her son back to the tiny Maine island where she grew up—she runs into her lifelong friend Harry, one of the island's summer residents, setting off a chain of events as unexpected and life altering as the shifts in climate affecting the whole ecosystem of the island...from generations of fishing families to the lobsters and the butterflies.

After Happily Ever: An Epic Novel of Midlife Rebellion
BY JENNIFER SAFREY

FICTION, FANTASY
Trade Paper, 388 pages (5.315 x 8.465) | $22
ISBN: 9781960573179
Also available as an ebook and audiobook

Princesses Neve, Della, and Bry are sisters-in-law, having married into the royal Charming family, and for the last thirty-plus years, they've been living a coveted happily-ever-after life in the idyllic kingdom of Foreverness. As they each turn 50 however, they begin to question the kingdom's "perfection." Can each of the women create a new happily-ever-after and will the kingdom of Foreverness survive it?

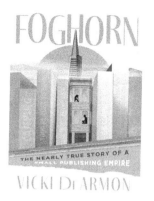

Foghorn: The Nearly True Story of a Small Publishing Empire

BY VICKI DEARMON

MEMOIR
Trade Paper, 320 pages (5.315 x 8.465) | $20
ISBN: 9781960573926
Also available as an ebook and audiobook

The heyday of small press publishing in the San Francisco Bay Area in the 1980s and 1990s lives again in this never-before-told story of how small presses—armed with arrogance and personal computers—took the publishing field. Vicki Morgan was an ambitious young woman publisher, coming-of-age while quixotically building Foghorn Press from scratch with her eccentric brother to help.

Charlotte Salomon Paints Her Life: A Novel

BY PAMELA REITMAN

HISTORICAL FICTION
Trade Paper, 392 pages (5.315 x 8.465) | $22
ISBN: 9781960573919
Also available as an ebook and audiobook

This historical fiction depicts the encroaching terror of the Third Reich and the threat of psychological disintegration of the artist Charlotte Salomon as she clings to her determination to become a serious modernist painter, to complete her monumental work "Life? Or Theater?" and get it into safekeeping in a race against time before capture by the Nazis.

For more books from **Sibylline Press**, please visit our website at **sibyllinepress.com**